The
DELIGHT MAKERS

BY

ADOLF FRANCIS BANDELIER

APPLEWOOD BOOKS
Carlisle, Massachusetts

The Delight Makers
was originally published in 1890

ISBN: 978-1-4290-4680-0

Thank you for purchasing an Applewood book. Applewood reprints America's lively classics—books from the past that are still of interest to modern readers. This facsimile was printed using many new technologies together to bring our tradition-bound mission to you. Applewood's facsimile edition of this work may include library stamps, scribbles, and margin notes as they exist in the original book. These interesting historical artifacts celebrate the place the book was read or the person who read the book. In addition to these artifacts, the work may have additional errors that were either in the original, in the digital scans, or introduced as we prepared the book for printing. If you believe the work has such errors, please let us know by writing to us at the address below.

For a free copy of our current print catalog featuring our bestselling books, write to:

APPLEWOOD BOOKS
P.O. Box 27
Carlisle, MA 01741

For more complete listings,
visit us on the web at:
awb.com

Prepared for publishing by HP

THE DELIGHT MAKERS

THE
DELIGHT MAKERS

BY

ADOLF F. BANDELIER

WITH AN INTRODUCTION
By CHARLES F. LUMMIS

ILLUSTRATED

NEW YORK
DODD, MEAD AND COMPANY

PREFACE

THIS story is the result of eight years spent in ethnological and archæological study among the Pueblo Indians of New Mexico. The first chapters were written more than six years ago at the Pueblo of Cochiti. The greater part was composed in 1885, at Santa Fé, after I had bestowed upon the Tehuas the same interest and attention I had previously paid to their neighbours the Queres. I was prompted to perform the work by a conviction that however scientific works may tell the truth about the Indian, they exercise always a limited influence upon the general public; and to that public, in our country as well as abroad, the Indian has remained as good as unknown. By clothing sober facts in the garb of romance I have hoped to make the " Truth about the Pueblo Indians " more accessible and perhaps more acceptable to the public in general.

The sober facts which I desire to convey may be divided into three classes, — geographical, ethnologi- cal, and archæological. The descriptions of the country and of its nature are real. The descrip- tions of manners and customs, of creed and rites, are from actual observations by myself and other ethnologists, from the statements of trustworthy Indians, and from a great number of Spanish sources of old date, in which the Pueblo Indian is represented as he lived when still unchanged by contact with European civilization.

The descriptions of architecture are based upon investigations of ruins still in existence on the sites where they are placed in the story.

The plot is my own. But most of the scenes described I have witnessed; and there is a basis for it in a dim tradition preserved by the Queres of Cochiti that their ancestors dwelt on the Rito de los Frijoles a number of centuries ago, and in a similar tradition among the Tehuas of the Pueblo of Santa Clara in regard to the cave-dwellings of the Puye.

A word to the linguist. The dialect spoken by the actors is that of Cochiti for the Queres, that of San Juan for the Tehuas. In order to avoid the complicated orthography latterly adopted by scientists for Indian dialects, I have written Indian words and phrases as they would be pronounced in continental languages. The letter ā is used to denote the sound of a in " hare."

To those who have so kindly assisted me, — in particular to Rev. E. W. Meany of Santa Fé, and to Dr. Norton B. Strong, of the United States Army, — I herewith tender my heartfelt thanks.

AD. F. BANDELIER

SANTA Fé, NEW MEXICO.

PREFACE TO THE SECOND EDITION

THE aim of our good and lamented friend in writing this book was to place before the public, in novelistic garb, an account of the life and activities of the Pueblo Indians before the coming of white men. The information on which it is based was the result of his personal observations during many years of study among the sedentary tribes of New Mexico and in Spanish archives pertaining thereto in connection with his researches for the Archæological Institute of America. He spent months in continuous study at the Tehua pueblo of San Juan and the Queres pueblo of Cochití, and the regard in which he was held by the simple folk of those and other native villages was sincerely affectionate. Bandelier's labors in his chosen field were commenced at a time when a battle with hardship was a part of the daily routine, and his method of performing the tasks before him was of the kind that produced important results often at the expense of great suffering, which on more than one occasion almost shut out his life.

Because not understood, *The Delight Makers* was not received at first with enthusiastic favor. It seemed unlike the great student of technical problems deliberately to write a book the layman might read with interest and profit; but his object once comprehended, the volume was received in the spirit in which the venture was initiated and for a long while search for a copy has often been in vain.

Bandelier has come unto his own. More than one serious student of the ethno-history of our Southwest has frankly declared that the basis of future investigation of the kind that Bandelier inaugurated will always be the writings of that eminent man. Had he been permitted to live and labor, nothing would have given him greater satisfaction than the knowledge that the people among whom he spent so many years are of those who fully appreciate the breadth of his learning and who have been instrumental in the creation, by proclamation of the President, of the " Bandelier National Monument," for the purpose of preserving for future generations some of the archæological remains he was the first to observe and describe.

F. W. HODGE.

Smithsonian Institution,
Washington, D. C.,
September 25, 1916.

NOTE

A SPECIAL interest attaches to the illustrations, now first included in this edition. Many of them are from photographs made by Chas. F. Lummis in 1890, under the supervision of Bandelier, and with special reference to "The Delight Makers,' then being written. These two friends were the first students to explore the Tyuonyi and its neighborhood. In rain and shine, afoot, without blankets or overcoats, with no more provision than a little *atole* (pop-corn meal) and sweet chocolate, they climbed the cliffs, threaded the cañons, slept in caves or under trees, measured, mapped and photographed the ruins and landscapes with a 40-pound camera, and laid the basis-notes for part of Bandelier's monumental "Final Report" to the Archæological Institute of America.

A few later photographs from the same hand show part of the excavation done in the Tyuonyi by the School of American Archæology—through whose loving and grateful efforts this cañon has been set apart as a National Monument bearing the name of its discoverer and chronicler,

ADOLF F. BANDELIER.

Thanks are due also to Hon. Frederick C. Hicks, M.C., for six very interesting photographs of the Zuñis and their country.

IN MEMORY

———

ONE day of August, 1888, in the teeth of a particular New Mexico sand-storm that whipped pebbles the size of a bean straight to your face, a ruddy, bronzed, middle-aged man, dusty but unweary with his sixty-mile tramp from Zuñi, walked into my solitary camp at Los Alamitos. Within the afternoon I knew that here was the most exraordinary mind I had met. There and then began the uncommon friendship which lasted till his death, a quarter of a century later; and a love and admiration which will be of my dearest memories so long as I shall live. I was at first suspicious of the "pigeon-hole memory" which could not only tell me some Queres word I was searching for, but add: "Policárpio explained that to me in Cochití, November 23, 1881." But I discovered that this classified memory was an integral part of this extraordinary genius. The acid tests of life-long collaboration proved not only this but the judicial poise, the marvelous insight and the intellectual chastity of Bandelier's mind. I cannot conceive of anything in the world which would have made him trim his sails as a historian or a student for any advantage here or hereafter.

Aside from keen mutual interests of documentary and ethnologic study, we came to know one another humanly by the hard proof of the Frontier. Thousands of miles of wilderness and desert we trudged side by side—camped, starved, shivered, learned and were Glad together. Our joint pursuits in comfort at our homes (in Santa Fé and Isleta, respectively) will always be memorable to me; but never so wonderful as that companioning in the hardships of what was, in our day, the really difficult fringe of the Southwest. There was not a decent road. We had no endowment, no vehicles. Bandelier was once loaned a horse; and after riding two miles, led it the rest of the thirty. So we went always by foot; my big camera and glass plates in the knapsack on my back, the heavy tripod under my arm; his aneroid, surveying instruments, and satchel of the almost microscopic notes which he kept fully and precisely every night by the camp-fire (even when I had to crouch over him and the precious paper with my water-proof focusing cloth) somehow bestowed about him. Up and down pathless cliffs, through tangled cañons, fording icy streams and ankle-deep sands, we travailed; no blankets, overcoats, or other shelter; and the only commissary a few cakes of sweet chocolate, and a small sack of parched popcorn meal. Our "lodging was the cold ground." When we could find a cave, a tree, or anything to temper the wind or keep off part of the rain, all right. If not, the Open. So I came to love him as well as revere. I had known many "scientists" and what happened when they really got Outdoors. He was in no way an athlete—nor even muscular. I was both—and not very long before had completed my thirty-five-hundred-mile "Tramp Across the Conti-

nent." But I never had to "slow down" for him.
Sometimes it was necessary to use laughing force to
detain him at dark where we had water and a leaning
cliff, instead of stumbling on through the trackless
night to an unknown "Somewheres." He has always
reminded me of John Muir, the only other man I have
known intimately who was as insatiate a climber and
inspiring a talker. But Bandelier had one advantage.
He could find common ground with *anyone*. I have
seen him with Presidents, diplomats, Irish section-
hands, Mexican peons, Indians, authors, scientists and
"society." Within an hour or so he was easily the
Center. Not unconscious of his power, he had an
extraordinary and sensitive modesty, which handi-
capped him through life among those who had the
"gift of push." He never put himself forward either
in person or in his writing. But something about him
fascinated all these far-apart classes of people, when
he spoke. His command of English, French, Spanish,
and German might have been expected; but his facil-
ity in acquiring the "dialects" of railroad men and
cowboys, or the language of an Indian tribe, was
almost uncanny. When he first visited me, in Isleta,
he knew just three words of Tigua. In ten days he
could make himself understood by the hour with the
Principales in their own unwritten tongue. Of course,
this was one secret of his extraordinary success in
learning the inner heart of the Indians.

I saw it proved again in our contact with the Qui-
chua and Aymará and other tribes of Peru and
Bolivia.

I have known many scholars and some heroes—but they seldom come in the same original package. As I remember Bandelier with smallpox alone in the two-foot snows of the Manzanos; his tens of thousands of miles of tramping, exploring, measuring, describing, in the Southwest; his year afoot and alone in Northern Mexico, with no more weapon than a pen-knife, on the trails of raiding Apaches (where "scientific expeditions" ten years later, when the Apache was eliminated, needed armed convoys and pack-trains enough for a punitive expedition, and wrote pretentious books about what every scholar has known for three hundred years) I deeply wonder at the dual quality of his intellect. Among them all, I have never known such student and such explorer lodged in one tenement.

We were knit not only thus but in the very intimacies of life—sharing hopes and bereavements. My first son, named for him, should now be twenty-two. The old home in Santa Fé was as my own. The truly wonderful little woman he found in Peru for mate—who shared his hardships among the cannibals of the Amazonas and elsewhere, and so aided and still carries on his work—I met in her maiden home, and am glad I may still call her friend.

Naturally, among my dearest memories of our trampings together is that of the Rito, the Tyuonyi. It had never in any way been pictured before. We were the first students that ever explored it. He had discovered it, and was writing "The Delight Makers." What days those were! The weather was no friend of ours, nor of the camera's. We were wet and half-fed, and cold by night, even in the ancient tiny caves. But the unforgettable glory of it all!

To-day thousands of people annually visit the Tyuonyi at ease, and camp for weeks in comfort. The School of American Archæology has a summer ses-session there; and its excavations verify Bandelier's surmises. Normal students and budding archæolo-gists sleep in the very caves (identified) of the Eagle People, the Turquoise, Snake and other clans. And in that enchanted valley we remember not only the Ancients, but the man who gave all this to the world.

During the six years I was Librarian of the Los Angeles Public Library, far later, no other out-of-print book on the Southwest was so eagerly sought as "The Delight Makers." We had great trouble in get-ting our own copy, which slept in the safe. The many students who wished copies of their very own were referred to dealers in Americana, who searched for this already rare volume; and many were proud to get it, at last, at ten, fifteen and even twenty times its orig-inal price. It will always be a standard—the most photographic story yet printed of the life of the prehistoric Americans.

CHARLES F. LUMMIS.

THE DELIGHT MAKERS

THE DELIGHT MAKERS

——◆——

CHAPTER I.

THE mountain ranges skirting the Rio Grande del Norte on the west, nearly opposite the town of Santa Fé, in the Territory of New Mexico, are to-day but little known. The interior of the chain, the Sierra de los Valles, is as yet imperfectly explored. Still, these bald-crested mountains, dark and forbidding as they appear from a distance, conceal and shelter in their deep gorges and clefts many a spot of great natural beauty, surprisingly picturesque, but difficult of access. From the river these cañons, as they are called in New Mexico, can be reached only by dint of toilsome climbing and clambering; for their western openings are either narrow gaps, or access to them is barred by colossal walls and pillars of volcanic rocks. The entire formation of the chain, as far as it faces the Rio Grande, is volcanic, the walls of the gorges consisting generally of a friable white or yellowish tufa containing nodules of black, translucent obsidian. The rock is so soft that in many places it can be scooped out or detached with the most primitive tools, or even with the fingers alone. Owing to this peculiarity the slopes exposed to the south and east, whence most of the heavy rains strike them, are invariably abrupt, and often even perpendicular; whereas the opposite declivities, though steep, still afford room for scanty vegetation. The gorges run from west to east, — that is, they descend from the moun-

tain crests to the Rio Grande, cutting the long and narrow
pedestal on which the high summits are resting.

Through some but not all of these gorges run never-fail-
ing streams of clear water. In a few instances the gorge
expands and takes the proportions of a narrow vale. Then
the high timber that usually skirts the rivulets shrinks to
detached groves, and patches of clear land appear, which,
if cultivated, would afford scanty support to one or two
modern families. To the village Indian such tillable spots
were of the greatest value. The deep ravine afforded shelter
not only against the climate but against roving enemies, and
the land was sufficient for his modest crops ; since his wants
were limited, and game was abundant.

The material of which the walls of these cañons are composed, suggested in times past to the house-building Indian
the idea of using them as a home. The tufa and pumice-
stone are so friable that, as we have said, the rock can be
dug or burrowed with the most primitive implements. It
was easier, in fact, to excavate dwellings than to pile up
walls in the open air.

Therefore the northern sides of these secluded gorges
are perforated in many places by openings similar in appearance to pigeon-holes. These openings are the points of
exit and entrance of artificial caves, dug out by sedentary
aborigines in times long past. They are met with in clusters of as many as several hundred ; more frequently, however, the groups are small. Sometimes two or more tiers
of caves are superimposed. From the objects scattered
about and in the cells, and from the size and disposition of
the latter, it becomes evident that the people who excavated
and inhabited them were on the same level of culture as
the so-called Pueblo Indians of New Mexico.

It is not surprising, therefore, that some traditions and
myths are preserved to-day among the Pueblos concerning

these cave-villages. Thus the Tehua Indians of the pueblo
of Santa Clara assert that the artificial grottos of what they
call the Puiye and the Shufinne, west of their present abodes,
were the homes of their ancestors at one time. The Queres
of Cochiti in turn declare that the tribe to which they belong, occupied, many centuries before the first coming of
Europeans to New Mexico, the cluster of cave-dwellings,
visible at this day although abandoned and in ruins, in that
romantic and picturesquely secluded gorge called in the
Queres dialect Tyuonyi, and in Spanish "El Rito de los
Frijoles."

The Rito is a beautiful spot. Situated in a direct line
not over twenty miles west of Santa Fé, it can still be
reached only after a long day's tedious travel. It is a narrow valley, nowhere broader than half a mile ; and from where
it begins in the west to where it closes in a dark and
gloomy entrance, scarcely wide enough for two men to pass
abreast, in the east, its length does not exceed six miles.
Its southern rim is formed by the slope of a timbered mesa,
and that slope is partly overgrown by shrubbery. The
northern border constitutes a line of vertical cliffs of yellowish and white pumice, projecting and re-entering like deco-
rations of a stage, — now perpendicular and smooth for some
distance, now sweeping back in the shape of an arched
segment. These cliffs vary in height, although nowhere are
they less than two hundred feet. Their tops rise in huge
pillars, in crags and pinnacles. Brushwood and pine timber crown the mesa of which these fantastic projections are
but the shaggy border.

Through the vale itself rustles the clear and cool brook
to which the name of Rito de los Frijoles is applied. It
meanders on, hugging the southern slope, partly through
open spaces, partly through groves of timber, and again
past tall stately pine-trees standing isolated in the valley.

Willows, cherry-trees, cottonwoods, and elders form small thickets along its banks. The Rito is a permanent stream-let notwithstanding its small size. Its water freezes in win-ter, but it never dries up completely during the summer months.

Bunches of tall grass, low shrubbery, and cactus grow in the open spaces between rocky débris fallen from above. They also cover in part low mounds of rubbish, and ruins of a large pentagonal building erected formerly at the foot of a slope leading to the cliffs. In the cliffs themselves, for a distance of about two miles, numerous caves dug out by the hand of man are visible. Some of these are yet perfect; others have wholly crumbled away except the rear wall. From a distance the port-holes and indentations appear like so many pigeons' nests in the naked rock. Together with the cavities formed by amygdaloid cham-bers and crevices caused by erosion, they give the cliffs the appearance of a huge, irregular honeycomb.

These ruins, inside as well as outside the northern walls of the cañon of the Rito, bear testimony to the tradition still current among the Queres Indians of New Mexico that the Rito, or Tyuonyi, was once inhabited by people of their kind, nay, even of their own stock. But the time when those people wooed and wed, lived and died, in that secluded vale is past long, long ago. Centuries previous to the ad-vent of the Spaniards, the Rito was already deserted. Noth-ing remains but the ruins of former abodes and the memory of their inhabitants among their descendants. These an-cient people of the Rito are the actors in the story which is now to be told; the stage in the main is the Rito itself. The language of the actors is the Queres dialect, and the time when the events occurred is much anterior to the dis-covery of America, to the invention of gunpowder and the printing-press in Europe. Still the Rito must have appeared then much as it appears now, — a quiet, lovely, picturesque retreat, peaceful when basking in the sunlight, wonderfully quiet when the stars sparkled over it, or the moon shed its floods of silver on the cliffs and on the murmuring brook below.

In the lower or western part of its course the Tyuonyi rushes in places through thickets and small groves, out of which rise tall pine-trees. It is very still on the banks of the brook when, on a warm June day, noon-time is just past and no breeze fans the air; not a sound is heard beyond the rippling of the water; the birds are asleep, and the noise of human activity does not reach there from the cliffs. Still, on the day of which we are now speaking, a voice arose from the thicket, calling aloud, —

"Umo, — 'grandfather!'"[1]

"To ima satyumishe, — 'come hither, my brother,'" another voice replied in the same dialect, adding, "See what a big fish I have caught."

It sounded as though this second voice had issued from the very waters of the streamlet.

Pine boughs rustled, branches bent, and leaves shook. A step scarcely audible was followed by a noiseless leap. On a boulder around which flowed streams of limpid water there alighted a young Indian.

He was of medium height and well-proportioned. His hands and feet were rather small and delicate. He carried his head erect with ease and freedom. Jet-black hair, slightly waving, streamed loose over temples and cheeks, and was gathered at the back in a short thick knot. In front it parted naturally, leaving exposed a narrow strip of

[1] The word "umo" properly signifies "grandfather;" but it is used indiscriminately for all ages and sexes in calling. An old man, for instance, will call his grandchild "umo;" so will a wife her husband, a brother his sister, etc.

the brow. The features of the face, though not regular, were still attractive, for large black eyes, almond-shaped, shone bright from underneath heavy lashes. The complexion was dusky, and the skin had a velvety gloss. Form, carriage, and face together betokened a youth of about eighteen years.

His costume was very plain. A garment of unbleached cotton, coarsely woven, covered the body as low as the knee. This garment, sleeveless and soiled by wear, was tied over the right shoulder. A reddish-brown scarf or belt of the same material fastened it around the waist. Feet, arms, and the left shoulder were bare. Primitive as was this costume, there was, nevertheless, an attempt here and there at decoration. The belt was ornamented with black and white stitches; from each ear hung a turquoise suspended by a cotton thread, and a necklace of coloured pebbles strung on yucca fibre encircled the neck.

Like a statue of light-coloured bronze decked with scanty drapery, and adorned with crude trinkets, holding a bow in the right hand, while the left clenched a few untipped arrows, the youth stood on the boulder outlined against the shrubbery, immovable above the running brook. His gaze was fixed on the opposite bank, where a youngster was kneeling.

The latter was a boy of perhaps nine years. A dirty wrap hung loosely over shoulders and back, and no necklace or ear-pendants decorated his body. But the childish features were enlivened by a broad grin of satisfaction, and his eyes sparkled like coals just igniting, while he pointed to a large mountain trout which he pressed against a stone with both hands. He looked at the older youth with an expression not merely of pleasure, but of familiar intimacy also. It was clear that both boys were children of the same parents.

The younger one spoke first, —

"See here, Okoya," he began, grinning; "while you are older than I, and bigger and stronger, I am more cunning than you. Ever since the sun came out you have followed the turkeys, and what have you? Nothing! Your hands are empty! I have just come down from the field, and look! I caught this fish in the water. Shall we fry and eat it here, or carry it home to the mother?"

The older brother did not relish the taunt; his lips curled. He replied scornfully, —

"Any child may catch a fish, but only men can follow turkeys. The tzina is shy and wary; it knows how sure my aim is, therefore it hides when I go out to hunt."

The little one replied to this pompous explanation with a clear mocking laugh.

"Turkeys care nothing about you," he retorted. "It is nothing to them whether you go out or not!"

"Shyuote," his brother scolded, "stop prating about things of which you do not know. It is true I am not one of the order of hunters, Shyayak, but I may become so soon." He stopped, as if a sudden thought had struck him, and then exclaimed: "Now I know why luck has failed me this morning! When I left our houses I should have scattered meal, and placed a pebble on the heap beside the trail, and offered a plume to our Mother Above. All this I neglected. Now I am punished for it by the birds concealing themselves. For had they come out — "

"You would have missed them," tauntingly replied the other. "If you want to kill turkeys join the Koshare. Then you will catch them with roots and flowers."

Okoya grew angry.

"Hush! foolish boy," he retorted, "what are the Koshare to me? Don't speak about such things here. Come, take your fish, and let us go home."

With this Okoya leaped over the brook. Shyuote whis-pered audibly to him, "Yes; you are very fond of the Koshare." But the sarcastic remark was not heeded by the elder lad, who turned to go, Shyuote following him. Proudly the little boy tossed his fish from one hand to the other.

Beyond the straight and lofty pine trunks a whitish glare soon appeared. Brilliant sunlight broke through the tree-tops, and played around the dark needles, turning them into a brighter, lighter, emerald green. A background of yellow and cream-coloured rocks, visible now through open-ings in the shrubbery, showed that the boys were approach-ing a clear space.

Here the elder one suddenly stopped, turned to his brother, looked straight at him, and asked, —

"Shyuote, what have you heard about the Koshare?"

Instead of answering the child looked down, indifferent and silent, as if he had not heard the query.

"What have you heard, boy?" continued the other.

Shyuote shrugged his shoulders. He had no inclination to reply.

"Why don't you answer?" Okoya persisted.

His brother looked up, cast a furtive glance at the in-terlocutor, then stared vacantly, but with head erect, before him. His eyes were glassy and without any expression.

Whenever the Indian does not wish to speak on any subject, whatever it be, no power on earth can compel him to break silence. Okoya, as an Indian, felt rather than understood this; and the child's refusal to answer a very simple question aroused his suspicions. He looked at the stubborn boy for a moment, undecided whether he would not resort to force. The child's taunts had mortified his pride in the first place; now that child's reticence bred misgivings. He nevertheless restrained both anger and curiosity for the present, not because of indifference but for policy's sake, and turned to go. Shyuote looked for a moment as if he wished to confess to his brother all that the latter inquired about, but soon pouted, shrugged his shoulders, and set out after Okoya in a lively fox-trot again.

The valley lay before them; they had reached the end of the grove.

Smiling in the warm glow of a June day, with a sky of deepest azure, the vale of the Rito expanded between the spot which the boys had reached and the rocky gateways in the west, where that valley seemed to begin. Fields, small and covered with young, bushy maize-plants, skirted the brook, whose silvery thread was seen here and there as its meanderings carried it beneath the shadow of shrubs and trees, or exposed it to the full light of the dazzling sun. In the plantations human forms appeared, now erect, now bent down over their work. A ditch of medium size bordered the fields on the north, carrying water from the brook for purposes of irrigation. Still north of the ditch, and between it and the cliffs, arose a tall building, which from a distance looked like a high clumsy pile of clay or reddish earth.

This pile was irregularly terraced. Human beings stood on the terraces or moved along them. Now and then one was seen to rise from the interior of the pile to one of the terraced roofs, or another slowly sank from sight, as if descending into the interior of the earthy heap. On the outside, beams leaned against it, and on them people went up and down, as if climbing ladders. Thin films of smoke quivered in the air from imperceptible flues.

The cliffs themselves extended north of this building and east and west as far as the range of view permitted, like a

yellowish ribbon of towering height with innumerable flexures and alternations of light and shade. Their base was
enlivened by the bustle of those who dwelt in caves all
along the foot of the imposing rocky wall. Where to-day
only vacant holes stare at the visitor, at the hour on the day
when our story begins, human eyes peered through. Other
doors were closed by deer-hides or robes. Sometimes a
man, a woman, or a child, would creep out of one of these
openings, and climbing upward, disappear in the entrance
of an upper tier of cave-dwellings. Others would descend
the slope from the cliffs to the fields, while still others
returned from the banks of the ditch or of the brook. At
the distance from which the boys viewed the landscape all
passed noiselessly; no human voice, no clamour disturbed
the stillness of the scene.

Peaceful as Nature appeared, neither of the youth were in
the least struck by its charms or influenced by the spell
which such a tranquil and cheerful landscape is likely to
exercise upon thinking and feeling man. With both it was
indifference; for the Indian views Nature with the eyes of a
materially interested spectator only. But the elder brother
had another reason for not noticing the beauty of the scene.
He was not only troubled, he was seriously embarrassed.
The hint thrown out by his little brother about the Koshare
had struck him; for it led to the inference that the child
had knowledge of secret arts and occult practices of which
even he, Okoya, although on the verge of manhood, had
never received any intimation. Far more yet than this
knowledge, which Shyuote might have obtained through
mere accident, the hint at unpleasant relations between
Okoya and the Koshare startled the latter.

It was perfectly true that he not only disliked but even
hated the cluster of men to which the name of Koshare was
given in the tribe; but he had concealed his feelings as care-

fully as possible until now. Only once, as far as he could
remember, had he spoken of his aversion; and then it was
during an absolutely confidential conversation with his own
mother, who seemed to entertain like sentiments.

To his father he had never uttered a word; because his
father was himself a Koshare. Whatever Shyuote knew, he
could only have gathered by overhearing a conversation of
the Koshare among themselves, in which it was mentioned
that he, Okoya, harboured ill-feelings toward that brother-
hood. In that case he might be exposed to serious danger,
since, as he believed, those people were in possession of
knowledge of a higher order, and practised arts of an occult
nature. Against danger arising from such a source, Okoya
considered himself utterly defenceless.

The more he tried to think over these matters, the more
troubled his mind became. Only one thought appeared
logical and probable and that was that the boy had overheard one or other of the Koshare's intimate conversations.
But how came it that the Koshare knew about Okoya's
aversion toward them? Who could have told them? Only
his mother knew the secret! Had she, perhaps, she —
The thought was like a spark which glowed for a while, grew
to a flame, flared and flickered unsteadily within his heart,
then began to shrink. No, no; it was impossible! it could
not be! His mother would never betray her child! The
flame died out, the spark remained fast dying. Suddenly it
blazed up again as if some breath had fanned it.

With renewed insistence, it struck Okoya that even if
Shyuote had merely overheard a conversation and the child's
knowledge was derived from that source, the most extraordinary part of the information could only have come from
one source, — the person in whom he had confided, his
mother! She alone could have told the Koshare that
Okoya hated them. The spark flared up anew; it burst ou*

in a wild flame of suspicion. It singed the heart and smothered feeling as well as reason. It so completely absorbed his thoughts, that Okoya forgot everything else. Instead of walking along at a quiet easy gait, he rushed fast and faster, wrapped in dismal despair and in wild impotent wrath. Heedless of his little companion he ran, panting with agitation, until Shyuote, unable to keep pace and startled at his wild gait, pulled his garment and begged him to stop.

"Brother," he cried, "why do you go so fast? I cannot follow you!"

Okoya came to a sudden halt, and turned toward the boy like one aroused from a sinister dream. Shyuote stared at him with surprise akin to fright. How changed was his appearance! Never before had he seen him with a countenance so haggard, with eyes hollow and yet burning with a lurid glow. Loose hair hung down over forehead and cheeks, perspiration stood on the brow in big drops. The child involuntarily shrunk back, and Okoya, noticing it, gasped, —

"You are right, the day is long yet and the houses near. We will go slower."

Bowing his head again he went on at a slower gait.

Shyuote followed in silence. Although surprised at the change in his brother's looks, he did not for a moment entertain the thought or desire of inquiring into the cause of it. He was fully satisfied that as long as Okoya did not see fit to speak of the matter, he had no right to ask about it: in short, that it was none of his business.

Meanwhile dark and dismal thoughts were chasing each other within the elder brother's soul. Doubt and suspicion became more and more crushing. He was tempted to break the spell and interrogate Shyuote once more, even to wrench from him, if needs be, a full explanation. The boy

Portrait of the Author

The east end of the Cañon of the Tyuonyi

(Upper picture) A modern Indian Dance
(Lower picture) An estufa

Rito de los Frijoles

Cavate rooms in cliff; Ruins of Talus Pueblo at the foot of cliff

A westerly cliff of the habitations of the Tyuonyi, showing second and third story caves, and some high lookout caves

(Upper picture) A Navajo Hogan
(Lower picture) The Heart of the Tyuonyi: The excavated
lower story of the great terraced Communal House

Rito de los Frijoles
A cliff estufa of the Snake-Clan

The Dance of the Ayash Tyucotz

Indian Pueblo Dances of To-day
(Upper picture) Lining up for the dance
(Lower picture) The "Clowns"

Type of old Indian woman

Juanico: A member of the modern village-council

The Hishtanyi Chayan, or Chief Medicine Man

Looking out from one of the weathered Cave-Rooms of the
Snake-Clan

Rito de los Frijoles

Ruins of an Ancient Pueblo

A Modern Pueblo

was old enough to enjoy that great and often disagreeable quality of the American Indian, reticence. Furthermore, he might have been forbidden to speak.

If the Indian is not an ideal being, he is still less a stolid mentally squalid brute. He is not reticent out of imbecility or mental weakness. He fails properly to understand much of what takes place around him, especially what happens within the circle of our modern civilization, but withal he is far from indifferent toward his surroundings. He observes, compares, thinks, reasons, upon whatever he sees or hears, and forms opinions from the basis of his own peculiar culture. His senses are very acute for natural phenomena; his memory is excellent, as often as he sees fit to make use of it. There is no difference between him and the Caucasian in original faculties, and the reticence peculiar to him under certain circumstances is not due to lack of mental aptitude.

He does not practise that reticence alike toward all. A great number of examples seems to establish the fact that the Indian has developed a system of casuistry, based upon a remarkably thorough knowledge of human nature. Certain matters are kept concealed from some people, whereas they are freely discussed with others, and *vice versa*. The Indian hardly ever keeps a secret to himself alone; it is nearly always shared by others whom the matter directly concerns. It may be said of the red man that he keeps secrets in the same manner that he lives, — namely, in groups or clusters. The reason is that with him individualism, or the mental and moral independence of the individual, has not attained the high degree of development which prevails among white races.

When Europeans began to colonize America in the fifteenth and sixteenth centuries, the social organization of its inhabitants presented a picture such as had disap-

peared long before on the continent of Europe. Everywhere there prevailed linguistic segregation, — divisions into
autonomous groups called tribes or stocks, and within each
of these, equally autonomous clusters, whose mutual alli-
ance for purposes of sustenance and defence constituted
the basis of tribal society. The latter clusters were the
clans, and they originated during the beginnings of the
human family. Every clan formed a group of supposed
blood-relatives, looking back to a mythical or traditional
common ancestor. Descent from the mother being always
plain, the clan claimed descent in the female line even if
every recollection of the female ancestor were lost, and
theoretically all the members of one clan were so many
brothers and sisters. This organization still exists in the
majority of tribes; the members of one clan cannot inter-
marry, and, if all the women of a clan die, that clan dies
out also, since there is nobody left to perpetuate it. The
tribe is in reality but a league; the clan is the unit.
At the time we speak of, the affairs of each tribe were
administered by an assembly of delegates from all its clans
who at the same time arbitrated inevitable disputes between
the several blood-relations.

Each clan managed its own affairs, of which no one
outside of its members needed to know anything. Since
the husbands always belonged to a different consanguine
group from their wives, and the children followed their
mother's line of descent, the family was permanently divided. There was really no family in our sense of the
word. The Indian has an individual name only. He
is, in addition, distinguished by the name of his clan,
which in turn has its proper cognomen. The affairs of
the father's clan did not concern his wife or his children,
whereas a neighbour might be his confidant on such matters. The mother, son, and daughter spoke among them-

selves of matters of which the father was not entitled to
know, and about which he scarcely ever felt enough curiosity to inquire. Consequently there grew a habit of not
caring about other people's affairs unless they affected one's
own, and of confiding secrets to those only whom they
could concern, and who were entitled to know them.
In the course of time the habit became a rule of education.   Reticence, secrecy, discretion, are therefore no
virtues with the Indian; they are simply the result of
training.

Okoya too had been under the influence of such training, and he knew that Shyuote, young as he was, had already similar seeds planted within him.   But uncertainty
was insufferable; it weighed too heavily upon him, he
could no longer bear it.

"Umo," he burst out, turning abruptly and looking at
the boy in an almost threatening manner, "how do you
know that I dislike the Koshare?"

Shyuote cast his eyes to the ground, and remained silent.   His brother repeated the query; the little fellow
only shrugged his shoulders.   With greater insistence the
elder proceeded, —

"Shyuote Tihua, who told you that the Delight Makers
are not precious to me, nor I to them?"

Shyuote shook his head, pouted, and stared vacantly to
one side.   He manifestly refused to answer.

Cold perspiration stood on the brow of the elder brother;
his body quivered in anguish; he realized the truth of
his suspicions.   Unable any longer to control himself he
cried, —

"It is my mother who told them!"

Trembling, with clenched hands and gnashing teeth, he
gazed at the child unconsciously.   Shyuote, frightened at
his wild and menacing attitude, and ignorant of the real

cause of his brother's excitement, raised his hand to his
forehead and began to sob.

A shout coming from the immediate vicinity aroused and
startled Okoya. A voice called out to him, —

"Umo!"

He looked around in surprise. They were standing
close to the cultivated plots, and a man loomed up from
between the maize-plants. He it was who called, and as
soon as Okoya turned toward him he beckoned the youth
to come nearer. Okoya's face darkened; he reluctantly
complied, leaped over the ditch, walked up to the interlocutor, and stood still before him in the attitude of quiet
expectancy with downcast eyes. Shyuote had dropped to
the ground; the call did not interfere with his sobs; he
pouted rather than grieved.

Okoya's interlocutor was a man of strong build, apparently in the forties. His features, although somewhat flat
and broad, created a favourable impression at first; upon
closer scrutiny, however, the eyes modified that impression. They were small, and their look piercing rather
than bright. His costume was limited to a tattered
breechclout of buckskin. A collar of small white shells
encircled the neck, and from this necklace dangled a
triangular piece of alabaster, flat, and with a carving
on it suggesting the shape of a dragon-fly. His hair
streamed loose over the left ear, where there was fastened to the black coarse strands a tuft of grayish
down.

This individual eyed Okoya in silence for a moment,
as if inspecting his person; then he inquired, —

"Where do you come from?"

The young fellow looked up and replied, —

"From below," pointing to the lower end of the
gorge.

"What did you hunt?" the other continued, glancing at the bow and arrows of the boy.

"Tzina;" and with perceptible embarrassment Okoya added, "but I killed nothing."

The man seemed not to heed the humiliation which this confession entailed, and asked, —

"Have you seen tracks of the mountain-sheep down yonder?"

"Not one; but I saw at a distance on the slope two bears very large and strong."

The other shook his head.

"Then there are no mountain sheep toward that end of the Tyuonyi," he said, waving his left hand toward the southeast, "thank you, boy," at the same time extending his right to the youth. Okoya grasped it, and breathed on the outside of the hand. Then he said, "hoa umo," and turned and sauntered back to where his little brother was still squatting and pouting, morose and silent.

The man had also turned around, bent down, and gone on weeding the corn. Withal he did not lose sight of the boys; on the contrary, an occasional stealthy glance from his half-closed eyes shot over where they met.

Shyuote rose from the ground. His eyes were dry, but he glanced at his brother with misgivings as well as with curiosity. The latter felt a sudden pang upon beholding the childish features. The short interruption, though annoying at first, had diverted him from gloomy thoughts. Now, everything came back to his mind with renewed force, — the same anguish, the feeling of utter helplessness in case of impending danger, indignation at what he believed to have been base treason on the part of his mother, — all this rushed upon him with fearful force, and he stood again motionless, a picture of wild perplexity. His face betokened the state of his mind. Shyuote did not dare to

inquire of him further than to ask a very insignificant question, — namely, who the man was that had called.

Okoya answered readily, for this query was almost a relief, — a diversion which enabled him to subdue his agitation. "Tyope Tihua," he said hastily, "wanted to know if
I had seen any mountain sheep. I told him that I had
only seen bear-tracks. Let him follow those," he growled.
"Come on, satyumishe, it is getting late."

While this conversation had been carried on, the boys,
now hurrying and now slackening their pace, had arrived
within a short distance of the tall clay-pile, which was seen
to be a high polygonal building, apparently closed on all
sides. Between them and this edifice there was still another lower one, not unlike an irregular honey-comb.
About forty cells, separated from each other by walls of
earth, carried up from the ground to a few inches above
the terraced roof, constituted a ground-floor on which
rested a group of not more than a dozen similar cells.
The walls of this structure were of stones, irregularly broken and clumsily piled, but they were covered by a thick
coating of clay so that nothing of the rough core remained
visible. Instead of doors or entrances, air-holes, round or
oval, perforated these walls.

The house appeared empty. No smoke flitted over the
flat roof; the coating was so recent that many places were
hardly dry.

North of this building, a circular structure thirty feet in
diameter rose a few feet only above the soil, like the upper
part of a sunken cylinder. Its top was flat, and large flags
of stone formed a rough staircase leading to its roof. In the
centre, a square opening appeared, out of which a tall beam,
notched at regular intervals like a primitive ladder, protruded, and down which also the beam disappeared as if
extended into the bowels of the earth. This edifice, half

underground, half above the soil, was what to-day is called in New Mexico an *estufa*.[1] This Spanish word has become a technical term, and we shall hereafter use it in the course of the story as well as the designations *tshikia* and *kaaptsh* of the Queres Indians.

The estufas were more numerous in a single pueblo formerly than they are now. Nor are they always sunken. At the Rito there were at least ten, five of which were circular chambers in the rock of the cliffs. These chambers or halls were, in the times we speak of, gathering places for men exclusively. No woman was permitted to enter, unless for the purpose of carrying food to the inmates. Each clan had its own estufa, and the young men slept in it under the surveillance of one or more of the aged principals, until they married, and frequently even afterward.

There the young men became acquainted with the affairs of their individual connections, and little by little also with the business of the tribe. There, during the long evenings of winter, old men taught them the songs and prayers embodying traditions and myths, first of their own clan, then of the tribe.[2] The estufa was school, club-house, nay, armory to a certain extent. It was more. Many of the prominent religious exercises took place in it. The estufa on special occasions became transformed into a temple for the clan who had reared it.

From the depths of this structure there came a series of

[1] *Estufa* properly means a stove, and the name was applied to those semi-subterranean places by the Spaniards on account of their comfortable temperature in winter. They recalled to them the *temazcalli*, or sweat-houses, of Mexico.

[2] The preservation of traditions is much systematized among the Pueblo Indians. Certain societies know hardly any other but the folk-tales relating to their own particular origin. To obtain correct tradition it is necessary to gain the confidence of men high in degree. That is mostly very difficult.

dull sounds like beats of a drum. The youngsters stopped short, and looked at each other in surprise.

"The new house," whispered Okoya, "which the Corn-clan have built here is empty, yet there is somebody in its estufa. What may this mean?"

"Let us look into it," eagerly suggested Shyuote.

"Go you alone!" directed the elder brother. "I will walk on, and you can overtake me by-and-by."

That suited Shyuote. He crept stealthily toward the round building. There was an air-hole in the rim which rose above the ground. Crouching like a cat, the boy cautiously peered through this opening, but quickly withdrew with an expression of disappointment. The underground chamber was not even finished; its walls were dark and raw, the floor rough, and on this floor a half-dozen young fellows in every stage of dress or undress were lounging. One of them mechanically touched a small drum with a stick, while two or three of the others were humming a monotonous tune to the rhythm of his rappings. Shyuote stole away in evident discontent; his curiosity was satisfied, but at the expense of his expectations.

Loud laughter, screams, and animated talking diverted his attention, and caused him to run in the direction of the new house of the Corn clan. He heard the voice of his brother, but at the same time women's voices also, and as soon as he turned the farther corner of the building, he saw what was plainly a playful encounter between Okoya and a pair of young girls.

The former had his bow in hand ready to shoot, and he pointed the arrow at the maidens alternately; they, utterly unconcerned about his weapon, were pressing him with weapons of their own, which he was much more anxious to avoid than they his missiles. These were two pairs of very dirty hands filled and covered with liquid mud with which

the damsels attempted to decorate his person. Okoya was
clearly on the defensive, and the advantage so far seemed
on the side of his agressors. Shyuote flew to his assistance.
Rushing to a large vessel of burnt clay, standing alongside
the wall and filled with water, he plunged both hands into it,
and began to bespatter the assailants with the not very
clean liquid. Forthwith one of the girls turned against the
new enemy. She was older and taller than Shyuote. Seiz-
ing his raven locks she pulled him to the ground on his
face, knelt on the prostrate form, and then and there gave
the boy a series of energetic cuffs against which the youngster struggled and wriggled in the most desperate but
absolutely ineffectual manner. The fair sex held the balance of power and wielded it. At every attempt of Shyuote
to rise or to roll over, she pushed his face back into the
moist ground, she pulled his hair, thumped his shoulders,
and boxed his ears. She was in earnest, and Shyuote was
powerless in her firm grasp. He could not even scream,
for a thick coating of soil had fastened itself to his features,
had penetrated into eye, mouth, and nostrils. His fate was
as melancholy as it was ludicrous; it brought about a truce
between Okoya and the other maiden. They dropped, he
the weapon, she her muddy arms, and looked at the other
set of combatants with surprise and with immoderate
laughter. The Indian is not tender-hearted on such occasions. When the victorious beauty at last arose, suffering
her victim to turn over again, the merriment became uproarious, for Shyuote presented the appearance of a blowing, spitting, coughing, statue of dirt. His looks were in
no manner improved by his frenzy after the boy had rubbed
his eyes, and recovered his breath. Tears of rage rolled
down his cheeks over patches of sand and mud, and when
he noticed the mirth of the others Shyuote's fury knew no
bounds. He rushed madly at the triumphant lass, who

did not shrink from the hostile approach. The contest was threatening to assume serious proportions, when another person appeared upon the scene, at the sight of whom even Shyuote temporarily stayed all demonstrations, while Okoya seemed both startled and embarrassed. The new-comer was a young girl too; she carried on her head a vessel of burnt clay similar to a flat urn, decorated with black and red designs on cream-coloured ground, and filled with water.

To understand this scene we must know that the two girls had been engaged in putting on the last coat of plaster to the walls of the abode of the Corn people, when Okoya suddenly came upon them. At a glance they saw that he had been on a hunt, and also that he had hunted in vain. Here was a welcome opportunity for jeering and mockery. They interrupted their plastic labour, and turned against him with such merciless allusions to his ill-success, that unable any longer to reply to their sarcasm Okoya threatened them, in jest of course, with his bow. Instead of desisting, the girls at once moved upon him with muddy hands. The one who last appeared upon the scene, although assistant to the others, inasmuch as she carried the water needed in the preparation of the mud for plastering, had not seen the engagement just fought. She looked at the group in blank surprise, stood still without lifting the bowl from her head, and presented thus the appearance of a handsome statue, dusky and graceful, whose lustrous black eyes alone moved, glancing from one of the members of the group to the other. Those large expressive eyes plainly asked, "What does all this mean?"

The antagonists of Okoya and Shyuote were buxom lasses, rather short, thick-waisted, full-chested, with flat faces, prominent cheek-bones, and bright eyes. The third maiden was taller and much more graceful; her features were less coarse, less prominently distinctive. The nose was well-proportioned, the mouth also, although the lips were rather heavy. The eyes were large and beaming, soft yet not without an intelligent expression. All three girls were dressed nearly alike. A dark-blue cotton garment descended as far as the knees; it was tied over the left shoulder, and the right was exposed. A red-tinged scarf served as belt around the waist. Arms and feet were bare. The long black hair streamed loosely. Two of them wore heavy necklaces of green stones, red pebbles, and shell beads. The last comer carried only a single string of shell beads with an iridescent conch fastened to it in front. Ear-pendants of turquoises hung from the ears of all three.

The attention of the girl with the urn on her head soon rested on Shyuote, and she was the first to break the silence by a hearty peal of laughter. This started her companions again, and the one nearest to Okoya exclaimed, —

"Mitsha help us throw the water in your urn over the head of the boy. Okoya began it all, give it to him, too. You are strong enough."

At the mention of Okoya's name the maiden addressed as Mitsha started. She threw a quick glance like a flash at him. Her face quivered and coloured slightly. Turning away, she deposited the water-urn at the foot of the wall, and remained standing, her eyes directed to the cliffs, her lithe fingers carelessly playing with the beads of her necklace. She was disinclined to take any part in the fray, and her behaviour acted as a damper on the buoyancy of the others. Okoya hastily gathered up his arrows, and called Shyuote to his side. But the boy did not care to obey. Thirst for revenge held him to the spot of his defeat; he shook his fists at the girls, clenched his teeth, and began to threaten vengeance, and to shower uncomplimentary expressions upon them. As soon, however. as the one who

had so effectually routed him showed again a decided
movement toward his raven locks, he beat a hasty retreat to
his elder brother.   This change of base excited new hilarity,
and under a shower of jokes and sarcasms the two boys departed.   Okoya walked along at a steady gait; but Shyuote,
as soon as he considered the distance safe enough, turned
around, making grimaces at the belligerent damsels, vowing
vengeance, and uttering opprobrious epithets of the choicest
kind.   He noticed that the two returned his compliments
without reserve, whereas Mitsha stood in silence leaning
against the house-wall.   One single look, one earnest
almost sad glance, she sent after the disappearing form
of Shyuote's elder brother.

The main building was now close at hand.   It was an
irregular pentagon, and at places two, at others three
stories high.   With one single exception these stories
formed terraces, retreating successively from the ground to
the top like so many steps of a staircase.   Nowhere did
there appear any entrance.   Notched beams led up to trap-
doors in the roofs, similar beams penetrated into the interior below.   Absolute stillness reigned about the edifice.
Some women scoured scanty clothing in the ditch running
past the structure; on the terraces not a soul appeared.
The lads directed their course toward that side where the
three stories presented a perpendicular wall, and as they
neared it an entrance, or doorway, high enough for a man
and wide enough for four abreast appeared in the vertical
front.   It led them through a dark passage into an interior
court which was fairly clean and contained three estufas.
Its diameter did not exceed one hundred and fifty feet.

Toward this court, or yard, the stories of the building
descended in terraces also; but though everywhere beams
leaned up as ladders, access to the ground-floor was also
afforded by narrow doorways closed with hides or mats.   It

was hot and quiet in this yard; the sun shed glaring light into it and over the roofs. Naked urchins played and squirmed below, whereas above, an old woman or some aged man would cower motionless, shading their blear eyes with one hand and warming their cold frames in the heat. Okoya went directly to one of the ground-floor openings, lifted the deer-skin that hung over it, and called out the usual greeting, —

"Guatzena!"

"Opona, — 'come in,'" responded a woman's voice. Both lads obeyed the summons. At first the room seemed dark on account of the sudden contrast with the glare outside, but as soon as this first impression was overcome, it appeared moderately lighted. It was a chamber about fourteen feet long and ten feet wide, and its walls were whitewashed with burnt gypsum. Deer-hides and a mat plaited of yucca-leaves lay rolled up in one corner. A niche contained a small earthen bowl, painted white with black symbolic figures. A doorway to the right led into another compartment which seemed darker than the first. As soon as the boys entered the room, a woman appeared in this side doorway. She was small, slender, and apparently thirty-five years of age. Her features, notwithstanding the high cheek-bones, were attractive though wan and thin. An air of physical suffering lay over them like a thin cloudy veil. At the sight of this woman, Okoya's heart began to throb again; for she it was whom he so direly suspected, nay, accused of treachery and deceit. This woman was his mother.

CHAPTER II.

THE homes of the Pueblo Indians of New Mexico, especially as regards the size and disposition of the rooms, are
to-day slightly modified from what they were in former
times. An advance has been made, inasmuch as the buildings are not any longer the vast and ill-ventilated honey-
combs composed of hundreds of dingy shells, which they
were centuries ago. The houses, while large and many-
storied, are compartively less extensive, and the apartments less roomy than at the time when the Queres lived
in the Rito de los Frijoles.

The two rooms where we left the lads and their mother
at the close of the preceding chapter formed such a home.
In the front one the family slept at night, with the exception of Okoya who was obliged to join the other youths in
the estufa of his clan. The husband was not always at
home after sunset. But the mother, Shyuote, and a little
girl four years old invariably took their nightly rest there.
To the little girl we have not yet been introduced. When
the boys returned she was in the court-yard at play, and in
the usual state of complete undress which is the regular
condition of Indian children of her age.

The inner cell was kitchen and store-room, and there
the family partook of their meals.

Among the Pueblos the house was in charge of the
women exclusively, everything within the walls of the house,
the men's clothing and weapons excepted, belonging to the

housekeeper. Even the crops if once housed were controlled by her. As long as they were in the field, the
husband or masculine head of the family could dispose of
them. Afterward he must consult the woman, and he could
not sell an ear of corn without her consent. It is still so
to-day in many villages. Formerly all the field-products
were gathered and stored in the granaries of the several
clans whence each household drew its supplies. Even the
proceeds of communal hunts and fisheries were treated in
this manner. Only where the husband, son, or brother
killed game while out alone, could he do with it as he
pleased.

Not many centuries ago the members of each clan, or
rather the women, their offspring, and aged people who
were taken care of by their children, lived together. They
occupied a certain section of the great hive which the communal dwelling represented, and such a section was not un-
appropriately called in Spanish a *quartel* or quarter. The
husband also stayed with his wife and the younger children,
but he had no rights as owner, or proprietor, to his abode.
Since it was the custom for women to raise the walls of
buildings, and to finish the house inside and outside, they
owned it also. The man was only tolerated. His home
was properly with his clan, whither he must return in case
his spouse departed this life before him.

It was different in regard to the fields. Each clan had
its particular holding, and since the field-work devolved
upon the men, the cultivated plots belonged to them alone.
Within each allotment every member who was of age, or
so situated as to have to support himself or a family, owned
and tilled a certain plot which was his by common consent,
although in no manner determined by metes or bounds.
The condition of ownership was regular improvement of the
plot, and if that condition was not complied with, any other

member of the same clan could step in and work it for his
own benefit. In case of death the field reverted to the maternal relative of its owner, whereas the widow and children
fell back for support upon the resources of their own clan.
Hence the singular feature that each household got its live-
lihood from two distinct groups of blood-relatives. The
home which we have entered belonged to the quarters of
the Gourd people, or clan Tanyi hanutsh, from which the
mother descended; and Okoya had slept at night in the
estufa of that cluster ever since his thirteenth year. But
the cultivated patch which the father tilled pertained to the
fields of his clan, that of Water, Tzitz hanutsh. Though
the Water people were his relatives, the crop raised by him
found its way into the store-room of Tanyi for the support
of the family which he claimed as his own.

Okoya's mother scanned her boys with a sober glance,
and turned back into the kitchen without uttering a
word.

Soon a grating sound issued from that apartment, indicating that toasted corn was being ground on the flat slab
called in Queres, *yakkat,* and now usually termed *metate* in
New Mexico. The boys meanwhile had approached a
niche in the wall. Each one took a pinch of yellow corn-
meal from the painted bowl, and scattered it successively
to the north, west, south, east; then threw a little of it up
in the air and to the ground before him. During this performance their lips moved as if in prayer. Then they
separated, for the spirits had been appealed to, and their
entrance into their home was under the special protection
of Those Above. Shyuote, whose trout had been ruined
during the combat with the girls, threw himself on the roll
in the corner, there to mourn over his defeat. Okoya went
out into the courtyard. Both expected an early meal, for
the fire crackled in the dark kitchen, and a clapping of

hands gave evidence that corn-cakes were being moulded to appease their hungry stomachs.

The court-yard had become very quiet. Even the children had gone to rest in a shady place, where they slept in a promiscuous heap, a conglomerate of human bodies, heads, and limbs, intermingled. The form of an old man rose out of a hatchway in the ground-floor, and a tall figure, slightly stooping, clad in a garment, and with a head of iron gray hair, stood on the flat roof. He walked toward a beam leading down into the court, seized its upper end and descended with his face toward the wall, but without faltering. A few steps along the house brought him in front of Okoya, who had squatted near the doorway of his mother's dwelling. The youth was so absorbed in gloomy thoughts that the man's appearance was unexpected. Starting in surprise and hastily rising, Okoya called into the house, —

" Yaya, sa umo, — ' Mother, my grandfather ! ' "

The old man gave a friendly nod to his grandchild, and crossed the threshold, stooping low. Still lower the tall form had to bend while entering the kitchen door. He announced his coming to the inmate in a husky voice and the common formula, —

" Guatzena ! "

" Raua, — ' good,' " the woman replied.

Her father squatted close to the fire and fixed his gaze on his daughter. She knelt on the floor busy spreading dough or thick batter on a heated slab over the fire. She was baking corn-cakes, — the well-known *tortillas* as they are called to-day.

After a short pause the old man quietly inquired, —

" My child, where is your husband ? "

" Zashue Tihua," the woman answered, without looking up or interrupting her work, " is in the fields."

" When will he come ? "

The woman raised her right hand, and pointed to the hole in the wall, whence light came in from the outside. The wall faced the west, and the height of the loop-hole corresponded to that of the sun about one hour before sunset.

"Give food to the children," directed the old man. "When they have eaten and are gone I shall speak to you."

The fire crackled and blazed, and ruddy flashes shot across the features of the woman. Was it a mere reflection of the fire, or had her features quivered and coloured? The old man scanned those features with a cold, steady look.

She removed from the fire the sooty pot of clay in which venison cut in small pieces was stewing together with corn, dark beans, and a few roots and herbs as seasoning. Then she called out, —

"Shyuote, come and eat! Where is Okoya?"

The latter alone heard the invitation, for Shyuote had gone to sleep on the hides. The elder brother shook him, and went into the kitchen. He was followed by the child who staggered from drowsiness. The mother meanwhile had placed on the floor a pile of corn-cakes. Beside it, in an earthen bowl decorated inside and out with geometrical lines, steamed the stew. Dinner was ready; the table spread.

To enjoy this meal both lads squatted, but Shyuote, still half asleep, lost his balance and tumbled over. Angry at the merriment which this created, the boy hastily grabbed the food, but his mother interfered.

"Don't be so greedy, uak, — 'urchin.' Remember Those Above," she said; and Shyuote, imitating the example of Okoya, crossly muttered a prayer, and scattered crumbs before him. Then only, both fell to eating.

This was done by simply folding a slice of the cake to form a primitive ladle, and dipping the contents of the stew out with it. Thus they swallowed meat, broth, and finally the ladle also. Okoya arose first, uttering a plainly audible hoa. Shyuote ate longer; at last he wiped his mouth with the seam of his wrap, grumbled something intended for thanksgiving, and strolled back to his resting place in the front room. Okoya went out into the court-yard to be alone with his forebodings. The sight of his mother seemed oppressive to him.

After the boys had gone the woman emptied the remainder of the stew back into the pot, filled the painted bowl with water, and put both vessels in a corner. Then she sat down, leaning against the wall, looking directly toward her father. Her face was thin and wan, her cheeks were hollow, and her eyes had a suppressed look of uneasiness.

The old man remained quietly indifferent as long as the meal lasted; then he rose, peeped cautiously into the outer apartment, resumed his seat, and spoke in a low tone, —

"Is it true that you have listened to kamonyitza, — 'black corn'?"

The woman started. "Who says so?" she answered with sudden haste.

"The Koshare," replied the old man, looking at her with a cold steady gaze.

"What do I care for them," exclaimed his daughter. Her lips curled with an air of disdain.

"It may be," spoke her father, in measured tones, "that you do not wish to hear from them; but I know that they care for your doings."

"Let them do as they please."

"Woman," he warned, "speak not thus. Their disposition toward you is not a matter for indifference."

"What reason have they to follow my path? I am a

woman like many others in the tribe, nothing more or less. I stay with my husband," she went on with greater animation, " I do my duty. What have the Delight Makers to say that might not be for my good?"

" And yet, you are not precious to them — "

" Neither are they precious to me," she cried. Her eyes sparkled.

Her father heaved a deep sigh. He shook his head and said in a husky tone, —

"Woman, your ways are wrong. I know it, and the Koshare know it also. They may know more, much more than I could wish," he added, and looked into her eyes with a searching sorrowful glance. An awful suspicion lay in this penetrating look. Her face flushed, she bent her head to avoid his gaze.

To the gloomy talk succeeded a still more gloomy silence. Then the woman lifted her head, and began entreatingly, —

" My father, I do not ask you to tell me how you come to know all this; but tell me, umo, what are these Delight Makers, the Koshare? At every dance they appear and always make merry. The people feel glad when they see them. They must be very wise. They know of everything going on, and drag it before the people to excite their mirth at the expense of others. How is it that they know so much? I am but a woman, and the ways of the men are not mine," she raised her face and her eyes flamed ; "but since I hear that the Delight Makers wish me no good, I want to know at least what those enemies of mine are."

The old man lowered his glance and sighed.

" My child," he began softly, " when I was young and a boy like your son Okoya, I cared little about the Koshare. Now I have learned more." He leaned his head against the wall, pressed his lips firmly together, and continued,

"The holders of the paths of our lives, those who can close them when the time comes for us to go to Shipapu, where there is neither sorrow nor pain, have many agents among us. Pāyatyama our Father, and Sanashtyaya our Mother saw that the world existed ere there was light, and so the tribe lived in the dark. Four are the wombs in which people grew up and lived, ere Maseua and Oyoyāuā his brother led them to where we are now, and this world which is round like a shield is the fourth womb."

The woman listened with childlike eagerness. Her parted lips and sparkling eyes testified that everything was new to her.

"Father," she interrupted, "I knew nothing of this. You are very wise. But why are women never told such things?"

"Don't cut off my speech," he said. "Because women are so forward, that is why many things are concealed from them."

"But," she continued, heedless of his rebuke, "where are the other three worlds?"

"This question I shall answer," he said, "for it is wise in you to speak so. Haatze the earth is round and flat, but it is also thick like a cake. The other three wombs are down below inside, one beneath the other. At Shipapu the people came out upon this world which is the fourth womb, but it was cold and dark. Then the great sun rose in the heavens above. In it Pāyatyama dwells, and on it he rides around the world in one day and one night to see everything which happens. It is day and light, night and dark. We have also summer and heat, winter and cold. For this reason there are summer-people and winter-people, some who like to live when it is cold and others who enjoy the heat. Every tribe, every clan, has some of both kinds. Thus they came out of the third world, and thus they have

3

remained until this day. It was cold at Shipapu when the
people came out on the surface, and Those Above saw that
they felt weak.   Toward the south it was warm and bright,
so Maseua and his brother said to their children, the men of
our tribe, ' Go you where there is more light; ' and the
summer people they directed to go along the Rio Grande;
the winter people they sent south also but far around by
the east over the plains where the great buffalo is roaming,
where the wind blows and it is cold and dry.   To both
kinds of men they said, besides, ' Come together in the
mountains and live there in peace, each one getting food
for himself and others as you are wont to do.'   But, lest the
people might get weary on their long journey, Maseua and
his brother commanded that from Shipapu there should
come forth a man whose body was painted white and black,
and who carried on his head dried corn-leaves instead of
feathers.   This man began at once to dance, to jump, and
to tumble, so that the people laughed and their hearts became glad.   This man led the summer-men southward,
and as often as they grew tired he danced again and made
jests ; and the tribe followed him until they came to where
we are now, and all met again.   The summer-people never
suffered hunger in all their wanderings, for their leader was
precious, and wherever they went he caused the fruits to be
ripe.   That man was the Koshare.[1]   Since that time there
have been Koshare in every tribe.   Their task it is to keep
the people happy and merry ; but they must also fast, mortify
themselves, and pray to Those Above that every kind of
fruit may ripen in its time, even the fruit in woman's womb.
To them is given the yellow flower from the fertile bottoms
which makes the hearts of men glad.   Now you know what
the Koshare are and," he added emphatically, " why you

[1] This tradition was told me by Tehua Indians, and some friends
among the Queres subsequently confirmed it.

should not laugh and make merry when you are not precious to them."

The woman had listened with breathless attention. At the close, however, she hung her head and sighed. The old man gazed at her in silence. In the outer room the regular breathings of the sleeping boy were heard, otherwise all was as still as a grave.

At last she lifted her face again.

"Father," she asked, "are those who are precious to the holders of our paths, are they always good?"

"I need not tell you about this," he replied, fixing upon her a penetrating glance.

"I know of nothing evil," she stammered, "unless it be bad men."

"And yet you have used owl's feathers!"

Her face grew pale. She asked hoarsely, —

"Where should I keep them?"

"The Koshare know it," was the equally husky reply.

She started, her eyes gleamed like living coals.

"Have the Koshare sent you here, father?"

"No," was the gloomy answer; "but if the old men come to me and say, 'kill the witch,' I must do it. For you know I am Maseua, head-war-chief, and whatever the principals command I must do, even if it takes the life of my only child!"

The woman rose to her feet; her attitude was one of defiance.

"Let the Koshare speak, and do you as you are commanded. The time must come when I shall have to die. The sooner it comes, the sooner shall I find rest and peace with our mother at Shipapu."

Her father also had risen, he clutched his cotton garment as if a sudden chill went through his body. Without a word he turned and went off dejected, stooping, with a heavy sigh.

The woman dropped to the floor beside the hearth with a plaintive moan. She drew her hair over her face, weep she could not. The embers on the hearth glowed again, casting a dull light over the chamber.

Say Koitza, as this wretched woman was called, was the only child of him with whom she had just had this dismal interview. His name was Topanashka Tihua, and he was maseua, or head-war-chief, of the tribe. In times of peace the maseua is subordinate to the tapop, or civil governor, and as often as the latter communicates to him any decision of the tribal council he is bound to execute it. Otherwise the maseua is really a superior functionary, for he stands in direct relation to the religious powers of which we shall hereafter speak, and these in reality guide and command through oracles and prophetic utterances. In war the maseua has supreme command, and the civil chief and the diviners, or medicine-men, must obey him implicitly as soon as any campaign is started.

Topanashka was a man of great physical vigour notwithstanding his age. He was highly respected for his skill and bravery, and for his stern rectitude and obedience to strict duty. He feared nothing except the supernatural powers of evil. There is nothing the Indian fears, nay hates, so much as sorcery. Topanashka could scarcely believe that his daughter had tampered with magic by causing the dark-coloured corn to speak, and keeping owl's feathers in her possession. Still, if such were really the case, he knew of no other course to pursue but to execute the penalty which according to Indian ideas she deserved, and which the leading men of the tribe composing its council would undoubtedly mete out to her, — death; a cruel, terrible death. But she was his only child, and ere he placed faith in the suspicion communicated to him in secret by one of the shamans in the tribe, he wanted to satisfy himself from her own behaviour whether it was true or not. To his deepest sorrow Say Koitza's behaviour seemed to prove that she was not falsely accused. It was a terrible blow to the old man, who for the first time in his life rose from a task bewildered and hopeless. Duty was to him paramount, and yet he could not utterly stifle the longing to save his only child from a cruel and ignominious fate.

His daughter too felt utterly wretched, and despondent in the highest degree. For the accusation against her was true. She had practised the dread art; and yet, strange to say, while conscious of guilt, in the bottom of her heart she felt herself innocent. Let us recall the past life of the unhappy being to see whether there is in it anything to explain this apparent anomaly.

When Say Koitza was fourteen years of age her husband Zashue Tihua began to pay her his first attentions. He called at her mother's home oftener than any other youth of her tribe, and one afternoon, when she was returning from the brook with a jar filled with water on her head, he stopped her, dipped some water out of the urn, drank it, and whispered something to which she gave no reply, hurrying home as rapidly as possible. She could not speak to her mother about this, for her mother was hopelessly deaf, and it would not have been proper to consult her father, since the father belonged of course to another clan. A whole night and one full day Say pondered over the case; at last her mind was made up. The girl took a dish filled with corn-cakes and rolls of sweet paste of the yucca-fruit, and placed it on her head. With this load she climbed up the rugged slope leading to the dwellings of the Water clan, to which Zashue belonged. The lad was sitting in the cave inhabited by his family, busying himself with straightening arrow shafts over the fire, when the girl, pushing before her the loaded tray, crept through the port-hole. Silently she placed the food before him, and went out again without a word. This was her affirmative reply to his wooing. Thereafter, Zashue visited the quarters of the Gourd people at the big house every night. Along the foot of the cliffs, in soft ground, and in a lonely sheltered spot, he meanwhile planted four stakes connected by cross-poles. From end to end cotton threads were drawn lengthwise, and here Zashue wove a cotton wrap day after day. The girl would steal out to this place also, carrying food to the young artisan. She would cleanse his hair while they chatted quietly, shyly at first, about the present and the future. When the mantle was done and it looked white and firm, Zashue brought it to Say Koitza's mother, who forthwith understood the intention of his gift, and felt gratified at the prospect of securing a son-in-law who possessed cotton. The plant was not cultivated near the upper Rio Grande at that time, and had to be obtained from the far south by barter. Many journeys distant, Pueblo Indians lived also, and thither the Queres went at long intervals to trade and to hunt the buffalo on the southwestern plains.

Topanashka also was pleased with the suitor. In due course of time Zashue Tihua and Say Koitza, therefore, became man and wife.

Zashue proved to be a good husband, according to Indian ideas. He worked and hunted dutifully, providing the store-rooms of Tanyi Hanutsh with supplies of which his wife, and through her he also, enjoyed the benefit. He spun cotton and wove it into wraps, scarfs, and sashes. Furthermore, he was always good-natured and merry. He did not spend too many nights out of his wife's home, either. They had three children, Okoya, Shyuote, and a little girl. Of these Shyuote became the father's favourite, for when the child was yet small it happened that his father made a vow to make a Koshare of him. Zashue was a Delight Maker himself, and one of the merriest of that singular crew. Among them he was perhaps the most popular; for while good-looking, his strength and agility enabled him to perform in a conspicuous manner, and his ready wit and quick conception of everything ludicrous caused him to shine as a great light among that society of official jesters.

So the two lived in quiet and sober content. Zashue was pleased with his spouse. She kept her looks well with advancing years, and while there is never among Indians that complete intimacy between man and wife which engenders fidelity under all circumstances, while a certain freedom of action is always permitted to the man toward the other sex, Say had natural tact enough to never pry into such matters. She, in turn, did her duty. Always at home, she faithfully fulfilled her obligations as head of the house, and naturally shrank from all society but that of her own sex and such men as were allied to her by near ties of relationship. When she told her father in that sad interview that she was faithful to her husband, Say had told the truth. And yet there was something that caused her to plead guilty.

The family had lived contentedly, and no cloud appeared to hang over them until, a few years previous to the date of our story, Say Koitza fell ill from want of proper care. Mountain fever is not infrequently fatal, and it was mountain fever that had seized upon the delicate frame of the little woman. This fever is often tenacious and intermittent; sometimes it is congestive. Indian medicine may cure a slight attack, and prevent too frequent returns of more violent ones; but if the case is a serious one, Indian remedies are of no avail. Say suffered from a slight attack at first, and recovered from it. A primitive cold-water treatment was effective for the time being; but in the year ensuing fever set in again, and no sudorific was of any use. She tried a decoction of willow bark, but it did her no good. She took the root of the yucca, or soapweed, and drank the froth produced by whipping water with it, but gained no relief. The poor woman did not know that these remedies are not employed by the Indians in a case like hers, but only for toothache and, in the case of soapweed, for consumption.

Thus it went on for three years. During the dry seasons there were no signs of the illness; but as soon as, in July or August, thunderstorms shed their moisture over the mountains, and chilly nights alternated with warm sunshine, the fever made its appearance. Two years before the rainy season had lasted unusually long, and it was followed immediately by snow-falls. The attacks from the disease were therefore unusually violent, and by November Say Koitza thought herself dying from weakness and exhaustion. Her condition was such that her husband felt alarmed, and every effort was made to relieve her by the aid of such arts as the Indian believes in. The chief medicine-man, or great shaman, of the tribe had to come and see the patient, pray by her side, and then go home to fast and mortify himself for four consecutive days. His efforts had no effect whatever. Every indigenous medicine that was thought of had been already used, and none had been of any avail.

At last the shaman, encouraged by the many blue and green stones, cotton wraps, and quantities of corn meal which Zashue Tihua contributed in reward of his jugleries, resolved to make a final trial by submitting himself and his associates to the dangerous ordeal of fire-eating for the invalid's sake. This ceremony was always performed by a certain group of medicine-men, called therefore Hakanyi Chayani, or Fire Shamans. The Hishtanyi

Chayan was their official head, and he, with the four others belonging to the fire-eating crew, fasted rigorously for four days and nights. Then they went to the house of Say Koitza, and in her presence sang the powerful song, while each one of them in turn waved a burning bunch of long dry grass to the six sacred regions, and each time bit off a piece of the burning weed and chewed it. When all had gone through the performances, and their mouths were well filled with ashes, each one gravely stepped up to the invalid, and spat the contents of his mouth in her face. Then they departed as quietly as they had come, and went home to await the results of the wonderful remedy.[1] It was a last, a supreme effort.

The condition of Say could not fail to arouse the sympathies of her own sex, even outside of her clan. Many were the calls from compassionate women. They would drop in, squat down, tender their services, suggest remedies, and gossip. Only one woman made herself directly useful, and that was Shotaye, a member of the Water clan. Shotaye was a strange woman. Nobody liked her, and yet many applied to her for relief in secret; for Shotaye possessed great knowledge of plants and other remedies, and she had a keen practical sense. But people dreaded her; she lived alone in her cave among the abodes of the Water people, and nobody knew but she might know more than the official medicine-men themselves. In short, the majority of the tribe believed that Shotaye was a witch; but the woman was so wary that nobody could prove her to be one.

Shotaye was not an old woman. Her appearance was not in the least repulsive, on the contrary. The men knew that the woman showed no objections to occasional

[1] This fire-cure was still practised by the Queres not very long ago.

attentions, even to intimacy. For this reason, also, she was not popular among her own sex.

Shotaye had had a husband once; but he had left her and was living with another woman. That husband was called Tyope, badger, a man of strong physique and one averse to monotony in conjugal life. Tyope was a scheming man, cunning and unscrupulous in the highest degree; Shotaye an energetic woman, endowed with a powerful will of her own. Had there not been the little cloud of marital inconstancy on both sides, the pair would have been well-assorted for good as well as for evil. Tyope was a Koshare rather than an agriculturist, he spent his time mostly in other people's homes and in the estufa of the Delight Makers, leaving his wife to provide for herself and for him also, whenever he chose to remain at her house. In short there were flaws on both sides, and Shotaye being the house-mistress held the main power. One fine evening when Tyope presented himself in the grotto occupied by his wife, she refused to recognize him any longer. He protested, he stormed, he menaced her; it was of no avail. Shotaye told him to go, and he left. Henceforth the two were mortal enemies. The woman said little; but he was bent upon her destruction by every possible means. She kept on the defensive, avoided all conflicts, and was very careful not to give any cause for a direct accusation of sorcery. She cured people incidentally, never asking any compensation for it. She lived alone, and thus earned enough to be independent of her own clan if need be.

This woman called on Say occasionally, but only between the periods of the attacks of fever. On such visits she would assist the patient, do the housework, and arrange the hides or covers for her. Say harboured a wish to consult her about her disease; but Shotaye studiously avoided any opportunity for confidential talk. One day, however, when

the two were alone in the kitchen, and the invalid felt somewhat relieved, she opened her heart to her visitor. Shotaye
listened very attentively, and when Say had concluded, instead of asking for further details, she abruptly asked
whether Say had no suspicion of being bewitched.

If such a question were put to us, we should doubt the
sanity of the questioner. Not so the Indian. Say felt like
one from whose eyes thick scales are suddenly removed.
Indeed, she thought this was the cause of her evil, this
alone could explain the tenacity of the disease, its mysterious intermittence. She told her interlocutor that she must
be right, or else why these regular returns and always during
the season of rain? Shotaye listened and listened; every
word she heard was in confirmation of her own thoughts.
Say must be under the influence of some evil charm, and
unless counteracted by magic, it was clear to her that the
poor woman must succumb to its workings.

Whatever there is in nature which the Indian cannot
grasp at once, he attributes to mysterious supernatural
agencies. He believes that nature is pervaded by spiritual
essence individualized into an infinite number of distinct
powers. Everything in nature has a soul according to him,
and it is that soul which causes it to move or to act upon
its surroundings in general. Thus the medical properties
of animals, of plants, or minerals, are due to spiritual mani-
festations. His medical art therefore does not consist
merely in eliminating the physical cause of disease. As
soon as any disease is stubborn there must be at the bottom
of it some spiritual source, and this source can be discovered and removed only by magic.

Incantations therefore form an important part of Indian
medicine. The formulas therefor are the special property of
the medicine-men, whom we shall hereafter designate with
the much more appropriate name of Shamans. The shaman

is wizard and physician at the same time. He is also a prophet, augur, and oracle. His duty it is not only to protect from evil, but to counteract it. He has charms and incantations which he offers for the production of beneficial natural phenomena.

Magic for such purposes is regarded by the Indian as essential to the existence of man. Magic, however, as a black art is the most heinous crime which he can conceive. The difference between the two consists mainly in their purpose ; the manipulations are substantially the same, so are the objects. To know those details is one of the attributes of the shamans.

The latter constitute a circle of their own, — a cluster of adepts, nominally in the arts of healing, but really in the arts of magic. That circle is wide, and whoever stands outside of it has no right to infringe upon the duties of its members by attempting to follow their example. It is an institution, and its origin dates from untold centuries. It is subdivided into groups, each of which practises charms, incantations, or magic, relating to certain human interests. The Shyayak are in possession of the spell which charms game, in other words they are the shamans of the hunt. The Uakanyi practise magic in warfare, they are the shamans of war. The Chayani are physicians who combine with the knowledge of medicine proper, the knowledge of magic curative powers. They are the shamans of medicine. Lastly the Yaya combine a knowledge of all these different branches in their essence. They are the prophets and priests. These groups may be described as, in a certain sense, guilds. But they are secret societies also, inasmuch as the arts and practices of each are special property which is kept secret from the others, and from the uninitiated members in the tribe. In order to become a member of a society of that kind secrecy is required and long apprentice-

ship. The novice rises slowly from one degree of knowledge to another, and only few attain the higher positions.

The members of these secret societies are therefore
magicians or wizards, and when any one dreads danger from
evil sorcery it is his duty to consult the proper shaman for
relief, unless he should be sure of the person of the sorcerer,
in which case he may kill him outright without even men-
tioning the deed. In the present instance Say could not
resort to such a summary expedient. It was therefore the
duty of Shotaye, who was better informed on institutions
and customs, to direct her sick friend to a shaman. But
Shotaye was not on good terms with the official wizards,
particularly the Chayani, those who cured, and still less with
the highest religious powers, the Yaya. It suited her pride
to attempt the experiment at her own risk, conscious all the
while that it was dangerous, — dangerous for herself, as well
as for her patient. For it entailed performances which
only the shaman can undertake, and should they be detected, the very crime of sorcery, against which their experi-
ments were directed, would be charged against them.

Shotaye had still another reason for not encouraging her
friend to speak to the higher chayani. The fever coincided
with the rainy season. As soon as this was over it subsided.
Natural as this was, both women attributed it to a mysterious cause; and Shotaye, suspicious and vindictive even,
thought she had discovered a clew to the guilty party.

The rainy season in New Mexico is of course essential to
the growth of the chief staple of the Indian, — maize or
Indian corn. When, therefore, in July daily showers should
occur, the principal shamans of each tribe and the yaya
must pray, fast, and mortify themselves, in order that
Those Above may send the needed rain. The hishtanyi
chayan scatters the powder of the white flower to the winds
meanwhile murmuring incantations. At night he imitate

thunder, by whirling a flint knife attached to the end of a
long string, and draws brilliant flashes from pebbles which
he strikes together in a peculiar manner. For the Indian
reasons that since rain is preceded in summer by lightning
and thunder, man by imitating those heralds is calling the
desired precipitation, — beckoning it to come.

This is the time of the year when the Koshare perform
their chief work. Four days and four nights, sometimes
longer, they must fast and pray in order that the crops
may obtain the moisture indispensable for ripening. The
people look upon the Delight Makers with a degree of respect akin to fear at all times, for they are regarded as
powerful intermediaries in matters of life and death to the
tribe; but during that particular time they are considered
as specially precious to the higher powers. Shotaye hated
the Koshare. They in turn disliked the woman, and gave
vent to their dislike by turning her into ridicule at public
dances as often as possible. This she resented greatly;
but she was powerless to retaliate, since the Delight Makers
enjoy special privileges on festive days. The medicine
woman's hatred was still increased by the fact that her
former husband, Tyope, was a leading Koshare. To his
influence she attributed the insults which the jesters offered
her, and she saw in the whole group but a crowd of willing
tools handled by her personal enemy.

Since Say's illness coincided with the beginning of the
rainy season, the principal activity of the Koshare immediately preceded the outbreak of the fever. Urged by hate
and desire for revenge, Shotaye combined the two facts in
her mind, and drew the conclusion that the disease was
due to the magic power of the Koshare, directed against
Say for some unknown reason and purpose.

If the Koshare were guilty, it was not only useless, it
was dangerous even, to call upon any chayan for relief.

The Delight Makers were the chief assistants of the shamans in any public ceremony, and indispensable to them
in many ways. Beside, Say Koitza could not have applied
to a chayan without her husband's knowledge, and that
husband was a Koshare.

So after explaining to the invalid her suspicions and inferences, she suggested direct inquiry about the principals
in the supposed evil actions against her. That inquiry
could be conducted only through sorcery itself, and Say
at first trembled. She feared, and not without good cause,
an appeal to evil powers. Still Shotaye spoke so plausibly;
she assured so strongly her friend of her own discretion and
fidelity, and was so insistant upon her constant success in
everything she had undertaken as yet, — that the woman
yielded at last against her own convictions. Something
within her seemed to speak and say, " Do not tread forbidden paths, speak to your husband first." But the arguments on the other side were too strong, her own physical
condition too weak; she grasped the expected relief regardless of the warnings of her conscience.

Among the objects connected with evil magic, a certain
kind of maize had the power of speech attributed to it.
It is the dark-coloured variety, called in the Queres language
ka monyi tza. Ears of this corn belonging to a witch are
said to speak in the absence of their owner, and to tell of
her whereabouts and doings. Shotaye knew this, and herself but indifferently versed in the black art, concluded that
the black corn would also reveal, if properly handled, the
agent whose manipulations caused Say Koitza's sufferings.
She hoped also that by combining the dreaded grain with
another more powerful implement of sorcery, owl's plumage, she would succeed in eliciting from the former all the
information desired. The woman was quite ignorant of the
evil ways in which she was about to wander; but she was

bold and daring, and the hope of injuring her enemies was a greater inducement than the desire to relieve her friend. The proposed manipulation was directed in fact much more against her former husband than against the disease.

But how to obtain the necessary objects ! How to secure black corn, and how and where to get the feathers of an owl ! Both were so well known and so generally tabooed that inquiry after them would forthwith arouse suspicion. Black maize might be procured on the sly ; but the other could be found by chance only, — by meeting with the body of a dead owl on the heights surrounding the Tyuonyi

Shotaye was in the habit of strolling alone all around the Rito, over the timbered mesa as well as through the gorges which descend from the mountains. On such excursions the woman observed the most minute precautions, for there was danger, — danger from roaming Indians of the Navajo or Dinne tribe, and danger from spies of her own tribe. Frequently people had followed stealthily in the hope of surprising her at some illicit practice, but she had been lucky enough to notice them in time. Of what is called to-day the mesa del Rito, the high table-land bordering the Tyuonyi on the south, Shotaye knew every inch of ground, every tree and shrub.

On a clear, cool November day she strolled again in that direction, climbing the heights and penetrating into the scrubby timber, interspersed with tall pines, which covers the plateau for miles. To her delight she discovered the remains of an owl at no great distance from the declivity of the Rito beneath a rotten pine. Instead of picking up the carcass she kicked it aside disdainfully, but took good care to notice whither so as to remember the place. It landed on a juniper-bush and remained suspended from its branches. Shotaye went onward carelessly. She looked

for herbs and plants, picking up a handful here, pulling out
a root there, until she had made a long circuit, which however brought her back to the place where the dead owl
was. Here she stopped, listening, all the while looking
out for plants. As if by accident she neared the bush on
which the carcass was still hanging, and after assuring herself that the body had not been disturbed, she brushed
past so as to cause it to drop to the ground. She hastily
plucked a few feathers, put them with the herbs and roots
already gathered, and turned homeward. Everything was
quiet and still around her, only at a short distance two
crows flew up croaking.

Say Koitza was not strong enough to walk up to the
cliffs; therefore Shotaye, when she came to announce to
her friend that the necessary material was at last secured,
suggested that the incantation be performed at the home
of the invalid. A certain evening when Zashue was sure
to be absent, owing to a gathering of the Koshare, was
appointed for the purpose. On that evening the two
women sat alone in the kitchen. Okoya was away in the
estufa of Tanyi hanutsh. The two younger children were
fast asleep in the outer room. It was a cold night, but
the fire on the hearth had almost completely subsided,
only a few embers remaining. Through the loophole in
the wall an occasional draught of chilly air entered. Say
Koitza clung to her friend's shoulder, shivering and trembling from fear as well as from cold.

In the centre of the dark room Shotaye had placed a
few ears of black corn, and on them two bundles of owl's
feathers, each tied to a chip of obsidian. She had also
brought along some bark of the red willow; this she pul-
verized in the hand, and made into two cigarettes with
corn husks. At that time tobacco was unknown to the
Pueblos, and red willow-bark was the only thing used for

smoking, while smoking itself was not a relish but exclusively a sacrifice.

Handing one of the cigarettes to her friend, Shotaye directed her to light it and then puff the smoke successively to the six mythical regions. After this she was to cast the glowing stub on the pile of corn and feathers. With a shudder Say Koitza obeyed these instructions; her teeth chattered while the cave-woman recited an invocation. Then both huddled together to listen. Even Shotaye felt afraid of the consequences. For a long time everything was silent; the cold draught from the outside had stopped; the women sat in breathless silence; they listened and listened. Nothing moved. Not a sound was heard.

Shotaye overcame her first anxiety and repeated the dread formula. All was silent. Suddenly a cold blast pervaded the room again. It fanned the embers to renewed life; they shed a faint glimmer over the chamber. The women started; there was a crackling heard; the feathers moved; the ears of corn seemed to change position. One of the feather bunches rolled on the floor. They nearly screamed in terror, for their excited imagination caused them to hear ghostly sounds, — disconnected, uncomprehended words. It was clear that the black corn had spoken. What it said neither could tell; but the fact of having heard the noise was sufficient to convince them that Say was under the influence of an evil charm, and Shotaye took care to add that that charm was exercised by the Koshare or by some one belonging to their society.

So powerful was the effect of this incantation scene upon Say that she fainted. After a while she recovered and Shotaye led her back to the outer room, where, after some time, she began to slumber from sheer exhaustion.

Then the medicine-woman returned to the caves, taking with her every vestige of the conjuration.

It was wise on her part, for as soon as Say awoke from feverish and anxious dreams, her first thought was about the dismal objects. Everything was quiet. Zashue had returned, and was quietly asleep by her side. She arose and glided into the kitchen, noiselessly, stealthily. The floor was clean. She felt around; not a trace of the objectionable pile could be noticed. Unspeakable was the feeling of relief with which she returned to her husband's side and extended herself on the hides again; sound sleep came to her, and when she awoke it was daylight. She felt stronger, brighter. Yet thereafter, as often as Zashue approached her in his harmless, bantering manner, she experienced a strange, sudden pang. She was reminded of having done wrong in not having been open with him. The Indian's conscience is hemmed in by bonds arising from his social and religious organization; why, for instance, should she have told her spouse? He was neither of her clan nor of her party. He belonged to the summer people, she to those of winter. She stood outside of all secret associations, whereas he was a Koshare.

The winter following proved to be mild and dry. Say recovered slowly. Shotaye kept aloof after the conjuration, for a long time at least. All of a sudden she made her appearance at the home of her convalescent friend. It was in order to remind her that the first step was only a preliminary, and that it could not effect a radical cure. All that had been achieved was to prove that an evil charm existed, and that the Koshare were the wrongdoers. It remained now to remove the spell by breaking the charm. This, she represented, had to be attempted when the Koshare were in their greatest power, and could

only be effected by means of the owl's feathers. By bury-
ing these feathers near the place where the Delight Makers used to assemble, Shotaye asserted that not only would
the disease be eliminated forever, but the guilty one be
punished according to the measure of his crime.

Say would not listen to any such proposals. She saw
no necessity for going any further in forbidden tracks.
Now that her health was restored, why should she attempt
to harm a cluster of men to which her husband belonged,
and thus perhaps imperil his life? Shotaye met this objection with the assurance that the remedy was directed
against the guilty ones only, and that she herself did not
for a moment think that Zashue had participated in the
evil manipulations against his wife; that consequently he
was in no manner exposed to danger. Say finally told
her visitor that she would wait and see, and then decide.

Winter went and spring came. Warm summer followed
with a dark-blue sky and sporadic thunderclouds. All the
crops were planted, irrigated, and scantily weeded. Now
they awaited the rains in order to complete growth and prepare for maturity. The great chayani had gone through
their official fasts, they had made their sacrificial offerings
in the sacred bowls dedicated to rain-medicine. Every
day clouds loomed up in the west, distant thunder rumbled,
but not a drop of rain fell in the Rito and the people began
to look gloomy. The Koshare were therefore required to
go to work earlier than usual. They were to fast four consecutive days between two full moons.

The estufa in which the Delight Makers used to assemble
is situated at the eastern end of the cliffs, and its access is
difficult to-day. It is a circular chamber in the rock twenty
feet in diameter. At present the outer wall has fallen in,
but a crease in the floor indicates the place where a little
port-hole led into the cave. The cave lies high, so that

from it a view of the whole valley presents itself, and at its feet opens a narrow chasm of considerable depth. This is a mere fissure, so narrow that cross-beams were fastened into its sides like the rounds of a step-ladder; and on these the people ascended to a narrow trail leading up to the entrance. Other cave-dwellings were scattered along this trail and farther below. They were inhabited by the people of the Turquoise clan.

All the Koshare had retired to this secluded spot, and the first day of fasting was nearly over when Shotaye called once more at the home of Say. The latter guessed the object of her coming and felt afraid. Without preamble, in a sober, matter-of-fact way, the cave-woman stated that the time had come for a decisive step; and with this she placed three bunches of owl's feathers on the floor. In vain Say Koitza protested, affirming that her health was fully restored. Shotaye would not listen to refusal or excuse. Now or never, she commanded. She repeated her former assertion that the charm could not hurt Zashue as long as he was not guilty. For a long while the women sat arguing the matter; at last Say Koitza yielded, and promised to comply.

Night came, and the people of the Rito went to rest. The moon rose behind the lava-ridge of the Tetilla; the rocky battlements of the cliffs shone brightly above the gorge, whose depths rested in dark shadow. A tiny figure crept out of the big building and hurried down the vale along the fields. When she reached the grove where we met Okoya and his little brother for the first time, she crouched beneath a tree, covered her head, and sobbed aloud. It was a dire task for Say Koitza, this errand out of which harm might arise to the whole cluster to which her husband belonged. If the charm which she clutched with trembling fingers should work against him, then he was the guilty party. So Shotaye had insinuated, and the word had stung her like the bite of a serpent. It came back to her mind as she hurried to perform the deed, and caused her to start. She rose hastily and turned toward the cliffs.

The uppermost rocks glistened fairly in the light of the moon; and where the sharp line of the shadows commenced, the ruddy glow of a fire burst from an oblong aperture. There was the estufa of the Koshare. From it issued the sound of hollow drumming intermingled with the cadence of a chorus of hoarse voices. A thrill went through Say, she stopped again and listened. Was not her husband's voice among them? Certainly he was there, doing his duty with the rest. And if he was as guilty toward her as the others? That monstrous thought rose again, it pushed her onward. She crawled ahead slowly, scarcely conscious of the danger attending her mission. Large blocks of débris, tent-shaped erosive hillocks, impeded her progress; they crowded along the foot of the cliffs like protecting bulwarks, and the trail wound around them on a higher plane. But this trail she dared not follow, there was not enough darkness on it. She crept along the base, the sense of danger coming to her with the increasing obscurity, until suddenly she stood before a cleft of almost inky hue. Here she remembered was the ascent to the estufa, here she had to perform the work, and here overpowered by emotion and excitement she dropped behind an angular block of stone unconscious.

When she recovered, the chorus sounded directly above her, and the chant seemed to soar away like voices from an upper world. She glanced up the dark fissure as through a flume. The cross-beams were faintly visible. Over the cleft rested a moonlit sky, but to the rocks clung the figure of a man. That man stood there a moment only, then shouting a few words as if calling to somebody within, he disappeared. The song was hushed. Say recognized the speaker; it was Tyope, Shotaye's former husband, and the one whom the woman suspected of having done her harm. Resolutely she went at her task.

Taking a bundle of owl's feathers from her wrap, she presented it successively to the six regions, and then buried it carefully in the sand, below where the first cross-beam traversed the fissure. Again she listened and spied, and creeping forward concealed the second bunch in another place near by. Then she whispered the sinister prayer which was to give to the feathers the power to do harm. At the close the drum rumbled again within the cliffs above her, and the chant rose strong and rude. Covering her head, shaking and shivering with sudden fear, Say Koitza rushed from the spot. Ere day broke she had reached home again, and extended her weary frame by the side of her sleeping children.

Say slept for the remainder of the night a long sleep of exhaustion. The next morning her first task was to bury the last bunch of owl's feathers in the kitchen, close to the fireplace, where it was to protect her from the inroads of enemies. She felt weak but rather comfortable. Her only anxiety was now the return of her husband.

Zashue came home at last, good-humoured as ever, but with a lively appetite akin to hunger. His wife received him in a subdued manner bordering on obsequiousness; she was more than ever bent on anticipating any desire on his part. All the while afraid of detection, every kind word spoken to her caused remorse, every joke pained her in secret. It recalled what she had done to his companions, perhaps to him also.

The incantations of the chayani and the fasts of the Koshare seemed to have no effect whatever upon the course of the rain-clouds. The heavens clouded regularly every day; they shed their moisture all around the Tyuonyi, but not a drop fell in the valley-gorge. Now the three chief penitents of the tribe, the Hotshanyi, the shaykatze, and the uishtyaka, were called upon to use their means of intercession with Those Above. They fasted, prayed, and made sacrifices alternately for an entire moon; still it rained not. In New Mexico local droughts are sometimes very pertinacious. Plants withered, the corn and beans suffered, languished, and died. The tribe looked forward to a winter without vegetable food. But Say Koitza was secretly glad, for drought killed her disease. She felt stronger every day, and worked zealously, anxious to please her husband and to remove every suspicion. Shotaye called on her frequently; she, too, felt proud of the success of her cure, sure of the revenge she had taken upon her enemies.

When a few rains swept at last down upon the vale, it was too late for the crops. Only the few stores kept in reserve and the proceeds of the hunt could save the tribe from a famine. Women and children put on red wristbands to comfort their hearts in the prospective distress, for a winter without vegetable supplies was until then an unknown disaster. Say Koitza also placed strips of red buckskin around her arms. Ostensibly she mourned for her tribe; in reality it was to relieve her heart from the reproaches of her own conscience.

But when winter set in and the fever had not put in its appearance, her mind gradually changed. She lost all fear of discovery, and finally felt proud of what she had done. Had she not preserved herself for her own husband, for her children? Instead of performing a crime, it was a meritorious act. Shotaye encouraged her in such thoughts. To her it was less the recovery of her friend than the blow dealt the Koshare, particularly her former husband, that excited her satisfaction and tickled her pride.

Say thus felt happy and at rest, but that fatal interview with her father suddenly dispelled all her fond dreams. The old man's revelations annihilated everything at one fell blow. No hope was left; her life was gone, her doom sealed. As if lightning had struck her she lay down by the hearth, motionless, for a long while. She heard nothing; she stared vacantly; her thoughts came and went like nebulous phantoms. At last somebody entered the outer room, but the woman noticed him not. Three times the new-comer called her name; she gave no reply. At the fourth call, " Koitza ! " she started at last, and faintly answered, —

" Opona."

Zashue, her husband, entered the kitchen and good-naturedly inquired, —

" Are you ill? "

She raised herself hastily and replied, —

" No ; but I was asleep."

" The sun is resting on the western mountains," said Zashue ; " give me something to eat, I am tired."

She stirred the fire, and when dry brush flamed over the hearth she placed the stew-pot on it. The remainder of the cornmeal she stirred with water, and began to mix cakes in the usual way. Her husband watched her pleasantly.

Zashue was indeed a good-looking Indian. Lithe and of a fair height, with black hair and large bright eyes, he appeared the picture of vigour and mirth. He chatted with the utmost nonchalance, telling his wife about the insignificant happenings of the day, the prospects of the crops, what such and such a one had said to him, and what he had told the other in return. It was innocent gossip, intimate chat, such as a contented husband may tell a wife in whom he places entire confidence. How happy she felt at the harmless chatter, and yet how intensely miserable. His inquiry, "Are you ill?" rang in her ears with a sickening clang, like some overwhelming reproach. Why, oh why, had she not spoken to him in time? He was so good to her. Now it was too late; and beside, why anticipate the fatal hour when he must know all? Why not improve the few moments of respite granted ere death came?

Say Koitza suffered him to continue, and listened with increasing interest to the talk of her husband. It might be the last time. Little by little, as he went on, with harmless, sometimes very clumsy, jokes and jests, she became oblivious of her wretched prospects, and her soul rested in the present. She began to smile shyly at first, then she even laughed. As Zashue ate he praised her cooking; and that gratified her, although it filled her with remorse and anguish. The children came also and squatted around the hearth, Okoya alone keeping at a distance and eyeing his mother suspiciously. Could she in his presence really feel as merry as she acted? Was it not evidence of the basest deception on her part? So the boy reasoned from his own standpoint, and went out into the court-yard in disgust.

The sun set, and a calm, still night sank down on the Rito de los Frijoles. As the sky darkened, evidences of life and mirth began to show themselves at the bottom of the gorge as well as along the cliffs. Monotonous singing sounded from the roofs of the big house, from caves, and from slopes leading up to them. Noisy talking, clear, ringing laughter, rose into the night. Old as well as young seemed to enjoy the balmy evening. Few remained indoors. Among these were Zashue and his wife. The woman leaned against him, and often looked up to his face with a smile. She felt happy by the side of her husband, and however harrowing the thought of her future seemed to be, the present was blissful to her.

After a while Zashue rose, and his spouse followed him anxiously to the door, trembling lest he should leave her alone for the night. She grasped his hand, and he stood for a while in the outer doorway gazing at the sky. Every sound was hushed except the rushing of the brook. The canopy of heaven sparkled in wonderful splendour. Its stars blazed, shedding peace upon earth and good-will to man The woman's hand quivered in that of her spouse. He turned and retired with her to the interior of the dwelling.

CHAPTER III.

WE must now return to the fields of the Rito, and to the spot where, in the first chapter of our story, Okoya had been hailed by a man whom he afterward designated as Tyope Tihua. That individual was, as we have since found, the former husband of Shotaye, Say's ill-chosen friend. After the boys had left, Tyope had continued to weed his corn, not with any pretence of activity or haste, but in the slow, persistent way peculiar to the sedentary Indian, which makes of him a steady though not a very profitable worker. Tyope's only implement was a piece of basalt resembling a knife, and he weeded on without interruption until the shadows of the plants extended from row to row. Then he straightened himself and scanned quietly the whole valley as far as visible, like one who is tired and is taking a last survey of the scene of his daily toil.

The fields were deserted. Everybody had left them except himself. Tyope pushed aside the stone implement and turned to go. After leaving the corn he turned to the right, and gradually stooping went toward a grove of low pines. Into that grove he penetrated slowly, cautiously, avoiding the least noise. It was clearly his intention to conceal himself. Once inside of the thicket of pine boughs he cowered, and after listening again and satisfying himself that nobody was around, he plunged his right arm beneath the branches that drooped down to the surface. When he withdrew it his hand grasped a bow. He placed this bow near his feet and dived a second time under the branches, pulling out another object, which proved to be a quiver made of panther-skin filled with arrows. He examined each of these arrows carefully, trying their heads of flint and obsidian, and replaced them in such a manner that the feathered ends projected from the quiver. A third time he ransacked the hiding-place, and produced from beneath the boughs a short wooden war-club. His last essay brought to light a cap of buffalo-hide thick enough to repel an arrow fired at short range, and so fashioned as to protect the forehead to the eyebrows, while behind, it descended low upon the neck. This cap, or helmet, he forthwith placed upon his head. Then he slung the quiver across his shoulders, wound the thong of the club around his right wrist, grasped the bow with the left hand, and rose to his feet.

Daylight was gone. Only a flat golden segment blazed above the western peaks. The peaks themselves, with the mountains, formed a huge mass of dark purple. Over the valley night hovered already, but a streak of mist trailing here and there like a thin veil marked the course of the little brook. It was so dark that Tyope could move without any fear of being seen. He nevertheless maintained a stooping position as long as he was on open ground. Once in the corn he followed its rows instead of traversing them, as if afraid of injuring the plants. He also examined carefully the edge of the brook before crossing it to the south side. Once on the declivity leading up to the mesa, he climbed nimbly and with greater unconcern, for there the shadow was so dense that nobody could notice him from below.

From the brink of the table-land Tyope looked back upon the Rito. He stopped not so much in order to see, for it was too dark, but in order to listen. Everything was quiet. A bear snarled far away, but this did not concern the listener.   He strolled on through the scrubby timber of the mesa until he arrived at a place where tall pines towered up into the starry sky, when he stopped again and remained for quite a while looking up at the heavens.   The great bear — the seven stars, as the Pueblos term it — sparkled near the northern horizon, and Tyope seemed to watch that constellation with unusual interest.   Now a hoarse dismal yelping struck his ear, the barking of the coyote, or prairie wolf. Twice, three times, the howl was repeated in the distance ; then Tyope replied to it, imitating its cry.   All was still again.

Suddenly the barking sounded much nearer, and Tyope moved toward the place whence the sound issued, brushing past the shrubs.   Reaching a clear space, he saw before him the form of a big wolf.   The animal was standing immovable, his tail drooping, his head horizontal.

"Are you alone?" Tyope whispered.   The apparition or beast, whatever it might be, seemed not to excite the least apprehension.   The wolf bent its head in reply without uttering a sound.

"Where are the Dinne?" Tyope continued.

A hollow chuckle seemed to proceed from the skull of the animal; it turned and disappeared in the darkness, but a rustling of boughs and creaking of branches made known the direction.   Tyope followed.

The wolf moved swiftly.   From time to time its husky barkings were heard ; and the Indian from the Rito, guided by these signals, followed as rapidly as possible.   At last he saw the outlines of a juniper-bush against a faint glow. Behind it sounded the crackling of freshly ignited brushwood, and soon a light spread over the surrounding neighbourhood.   Stepping into the illuminated circle Tyope stood before a man squatting by the fire.

The man was heaping wood on the fire which he had

just started. By his side lay the skin of a large wolf. He seemed not to notice Tyope, although his face was directed toward him, for his eyes disappeared below projecting brows, so projecting that only now and then a sudden flash, quick as lightning, broke out from beneath their shadow. His form indicated strength and endurance; he was of stronger build than the man from the Tyuonyi. A kilt of deer-hide was his only dress. His hair was wound around his skull like a turban. As ornaments the stranger wore a necklace of panther claws. A bow and some arrows were lying on the wolf's skin beside him.[1]

Without a word Tyope squatted down near the fire, facing the other Indian. It had turned cold, and both men held their hands up to the flame. The former glanced at the latter furtively from time to time, but neither uttered a word. The fire was beginning to decline; its light grew faint. At last the other Indian said, —

"When will the Koshare go into the round house?"

"As soon as the moon gives light," Tyope carelessly replied.

"How many are there of you?"

"Why do you want to know this?" inquired the man from the Rito, in a husky voice.

His companion chuckled again and said nothing. He had put an imprudent question. He turned away carelessly, placed more wood on the fire, and poked the embers. Tyope looked up at the sky, and thus the vivid, scornful glance the other threw on his figure escaped him.

So far the conversation had been carried on in the Queres language; now the stranger suddenly spoke in another dialect and in a more imperious tone.

---

[1] This custom of taking the disguise of a wolf is or has been used by the Navajos frequently in order to surprise herds of cattle and horses

" Art thou afraid of the Dinne? "

" Why should I be afraid of them? " responded Tyope in his native tongue.

" Speak the tongue of the Dinne," the other sternly commanded, and a flash burst from beneath his eyebrows, almost as savage as that of a wolf. " Thou hast courted the people of my tribe. They have not sought after thee. Thou knowest their language. Speak it, therefore, and then we shall see." He straightened himself, displaying a youthful figure full of strength and elasticity.

Tyope took this change of manner very composedly. He answered quietly in the same dialect, —

" If thou wilt, Nacaytzusle, I can speak like thy people also. It is true I came for them, but what I wanted"—he emphasized the word — " was as much for their benefit as my own. Thou, first of all, wast to gain by my scheme." His eyes closed, and the glance became as sharp as that of a rattlesnake.

Nacaytzusle poked the embers with a dry stick as if thinking over the speech of the other. Then he asked, —

" Thou sayest thou hast wanted. Wantest thou no more? "

" Not so much as hitherto," Tyope stated positively.

" What shall it be now? " inquired the Dinne.

" I will speak to thee so as to be understood," explained the man from the Rito, " but thou shalt tell thy people only so much of it as I shall allow thee to say. Thou art Dinne, it is true, and their tongue is thy language, but many a time hast thou seen the sun set and rise while the houses wherein we dwell on the brook were thy home. When they brought thee to us after the day on which Topanashka slaughtered thy people beyond the mountains, thou didst not remain with us long. The moon has not been bright often since thou left us to join thy people. Is it not so, Nacaytzusle? Answer me."

The Navajo shrugged his shoulders.

"It is true," he said, "but I have nothing in common with the House people."

"It may be so now, but if thou dost not care for the men, the women are not without interest to thee. Is it not thus?"

"The tzane on the brook," replied the Navajo, disdainfully, "amount to nothing."

"In that case" — Tyope flared up and grasped his club, speaking in the Queres language and with a vibrating tone — "why don't you look for a companion in your own tribe? Mitsha Koitza does not care for a husband who sneaks around in the timber like a wolf, and whose only feat consists in frightening the old women of the Tyuonyi!"

The Navajo stared before him with apparent stolidity. Tyope continued, —

"You pretend to despise us now, yet enough has remained within your heart, from the time when you lived at the Tyuonyi and slept in the estufa of Shyuamo hanutsh, to make my daughter appear in your eyes better, more handsome, and more useful, than the girls of the Dinne!"

The features of the Dinne did not move; he kept silent But his right hand played with the string of the bow that lay on the wolf's skin.

"Nacaytzusle," the other began again, "I promised to assist you to obtain the girl against her will. Mind! Mitsha, my daughter, will never go to a home of the Dinne of her own accord, but I would have stolen her for your sake. Now I say to you that I have promised you this child of mine, and I have promised your people all the green stones of my tribe. The first promise I shall fulfil if you wish. The other, you may tell your tribe, I will not hold to longer."

The Navajo looked at him in a strange, doubtful way and replied, —

" You have asked me to be around the Tyuonyi day after day, night after night, to watch every tree, every shrub, merely in order to find out what your former wife, Shotaye, was doing, and to kill her if I could.   You have demanded," he continued, raising his voice, while he bent forward and darted at the Indian from the Rito a look of suppressed rage, " that the Dinne should come down upon the Tyuonyi at the time when the Koshare should fast and pray, and should kill Topanashka, the great warrior, so that you might become maseua in his place !   Now I tell you that I shall not do either ! "

The eyes of the young savage flamed like living coals.

" Then you shall not have my child ! " exclaimed Tyope.

" I will get her.   You may help me or not ! "

" I dare you to do it," Tyope hissed.

Nacaytzusle looked straight at him.

" Do you believe," he hissed in turn, " that if I were to go down to the brook and tell the tapop what you have urged me and my people to do against your kin that he would not reward me ? "

Tyope Tihua became very quiet; his features lost the threatening tension which they had displayed, his eyes opened, and he said in a softer tone, —

" That is just what I want you to do.   But I want this from you alone.   Go and see the tapop.   Tell him not the small talk about this and that, but what you have seen with your own eyes about Shotaye, that witch, that snake, — of her dark ways, how she sneaked through the brush on the mesa, and how she found and gathered the plumage of the accursed owl.   Tell him all, and I will carry Mitsha to your lodges, tied and gagged if needs be."

" Why don't you send the girl out alone ?   I will wait for her wherever you say."

"Do you think that I would be so silly?" the Pueblo retorted with a scornful laugh. "Do you really believe I
would do such a thing? No, Dinne, you and your people
may be much more cunning than mine in many ways, but
we are not so stupid as that. If I were to do that, you
would rob me of my handsome maiden and that would be
the last of it. No, Dinne, I do not need you to such
an extent, I am not obliged to have you. But if you go to
the Tyuonyi and accuse the witch, then you shall go out
free, and Mitsha must follow you to the hogans of your
people, whether she will or not. Do what I tell you, and I
will do as I promise. If you will not neither will I, for
mind, I do not need you any longer."

Tyope glanced at the stars with an air of the utmost indifference. Nacaytzusle had listened quietly. Now he
said without raising his eyes, —

"Tyope, you ask me to do all this, and do not even give
me a pledge. You are wise, Tyope, much wiser than we
people of the hogans. Give me some token that you also
will do what you have said when I have performed my
part. Give me"—he pointed to the alabaster tablet hanging
on Tyope's necklace — "that okpanyi on your neck."

It was so dark that Nacaytzusle in extending his arm involuntarily touched the other's chest. Tyope drew back at
the touch and replied, rather excitedly, —

"No, I will not give you any pledge!"

"Nothing at all?" asked the Navajo. A slight rustling
noise was heard at the same time.

"Nothing!" Tyope exclaimed hoarsely.

The savage thrust his arm out at the Pueblo with the ra-
pidity of lightning. A dull thud followed, his arm dropped,
and something fell to the ground. It was an arrow, whose
head of flint falling on the ashes caused the embers to glow
for an instant. Both men sprang in opposite directions.

like snakes darting through the grass. Each one concealed himself behind a bush. The branches rustled and cracked for a short space. The place around the fire was vacant; nothing remained but a dim streak of ruddy light.

Tyope, after repelling the assault upon him, had taken refuge behind a low juniper-bush. When the Navajo thrust a pointed arrow at his chest he had numbed the arm of the savage by a blow from his club, and then both men, like true Indians, hurriedly placed themselves under cover, whence each listened eagerly to discover the movements of his foe. Tyope could have killed the Navajo while close to him, for he had the advantage in weapons; but, although he really had no further use for the young man, he was not so angry as to take his life.

Still, under the circumstances, the greater the caution displayed the better. Intimately acquainted with the character of the Dinne Indians, and that of Nacaytzusle in particular, Tyope had gone on this errand well armed. Open hostility had resulted from the interview; it was useless to make any attempt at conciliation. Speedy return to the Rito was the only thing left. This return might become not only difficult, but dangerous, with the young Navajo concealed on the mesa. Tyope had known Nacaytzusle thoroughly from childhood.

Twenty years before, the Dinne had killed an old woman from the Tyuonyi. The murder took place near the gorge, on the mesa north of it, whither she had gone to collect the edible fruit of the piñon tree. When the corpse was discovered the scalp had been taken; and this, rather than the killing, demanded speedy revenge. A number of able-bodied men of the clan to which the grandmother belonged gathered in order to fast and make the usual sacrifices preliminary to the formation of a war party. On the last night of their fast a delegate from the hishtanyi chayani appeared in their midst, and performed the customary incantations. He painted their bodies with the black lustrous powder of iron and manganese ore which is believed to strike terror into the hearts of enemies. He seiected their leader, invested him with the office, and blessed the war-fetiches. To the leader he gave a little bag of buckskin filled with the powder of the yerba del manso, which still further produces dismay among the foe. That leader was Topanashka Tihua, then in the full vigour of manhood.

On the following morning Topanashka left before daybreak with five picked men in the hideous garb of Indian braves. They penetrated cautiously the mountain labyrinth west of the Rito, concealing themselves during the day and travelling at night. On the morning of the fifth day they discovered a few huts of the Navajo. Whether or no their inmates had participated in the murder of the old woman they did not stop to inquire, but pounced upon the people who were still asleep. The results of the surprise were nine scalps and one captive. This captive was a little boy, and that boy was Nacaytzusle.

Although barely three years old, he was dragged to the Rito and had to take part in the solemn dance, during which the scalps of his parents were triumphantly waved by those who had killed them. Afterward he was adopted into the Turquoise clan, for the people of the Eagle clan refused to receive him, the privilege of so doing being theirs. Topanashka disliked the appearance of the child, and his counsels weighed heavily. Thus Nacaytzusle became an adopted son of the Queres, but it did not change his nature. His physique at once indicated foreign origin ; he grew up to be taller, more raw-boned, than the youth of the House people, and his dark, wolfish look and the angular cut of his features betrayed his Dinne blood.

Like all the other youth, he received the rude education

which was imparted at the estufas. He showed considerable aptitude for mastering songs and prayers, after once
acquiring the language of his captors. He also watched the
wizards as often as opportunity was afforded, and learned
many a trick of jugglery. Tyope was struck by the youth's
aptitude for such arts and practices. It revealed natural ten-
dencies, and confirmed Tyope in the belief that the Navajos
were born wizards, that their juggleries and performances,
some of which are indeed startling, revealed the possession
of higher powers. The Pueblos hold the Navajos in quite
superstitious respect. Tyope therefore looked upon the
young fellow as one who in course of time might become an invaluable assistant. He observed the boy's ways,
and became intimately acquainted with all his traits, bad
and good.

Nacaytzusle was a successful hunter ; he was very nimble,
quick, and exceedingly persevering, in everything he undertook. But he was also a natural lounger and idler, whenever he was not busy with preparations for the hunt or
repairing his own scanty clothing. Work in the fields he
avoided. He even showed marked contempt for the people
of the Rito, because the men performed toil which he
regarded as degrading. Keeping aloof from the men's
society to a certain extent, he was more attracted by the
women. It was especially Mitsha Koitza, Tyope's good-
looking daughter, who attracted him ; and he began to pay
attentions to her in a manner in keeping with his wild
temperament. Tyope, strange to say, was pleased to notice
this. He would have been happy to have given his child
to the savage, but he had no right to interfere in the matter
of marriage, for this belonged to the girl's own clan to
arrange. The clan was that of the Eagle, and Topanashka
was its most influential member, its leading spirit. Mitsha
avoided the Navajo ; and when Nacaytzusle attempted to

press his suit, the girl repelled his addresses in a manner
that showed her aversion to him beyond any possible
question.

Had Mitsha been less positive in her behaviour, it is quite
likely that the character of the young captive might have
changed, — that he might have softened little by little, entering into the path traced by the customs of sedentary Indians. As it was, his hatred to them increased, and with it
the desire to recover his independence by returning to his
kindred.

About a year before, then, Nacaytzusle disappeared from
the Tyuonyi. Shortly afterward Tyope was suddenly ac-
costed by him while hunting on the mesa, and a secret
intercourse began, which led to the negotiations of which
we have just heard the main purport. These negotiations
were now broken, and in a manner that made a return to
the Rito rather dangerous. The very qualities which had
fascinated Tyope — the wariness, agility, and persistency
of the Navajo, his physical strength, and above all his supposed natural faculties for magic, coupled with his thorough knowledge of the country — caused Tyope to ponder
upon his means of escape.

The blow which he dealt the savage was sufficient to
teach him that a hand-to-hand encounter would not result
favourably to him. At the same time this slight injury could
not fail to exasperate the Navajo, and Tyope knew that the
savage would lie in wait for him at some point which he had
to pass on his return. For the present, Nacaytzusle was
very likely concealed in the vicinity, in the same manner
and for the same reasons as the Pueblo Indian himself; but
he was sure to leave his hiding-place and make some movement toward preparing either an ambush or a sudden surprise. Tyope remained motionless for a while. He glanced
across the space where the fire had been burning; but every

spark was gone, and it was too dark to discern anything. He finally rose to his knees slowly and cautiously, and turned his eyes in the opposite direction. There also was an open space, and the dim starlight enabled him to discover that between his station and the nearest tree something similar to a rock or ledge protruded. He peered and listened, then turned around on his knees and flattening his body on the ground began to creep toward the tree. As soon as he reached its foot he rose to full height, leaned against the trunk, and glanced at the stars. They indicated that it was past midnight, and Tyope felt uneasy. In case he should be delayed, and reach the Rito after daylight, it might excite suspicions. Yet his only safety lay in making a wide circuit.

The dismal yelping of a prairie wolf struck his ear, and to his alarm there was at once a reply near where the interview had taken place, but slightly to the east and more toward the deep gorge in which the Rio Grande flows. He concluded that Nacaytzusle had shifted his position, by placing himself on Tyope's supposed line of retreat. But it was also manifest that the boy had not come to the meeting alone, — that at least one more Navajo lurked in the vicinity. At least one, perhaps more.

Another wolf now howled in the direction of the south. A fourth one was heard farther off, and both voices united in a plaintive wail. Any one unacquainted with the remarkable perfection with which the Navajos imitate the nocturnal chant of the so-called coyote, would have been deceived, and have taken the sounds for the voices of the animals themselves; but Tyope recognized them as signals through which four Navajo Indians prowling around him informed each other of their positions and movements. This made his own situation exceedingly critical. The only mitigating circumstance was that the four were dispersed, and only one of them could as yet have an idea of his whereabouts.

The Indian from the Rito braced himself against the tree, and taking off his helmet laid it carefully beside him on the ground. Then he took off the quiver, emptied it, and tied the strap to which it was fastened around his waist. To this belt he tied both the quiver and the helmet, distributing them in such a manner that in the prevailing darkness they appeared like one of the ragged kilts of deer-skin which formed the main part of a Navajo's costume. Next Tyope untied the knot which held his hair on the back of the head, divided the long strands into switches, and began to wind those around his skull. Necklace, fetich, and the plume that adorned his sidelock, he put in the quiver. He was now so far transformed that any one, Nacaytzusle excepted, might have taken him in the night for a Navajo warrior. This metamorphosis was performed rapidly, but without anxious haste or confusion. The howls had meanwhile been repeated. They sounded nearer than before from the east, the south, and the southeast. Nacaytzusle alone, to judge from the signals which he gave, remained stationary.

Tyope, abandoning his position at the foot of the tree, glided to the nearest shrub. Thence he struck northward in the direction of the Rito. He walked erect, but scrupulously avoided everything that might create noise. When near the fireplace he stood still and listened. A wolf yelped to the right of where the Dinne of whom Tyope was most afraid seemed to be listening, about two hundred steps from him, on the swelling of the mesa. He manifestly expected the Queres to return the same way he came. It was not a sign of much wisdom, but the boy was young and inexperienced in the stratagems of Indian warfare. Tyope felt relieved.

Suddenly loud barking sounded directly in front of

him, and at no great distance. Tyope dropped on the
ground and began to glide like a snake toward the
place whence this last signal came. He crouched behind
a flat rock and raised his eyes. It was in vain; nothing
could be seen in the obscurity. He felt puzzled. Was
this last signal the voice of another enemy who had hitherto
remained silent, or was it Nacaytzusle who had changed
his position? At all events it was safer to rise and go
directly toward the spot, rather than approach it in a
creeping posture. He walked deliberately onward, at the
same time calling out in a low tone, —

"Nacaytzusle!"

Nothing moved.

He advanced a few steps and repeated, —

"Nacaytzusle! Hast thou seen anything?"

"No," said a hollow voice near by, and a human form
arose as if from beneath the surface. The man stepped
up to Tyope; and to the latter's unpeakable relief, he
looked stouter and shorter than Nacaytzusle. The Indian
was unknown to him, and Tyope said eagerly, —

"The badger must be hiding near where the fire is.
We should cut off his trail to the north. Nacaytzusle
went too far east; there " — he pointed toward the northeast — "is where he ought to stand."

Tyope spoke the Navajo language fluently.

"Thou art right," said the other; "go thither, and we
will be closer together."

Tyope felt loath to follow this advice, for it would have
brought him uncomfortably near his most dangerous foe;
yet, under the circumstances and to avoid all suspicion
he accepted the suggestion, and was about to turn in the
direction indicated when the signals sounded again and
simultaneously from every quarter. The strange Indian
held him back, asking, —

"How is this? We are five, and four have shouted now. Who art thou, and where dost thou come from?"

"I came from above," Tyope replied, with affected composure.

They stood so close together that the Navajo could notice some details of Tyope's accoutrements. Grasping the cap of buffalo hide which dangled from the belt of the Queres, he inquired, —

"What dost thou carry here?"

All was lost, for the Navajos were well acquainted with this garment, peculiar to the war dress of the Pueblos. Tyope saw that only the most reckless act could save him. So he dropped all his arrows, which until now he had carried in his right hand, and thrust his club like a slung-shot into the other's face. With a yell of pain and surprise the Navajo tumbled backward into a bush, while Tyope darted forward in the direction of the Rito. Behind him sounded the hoarse cries of the wounded man, loud yells answering. They came from four sides; all the pursuers were running at full speed to the assistance of their companion.

Madly, like a deer pursued by wolves, Tyope bounded onward. But soon his speed slackened; he believed that he was safe, and there was no use in tiring himself. His movements were no longer noiseless as before. During his first run he had made so much noise as to lead the pursuers directly on his trail. These pursuers had suddenly become silent. Nevertheless, from time to time, rustling sounds struck the ear of Tyope, and proved that the pursuit was carried on unrelentingly. He noticed a suspicious twittering and cracking, not behind him, but at one side; and it approached.

He comprehended at once that one of the Navajos, instead of rushing to the rescue of the one whom Tyope had struck down, had taken a direction diagonal to his own, with the hope of intercepting him near the brink of the declivity leading down into the Rito, or perhaps sooner. A change in his line of flight was thereby rendered necessary, but in what direction? The warning sounds were heard directly north of him; then everything became quiet. The same stillness reigned all around; and this proved that the pursuers, while certainly approaching with the greatest possible alacrity, were anxious to cover their movements. Tyope stood still, undecided what to do. The sound of a breaking or bending twig, faint though audible, caused him to crouch behind a cedar bush again. He held his breath, listened, and peered through the branches. Soon a man appeared, — a Navajo; but whether it was Nacaytzusle or not, he could not discover. The Indian glided across the open space as noiselessly as a spectre, and disappeared in a northerly direction. Tyope remained in his concealment for a while, and as nothing more was heard or seen, he crawled to the nearest shrub to the west. There he again listened and watched, then rose to his feet and moved in a westerly direction.

The moon had risen, and its crescent shed a glimmer over the tree-tops. For some time Tyope walked on. Frequently he halted to listen; everything was still. From this he inferred that his enemies had passed him, and were now stationed along the brink of the gorge in order to intercept him, and that he had gone far enough to risk a descent from where he stood. It did not seem likely that the Navajos had posted themselves so far up the brink, since he knew it to be beyond the highest cave-dwellings. Turning to the north, therefore, he soon found himself under the last trees of the mesa. Beyond opened a whitish chasm, and the northern cliffs of the Rito rose like dim gigantic phantoms. Here he knew the descent had to be made, but here also the most imminent danger was lurking.

The brink of the Rito on the south side is lined by shrubbery, with high timber interspersed; but ledges of friable volcanic rocks advance in places beyond this shade. crowning the heights like irregular battlements. Their surface is bare, and anything moving on them might become visible to a watchful eye, notwithstanding the dimness of the moonlight.

Tyope lay down, and began to glide like a snake. He moved slowly, pushing his body into every depression, hugging closely every protuberance. Thus he succeeded in crossing the open space between the woods and the rim of the declivity. Now he could overlook the valley beneath and glance down the slope. It was not very steep, and thickets covered it in places. But between him and the nearest brush a bare ledge had yet to be crossed. He crept into a wide fissure, and then down. The crags were not high, scarcely ten feet. Then he pushed cautiously on to the open space. When near the middle of it he raised his head to look around. Immediately a twang sounded from the heights above him, and a whiz followed. Tyope bounded to his feet, reeled for a moment; another twang and another whizzing, — an arrow struck the ground where he had lain; but already the Queres was away, leaping from rock to rock, tearing through shrubbery and thickets like a frightened mountain sheep. Stones rolled from above; somebody was hastening down in pursuit; arrow upon arrow sped after the fugitive. But Tyope was safely out of reach and in the bottom, whither the Navajo did not dare to follow. A drizzling noise, like that of pebbles dropping from a height, told that the pursuer had withdrawn to the woods again : then all was still.

Down below on the edge of the brook lay Tyope, panting from exhaustion. His life was safe and he felt unhurt, but he was overcome by emotion and effort. As long as the excitement had lasted his physical strength had held out. Now that all was over he felt tired and weak. Yet he could not think of rest, for daybreak was close at hand. He dipped some water from the brook and moistened his parched lips, taking care not to touch his face or body with the liquid. Tyope was tired and worn out, but at the same time angry; and when the Indian suffers or when he is angry he neither washes nor bathes. Physical or mental pain, disappointment, and wrath, are with him compatible only with lack of cleanliness, and since he becomes wrathful or disappointed or sick quite as often as we do, his bodily condition is frequently far from pleasant.

Tyope felt angry and disappointed at himself. The failure in regard to Nacaytzusle was not the cause of his disappointment. What angered him was that he had not killed the Navajo whom he struck down on the mesa, and taken his scalp. There would have been ample time, and he could have concealed the trophy, returning for it in the daytime. He had already taken one scalp in his life, but to have missed this opportunity of securing a second one was an unpardonable failure. It was this which caused him to avoid the cooling waters and forget the demands of cleanliness.

He rose and walked on. The valley opened before him; the dim light of a waning moon shone into it, allowing a practised eye to discern grotto after grotto in the cliffs. As Tyope proceeded down the gorge, following the brook's course, he glanced at the caves. They were those of the Water clan. He frowned and clenched his fist in anger. There lived his enemy, Shotaye, his former spouse. There was her den, the abode of the hated witch. How often had she crossed his path, how often warned those whom he had planned to injure ! Yes, she was a sorceress, for she knew too much about his ways. But now his time would come, for he too knew something concerning her that must ruin her forever. He had known it for some time, but only now was it possible to accuse her. He shook his fist at the cliffs in silent rage; the thought of taking revenge filled his heart with sinister joy, and made him forget the fatigue and disappointment of the past hours.

He soon stood in front of the place where the cliffs form a perpendicular wall, and where instead of excavating dwell-ings the people of the Eagle clan had built their quarters outside, using the smooth surface of the rock as a rear wall. A row of terraced houses, some three, some two stories high, others with a ground-floor only, extended along the base of the rocks, looking like a shapeless ruin in the faint glow of the moon. Toward this edifice Tyope walked. All was silent, for nobody had as yet risen from sleep. He climbed on the roof of a one-story house and stooped over the hatchway to listen. It was dark inside, and only the sound of regular breathings could be heard. Tyope descended into the room. Two persons lay on the floor fast asleep. They were his wife and daughter. Concealing his weapons and war-accoutrements, he stretched himself at full length beside the others. The rushing of the brook was but faintly heard ; a cold blast entered through the loophole in the wall. Tyope heaved a deep sigh of relief and closed his weary eyes. The night was nearly over, but he had reached home before the dawn of day.

CHAPTER IV.

A BRIGHT morning followed the night on which Tyope underwent his adventures. He slept long, but it attracted no undue attention and called forth no remarks on the part of his wife and daughter. They were wont to see him come and go at any hour of the night. It was very near noon when he awoke at last, and after disposing of his late breakfast, *à la mode du pays*, sauntered off to parts unknown to the others. The day was one of remarkable beauty. No dim foggy city sun cast a sullen glance at the landscape. The sun stood in the zenith of a sky of the deepest azure, like a flaming, sparkling, dazzling meteor. Still its heat was not oppressive.

On the mesa above the Rito a fresh wind was blowing. The shrubbery was gently moved by the breeze. A faint rushing sound was heard, like distant waves surging back and forth. In the gorge a zephyr only fanned the tops of the tallest pines; a quietness reigned, a stillness, like that which the poets of old ascribe to the Elysian fields.

There is not much bustle about the big house on the Tyuonyi. The men are out and at work, and the children have retired to the court-yard. A group of girls alone enlivens the space between the main building and the new home of the Corn people. They are gathered in a throng while they talk, laugh, and chatter, pointing at the fresh coat of clay which they have finished applying to the outside of the new building. Their hands are yet filled with the liquid material used for plastering, and they taunt each other as to the relative merits of their work.

One of the maidens, a plump little thing with a pair of lively eyes, calls out to another, pointing at a spot where the plaster appears less smooth and even, —

"See there, Aistshie, you did that! You were too lazy to go over it again. Look at my work; how even it is compared with yours!"

The other girl shrugged her shoulders and retorted, —

"It may be, but it is not my fault, it is yours, Sayap. You did it yesterday when we beat off the boys. You pushed Shyuote against the wall and he thumped his head here. See, this is the mark where he struck the clay. You did this, Sayap, not I."

Sayap laughed, and her buxom form shook.

"You are right; I did it, I served the urchin right. It was good, was it not, Aistshie? How I punished the brat, and how he looked afterward with his face all one mud-patch!"

"Yes," Aistshie objected, "but I did more. I faced Okoya, despite his bow and arrows. That was more than you did."

The other girls interrupted the scornful reply which Sayap was on the point of giving. They crowded around the two with a number of eager questions.

"What was it?" queried one.

"What happened yesterday?" another.

"Did you have a quarrel with boys," a third; and so on. All pressed around begging and coaxing them to tell the story of yesterday's adventure. The heroines themselves looked at each other in embarrassment. At last Aistshie broke out, —

"You tell it, Sayap."

"Well," began the latter, "it was yesterday afternoon

6

and we were just putting on the last touches of the coating, when Okoya and little Shyuote his brother — "

A clod, skilfully hurled, struck her right ear, filling it with sand and cutting off the thread of her narrative rather abruptly. Sayap wheeled around to see whence the blow had come. The other girls all laughed, but she was angry. Her wrath was raised to the highest pitch however, when she discovered that Shyuote was the aggressor. On a little eminence near by stood the scamp, dancing, cutting capers, and yelling triumphantly.

" Shyuote is small, but he knows how to throw."

" Fiend," cried Sayap in reply. She picked up a stone, raised it in the awkward manner in which most girls handle missiles, and running toward the boy hurled it at him. It fell far short of its mark, of course, and Shyuote only laughed, danced, and grimaced so much the more. As Sayap kept advancing and the other girls followed, he threw a second clod, which struck her squarely in the face, and so sharply that blood flowed from her nose and mouth. At the same time the rogue shouted at the top of his voice, —

" Come on ! All of you ! I am not afraid. You will never catch me ! "

And as the majority of his pursuers came on, while two or three remained behind soothing and consoling Sayap, who stood still, crying and bleeding, he thrust out his tongue at them its full length, performed a number of odious grimaces, and then nimbly clambered up between a group of erosive cones that lay in front of the cliff. He turned around once more to yell defiance and scorn at his pursuers, and disappeared on the other side. Farther pursuit being hopeless, the girls clustered around the weeping Sayap and held a council of war. They vowed dire vengeance on the lad, and promised their injured sister to improve the first opportunity that should present itself.

Shyuote, on the other hand, felt proud of his success. His revenge was, he felt, a glorious one. Still he was careful not to forget the counsels of prudence, and instead of returning to the house by a direct route, which might have carried him too near the enraged damsels, he sauntered along, hugging the cliffs for some distance, and then cautiously sneaked into the fields below the new homes of the Maize clan. Once in the corn he felt safe, and was about to cross the brook to the south side, when the willows bordering the streamlet rustled and tossed, and a voice called to him from the thicket, —

"Where are you going, uak?"

Shyuote stopped, and looked around for the speaker; but nobody was visible. Again the boughs rustled and shook, and there emerged from the willows an old man of low stature, with iron-gray hair and shrivelled features. He wore no ornaments at all; his wrap was without belt and very dirty. In his left hand he held a plant which he had pulled up by the roots. He stepped up to Shyuote, stood close by his side, and growled at him rather than spoke.

"I asked you where you were going. Why don't you answer?"

Shyuote was frightened, and stammered in reply, —

"To see my father."

"Who is your father?"

"Zashue Tihua."

The features of the interlocutor took on a singular expression. It was not one of pleasure, neither did it betoken anger; if anything, it denoted a sort of grim satisfaction.

"If Zashue is your father," continued he, and his eyes twinkled strangely, "Say Koitza must be your mother."

"Of course," retorted the boy, to whom this interrogatory seemed ludicrous.

"And Okoya your brother," the old man persisted.

"Why do you ask all this?" inquired the child, laughingly.

A look, piercing and venomous, darted from the eyes of the questioning man. He snarled angrily, —

"Because I ask it. I ask, and you shall answer me without inquiring why and wherefore. Do you hear, uak?"

Shyuote hung his head; he felt afraid.

"I forbid you to say anything about what I say to you to your mother," continued the other, grasping the left arm of the boy.

Shyuote shook off the grip, and also shook his head in token of refusal. The old man seized the arm again and clutched it so firmly with his bony fingers that the lad screamed from pain.

"Let me go!" he cried. "You hurt me, let me go!"

"Will you do as I bid you?" asked his tormentor.

"Yes," sobbed the child. "I will obey. My mother shall not know anything. Let me go, you hurt!"

The man loosened his grip slightly.

"To your father you shall say that I, the Koshare Naua," — the boy looked up at him at these words in astonishment, — "send word to him through you to come to my house on the night after the one that will follow this day, when the new moon sets behind the mountains. Do you hear me, boy?"

Shyuote stared at the interlocutor with mouth wide open, and with an expression of fear and surprise that evidently amused the other. He gave him a last look, a sharp, threatening, penetrating glance; then his features became less stern.

"Have no fear," he said in a milder tone. "I will not do you any harm; but you must do as I say. Go to your nashtio now, and tell him what I said." With this he wheeled about and left the boy as abruptly as he had appeared. Shyuote stood gaping and perplexed.

He felt very much like crying. His arm still ached from the grip of the old man, and while he was rubbing the sore spot his anger rose at the harsh and cruel treatment he had suffered. He thought of rushing home to his mother forthwith and telling her all about the bad old man, and how he had forbidden him to say anything to her. Still, the Koshare Naua was not to be trifled with, and Shyuote, young and childish as he was, had some misgivings about betraying his confidence. His father had told him that the Naua, or chief leader of the Koshare, was a very wise and therefore a very powerful man. Zashue, who as soon as Shyuote was born had pledged the child to become one of the Delight Makers, was educating the lad gradually in his duties; and Shyuote had already imbibed enough of that discipline to feel a tremendous respect for the leader of the society to which he was pledged to belong. He suppressed the thoughts of rebellion that had arisen, and strolled on, crossing the creek and hunting for his father among the corn-patches on the other side. But his good-humour had left him. Instead of being triumphantly buoyant, he felt morose and humiliated.

Zashue Tihua was at work in the fields of the Water clan, on the southern border of the cultivated plots. He was not alone; another young man kept him company. It was his younger brother, Hayoue. They were weeding side by side, and exchanging remarks while the work went on. Zashue looked up, and his handsome face brightened when he discovered Shyuote coming toward them through the maize. A visit from his favourite child, although by no means an unusual occurrence, was always a source of pleasure. He liked to have Shyuote around him when he was at work.

Throwing a small, sharp stone-splinter toward the boy, he called out to him, —

"Come, take this okpanyi and begin weeding where you stand. Weed toward us until we meet, and we will go home together to the yaya."

This was still further a source of displeasure to Shyuote, who above all things disliked work. He had not come down to the fields to toil. What he sought for was a friendly chat with his father, a few hours of lounging and loafing near him. Disappointed and pouting, he bent over the work assigned, while the two men went on with their task as well as with their conversation.

Hayoue was taller than his brother, and a strikingly handsome young Indian. His eyes had a more serious and less mischievous expression than those of Zashue. He was yet unmarried; but, notwithstanding, a marked predilection for the fair sex formed one of his characteristics. He was held in high esteem by the leading men of the tribe, Tyope and his adherents excepted, for his sagacity, good judgment, and personal valour.

"I tell you," Zashue spoke up, "Shyuote will become a good one."

Hayoue shrugged his shoulders and replied, —

"You should know your own children better than I, yet I tell you Okoya also is good; besides, he is wise and reserved."

"Yes; but he is too much with the women, and his mother stands nearer to him than his father. He never follows me to the fields unless I tell him. Look at the little one, on the other hand. He will be a man."

While his brother spoke Hayoue had quietly observed Shyuote; and the slow, loitering way in which the boy performed his work had not escaped his observation. He said, —

"It may be. To-day he certainly acts rather like an old woman. See how loath he is to weed the plants."

"You always prefer Okoya," replied Zashue. "You like him because he never opens his mouth unless an arrow is forced between his teeth."

"And you prefer Shyuote because you are making a Koshare of him," Hayoue answered, with great composure.

"He surely will become a good one, a better one than I am."

"If he becomes as good a Delight Maker as you are, Zashue, we may be satisfied. Shall you soon retire to the estufa?" he inquired, changing the subject of the conversation.

"I don't know; the Naua has not said anything as yet, but the time is near at hand when we should begin to work. Before going into the round house in the rocks, we ought to be sure that there are no Navajos in the neighbourhood. You are Kauanyi, a member of the order of warriors," he added with a side-glance at his brother, "do you know anything of the sneaking wolves in the mountains?"

Hayoue denied any knowledge concerning the Navajos, adding, —

"I did not like it when that fellow Nacaytzusle ran away from us. He knew too much of our ways."

"He can do no harm. He is glad to stay among his people."

"Still I don't trust him," Hayoue muttered.

"Neither would I, if I were in your place," Zashue taunted, and a good-natured though mischievous smile lit up his features. "If I were you I would keep still better guard over Mitsha Koitza."

"What have I to do with the child of Tyope," exclaimed the other, rather contemptuously.

"Indeed?" queried Zashue, "so you, too, are against Tyope? What has he done to you?"

"Nothing, but I mistrust him as much as I do the Navajo."

These last words were uttered in such a positive manner — they were so earnestly emphasized — that they cut off the conversation. It was plain that Hayoue had made up his mind on the subject, and that he did not wish to have it broached again.

"Sa nashtio," called Shyuote over to where the brothers were weeding in silence, "come over here ; I must tell you something, but I must tell it to you alone."

Hayoue at once turned away, while Zashue called the lad to him. But Shyuote protested, saying that only his father was to hear his communication, and Zashue at last went where the boy was standing. It vexed him, and he inquired rather gruffly what he had to say. Shyuote made a very wise and important face, placed a finger to his lips, and whispered, —

"The Koshare Naua told me to tell you that you should go to see him, not to-morrow, but the day after, when the moon goes behind the mountains."

"Is that all !" exclaimed Zashue, disappointed and angry, — "is that all you had to say? That much you might have shouted to me. There was no need of being so secret about it, and " -- he glanced at the insignificant and careless work the boy had performed — "is that all you have done since you came? You are lazy, uak ! Go home. Go home at once to your mother and tell her that I shall not return for the evening, but will stay with Hayoue in the caves." And as Shyuote, dismayed and troubled, appeared loath to go, Zashue turned to him again, commanding in a very angry tone, —

"Go home ! Go home at once !"

Shyuote left in haste; he felt very much like crying. Hayoue said to his brother,—

"Didn't I tell you that Shyuote was lazy? Okoya is far, far more useful."

"Let me alone about Okoya," growled Zashue; and both went on with the work as before.

Shyuote stumbled across the patches of corn, rather than walked through them. He felt sad, dejected, and very wrathful. All the buoyancy with which his victory over the girls had inspired him was gone. Since that heroic feat nothing but ill-luck had crossed his path. He was angry at his father for scolding him and driving him home, in the presence of Hayoue, for whom the boy had as great a dislike as his uncle had for him. Why, it was worse than the threats and cuffs of the old Naua! It was not only an injustice, it was an insult! So the lad reasoned, and began to brood over vengeance. He was going to show his father that he, the ten-year-old boy, was not to be trifled with. Yes, he would show his teeth by refusing to become a Koshare. Would not that be a glorious revenge! The little fellow did not know that he was pledged to the Delight Makers by a sacred vow of his parent which it was not in his power to break. After a while his thoughts changed, and he concluded that it might be better to say nothing and to go home and ask for something to eat. But never, never again would he favour his father with a friendly call in the corn-patch. This latter resolve appeared to him so satisfactory, the revenge so ample for the injury received, that he forgot the past and fairly danced through the fields, hopping sometimes on one foot and sometimes on the other. He crossed the brook and reached the large house almost to his own surprise.

It was noon, and the full blaze of the sun flooded the valley with light. Not a breeze fanned the air, nothing stirred.   No vibrations troubled the picture which the cliffs, the caves, the buildings, presented in the dazzling glare. The cliffs had lost their yellowish hue and appeared white, with every protuberance, every indentation, or cavity, marked by intense shadows.   The houses inhabited by the Eagle clan along the foot of the rocks were like a row of irregularly piled cubes and prisms; each beam leaning against them cast a jet-black streak of shadow on the ground.   Below the projecting beams of the roofs a short black line descended along the wall, and the towering rocks jutted in and out from dark recesses like monsters. So strong were the contrasts between shadow and light that even Shyuote was struck by it.   He stood still and stared.

Something indefinite, a vague feeling of awe, crept over him.   For the real grandeur of the scenery he had no sense of appreciation, and yet it seemed to him as if everything about were new and strange.   Thousands of times had he gazed at the cliffs of his valley home, but never had they appeared to him as they did now.   So strong was this impression, and so sudden, too, that he shrank from the sight in amazement; then he turned his eyes away and walked rapidly toward home.   He was afraid to look at the colossal pillars and walls; they appeared to him like giants threatening to move.   All his plans for revenge, every thought of wrath and indignation, had vanished.

Suddenly his left knee was struck by a stone hurled with such force that Shyuote bounded and screamed.   At the same time six or seven boys, some apparently of his age while others were taller and older, rushed from the bushes skirting the ditch.   Two of them ran directly in front of him.   They were armed with sticks and short clubs, and the largest, who seemed to be of the same age as Okoya, shouted, —

"You have injured Sayap, and caused her blood to flow. You rotten squash, you shall suffer for it."

Shyuote took in the situation at a glance. He saw that only desperate running would save him from being roughly handled. He darted off like an arrow toward the cave-dwellings in front of him. Unfortunately these were the quarters of the Corn people who had not yet moved into their new homes. To them belonged Sayap and the boys that were assailing Shyuote; and as the fugitive approached the slope, he saw it occupied by other youth ready and eager to give him a warm reception. At the same time the tallest of his pursuers was gaining on him rapidly; rocks flew past his head; a stone struck him between the ribs, stopping his breath almost. In despair he turned to the left, and making a last effort flew towards the houses of the Eagle clan. Panting, blinded by exertion and by pain, he reached one of the beams leading to a roof, rushed upward along it, and was about to take refuge in the room below, when a young girl came up the primitive ladder down which he had intended to precipitate himself. Issuing from the hatchway she quietly pushed the lad to one side; then, as in that moment one of his pursuers appeared on the roof, she stepped between him and Shyuote.

"Get out of the way, Mitsha! Let me get at the wren!" cried the youth who had just climbed the roof. Shyuote fled to the very wall of the rock; he gave up all hope and thought himself lost. But the girl quietly asked, —

"What do you want with the boy?"

"He has hurt Sayap, our sister," the tall youngster answered. "He threw a stone at her and caused her to bleed. Now I am going to pay him for it."

"So will I!" shouted another one from below.

"I too!" "And I!" "He shall get it from all of

us !" yelled a number of youthful voices, and in an instant the roof was crowded with boys.

Mitsha had placed herself so as to shield the trembling lad with her own body. Very quietly she said, —

"Don't you see that he also is bleeding? Let him go now, it is enough." A stone had indeed grazed Shyuote's scalp, and blood was trickling down his cheek.

"It is not enough!" shouted one of the older boys, angrily. "Get out of the way, Mitsha!"

"You shall not hurt him on this roof," replied Mitsha, in a calm but very positive tone.

"Do you intend to protect him?" cried the tallest one of the pursuers, and another one exclaimed, —

"How does it concern you? You have nothing to do here." All turned against the girl. A little fellow, who carried several large pebbles in his hand for the occasion, endeavoured to steal a march around Mitsha in order to reach Shyuote; but she noticed it, and grasped his arm and pulled him back so vigourously that he reeled and fell at full length on the roof. Then she ordered them all to leave forthwith.

"You belong to the Corn clan," she said, "and have nothing to do here on the houses of the Eagle clan. Go down! Get away at once or I will call our men. As long as I am here you shall not touch the uak."

"So you take his part?" cried the biggest one of the invaders. He raised a stick to strike her.

"Lay down your club, you dirty ear of corn," replied the maiden, "or you will fare badly." With this she drew from under her wrap a heavy war-club; it was the same weapon which Tyope had used the night previous.

The boy's arm remained uplifted, but still the attitude of the girl, her threatening look and resolute appearance, checked the assailants. Mitsha stood with apparent composure, but her eyes sparkled and the expression of her face denoted the utmost determination. Besides she was fully as tall as most of her opponents, and the weapon she was holding in readiness looked quite formidable. But the superior number of her assailants exercised a certain pressure on these assailants themselves, and the Indian under such circumstances has no thought of chivalrous feeling. A dozen boys stood before the solitary maiden on the roof, and they were not to be intimidated by her. For an instant only neither said a word; then a threatening murmur arose. One of the lads called out to the tallest of the crowd, —

"Strike her down, Shohona!"

A stone was thrown at her but missed its aim. At this moment the boys nearest the brink of the roof were suddenly thrust aside right and left, the one who had threatened Mitsha with his stick was pulled back and jerked to one side violently, and before the astonished girl stood Okoya. Pale with emotion, breathless, with heaving chest, and quivering from excitement, he gasped to her, —

"Go down into the room; I will protect my brother." Then he turned to face the assailants.

The scene on the roof had attracted a large number of spectators, who had gathered below and were exchanging surmises and advice on the merits of a case about which none of them really knew anything. Now a woman's voice rose from amid this gaping and chattering crowd, — the sharp and screechy voice of an angry woman. She shouted to those who were on the roof, —

"Get down from my house! Get down, you scoundrels! If you want to kill each other do it elsewhere, and not on my home!" With this the woman climbed on to the roof. She seized the boy nearest to her by the hair and pulled him fairly to the ground, so that the poor fellow

howled from pain. With the other hand she dealt blows
and cuffs, and scratched and punched indiscriminately
among the youngsters, so that a sudden panic broke out
among these would-be heroes. Each sought to get out of
her reach with the greatest alacrity. She at last released
her hold on the first victim and reached out for another; but
the last of the young Corn people was just tumbling down
from the roof, and her clutch at his leg came too late. In
an instant the roof was cleared. The young braves from
the Maize clan were ungraciously received below. A number of their parents had assembled, and when the woman
began to expostulate, they looked at the matter from her
point of view. They saw that it was an infringement, a
trespass, upon the territory and rights of another clan, and
treated their pugnacious sons to another instalment of
bodily punishment as fast as they came tumbling from
above. The final result for the incipient warriors of the
Corn people was that they were ignominiously driven
home.

While peace was thus restored upon the ground it still
looked quite stormy on the roof. The woman who had so
energetically interfered at last discovered Okoya, who was
looking in blank amazement at this sudden change of affairs. Forthwith she made a vicious grab at his ebony
locks, with the pointed remark, —

"Down with you, you stinking weed!"

But Mitsha interfered.

"Mother," she said gently, "do not harm him. He was
defending his brother and me. He is none of the others."

"What!" the woman screamed, "was it you whom they
were about to strike, these night-owls made of black corn?
You, my child? Let me tell them again what they are,"
and she ran to the brink of the roof, raised handfuls of dust
from it and hurled them in the direction of the caves of the

offenders. She stamped, she spat; she raved, and heaped upon the heads of the Corn people, their ancestors, and their descendants, every invective the Queres language contains. To those below this appeared decidedly entertaining; the men especially enjoyed the performance, but Mitsha felt sorry, — she disliked to see her mother display such frenzy and to hear her use such vulgar language. She pulled her wrap, saying, —

"It is enough now, sanaya. Don't you see that those who wanted to hurt me are gone? Their fathers and mothers are not guilty. Be quiet, mother; it is all over now."

Her mother at last yielded to these gentle remonstrances, turned away from the brink, and surveyed the roof. She saw Okoya standing before weeping Shyuote, and scolding him.

"What are you doing to this child?" asked Mitsha's mother, still under the pressure of her former excitement. She was ready for another fray.

"He is my brother, and the cause of the whole trouble," Okoya explained to her. "I chide him for it, as it is my duty to do. Nevertheless, they had no right to kill him, still less to hurt the girl."

The woman had at last had time to scrutinize the looks of the young man. She herself was not old, and when not under the influence of passion was rather comely. Okoya's handsome figure attracted her attention, and she stepped nearer, eyeing him closely.

"Where do you belong?" she inquired in a quieter tone.

"I am Tanyi."

"Who is your father?"

"Zashue Tihua."

The woman smiled; she moved still nearer to the young man and continued, —

" I know your father well. He is one of us, a Koshare."
Her eyes remained fastened on his features ; she was manifestly more and more pleased with his appearance. But at
the same time she occasionally glanced toward her daughter Mitsha, and it struck her forcibly that Mitsha, too, was
handsome.

" I know who you are," she said smilingly. "You are
Okoya Tihua, your little brother is called Shyuote, and Say
Koitza is your mother's name. She is a good woman, but "
— and she shrugged her shoulders — " always sick. Have
you any cotton? " she suddenly asked, looking squarely into
the eyes of the boy.

" No," he replied, and his features coloured visibly, " but
I have some handsome skins."

Mitsha too seemed embarrassed ; she started to go into
the room below, but her mother called her back.

" Sa uishe," she coaxed, "won't you give the motātza
something to eat? "

The faces of both young people became fiery red. He
stood like a statue, and yet his chest heaved. He cast
his eyes to the ground. Mitsha had turned her face away ;
her whole body was trembling like a leaf. Her mother
persisted.

" Take him down into the room and feed him," she repeated, and smiled.

" I have nothing," murmured Mitsha.

" If such is the case I shall go and see myself." With
these words the woman descended the beam into the room
below, leaving the two alone on the roof, standing motionless, neither daring to look at the other.

While the colloquy between Okoya and Mitsha's mother
was going on, Shyuote had recovered somewhat from his
fright and grief and had sneaked off. Once on the ground he
walked — still trembling, and suspiciously scanning the cliff

wherein the Corn people had their abodes — as straight as possible toward the big house. Nobody interfered with him; not even his two defenders noticed that he had gone; they both remained standing silent, with hearts beating anxiously.

"Okoya," the woman called from below, "come and eat. Mitsha, come down and give sa uishe something to eat."

A thrill went through Okoya's whole frame. She had called him *sa uishe*, — " my child." He ventured to cast a furtive glance at the maiden. Mitsha had recovered her self-control; she returned his shy glance with an open, free, but sweet look, and said, —

" Come and partake of the food." There was no resisting an invitation from her. He smiled; she returned the smile in a timid way, as shy and embarrassed as his own.

She descended first and Okoya followed. On the floor of the room, the same chamber where Tyope had taken rest the night before, stood the usual meal; and Okoya partook of it modestly, said his prayer of thanks, and uttered a plain, sincere hoya at the end. But instead of rising, as he would have done at home, he remained squatting, glancing at the two women.

While he ate, the mother watched him eagerly; her cunning eyes moved from his face toward that of her daughter like sparks; and gradually an expression of satisfaction mingled with that of a settled resolve appeared on her features. There was no doubt that the two would be a handsome pair. They seemed, as the vulgar saying goes, made for each other; and there was something besides that told that they were fond of each other also. Okoya had never before entered this dwelling; but the woman thought that they had met before, nay, that her desire had been anticipated, inasmuch as the young people already stood to each other, if not in an intimate, in a more than merely friendly, relation.

"Why do you never come to see us?" asked the woman, after Okoya had finished his meal.

"I stay at the estufa during the night," was the modest reply.

"You need have no fear," she answered pleasantly, "Tyope and your father are good friends. You should become a Koshare!" she exclaimed.

Okoya's face clouded; he did not like the suggestion, but nevertheless asked, —

"Is she," looking at Mitsha, "a Koshare also?"

"No. We had another child, a boy. He was to have become a Delight Maker, but he died some time ago." The woman had it on her lips to say, "Do you become one in his place as our child," but she checked herself in time; it would have been too bold a proposal.

Okoya glanced at the daughter and said timidly, —

"If you like, I shall come again to see you;" and Mitsha's face displayed a happy smile at the words, while her mother eagerly nodded.

"Come as often as you can," she replied. "We" — emphasizing the word strongly — "like it. It is well."

"Then I will go now," said Okoya, rising. His face was radiant. "I must go home lest Shyuote get into more trouble. He is so mischievous and awkward. Good-bye." He grasped the woman's hand and breathed on it; gave a smiling look to the girl, who nodded at him with a happy face; and returned to the roof again. Thence he climbed down to the ground. How happy he felt! The sun seemed to shine twice as brightly as before; the air felt purer; all around him breathed life, hope, and bliss. At the foot of the slope he turned back once more to gaze at the house where so much joy had come to him. A pair of lustrous eyes appeared in the little air-hole of the wall. They were those of the maiden, which were following him on his homeward way.

Tyope's wife was right in supposing that her daughter
and Okoya were not strangers to each other. And yet not
a single word had passed between them before beyond a
casual greeting. As often as they had met he had said
" guatzena," and she had responded with " raua." But at
every meeting his voice was softer, and hers more timid
and trembling. Each felt happy at the sight of the other,
but neither thought of speaking, still less of making any advances. Okoya was aware of the fact — which he felt deeply
and keenly — that a wide breach, a seemingly impassable
chasm, existed between him and the girl. That gap was
the relation in which he stood toward Tyope, the girl's
father. Or rather the relation in which he fancied himself
to stand toward him. For Tyope had hardly ever spoken
to him, still less done him any wrong. But Okoya's mother
had spoken of Tyope as a bad man, as a dangerous man, as
one whom it was Okoya's duty to avoid. And so her son
feared Tyope, and dared not think of the bad man's
daughter as his future companion through life. Now everything was changed.

Mitsha's mother had said that Tyope was a friend of his
father, and that Tyope would not be angry if Okoya came
to her house. Then he was not, after all, the fiend that
Say Koitza had pictured him. On the contrary he appeared to Okoya, since the last interview, in the light of an
important personage. Okoya's faith in his mother was
shaken before ; now he began to think that Tyope after all,
while he was certainly to him an important man, was not as
bad as represented. The Koshare also appeared to him in
a new and more favourable light. The adroit suggestion
made by the woman that he should join the society bore its
fruits. Okoya felt not only relieved but happy ; he felt
elated over his success. He was well trained in the religious discipline of the Indians : and now that he saw hope

before him, his next thought was one of gratitude toward that mother of all who, though dwelling at the bottom of the lagune of Shipapu at times, and then again in the silvery moon, was still watching over the destinies of her children on earth, and to whose loving guidance he felt his bright prospects due.

He had no prayer-plumes with him. These painted sticks — to which feathers or down of various birds, according to the nature of the prayer they are to signify, are attached — the aborigine deposits wherever and whenever he feels like addressing himself to the higher powers, be it for a request, in adoration only, or for thanksgiving. In a certain way the prayer-plume or plume-stick is a substitute for prayer, inasmuch as he who has not time may deposit it hurriedly as a votive offering. The paint which covers the piece of stick to which the feather is attached becomes appropriately significant through its colours, the feather itself is the symbol of human thought, flitting as one set adrift in the air toward heaven, where dwell Those Above. But as in the present instance, the Indian has not always a prayer-plume with him. So he has recourse to an expedient, simple and primitive.

Two little sticks or twigs, placed crosswise and held to their place by a rock or stone, serve the same purpose in case of emergency. Such accumulations of rocks, little stone-heaps, are plentiful around Indian villages; and they represent votive offerings, symbolizing as many prayers. There were a number of them at the Rito around the big house, along the fields, and on the trails leading up to the mesa. Okoya went to the nearest one and placed two twigs crosswise on it, poising them with a stone. Then he scattered sacred meal, which he always carried with him in a small leather wallet, and thanked the Sanashtyaya, our mother, with an earnest ho-a-a, ho-a-a.

Then he turned homeward. The very thought of that home, however, made his heart heavy and sad. For more and more he became convinced that his mother was false to him. The assertion made by Tyope's wife that he was welcome in her house, and that Tyope would not object to his visiting there, worked another breach in the faith he was wont to place in his mother's words. Not that the invitation to join the Koshare had exercised any influence upon his opinion regarding that society of men and women. He mistrusted, he hated, he feared them as much as ever, but toward Tyope personally he felt differently. His thoughts were carried back to the gloomy subject; one by one his doubts and misgivings returned with them, and a longing after some friend to whom he might communicate his fears and whom he might consult with absolute confidence. As he was thus pondering and walking on, slowly and more slowly, he saw at some distance two men climbing up toward where the cave-dwellings of the Water clan lay. One of them was his father; he recognized him at once. Who was his companion? He stopped and looked. It was his father's brother, Hayoue; and with this it seemed as if a veil had suddenly dropped from his eyes. The tall, slender young man yonder, who was advancing up the declivity at such an easy gait, was the friend upon whom he could fully rely, the adviser who would not, at least purposely, lead him astray. Hayoue was but a few years older than Okoya. The relations between the two were those of two brothers and chums, rather than those of uncle and nephew. Hayoue was not a member of his clan, consequently not exposed to any influence which his mother, through her father, Topanashka, might attempt to exert. Hayoue, he knew, disliked the Koshare as much as he disliked them himself, and Hayoue was thoroughly trustworthy and discreet, though very outspoken if necessary, and fearless. Yes, Hayoue was the friend in need he so anxiously desired to find, and now that he had found him he resolved to seize upon the first opportunity of consulting him on the subject that so seriously troubled his mind. He was so delighted at this sudden discovery, as it might be called, that he attributed it to an inspiration from above, and stood for a moment in doubt whether he should not return to the stone-heap and offer another prayer of thanks to the mother above, for what he considered to have been a gift of her goodness to him. But the house was too near, and he bethought himself of Shyuote and what the mischievous urchin might have done since he had left him. He entered the front room of his mother's dwelling with a lighter and easier mind than the day before, and what he saw at once diverted his thoughts into another widely different channel.

Shyuote sat in a corner, and his eyes were red from crying. Beside him stood Say, agitated and angry. Without giving her elder son time to speak, she asked, —

"Who sent the boy to the fields?"

"I don't know," replied Okoya, in astonishment. He knew nothing of Shyuote's morning rambles. "He must know; how could I tell?"

"He says that they drove him from the corn because he threw mud at a girl," added the mother.

"That is quite likely," rejoined his elder brother. "That is why the lads of the Corn clan intended to beat him, I presume."

"Why did you not stay with your father?" cried Say.

"Because," — he held his arm up to his eyes and commenced to sob, — "because my father drove me off."

"Why did he drive you away?"

"Because — " He stopped, then raised his head as if a sudden and wicked thought had flashed across his mind.

His eyes sparkled. "I dare not tell." He cast his eyes to the ground, and a bitter smile passed over his lips.

"Why dare you not tell?" both Say and Okoya inquired. "Has sa nashtio told you not to say anything about it?"

"Not he, but the Koshare Naua." It was like an explosion. Say Koitza felt a terrible pang; she stared vacantly at the wicked lad for a moment, and then turned and went into the kitchen. Shyuote wept aloud; his brother looked down upon him with an expression of mingled compassion and curiosity.

The doorway was suddenly darkened by a human form, and with the usual *guatzena* the grandfather, Topanashka, entered the apartment. Okoya stood up quickly and replied, —

"Raua opona."

"What is the boy crying for?" inquired the old man.

"The Corn people tried to hurt him because he threw something at one of their girls," Okoya explained.

"Is that all? I heard scolding and crying going on here, and so I thought I would come and see what was the matter. Where is your yaya?"

Say, when she heard her father's voice, came out and leaned against the entrance to the kitchen. Her face was convulsed, her eyes glassy. Topanashka scanned her features quietly and then said in a cold tone, —

"Guatzena."

She understood the meaning of his cold, searching gaze, and gathered all her strength to meet it with composure.

"Shyuote cries also," she said, "because his father sent him home from the fields."

"Why did Zashue do that?"

"This he dare not tell, for the Koshare Naua" — her voice trembled at the mention of the name — "forbade him to say anything about it." Her eyes clung to the features of her father. Topanashka turned away slowly and quietly, and she followed him to the door. As he was crossing the threshold he whispered to her, —

"There is nothing new as yet."

CHAPTER V.

THE people of the Water clan dwelt at the western end of the cliffs which border the Tyuonyi on the north. They occupied some twenty caves scooped out along the base of the rock, and an upper tier of a dozen more, separated from the lower by a thickness of rock averaging not over three feet. This group of cave-dwellings — and vestiges thereof are still visible at this day — lay in a re-entering angle formed by the cliffs, which overhang in such a manner as to form a sheltered nook open to the south. Ascent to their base is quite steep, and great heaps of débris cover the slope. The gorge is narrow, a dense thicket interspersed with pine-trees lines the course of the brook, and the declivity forming the southern border of the Rito approaches the bottom in rocky steps, traversed laterally by ledges overgrown with scrubby vegetation.

Vestiges of former occupancy are still scattered about the caves. Some of these furnish a clew to the manner in which the dwellings were formed by scraping and burrowing. Splinters of obsidian and of basalt — sharp fragments, resembling clumsy chisels or knives — served to dig an oblong hole in the soft pumice or tufa of the cliff. After this narrow cavity had penetrated a depth of one or two feet, the artisan began to enlarge it inside, until a room was formed for which the tunnelled entrance served as a doorway. The room, or cell, was gradually finished in a quadrangular or polygonal shape, with a ceiling high enough to

permit a person of average size to stand erect. Not unfre-
quently side rooms were excavated connecting with the first
by low apertures, to pass through which it was necessary to
stoop, or even to creep on all fours. These passages were
too low for doorways, too short to deserve the name of tun-
nels. Into the front apartment light and air were admitted
through the entrance, and sometimes through small window-
like apertures. The side cells were utterly dark except
where excavated parallel to the face of the rock, when
sometimes another entrance was opened to the front,
sometimes an air-hole only admitted light and air.

If on the afternoon of the day when Shyuote had his
perilous adventure with the young people of the Corn clan,
we had been able to peep into the third one of the ground-
floor caves, counting from the west end of the group inhabited by the Water people, we should have found the
apartment empty; that is, as far as human occupancy was
concerned. But not deserted; for while its owner was not
there, ample signs of his presence only a short time before
could be detected everywhere. In the fireplace wood was
smouldering, and a faint smoke rising from this found
egress through a crude chimney. This was built over the
hearth, with two vertical side slabs of pumice supporting a
perforated square flag, over which a primitive flue, made of
rubble cemented by mud, led to a circular opening in the
front wall of the cave. In a corner stood the frame for the
grinding-slabs, or *metates*, and in it the three plates of lava
on which the Indian crushes and pulverizes his maize were
placed in the convenient slanting position. Not only the
prismatic crushing-pins, but freshly ground meal also, lay in
the stone casings of the primitive mill, and on these the
plates themselves. Deerskins and cotton wraps were rolled
in a bundle in another corner. Others hung on a line made
of rawhide and stretched across one end of the room, fast

ened to wooden pins driven into the soft rock. On the floor — to which a thick coating of mud, washed with blood and smoothed, gave a black, glossy appearance — there were beside, here a few stone axes with handles, there some black sooty pots, painted bowls, and finally the inevitable water-urn with wide body and narrow top, decorated in the usual style with geometrical and symbolical figures painted in red and black on whitish ground. The walls of the cave were burnished with burnt gypsum ; the ceiling was covered by a thick coat of soot ; and a band of yellow ochre, like wain-scoting, ran along the base of the sides.

The owner of this troglodytic home, however, is not to be seen ; but in a side chamber, which communicates with this apartment through one of the dark and low passages just described, a rustling sound is heard, as of some one rummaging about in darkness. After a while a woman's head peeps through the passage into the outer room, and little by little the whole body emerges, forcing itself through the narrow opening. She rises and stands erect in front of the hearth, and the sunbeam which still enters the apart-ment by the round hole above the fireplace strikes her features full and enables us to scan them. The woman into whose dwelling we have pryed, and who stands now in the dim chamber as sole occupant and owner, is Shotaye, Tyope's former wife, and the friend who has given Say Koitza such ill advice.

If Shotaye be a witch, she certainly is far from display-ing the hag-like appearance often attributed to the female sorcerer. There is even something decidedly fascinating about her. Shotaye, although near the forties, is for an Indian woman undoubtedly good-looking. No wonder some other women of the tribe are afraid of her. She is tall and well rounded, and her chest is of that fulness that develops at an early age in the women of the Pueblos.

Her face is even pretty, — her lips are pouting and sensual, the nose small and shaped like a short, pointed beak, the cheek-bones high, while the chin indicates remarkable determination. Magnificent black hair streams down her back. It is as full as a wave, as lustrous as polished obsidian.

Her dress consists of a buckskin wrap without girdle, embroidered at the lower end with multi-coloured porcupine-quills. Bracelets of white shells, a necklace of feldspar crystals and turquoises, and strings of yellow cotton threads around her ankles complete the costume. Such is the woman who has played and still plays an ominous part in the history of Okoya's mother, and in the history of the people at the Rito de los Frijoles. Now that we have seen her home and her person, let us proceed with the tale of her doings on the afternoon to which the close of the preceding chapter has been devoted.

Shotaye had been rummaging about in the inner cell of her rocky house in search of some medicinal plant, for that cell was her storeroom, laboratory, and workshop. But as the room was without light at all, she had entered it with a lighted stick in her hand; and just as she had begun her search the flame had died out. So after a vain attempt by groping in darkness, she crawled back to the exterior apartment and knelt down in front of the hearth to fan the coals with her breath and thus obtain another torch for her explorations. At that moment the deerskin robe closing the entrance to her grotto was timidly lifted, and a feeble voice called the usual greeting. "Opona," replied Shotaye, turning toward the doorway. A lithe figure crept into the cave. When near the fireplace it stood still, enabling the mistress of the dwelling to recognize the features of Say, her friend and now fully recovered patient.

But how different was Say's appearance from what it

was when Shotaye a few days ago saw her last? How changed, — how thin and wan her cheeks, how sunken her eyes, how sallow and sickly her complexion! Her face seemed to bear the seal of approaching death, for the eyes stared expressionless, the mouth twitched without speaking. But one thought seized Shotaye, that her friend must be ill, very, very ill, — that the old disease had returned in full force and had clutched her anew with perhaps irresistible power. Anxiously she rose to her feet, and scanned the face of the invalid.

"What ails you, my sister," she inquired tenderly. "Has disease come on you again? Speak, sa uishe, speak to me that I may know."

Her visitor only shook her head and glanced about as if seeking a place to rest herself. The medicine-woman gathered hurriedly a few robes, folded them so as to make a cushion near the hearth, and then gently urged Say to sit down on this soft and easy seat. She yielded, and then remained motionless, her glassy eyes staring vacantly at the floor.

"Sister," Shotaye reiterated, "sister, what ails you? Speak, and I will do all I can for you." But the other merely shook her head and began to shiver. Shotaye noticed the wristbands of red leather on her arms, and it startled her. She asked eagerly, —

"Why do you wear in trouble the colour that should make our hearts glad? What has happened to you that causes you to seek relief for your distress?" The tone of her voice sounded no longer like entreaty; it was an anxious, nay stern, command. Okoya's mother raised her eyes with an expression of intense misery; she threw toward her questioner a look imploring relief and protection, and finally gasped, —

"They know everything!" Then her head dropped or

her knees, she grasped her hair, covered her face and chest
with it, and broke out in convulsive sobs.

"They know everything!" Shotaye repeated, "Who
know everything?" Suddenly the truth seemed to flash
upon her mind.

"What, the Koshare?" she cried in terror.

Convulsive sobs and groans were the only reply to her
exclamation. They amply confirmed her worst apprehensions. "The Koshare know all." Unconsciously the cave-
dweller uttered these words while staring into the remnant
of gleaming coals on the hearth; then she became silent.
Neither could Say Koitza utter a word; only from time to
time her spasmodic sobs broke the stillness of the room.
The bright disk which the light from the outside painted
on the wall opposite was fading little by little, a sign of
approaching sunset.

Shotaye's features displayed few signs of the terror which
her friend's disclosures had produced. Soon her face betokened that fear could not retain its hold long on her
resolute mind, that intense reflection had superseded dismay. She turned to her visitor and asked, —

"Tell me, sister, how you came to know that the Delight Makers are acquainted with your doings? Tell me,
and do not weep." And as Say remained silent and immovable she crouched beside her, removed her hair gently
from her face, then raised her head and placed it so as to
rest on her bosom. Then she looked deep into the eyes
of the poor woman. They were glassy and almost lifeless.
While thus gazing intently at Say, Shotaye's features
changed and became sad and dejected.

It was for a moment only. Soon the expression of hope-
lessness vanished and the lines of her face became resolute,
hard, and determined. Surprise had yielded to reflection,
reflection to pity and remorse. Now remorse in turn gave

way to determination. Shotaye felt that she, much rather than her friend, was lost, irretrievably lost; but her energetic nature demanded that she should see the situation clearly. Although the spasmodic hints of Say, her broken words, spoke enough, she wanted more. Her mind craved the full truth, however terrible it might prove.

Say Koitza had slowly recovered from her stupor. She became quieter and quieter. In the arms of her resolute and sympathizing friend consciousness returned; she sobbed no more, and from time to time would raise her eyes with a look that besought pity, mercy, and assistance. The medicine-woman eagerly watched these changes and repeated her previous query.

" How do you know that the Koshare are aware of it? "

" Sa nashtio told me," moaned the poor woman.

Shotaye sighed. This was bad news indeed. She muttered, —

" This is bad, very bad. If the maseua knows it, then the tapop will not be long without notice."

" The tapop knows nothing," breathed Say.

" But how can the maseua have been informed without the knowledge of the other? " Shotaye asked with surprise.

" He is my father," replied Say, and wept aloud. " He is my father, and yet " — she started to rise and grasped her hair with both hands, screaming — " he has to kill me with his own hands ! "

So loud and piercing was her shriek that Shotaye was seized with sudden fright. Rising quickly, she ran to the doorway and peeped outside to see if the scream had attracted attention. But there appeared to be nobody about, except a few children who were playing and romping in front of the caves and whose cries had drowned the shriek. Reassured she returned to Say, who was lying with her face on the floor, tearing her hair and uttering low convulsive groans. Shotaye grew frightened, and brought water in a gourd. She moistened her forehead and hands with the liquid, rubbed her face, and thus finally brought her back to some composure. After drinking some water Say sat on the robes again, shivering and gasping. Her mind seemed entirely gone, the expression of her features was akin to idiocy. The room had grown darker, night was approaching.

As soon as she appeared to be quiet, Shotaye felt tempted to resume her questionings. But she bethought herself of the late hour, and of the suspicion which might arise in case Say Koitza should not be home in time. Still, she must ask some questions; her positive mind required some additional knowledge which must be gained ere she could afford to let her visitor return home. Shotaye returned to the entrance, looked stealthily outside, and listened. Dusk had set in, and the bottom of the gorge was wrapped in twilight. The shrubbery along the brook appeared dim and pale, the lofty pines looked like black monuments. On the southern declivity all detail had vanished, but the top of the southern mesa glistened yet like a golden seam. In the recess formed by the angle of the cliffs which contained her home, the usual bustle of the evening hours prevailed; and laughter, merry and boisterous, issued from a cave opposite that where Shotaye, concealed by folds of the half-lifted curtain, stood watching with eye and ear. In those caves fronting hers dwelt the family of Zashue, Say's husband. Thence sounded the merriment, and the woman recognized familiar voices. Surely enough Hayoue was there; and there could be no mistake, that clear good-natured laugh was from Zashue himself. Shotaye dropped the curtain and turned back considerably relieved. If Zashue was at his mother's and brother's home, she reasoned, he would not return to the big house that night; and since he was so gay, so merry, it was not likely that he knew anything of the terrible accusation against his wife and her. If that were the case there was no immediate danger, since all the Koshare were not informed of the matter. Returning to the hearth she poked the embers, placed on them another stick of pitchy wood, and fanned it with her breath until the flames burst forth, lively and bright. Until then Say had remained motionless in her seat. She had taken no notice of her friend's movements; but when the wood flamed and a warm glow began to spread over the apartment, she started like one whose dreams are suddenly disturbed and began to speak.

"I must go," she exclaimed anxiously. "I must go home. I must cook for Zashue! He is looking for me! I must go," and she attempted to rise.

Shotaye tried to quell her sudden apprehension, but she kept on with growing excitement, —

"I must! Let me go! Let me go! For he is looking for me."

"He is not," assured the other. "Be quiet. He is yonder with his people in the cave. There he sits and there he will stay till late."

A sudden tremor seized the body of Say. Her hands shook like aspen leaves. "Is he there?" she gasped. "Then he is coming after me. Is he not a Koshare?" Her eyes glistened with that peculiar glare which betokens aberration of the mind.

Any ordinary Indian woman would have concluded from the appearance and utterances of Say that she was hopelessly insane, and would either have resorted to incantations or left her in terror. Shotaye, although very much frightened, did not think of desertion, but only of relief.

8

With keen self-possession she said in a decided and convincing tone, —

"Fear nothing, sa tao; he will not come, for he knows
nothing."

"Nothing?" inquired Say, looking at her with the shy
and sly glance of a doubting maniac.

"Nothing at all!" Shotaye exclaimed, firmly. She had
recovered her ascendency. She directed her glance, commanding and convincing, straight at the wavering gaze of
the excited woman, whose look became dim and finally
meek. Shotaye took advantage of the change.

"Zashue knows nothing at all," she asserted, "and that
is very, very good; for it gives us hope."

"But if they tell him!" and the anxious look came back
to her face.

"Let them tell, if they choose," defiantly exclaimed the
other; "afterward we shall see."

Say shook her head in doubt.

"But how did the Koshare come to know about it?"
Shotaye again pressed the main question.

"I do not know," sighed Say; and she again stared into
the fire, and her face quivered suspiciously. The cave
dweller quickly interjected, —

"What do the Delight Makers really know about us?"

"They know — they know that I spoke to the dark-
coloured corn."

"Is that all?"

"No — yes — no. They know more." She spoke with
greater vivacity, and in a natural tone of voice; "they
know about the owl's feathers, too." A deep sigh followed
this reply, and tears came to her eyes. Say was herself
again.

Shotaye also heaved a deep sigh of relief. Her friend's
mind was restored, and she had gained the much-desired

information. But it would have been dangerous to proceed further in th:s conversation, lest the cloud which had threatened Say's mental powers should return and settle permanently. So, after a short silence, she turned to her friend, and said in a positive tone, —

"Sister, go home now and rest easy. Nothing is lost as yet. Go home, be quiet, and attend to your work as usual. I shall be on the watch."

"But the Koshare !" Say anxiously exclaimed.

"Leave them to me," the other answered; and so powerful was her influence on the timid mind of her visitor, so unbounded the confidence which the latter had in her abilities and her faithfulness, that Say rose without a word, and like an obedient child, covering her head with one corner of her wrap, went out and meekly strolled home. It was night, and nobody noticed her. Okoya was already at the estufa; Shyuote and the little girl were asleep. Say lay down beside her sleeping children and soon sank into a heavy slumber. Her body, weak from over-strain, compelled a rest which the mind might have denied to her.

In her dark chamber in the rock, Shotaye sat alone before the fire on the hearth. It began to flame lustily, for the woman fed it well. She wanted the glow, first in order to cook her food, next in order to brighten the room; for with the dark and tangled subject on her mind, she felt the need of light and warmth as her companions in musing. When the flames rustled and crackled, Shotaye squatted down in front of them, folded her arms around her knees, and began to think.

She felt far from being as reassured about the outlook as she had pretended to be when she sent Say Koitza home with soothing and comforting words. But the preservation of her friend's mental powers was an imperative necessity. Had Say been permitted to fall a prey to her momentary excitement, everything would have been lost for Shotaye. Had Say's mind given way permanently, the cause of that calamity would have been attributed to her, and she would have been charged with her friend's insanity in addition to the charge of witchcraft already being formulated.

These thoughts, however, came to her now in the stillness of the night and by the fireside. So long as her poor friend was with her she had acted almost instinctively, with the quick grasp of an active intellect and under the good impulses of compassion and attachment. Now that she was alone the time had come to ponder, and Shotaye weighed in her mind the liabilities and assets of her situation. She began to calculate the probabilities for and against.

It was not difficult for her to escape; but this was only possible when attempted alone. With Say Koitza flight was next to impossible. Beside, it appeared very unlikely to her that the woman would flee from her children.

As for Shotaye, the case was different; she might leave her cave and her scanty effects at any time, provided she knew where to go. This was not so easy to determine. The Navajos, or Dinne, haunted the country around the Tyuonyi; and in case she fell in with one or more of their number, it became a matter of life or death. The Moshome, or enemies of her tribe, might take a fancy to the woman and spare her; but they might feel wicked and kill her. Death appeared, after all, not such a terrible misfortune; for under present circumstances what else could she expect at the Rito but a horrible and atrocious death? But Shotaye was intent upon living, not so much for the sake of life itself — although it had many sensual charms for her — as out of a spirit of combativeness resulting from her resolute character, as well as from the constant struggles which she had undergone during the time of her separation from her husband. She felt inclined to live, if possible, in spite of her enemies. To endure the lot of a captive among the Navajos was repulsive to her instincts; she hated to be a drudge. Admitting that she succeeded in eluding those enemies, whither was she to direct her flight? That there were village communities similar to her own at a remote distance was known to her; but she was aware of only one in which she might be received, and that belonged to the Tehuas, of whom she knew that a branch dwelt in the mountains west of the river, inhabiting caves somewhere in the rocks at one day's journey, more or less, from the Rito. Between these Tehuas and the Queres of the Tyuonyi there was occasional intercourse, and a fairly beaten trail led from one place to the other; but this intercourse was so much interrupted by hostilities, and the Navajos rendered the trail so insecure beside, that she had never paid much attention to it. Still, there was no doubt in her mind that if she reached the habitations of the Tehuas, above where the pueblo of Santa Clara now stands, a hospitable reception would be extended to her. But could she leave Say alone to her dismal fate?

After all, death was not such a fearful thing, so long as no torture preceded or accompanied it. Death must come to her once, at all events, and then what of it? There need be no care for the hereafter, according to her creed. The Pueblo Indian knows of no atonement after dying; all sins, all crimes, are punished during this life. When the soul is released from the thralls of this body and its surrounding nature, it goes to Shipapu, at the bottom of the lagune, where there is eternal dancing and feasting, and where everything goes on as here upon earth, but with less pain, care, anguish, and danger. Why therefore shun death? Shotaye was in what we should call a philosophic mood.

Such careless philosophy may temporarily ease the mind, since it stifles for a moment the pangs of apprehension and dread. But with the temporary relief which Shotaye felt, the demands of physical nature grew more apparent. In other words she felt hungry, and the more so as, being now almost resolved to suffer death with resignation, it was imperative to live, and consequently to eat, until Death should knock at her door. She poured a good portion of the now boiling stew into a smaller bowl and began to fish out the morsels with her fingers, while between times she drank of the broth. The warm food comforted her, gave her strength, and aroused her vital powers, which arduous thinking had almost put to sleep.

She placed the pot with the stew in a corner and sat down again, leaning against the wall. No sleepiness affected her. There was too much to think of as yet. Her thoughts returned to the absorbing subject of the day, and with these thoughts, random at first, a pale, wan figure rose before her inner eye, — a form well, only too well, known to her; that of Say Koitza. She saw that figure as she had seen it not long ago, — crouching before that very fire in bitterest despair, bewailing her own lot, lamenting her imminent untimely death, and yet without one single word of reproach for her who had beguiled her into doing what now might result in the destruction of both. Was not that thin, trembling woman her victim? Was she not the one who had led Say astray? The Indian knows not what conscience is, but he feels it all the same; and Shotaye, ignorant of the nature of remorse, nevertheless grew sad.

Indeed she it was who had beguiled the poor frail creature, — she it was who had caused her to perform an act which, however immaterial in fact, still entailed punishment of the severest kind according to Indian notions and creed. She was the real culprit, not Say, — poor, innocent, weak-minded Say. Shotaye felt that she had done wrong, and that she alone deserved to suffer. But would her punishment save the other? Hardly, according to Indian ideas. Therefore, while it dawned upon her that by accus. ing herself boldly and publicly she might perhaps ward off the blow from the head of her meek and gentle accomplice, that thought was quickly stifled by the other, that it was impracticable. Again a voice within her spoke boldly, Save yourself regardless of the other.

Yet she discarded that advice. She could not forsake her victim. For in addition to the legitimate motives of sympathy, another and stronger reason prevailed,— the dread of the very powers whom she thought to have invoked in Say's behalf, and to whose dark realm she fancied that she would be fettered and still faster riveted by committing an action which she regarded as worse than all her other deeds. Dismissing every thought of self she resolved to remain true to Say, happen what might. Shotaye had almost become —

> " part of the power that still
> Produceth good, whilst ever scheming ill."

She believed that death stood plainly at her door. Nevertheless she hated to die. The philosophy of careless, frivolous resignation could not satisfy her strong vitality, still less her stronger feelings of hatred against her enemies. She felt that there might be a bare possibility of saving her companion ; and the wish to save herself at the same time, and in the very teeth as it were of the Koshare, grew stronger and stronger. It waxed to an intense longing for life and revenge? But what was to be done? There was the riddle, and to solve it she thought and thought. Shotaye became oblivious of all around her, completely absorbed in her musings.

It thus escaped her notice that the curtain over the doorway had been cautiously lifted several times, and that a human face had peered into the apartment. She even failed to hear the shuffling step of two men who stealthily entered the room. Only when they stood quite near her did the woman start and look up. Both men broke out into roaring laughter at her surprise. Shotaye grew angry.

"Why do you come in so unceremoniously," she cried. "Why do you sneak in here like a Moshome, or like a prairie wolf after carrion? Cannot you speak, you bear?" she scolded without rising.

Her anger increased the merriment of the intruders. One of them threw himself down by her side, forced his head into her lap, attempting to stroke her cheeks. She pushed him from her, and recognized in him the gallant Zashue, Say Koitza's husband. He grasped both her hands. This she allowed; but continued scolding.

"Go away, you hare, let me alone." He again reached toward her face, but she avoided him. "Go home to your woman; I have no use for you."

The men laughed and laughed; and the other one knelt down before her, looking straight into her face with immoderate merriment. Then she became seriously angry.

"What do you want here," she cried; and when the first one attempted to encircle her waist she pushed him from her with such force that he fell aside. Then she rose to her feet and Zashue followed.

"Be not angry, sister," he said good-naturedly, rubbing his sore shoulder; "we mean you no harm."

"Go home and be good to your woman."

"Later on I will," he continued, "but first we want to see you."

"And talk to you," said Hayoue, for he was Zashue's companion; "afterward I shall go." He emphasized the "I" and grinned.

"Yes, you are likely to go home," she exclaimed. "To Mitsha you will go, not to your mother's dwelling."

"Mitsha is a good girl," replied the young man, "but I never go to see her."

His brother meanwhile attempted to approach the woman again, but she forbade it.

"Go away, Zashue, I tell you for the last time." Her speech and manner of action were very positive.

"Why do you drive us away?" he said in a tone of good-natured disappointment.

"I do not drive you away," replied Shotaye. "You may stay here a while. But then both of you must leave me." Her eyes nevertheless gazed at the two handsome forms with evident pleasure, but soon another thought arose.

"Sit down," she added quietly, as she grasped after the stew-pot, placed it on the fire, and sat down so that she was in the shadow, whereas she could plainly see the features of both men. The visitors had squatted also ; they feared to arouse the woman's anger, and the surprise they had planned had failed.

Hayoue spoke up first, —

"You are good, sanaya, you give us food."

"Indeed," she remonstrated, "when I am not willing to do as you want, you call me mother and make an old woman of me." She looked at the young man, smiling, and winked at him.

"You are not very young after all," he teased ; "you might easily be my mother."

"What ! I your mother? The mother of such an elk? You have one mother already, and if you need another, go to Mitsha's mother." With these words she fixed her gaze on the youth searchingly and inquiringly. As her face was in the shadow Hayoue could not well notice its expression. But he said again, and very emphatically, —

"I tell you once more, koitza, that I will not have anything to do with the girl; she is all right, but—" he stopped and shrugged his shoulders. Zashue interjected, —

"Why not? Tyope would then be your nashtio."

"For that very reason I do not want his daughter," Hayoue exclaimed, looking straight at his brother. He was in earnest about this matter, and whenever Hayoue grew serious it was best not to tease him too much.

Shotaye had treasured every word, noticed every look and gesture. Of course she, as Tyope's former wife, took care not to take part in the conversation as far as Tyope was concerned.

Zashue turned to her with the query, —

"Samām, have you any feathers?"

Shotaye was startled; what might be the import of this suspicious inquiry? Did he know about her affair and come only as a spy? She withheld her answer for a moment, just time enough for reflection. It was better to seem unconcerned, so she replied quietly, —

"I have."

"If you have hawk's feathers, will you give me some?"

The mention of hawk's feathers reassured Shotaye. At the same time it indicated to her a prospective trade, and the woman had always an eye to business. So she placed both elbows on her knees, looked straight at Zashue, and inquired, —

"What will you give me for them?"

"Nothing," replied Zashue, with a laugh.

"Promise her the next owl that you may find," Hayoue taunted.

"Be still, you crow," scolded Shotaye, with well-feigned indignation; "you need owl's eyes that you may sneak about in the dark after the girls. There is not a single maiden safe when you are at the Tyuonyi."

"And no man is safe from you," retorted the young man.

"You are safe, at any rate."

"When you call me a turkey-buzzard you say the truth,"
he answered, "else I would not have come to you."

Shotaye understood the venomous allusion and was going
to retort, but bethought herself in time and only said in a
contemptuous tone, —

"Why should I quarrel with you, uak." Then turning to
Zashue and changing the subject, —

"How many feathers do you want, and what will you give
me for them?"

"Four, but they must be long ones."

"What will you give me for them?"

"Let me see the feathers." With this he rose.

Without replying Shotaye poured out two little bowls of
broth, placed them before her visitors, said "eat," took a
lighted stick from the hearth, and crawled into the dark passage leading to her magazine. Soon she was heard to rummage about in that apartment, and a faint glow illuminated
the low tunnel.

While the woman was busy searching for the feathers, the
two men partook of the food she had set before them spar-
ingly, as it was a mere matter of etiquette. But while eating
they exchanged sly glances and winks, like bad boys bent
upon some mischief. At last, as Shotaye did not return,
Zashue stealthily arose, removed one of the heavy grinding-
plates from its frame, and placed it across the mouth of the
gangway. Then he stretched himself at full length on the
floor with his back leaning against the slab. Hayoue
watched him and chuckled.

The light of the torch shone through the space which the
slab could not cover; the mistress of the cave was coming
back. Very soon however the light disappeared and all
grew silent. The firebrand had been extinguished; the
woman was inside, but kept perfectly still, giving no signs

of impatience or disappointment. The mischievous men looked at each other in astonishment; they had not expected that.

They waited and waited. Nothing stirred in the inner room; it grew late and later. Hayoue had intended to make other calls, and Zashue also became impatient to go. So he called into the dark passage, —

"Shotaye." No reply.

"Shotaye."

"Shotaye samām!"

All was as silent as the grave. They sat in expectation for a while; then he again shouted, —

"Shotaye samām! Come out!"

Nothing was heard. He noisily removed the grinding-slab from the entrance and cried, —

"Shotaye, we must go. Bring the feathers."

"Let me alone and go," sounded the dull reply at last.

"Give me the feathers first," Zashue demanded.

"Come and get them yourself," replied the voice inside.

This was rather an awkward invitation, for both men, like almost everybody else at the Rito, were afraid of the medicine-woman's private room.

"Do bring them," Zashue begged.

"Go! I will not come out any more," growled the voice within.

"Shotaye, sister, bring me the feathers. I will give you a fine deerskin for them," implored the husband of Say.

"What do you want them for?"

"For the dance."

"You lie! There is no dance now."

Anxiously and eagerly Zashue cried, —

"There will certainly be a dance. Three days hence we shall dance the ayash tyucotz!"

And Hayoue, who until then had quietly enjoyed the dialogue, now interjected emphatically, —

"Certainly, sanaya, in three days."

"What will you give me if I bring them?" came the dull query again from within.

"A hide."

"Go! I will keep my feathers."

"I will give you two turquoises."

"Give me four," demanded the cave-dweller.

"It is too much," cried both men at once.

No reply followed. Shotaye remained silent. The trade was broken off. Still the younger brother felt disinclined to give up. He went to the mouth of the passage and said aloud, —

"If you give us the feathers you shall have two green stones and one deerskin."

"Is it true; do both of you promise it?" asked the woman, after a while.

"Yes! yes!" cried both men together.

"Then put the things near the hearth and sit down," she commanded.

"We have them not with us."

"Go and get them."

"We cannot to-night."

"Then I will keep my feathers until you bring what you have promised;" and with these words Shotaye crept smiling out of the passage and planted herself before the discomfited men.

"Go home, now, children," she said. "I am tired. I am sleepy."

They attempted to beg, they pleaded and implored; but she was firm. All they finally obtained was her promise to deliver the feathers on the next day, provided the price agreed upon was paid. With this the two men had to be satisfied, and their exit was as crestfallen and disappointed as their entrance had been mischievous and buoyant.

They had been completely outwitted and foiled by the wily woman. Nevertheless, they never thought for a moment of obtaining by force what she so positively refused. It would have been easy for the two strong men to overpower her; but both were afraid of the supernatural powers attributed to Shotaye. For the same reason they were anxious to obtain the feathers. An object coming from her and having been in her possession was suspected of having acquired thereby virtues which it did not possess before. But these virtues were thought to be beneficial only as long as the object was obtained from her in a legitimate way, and with her own free will and kind consent. In the opposite case, the bad will of the woman went with the feathers, and was thought to work harm to their new owner. It was easy to taunt or to tease Shotaye, but to arouse her anger appeared a dangerous undertaking; and as for harming her person, none but the shamans would have attempted it.

After her guests' departure Shotaye felt wide awake. She had dismissed them, not in order to go to rest, but in order to be once more alone with her thoughts. For during the bantering conversation with the brothers, she had learned several important facts that changed materially her plans. In order to ponder carefully over the different aspect of matters, she poked the fire again and sat down by the hearth in the same position as before the interruption, and mused.

In the first place, it had become clear to her that Zashue was utterly ignorant of the accusation against his wife.

Next, she was convinced that Hayoue was far from being Tyope's friend; on the contrary, he seemed to dislike him thoroughly. Hayoue was known to be very outspoken in matters of sympathy and antipathy, and if he were not fond of Tyope, the latter certainly had come to feel it in some way or other. Then, for she knew Tyope well, he doubtless hated Hayoue cordially, and would have shown his enmity in the dark, underhand way peculiar to himself. If Hayoue, on the other hand, was not favourably inclined toward Tyope, it was quite certain that he, being Cuirana, nursed feelings of dislike toward the Koshare in general. Any accusation, therefore, which the Delight Makers would bring against Say Koitza was sure to meet at first with decided incredulity on the part of the young man, and this incredulity might possibly be converted, through adroit management, into active opposition.

But the most valuable piece of news she had heard from the intruders was that three days hence a solemn dance, the ayash tyucotz, was to be performed at the Rito. These ceremonies, which are always of a religious nature, are proposed generally by the principal shamans to the civil chiefs, — in council or privately, — either on the strength of some presage or dream, or as a public necessity. The proposal agreed to, as it usually is, the time is set; but no publication is made either of the performance or of the hour until the day on which it is to occur or the evening previous. But the matter is talked about at home, in the circle of friends, and thus it gradually becomes known to everybody as a public secret, and everybody has time to prepare for it. Shotaye mixed very little with the people at the Rito; she hardly ever went to see any one, and such as came to see her had other matters to talk about. It was no surprise to her to learn that an important dance was near at hand; but it was a source of much gratification nevertheless. For until the dance was over nothing could or would be undertaken against Say and herself. After the perform-

ance, it was equally sure that several days would elapse
ere the council could meet in full, as the religious heads
of the tribe had yet to go through ceremonies of a private nature. At all events, it proved to her that there
was no immediate danger, and that she still had time before her. With time, so the resolute and wary woman
reasoned, there was hope.

Thus musing and speculating, she sat for a long while.
The fire went out, but she did not notice it. At last
she arose, unfolded several robes and mantles, which she
easily found in the dark, and spread them out on the floor
for her couch. Shotaye could go to sleep; for at last
she saw, or thought she saw, her way clearly. She had
fully determined upon her plan of action.

CHAPTER VI.

"Hu–Hu–Hu–Hu–Hu–Hu–Hu–Hu–Hu-o-o-o-o !"

Shrill cries, succeeding one another in quick succession, ending in a prolonged shout, proceed from the outer exit of the gallery that opens upon the court-yard of the large building.

The final whoop, caught up by the cliffs of the Tyuonyi, echoes and re-echoes, a prolonged howl dying out in a wail. Men's voices, hoarse and untrained, are now heard chanting in rhythmic and monotonous chorus. They approach slowly, moving with measured regularity; and now strange figures begin to emerge from the passage-way, and as they file into the court-yard the chant grows louder and louder. A refrain —

"Ho-ā-ā! Heiti-na! Ho-ā-ā! Heiti-na!"

breaks clearly and distinctly upon the ear, mingled with the discordant rumblings of a drum. The fantastic procession advances, forming a double column, composed of men and women side by side. The former are stamping and the latter tripping lightly, but all are keeping time. They certainly present a weird appearance, tricked out in their gaudy apparel and ornamented with flashy trinkets. The hair of the men is worn loose; tufts of green and yellow feathers flutter over the forehead, while around their necks and dangling over their naked chests are seen strings of porcupine quills, shell beads, turquoises, bright pebbles, feldspar, apatite, — anything in short that glitters and shines. Bunches of similar material glisten in their ears. Fastened about the waist, and reaching as low as the knee, a rude

kilt-like garment composed of white cotton cloth or of
deerskin hangs and flaps. It is ornamented with an embroidery of red and black threads, and quills of the porcupine. Below the knee, garters of buckskin, tinged red and
yellow, form a fringe to which are attached tortoise-shell
rattles and bunches of elk-hoofs. The ankles are encased
with strips of the white and black fur of the skunk, and
from the waist a fox-skin hangs, fastened to the back and
reaching almost as far as the heel. Each man carries a
tuft of hawk's feathers in his left hand, while the right
grasps a rattle fashioned from a gourd and filled with
pebbles.

The women wear their ordinary dress, emphasized however with a profusion of necklaces, wristbands, and ear
pendants, while in each hand is borne a bunch of pine
twigs wagging from side to side as they move. But by far
the most striking feature of their costume is their headdress.
It consists of a piece of buffalo-hide scraped and flattened
like a board, about fifteen inches long and seven inches
wide, one end of which is cut square. The other terminates in what resembles a triple turret, squarely notched.
This is painted green, and decorated with symbolic figures
in red and yellow. White feathers flutter from each of the
three turret-shaped projections, and this peculiar headgear
is held in place by strips of buckskin attached to the
squared end, and knotted about meshes of the dark, streaming hair.

The faces of both sexes are generously daubed with white
clay, in addition to which the men have their naked chests,
upper arms, and hands also decorated with stripes and
blotches of the same substance.

The procession is a long one ; couple follows couple, the
men gravely stamping, the women gracefully tripping. At
the head are the tallest and most robust youths, the best

developed and most buxom girls. Following these, the
dancers are less and less carefully assorted and matched,
while boys and old women, little girls and old men, bring
up the rear.

As the last couple emerges, the chorus bursts out in full
force, the choristers themselves issuing from the dark passage-
way. These are twelve in number, all men, dressed or
undressed as each one's fancy dictates, their faces whitened
like the dancers'. Their rude chant or rhythmic shouting is
in the minor key. They advance in a body, keeping time
with their feet, gesticulating in a manner intended to convey the meaning of their song. In their midst goes the
drum-beater, an aged man adorned with an eagle's feather
behind each ear. Like the rest, his face is daubed with
white paint; his drum, which he thumps incessantly with a
single stick, being manufactured from a hollow tree. Both
ends of it are covered with rawhide, and the whole instrument is painted yellow. We recognize easily in this musi-
cian the head of the Koshare, Shyuote's late tormentor.

At no great distance from the exit, the chorus comes to
a halt, but the singing, gesticulation and beating of the
drum proceed. The dancers meanwhile move about the
whole court to the same step, but the couples separate and
change places; man steps beside man, woman joins woman,
all turning and passing each other, suggesting by their
movements the flexures of a closely folded ribbon. The
couples then re-form, the double rank strings out as at first,
tramping and tripping in a wide circle to the rhythm and
measure of the monotonous music.

This solemn perambulation and primitive concert is witnessed by numerous interested spectators, and listened to
by a large and attentive audience. The Rito's entire
population is assembled, eagerly, at times almost devoutly,
gazing and listening. The assemblage crowds the roofs

and lines the walls below, all confusedly gathered together. There is every imaginable posture, costume, or lack of costume, — men, women, children clothed in bright wraps or embroidered skins, scantily covered with dirty rags, or rejoicing in the freedom of undress. The several roofs of the large house, rising in successive terraces three stories high, form an irregular amphitheatre filled with humanity of all sizes, shapes, ages, clothing, in glaring contrast with one another. In the arena formed by the court-yard, form and colour intermingle with more order and regularity; and at the same time greater brilliancy is exhibited. The fantastic headdresses of the women nod and vibrate like waving plants of Indian corn; the lustrous hair and the gaudy costumes glisten and sparkle in the sunlight, fox pelts wag back and forth, plumes and feathers flit and dance, the monotonous chanting, the dull thumping and drumming rise into the deep blue sky, re-echoing from the towering cliffs, whose pinnacles look down upon the weird scene from heights far above the uppermost tier of spectators.

Among those looking on we may recognize some of our acquaintances. Seated upon one of the terraces, his chin resting on his hand, is Topanashka, who looks down upon the actors with a grave, cold, seemingly indifferent gaze. Say Koitza stands in the doorway of her dwelling, her wan face wearing an immobile expression. Her little girl, elegantly arrayed in a breechclout and turquoise necklace, clings to her mother's wrap with one hand while the other disappears in her gaping mouth. The child is half afraid, half curious; and has an anxious, troubled look. Shyuote, however, evinces no sign of embarrassment or humility. Planted solidly on his feet, with legs well apart and both arms arched, he gapes and stares at everybody and everything, occasionally fixing his glance upon the resplendent

sky overhead.   In vain we search for Zashue and his elder
son, Okoya.

The mass of spectators — hundreds are here already and
more are coming constantly — do not content themselves with
devout and reverent admiration.   Criticism is going on, and
it is exercised with the most unlimited freedom.   Should
any one attract attention to himself, either by the perfection
or imperfection of his dress measured by the standard of the
critic, he is not only mentioned by name and his garb audibly criticised, but pointed at approvingly or derisively.
The men are made the butt of their own sex among the
audience ; while the women praise or depreciate, according
as the occasion may seem to require, the female members
of the procession.   Frequently, when the costume of some
dusky beauty in the arena is the object of publicly expressed
admiration, some other within hearing may be seen casting
a covert glance of disappointment at her own less successful
apparel.   Or she fixes her eyes upon her gorgeous necklace
with evident gratification, satisfied that her own get-up is
handsomer than the one that the others so much admire,
while she soothes her injured vanity with haughty contempt for the taste of those who see so much in her rival to
admire.

The beat of the drum ceases, the wild song is hushed,
and the dancers break rank, seeking rest.   They collect in
groups or mingle with the bystanders, chatting, laughing,
panting.   Their violent exercise has played sad havoc with
the paint upon their faces and bodies, rendering them less
fantastic but more ludicrous.   The drummer occasionally
raps his instrument to satisfy himself that it is in order,
otherwise there is a lull of which all avail themselves to take
part in the general conversation.   Children resume their
sports in the court-yard.

Suddenly loud peals of laughter are heard on every side,

and all eyes turn simultaneously toward the passage-way whence are issuing half a dozen strange-looking creatures. They do not walk into the polygon, but rather tumble into it, running, hopping, stumbling, cutting capers, like a troop of clumsy, ill-trained clowns. When they have reached the centre of the open space, laughter becomes louder and more boisterous all around. Such expressions of mirth do not merely signify amusement, but are meant as demonstrations of applause. The Indian does not applaud by clapping his hands or stamping his feet, but evinces his approbation by laughter and smirks.

The appearance of the six men who have just tumbled into the arena is not merely strange, it is positively disgusting. They are covered with white paint, and with the exception of tattered breechclouts are absolutely naked. Their mouths and eyes are encircled with black rings; their hair is gathered in knots upon the tops of their heads, from which rise bunches of corn husks; a string of deer-hoofs dangles from each wrist; fragments of fossil wood hang from the loins; and to the knees are fastened tortoise-shells. Nothing is worn with a view to ornament. These seeming monstrosities, frightful in their ugliness, move about quite nimbly, and are boldly impudent to a degree approaching sublimity. Notwithstanding their uncouth figures and mountebank tricks their movements at times are undoubtedly graceful, and they appear to exercise a certain authority over the entire pageant.

White is the symbolic paint of the Koshare; hence all the actors who have performed their several parts, including the coarse jesters, make up and represent the society of the Delight Makers, whose office it is to open the ayash tyucotz. The association whose name has been selected as the title of our story is now before us fully represented, arrayed in its appropriate dress and engaged in the discharge of some ɾf its official duties. The clowns, too, the most agile and sprightly, in a word the most amusing of the company, are only an exaggeration of the rest, whose joint task it is to diffuse mirth, joy, buoyancy, delight, throughout the whole tribe. The jesters are also the heralds and marshals of the celebration. They gather together in the centre of the court and carry on a boisterous conversation accompanied with extravagant gestures. No one interrupts their noisy garrulity, but the entire assemblage listens eagerly, hailing their clumsy attempts at a joke and their coarse sallies of wit with shrieks of laughter. Their jests are necessarily of the coarsest; nevertheless excellent local hits are made and satiric personalities of considerable pungency are not infrequently indulged in. One of the clowns has tumbled down; he lies on his back, feet in the air; another takes hold of his legs and drags him around in the dust. The peals of laughter that greet this effort give testimony to the estimation in which it is held by the lookers-on. If one of the spectators has the misfortune to display immoderate enthusiasm, forthwith he is made the target of merciless jeering. One of the merrymakers goes up to him and mimics his manner and actions in the crudest possible way. The people on the terraced roofs exhibit their joy by showering down corn-cakes from their perches, which the performers greedily devour. These things are delightful according to Indian notions, and are well fitted to show how much of a child he still is, — a child however, it must be remembered, endowed with the physical strength, passions, and appetites of adult mankind.

The jesters scatter. One of their number runs up to Say Koitza, who shrinks at his approach. Nevertheless he plants himself squarely in front of her, bends his knees sidewise so as to describe a lozenge with his legs, and thrusts out his tongue to its fullest possible extent. Upon this the woman laughs, for in the grimacing abomination she has discovered

her own husband, Zashue, who thus pleasantly makes himself
known.   The hit is simply magnificent in the judgment of
his audience.   Meanwhile one of his colleagues is astride a
beam and endeavouring to crawl up it; a third is actually on
the roof and scatters the shrieking girls everywhere by his
impudent addresses; another bursts from a room on the
ground-floor holding ears of corn in each hand, and throwing himself upon the earth begins to gnaw them as a dog
would a bone, while one of his companions leaps on him,
and together they give a faithful representation of two prairie
wolves fighting over carrion.   The greatest uproar prevails all
about; the Koshare are outdoing themselves; they scatter
delirious joy, pleasure, delight, broadcast among the people.

The rumblings of the drum are heard again; the men
and women dancers take their places; once more the
chorus surround the musicians.   The clowns hush at once,
and squat or lie down along the walls, sober and dignified.
The strange *corps de ballet* re-forms in four lines, the second
and third facing each other, and the first and fourth fronting in opposite directions; men and women alternate.
Loud whoops and yells startle the air; the drum rolls and
thunders; each dancer brandishes his rattle.   Softly and
gently, at first, the chant begins, —

"Ho-ā-ā, Heiti-na, Heiti-na."

Gradually it increases in power, the dancers marking
time.   Livelier become the motions, stronger and stronger
the chanting, its text distinct and clearly enunciated, —

"Misho-homa Shi-pap, Na-ya Hate Ma-a-a-se-ua,
Uā-tir-anyi, Tya-au-era-nyi,
Shoto Ha-ya Ma-a-a-se-ua,
Nat-yu-o-o, Nat-yu-o-o, Ma-a-a-se-ua,
Heiti-na, Heiti-na, Ho-ā-ā, Ho-ā-ā."

The dancers intermingle; those in the front shift to the
rear rank; then all together utter a piercing shriek and dart

back to their former positions. The ceremony continues for upward of half an hour, during which the same words are sung, the same figures repeated. Then there is again a pause, and the actors disband to rest and recuperate. The clowns forget their dignity and set to work with redoubled energy, growing bolder and bolder. A party of them has penetrated into a ground-floor apartment, and are throwing the scanty furniture through the doorway. Now they spread robes and mats in the open court, lie down on them, crack jokes, and make faces at the audience. A specially gifted member of the fraternity hurries down a beam with a baby in his clutches, which he has powdered with ashes. He dances about with it, and exhibits the squalling brat in every attitude as a potential Koshare. The people scream and shout with unmixed pleasure. Now they point at a pair of monsters, one stamping and the other tripping daintily, who effectually mimic the late partners of the dance in the most heartless manner. Another of these hideous creatures is sitting down, his head covered with a dirty rag, staring, stuttering, and mumbling, like an imbecile. His pantomime is recognized at once as a cruel mimicry of the chief penitent while at prayer, and it is universally pronounced to be a superb performance. To the Koshare nothing is sacred; all things are permitted, so long as they contribute delight to the tribe.

Topanashka appeared to be lonesome in his exalted seat upon the roof. He arose quietly; and the by-standers made room for the tall man as with eyes fixed on an opposite terrace, he slowly descended and walked along the houses without deigning to take any notice of the gambols of the Koshare. He brushed past Say Koitza, and without looking at her or moving a feature muttered so that she alone could hear. —

"Watch, lest they discover the feathers."

Passing to the other side of the court he seated himself near a small, slender man, somewhat younger than himself. This was the tapop, or chief civil officer at the Rito.

The woman was greatly frightened by her father's words. It flashed upon her that should the Delight Makers raid her household and upset it, as they had others, the owl's feathers might be detected. In the troubled state of her mind she had failed to destroy or even remove them. Nevertheless, she could not immediately leave her post, through fear of awakening suspicion; she must wait until the dance should begin and the goblins become quiescent. Then? What then?

The feathers lay buried in the earthen floor of the inner room. Their removal must be accomplished with great care, in such a manner as to leave no signs of the earth having been recently disturbed.[1] There was no choice; they must be removed at all hazards. There would be ample time if she could only afterward obliterate all traces of her work. Luckily the kitchen was very dark, and the hearth covered with ashes. Water was there also, but she dare not use it lest the moistened spot betray her. Her mind was made up, however, and the attempt would be made as soon as the dance was renewed.

Singing and drumming are heard once more; the dancers fall into line; and when the chorus was shouting the second verse, —

[1] It was natural for her to think of removing the feathers, as they would in all probability be looked for just where she had put them; that is, under the floor. Such was the case at Nambé in March, 1855, when owl's feathers were found buried at several places in the Pueblo. The result of the discovery at Nambé was the slaughter of three men and one woman for alleged witchcraft by the infuriated mob of Indians.

"Na-ya, Ha-te Oyo-yā-uā,
Uā-tir-anyi Tya-au-era-nyi,"—

and the jokers had dispersed, Say slowly retreated within
the room, cowered down by the hearth, a sharp stone-
splinter in her hand and her eyes fixed upon the door,
watching lest anybody should appear. She listened with
throbbing heart to discover whether there was any shuffling
sound to betray the approach of one of the Koshare. She
saw nothing, and no sound was heard except the beats of
the drum and the monotonous rhythm, —

"Heiti-na, Heiti-na,
Nat-yu-o-o, Nat-yu-o-o, Ma-a-a-se-e-e-ua."

The woman began to dig. She dug with feverish haste.
The dance lacked interest for her; time and again had she
witnessed it, and well knew the figures now being performed. She made the hole as small as possible, digging
and digging, anxiously listening, eagerly looking up now
and then at the doorway, and starting timidly at the least
sound.

At last her instrument struck a resisting though elastic
object; it was the feathers.

Cautiously she pulled, pulled them up until she had
drawn them to the top of the hole, then peered about her,
intently listening. Nothing! Outside the uproar went
on, the chorus shouting at the top of their voices, —

"Ei-ni-a-ha, Ei-ni-a-ha-ay,
Tu-ua Se-na-si Tyit-i-na,
Tyit-i-na-a-a, Ma-a-a-se-ua."

Wrenching the bundle from its hiding-place, she concealed
it in her bosom; then carefully replaced the earth and
clay; put ashes on this, then clay; rubbed the latter with a
stone; threw on more ashes and more clay; and finally
stamped this with her feet, — all the while listening, and

glancing into the outer room. At last, when it seemed to her that the most rigid search could detect no trace of her labours, she brushed the ashes from her wrap and went out under the doorway again.

She appeared composed and more cheerful, but her heart was palpitating terribly; and at every pulsation she felt the dangerous bundle concealed beneath her clothing, and she tightened still more the belt encircling her waist.

The third act of the dance soon ended, and the jesters went to work once more,—women and girls now became the objects of their attentions. The screams and shrieks from the roof terraces when a Koshare is tearing about amongst the women, loud as they are, are drowned by the uproarious laughter of the men, who enjoy hugely the disgust and terror of the other sex.

From some of the houses the white painted horrors have taken out the grinding-slabs. Kneeling behind them, they heap dirt on their flat surfaces, moisten it with water, and grind the mud as the housewife does the corn, yelping and wailing the while in mimicry of the woman and her song while similarly engaged. The pranks of these fellows are simply silly and ugly; the folly borders on imbecility and the ugliness is disgusting, and yet nobody is shocked; everybody endures it and laughs.

Say Koitza herself enjoyed seeing her sex made a butt by coarse and vulgar satyrs. Suddenly two of the beasts stand before her, and one of them attempts an embrace. With a loud shriek she pushes him away, steps nimbly aside, and so saves the treacherous bundle from his grasp. Both the monsters storm into the house, where a terrific uproar begins. Corn is thrown about, grinding-slabs are disturbed, pots and bowls, robes and mats, are dragged hither and thither; they thump, scratch, and pound every corner of her little house. Gasping for breath, quaking from terror and distress, she leans against the wall, for in the fellow who sought to embrace her she recognizes Tyope.

All at once he darts out of the house, rushing past her with a large ear of corn in each hand which he forthwith hurls at the head of one of his comrades. This provokes intense merriment, increased still more by his lying down and rolling over several times. The climax of his humour is attained, and exhibits itself in his squatting on the ground close to one of the clay-grinding artists, where he begins to feed very eagerly upon the liquid mud, literally eating dirt. But a terrible weight has been lifted from the breast of the poor woman, for the dangerous man has, so she must conclude from his actions, discovered nothing.

Meanwhile the other Koshare had stepped out of the house with well-filled hands. Say is unconscious of his approach, and as he passes her he empties his treasures, fine ashes, upon her devoted head. So sudden is his disappearance and so loud the laughter which this display of subtle humour excites among the by-standers, that Say Koitza fails to recognize its author, Zashue, her own husband.

She feels much relieved, and her heart has grown light now that the immediate danger is past. And intently she tries to catch her father's eye, but the old man is quietly seated and does not look toward her.

The drum beats to signal the close of the intermission The clowns are becoming too impudent, too troublesome, so that an end must be made to their pranks. The society of the Koshare will appear now for the last time, as after the next dance they retire. While this is at its height, Topanashka rises and returns to his former place.

Walking slowly past his daughter, he looks at her. She meets his gaze cheerfully, and with a slight nod of approbation he moves onward.

The dance is over, and the Koshare depart to scatter beyond the large house and to rest. On the disappearance of the last of their number, including the jesters, whoops and shouts fill the air again from without, and a second procession similar to the former marches into the courtyard. It is composed of different persons similarly costumed, except that their paint is bluish instead of white. No clowns accompany them. They go through a similar performance, and sing the same songs; but everything is done with gravity and even solemnity. This band is more numerous by at least ten couples, and as a consequence the spectacle is more striking on account of a greater variety of dress and finery. A tall, slender young man opens the march. It is Hayoue. His partner is a buxom lass from the Bear clan, Kohayo hanutsh, a strong, thick-waisted creature, not so good-looking for a girl as he is for a man, yet of such proportion and figure as strike the Indian fancy. They pay each other little attention. During the pauses each one follows his own bent, and when the time calls they meet again.

In an Indian dance there is no need of engaging partners, though it is not unusual for such as fancy one another to seize the opportunity of so doing. The mere fact of a certain boy stamping the earth beside a certain girl on a certain occasion, or a certain maiden tripping by the side of a particular youth, does not call for that active gossiping which would result if a couple were to dance with one another alone at one of our balls. A civilized ball is professedly for enjoyment alone; an Indian dance is a religious act, a public duty.

The society who are now exercising their calisthenics in the court has much similarity to the Koshare, yet their main functions are distinct. They are called the Cuirana.

If, during the conversation in which Topanashka informed his daughter as to the origin of the Koshare and the ideas underlying their rôle in Indian society, Say Koitza had inquired of him about the Cuirana he might have given her very similar information.

With this marked distinction, however, that whereas the former consider themselves summer people, the latter are regarded as winter men. While the Koshare are specially charged with the duty of furthering the ripening of the fruit, the Cuirana assist the sprouting of the seed.

The main work of the Koshare is therefore to be done in the summer and autumn, that of the Cuirana in the spring; and, moreover, while on certain occasions the latter are masters of ceremonies also, they never act as clowns or official jesters. Their special dance is never obscene, like that of the Delight Makers.

During their performance, therefore, the public did not exhibit the unbounded hilarity which marked that of their predecessors. The audience looked on quietly, and even with stolidity. There was nothing to excite laughter, and since the figures were slavish repetitions, it became monotonous. Some of the spectators withdrew to their houses, and those who remained belonged to the cliffs, whence they had come to witness the rite, as a serious and even sacred duty.

While the dance of the Cuirana is in progress, two of the white painted clowns are standing outside of the big building, and at some distance from the new house of Yakka hanutsh, in earnest conversation. Heat and exercise have partially effaced the paint, so that the features of Tyope Tihua, and of Zashue, the husband of Say, can be easily recognized.

"I tell you, satyumishe," asserts the latter, "you are mistaken, or words have been spoken to you that are not true. This wife of mine is good. She has nothing to do with evil, nor has she tampered with it. You have done her wrong, Tyope, and that is not right." His features, already distorted by the paint, took on an expression of anger.

The other responded hastily, "And I tell you, Zashue Tihua, that I saw your wife sitting by the hearth with Shotaye," — his voice trembled at the mention of her name, — "and I heard when that mean, low aniehna " — his eyes flashed, giving a terrible expression to his already monstrously disfigured countenance — "spoke to the yellow corn ! "

" Did you understand what she said ? " Zashue interjected.

" No, but can any one ask aught of the yellow corn but evil ? I know, too, that this shuatyam picked up the body of an owl on the mesa " — he pointed to the southern heights — "and carried its feathers back to her foul hole in the rocks."

"But you did not see Say with them ? " Her husband looked in the eyes of the other inquiringly, and at the same time threateningly.

"That is the truth, but why does she go with the witch, and for what purpose does that female skunk need owl's plumage, if not to harm the tribe ? She has done harm, too," — he stamped his foot angrily, — "she is the cause of our having no rain last summer. She destroyed the maize-plant ere it could bring forth ears. She did it, and your wife helped her." Furious, and with flaming eyes, Tyope turned his head and stared into space.

"Are you sure that Shotaye has done this, and that it is not Pāyatyama's will ? "

"Did we not fast and mortify ourselves while it was yet time, all of us from the Hotshanyi down to the youngest Koshare ? " exclaimed Tyope. "Was it of any use ? No, for that base woman had power over us in order to destroy the tribe."

"I am not defending her," Zashue muttered, "but it is not certain that she is guilty, nor is it proven that she is the cause of the hunger we suffered last winter."

His companion threw at him a glance of intense rage. The other's incredulity exasperated Tyope, but he suppressed his feeling and spoke in a quieter tone.

"Come, satyumishe, the Naua is expecting us, and in his presence we shall speak further. Our father is wise and will teach oui hearts."

Say Koitza's husband stood motionless, looking away from his friend.

"Come," Tyope urged, placing his hand on the other's shoulder. Zashue at last turned around and reluctantly followed him. Both went toward the new estufa of the Maize clan.

From this circular building faint sounds, as of a drum beaten by a weak or lazy hand, were issuing. The principal Koshare and the Naua had retired thither for recuperation after the dance. Although the old man was not of the cluster to whom the estufa belonged, he had obtained permission from Yakka hanutsh to use the room on this occasion as a meeting and dressing place for himself and his associates. The club-house of the Corn people thus served to-day a twofold purpose, and was used by two distinct groups of the inhabitants of the Rito.

At this hour the Koshare Naua was its sole occupant. He sat on the floor, holding the drum in his lap and touching the instrument lightly from time to time. His vacant gaze was fixed upon a small heap of dying embers, nearly in the centre of the room and beneath the hatchway. Occasionally he raised his head to glance at the wall opposite him. The interior of the estufa appeared quite different from what it did on the day when Shyuote's peep into it was so poorly rewarded. Its walls had been whitened.

10

and were in addition covered with strange-looking paint
ings. The floor was partly occupied by a remarkable
display of equally strange objects.

The painting in front of which the old man sat, and at
which he gazed from time to time, represented in the first
place a green disk surrounded by short red rays, which
three white squares, bordered with black, converted into
something like the rude semblance of a human face. This
disk stood for a picture of the sun. Below it was the
symbol of the moon's white disk, encircled by a black and
red ring, and provided also with square eyes and mouth.
Still lower were painted two crosses, a red one and a white
one, both with black border.

Above the sun there appeared a form intended to be
human, painted in very gaudy colours. This was Pāyatyama, the sun-father.   On each side of him rose a terraced
pyramid painted green, and from the top of one of these
pyramids to that of the other there spanned or stretched a
tri-coloured arch, red, yellow, and blue, over the sun-father's
head.   On each side of sun and moon was the crudely
executed picture of an animal, — the one on the right,
being intended for a bear, painted green ; the one on the
left, for a panther, painted red. The heads of these beasts
were turned toward the central figures.   Still farther, beyond
these beasts of prey, two gigantic green serpents with horned
heads swept over the remainder of the wall, leaving but
a narrow space facing the sun, where four maize-plants,
two green ones and two of a reddish-brown hue, were
painted.

Below the central figures and not quite reaching up to
them, an arch of wood, painted green with a yellow middle
stripe, was held aloft by two poles driven into the floor of
the estufa. Under this arch stood a wooden screen, green
and black with a yellow border at the bottom, while the

upper edge was carved into four terraced pyramids surmounted by as many black arches. Both right and left of
the screen, pine-branches resembling Christmas-trees of
to-day were stuck into the floor. This strange decoration
expresses symbolically a meaning similar to that intended
to be conveyed by the dance of the ayash tyucotz.

The sun-father, soaring above the sun, moon, and stars, —
for the red cross is the star of morning, the white the evening star, — is surrounded by the symbols of the principal
phenomena in nature that are regarded as essentially benefi-
cent to mankind. Thus the terraced pyramids are the
clouds, for the clouds appear to the Indian as staircases
leading to heaven, and they in turn support the rainbow.
The two principal beasts of prey, who feed upon game, like
man, and whose strength, agility, and acute senses man
hopes to acquire, are represented as the bear in the colour
symbolic of the east, and the panther in that of the south.
Farther away from the sun-father are the two monstrous
water-snakes, genii of the fish-bearing and crop-irrigating
water-courses. The sun-father stands surrounded by all
these elements and beings; he fixes his blissful magic gaze
upon the nourishing maize-plants, that they may grow and
that their ripe fruit may sustain the tribe. Thus much for
the allegory on the wall.

But in order that the wish and hope which this allegoric
painting expresses on the part of man may become realized,
invocation rises before the picture in the shape of the screen,
denoting an altar on which the rainbow has again settled
down as a messenger from above. Both are green, since
it is summer; and the summer sun, or summer home of the
sun-father, is green also, like the earth, covered with luxuriant
vegetation.

Invocation alone does not suffice to incline the hearts
of Those Above kindly toward mankind: gratitude is re-

quired as an earnest of sincere worship.   But this gratitude
can be expressed by words as well as by deeds, and prayers
must precede, accompany, or follow the offering.   In front
of the altar a row of bunches artistically composed of snow-
white down are placed on the floor.   Each of these delicate
fabrics has sacred meal scattered about its base, and each
of them symbolizes the soul of one household.   They are
what the Queres Indian calls the *yaya*, or mother, dedicated
to the moon-mother, who specially protects every Indian
home.   All these stand below the altar in token of the
many prayers that each household sends up to the moon,
painted above, that the mother of all, who dwells in the
silvery orb, may thank her husband in the sun for all the
good received, and implore him to further shed his blessings on their children.   Between these feather-bushes and
the embers, a great number of other objects are placed, —
fetiches of stone, animal figures, prayer-plumes, sacrificial
bowls painted with symbolic devices and surmounted by
terraced prongs, and wooden images of household gods
decorated with feathers.   Sacred meal is in or about all of
them, and all stand for so many intercessors praying for the
good of the people, giving thanks in the name of the
people and offering their vows in token of gratitude.

Similar to this estufa of the Corn clan are to-day all the
other estufas on the Tyuonyi.   They contain similar pictures, and similar objects are grouped on the floors in front
of them.   Before the altars the swan-white mother-souls
glisten and flutter.   The estufas are without human occupants, their entrances alone are watched by old men or
women outside to prevent the work of invocation and gratitude performed inside by symbolic advocates from being
desecrated by rude or thoughtless intruders.

While this work is going on thus silently and without
direct intervention of man, man himself performs a similar

duty in the open air through the ceremonies of the great dance.

In this dance the Koshare came first, for their request was one of immediate importance. That the fruit may ripen is the object of their sacramental performances, — " even the fruit in woman's womb," Topanashka had explained. To this end man must contribute with delight and work with love. Whoever mourns or harbours ill-will cannot expect his task to prosper. In this manner even the obscene performances of the Koshare are symbolic, and their part in the great dance is above all an invocation.

Next the Cuirana came. Their labours are over; the germs which they were to protect with incantations have sprouted long ago, and the plants are ready for maturing. For these results of their work they give thanks to the sun-father, — thanks loud and emphatic, so that he may hear and see how grateful his children are. Their performance to-day is a testimonial of gratitude.

To close the dance, both societies will finally appear together, and with them representatives of the tribe at large. All together they will go through the same succession of ceremonies, in token that all acquiesce in the sentiments of the Koshare and the Cuirana, — that each individual for himself and in behalf of all the others joins in giving thanks for the past and praying for the future.

This is the signification of the ayash tyucotz when performed about the time of the summer solstice. However clumsy and meaningless it may seem, it is still a solemn performance   It gives public expression, under very strange forms, to the idea that has found its most perfect utterance in the German philosopher's[1] definition of " abject reliance upon God ; " whereas in its lowest form it is still " a vague and awful feeling about unity in the powers of nature, an

[1] Schleiermacher.

unconscious acknowledgment of the mysterious link connecting the material world with a realm beyond it."

Seated comfortably and alone, surrounded by the symbols of his creed, the old leader of the Koshare was tapping
his drum and humming softly a prayer. On a sudden the
hatchway above him became darkened, and as he looked
up he saw the legs of a man appearing on the uppermost
rounds of the ladder leading down into the subterranean
chamber. As that man continued to descend, the body,
and finally the head, of Tyope appeared. Then followed
Zashue Tihua. When both men were below, they went to
the nearest sacrificial bowl, each one took from it a pinch
of yellow corn-meal and scattered it in front of the altar.
Then they turned to the old man, but he did not take any
notice of either of them. Tyope squatted by his side, while
Zashue remained erect.

"Sa nashtio," began the former, "we have not found
anything."

"There is nothing," added Zashue, rather excitedly;
"my wife is innocent."

The Naua raised his eyes with an expression of astonishment and surprise, as if failing to understand.

"What is it that you have not found?" he asked, rather
dreamily.

"No coco—" Tyope stopped and looked at the pictures on the wall. It is improper to mention the names of
evil powers or agencies in presence of the symbols of Those
Above. So he corrected himself and said, —

"No hapi."

"Hapi?" the Naua inquired with a vacant stare, "what
sort of hapi? Where did you look for them?" He bent his
head, as if trying to remember.

"Hapi," exclaimed Tyope, "in the house of Say Koitza,
this motātza's wife;" and he pointed at his companion.

"Yes, indeed ;" the chief of the Koshare now recollected. "I know ; I recollect well." His eyes suddenly brightened ; they assumed an expression of cunning as well as of suspicion. His quick glance moved back and forth from one of his visitors to the other. "So you found nothing? Then there is nothing ! You were right, Zashue ; your wife is good." He gave a chuckle which he intended for a benevolent smile.

"See," Say's husband exclaimed, turning to Tyope ; "the Naua believes as I do. My wife is no — " the evil word he suppressed in time. He stopped, biting his lips in embarrassment.

Tyope's features moved not. He spoke to the chief of the Delight Makers as quietly and calmly as possible, —

"I believe as you do, nashtio ; but while Say may be guiltless, Shotaye is not."

"Hush !" the Naua sternly interrupted ; "think of those here." He pointed toward the symbols. "Don't you know that they must not hear the name of that woman?"

Tyope replied hastily, and eager to drown the reprimand his chief had given him, —

"What shall we do, Naua?"

The old man became impatient. "Don't you see that I am at work? I am busy. Those here," he again nodded at the idols, "leave me no peace. I must be with them until the last otshanyi begins. In three days we go to the kaaptsh, — you, he, all our brethren, — and then we may speak. Now leave me alone. Go! Leave me! Go! Go!" he cried, and waved his hand upward. He was not to be spoken to any longer ; he began to beat his drum and took up the low chant again. Zashue hurriedly climbed out of the estufa, and Tyope followed with an angry face. When the latter was on the open ground again, Zashue stepped up to him and said in a very decided tone, —

"You see now, satyumishe, that Say is innocent. Hereafter, Tyope, leave her alone." Turning about, he walked
toward the large house. Tyope cast after him a look less
of anger than of bitter disappointment.

The last act of the great ceremony began. A tremendous shout sounded from the outer entrance to the gallery
leading into the court-yard of the great house. The chant
arose stronger and louder than ever before, and several
drums rumbled at once. Again were the terraces filled
with people, the walls below lined with spectators. Topanashka sat on the roof, cold and impassable. Say Koitza
leaned in the doorway of her home, with a quiet, almost
smiling, countenance.

A long array of couples, dressed as before but painted
red, opened the procession; then came the Cuirana, and
last the Koshare. Topanashka arose and joined the dancers; the Tapop stood beside him, and both stamped
along, keeping time as if they were young once more.
The singers were reinforced by several aged men with
snow-white hair, three of whom wore dark wraps, sleeveless and covered with red embroidery. These were the
chief penitents; those without badges or distinctive dress,
the principal shamans of the tribe. A thrill of excitement
ran through the spectators; children on the roofs gathered
in groups, moving in harmony with the strong rhythmic
noise below. The jesters had become very quiet; they
went about gravely keeping order, for the court was now
filled with performers. The green headdresses waved like
reeds before the wind, and the whole space looked like
a rhythmically wafted cornfield. When the dancers were
executing the beautiful figure of the planting of maize, —
man and woman bending outward simultaneously, each
one to his side, and all the rattles sounding as if upon
command, — everything around was hushed; everybody

looked on in respectful silence, so correct were the motions, so well-timed and so impressive the sight. Say also
felt genuine delight. She thought of times long past when
she, too, had joined in the dance. Now, alas, she could not.
With all the relief this day had brought her, there still remained a dull weight in her bosom, and an inner voice forbade her to mingle with those so sincerely engaged in rites
of thanksgiving to the powers of good and happiness.

While she stood and gazed around, her attention was
directed to a young couple passing in front of her. The
handsome lad with the dark, streaming hair was Okoya,
and she recognized him proudly as the best-looking youth
on the ground, Hayoue perhaps excepted. But then, was
not Hayoue, Okoya's father's brother? But who was the
girl by Okoya's side? That slender figure of medium
height, that earnest, thoughtful expression of the face, those
lustrous eyes, — whose were they? The two were manifestly
a handsome pair, and the longer she watched them the
more she became satisfied that they were the prettiest
couple in the dance. They were certainly well matched;
her son's partner was the handsomest girl of the tribe; of
this she was convinced, and she felt proud of it. Motherly
pride caused her heart to flutter, and the instinct of woman
made her eager to know who the maiden was who appeared
such a fitting partner for her own good-looking son. Say
Koitza determined to improve the first opportunity that
might present itself for ascertaining who the girl was and
where she belonged.

The day was drawing to a close, a day of joyful excitement for the people of the Tyuonyi. The dance terminated. As the sun went down the dancers crowded out
of the passage-way; so did the visitors; it grew quieter
and quieter on and about the large house. The swarm of
people leaving it scattered toward the cliffs in little bands

and thin streams, separating and diverging from each other like the branches of an open fan. And yet, after night had come and the moon had risen in a cloudless sky, there was still bustle everywhere. Households ravaged by the visitations of the Koshare were being restored to order, the exhausted dancers were being feasted, and the estufas were being cleared of everything bearing a sacred character. Young men and boys still loitered in groups, repeating with hoarse voices the songs and chants they had lately addressed to the ruler of day.

On the terrace roof of the home of Tyope's wife a young girl stood quite alone, gazing at that moon where the mother of all mankind, the Sanatyaya, is supposed to reside. It was Mitsha Koitza, who had just returned from the estufa of her clan with the mother-soul of her own home, and who still lingered here holding in her hands the cluster of snowy, delicate feathers. She thinks, while her nimble fingers play with it, of the young man who has been her partner the whole day, who has danced beside her so quiet, modest, and yet so handsome, and who once appeared to her on this same roof brave and resolute in her defence. While she thus stands, gazes, and dreams, a flake of down becomes detached and quivers upward into the calm, still air. Involuntarily the maiden fastens her glance on the plumelet, which flits upward and upward in the direction of the moon's silvery orb. Such a flitting and floating plume is the symbol of prayer. Mitsha's whole heart goes anxiously with the feather. It rises and rises, and at last disappears as if absorbed by moonlight. The features of the maiden, which till now have carried an anxious, pleading look, brighten with a soft and happy smile. The mother above has listened to her entreaty, for the symbol of her thoughts, the feather, has gone to rest on the bosom of her who watches over every house, who feels with every loving and praying heart.

CHAPTER VII.

AMONG Indians any great feast, like the dance of the ayash tyucotz described in the preceding chapter, is not followed by the blue Monday with which modern civilization is often afflicted. Intoxicating drinks were unknown to the sedentary inhabitants of New Mexico previous to the advent of Europeans. If it happened, however, that one or other of the feasters overloaded his stomach with the good things set before him, after the ceremony was over a decoction made from juniper-twigs afforded prompt and energetic relief. Among the younger men it was not rare for some to remain in company with the fair sex until the small hours of morning, in which case the rising sun found them somewhat out of sleep. But the majority were glad to retire to their habitual quarters for a good rest after the day's exertions, and these woke up the following morning bright and active, as if nothing had happened to divert them from the duties and occupations of every-day life. To this majority belonged Okoya.

After the dance was over he had loitered and lounged about for a time with some companions of his own age, but as soon as the moon rose he had sauntered home. His mother was busy putting things into shape, for the Delight Makers had left behind a fearful disorder. Shyuote was there, too ; he was careful not to assist his mother, but to stand in her way as much as possible, which action on his part called forth some very active scolding. But it struck Okoya that she appeared more cheerful than before. Her motions were brisker, her step more elastic. Say Koitza placed the usual food before her eldest son, and at this moment Zashue came in also. He felt exceedingly proud of his exploits as a jester, and was jollier than ever before. Okoya listened for a while to the clumsy and not always chaste jokes of his parent, and then retired to the estufa. The next morning, bright and refreshed, he strolled back to the house for breakfast, expecting to meet his father, who would assign him his day's work.

Zashue had gone already. Nobody asked where, but it was taken for granted that he had gone to see the old chief of the Delight Makers about the approaching days of penitential retirement. His mother was up ; and she addressed her son in a pleasant manner, set food before him, and then inquired, —

"Sa uishe, who was the girl that danced by your side ? "

"It was Mitsha Koitza," Okoya replied without looking up.

"Mitsha Koitza," she repeated, "where does she belong ? "

"Tyame hanutsh."

"Who is her father ? "

"Tyope Tihua. Do you like her ? " and he looked at his mother pleadingly, as if asking her forgiveness and her consent to his choice.

The woman's brow clouded at the mention of a name so hateful to her. She looked hard at her son and said in a tone of bitter reproach, —

"And you go with that girl ? "

"Why not ! " His face darkened also.

"Have I not told you what kind of man Tyope is ? "

"The girl is no Koshare," he answered evasively.

"But her mother is, and he."

Both became silent. Okoya stared before him ; his appetite was gone ; he was angry, and could not eat any more.

What right had this woman, although she was his mother, to reprove him because he was fond of a girl whose father she did not like! Was the girl responsible for the deeds of her parents? No! So he reasoned at once, and then his temper overcame him. How could his mother dare to speak one single word against the Koshare! Had she not betrayed him to them? In his thoughts the hatred which she pretended to display against the Koshare appeared no longer sincere; it seemed to him hypocrisy, duplicity, deception. Such deceit could mean only the darkest, the most dangerous, designs. With the Indian the superlative of depravity is witchcraft. Okoya revolved in his mind whether his mother was not perhaps his most dangerous enemy.

On the other hand, Say Koitza, when she began to question her son, had in view a certain object. She was anxious to find out who the maiden was whose looks had at once charmed her. Next she was curious to know whether the meeting of the two was accidental or not. Therefore the leading question, " And you go with that girl? " Under ordinary circumstances his affirmative reply might have filled her motherly heart with joy, for Mitsha's appearance had struck her fancy; but now it filled her with dismay. Nothing good to her could result from a union between her child and the daughter of Tyope. That union would be sure to lead Okoya over to the home of his betrothed, which was the home of her mother, where he could not fail to gradually succumb to the influence which that mother of Mitsha, a sensual, cunning, sly woman utterly subservient to her husband, would undoubtedly exert upon him. It was not maternal jealousy that beset her now and filled her with flaming passion, it was fear for her own personal safety. Under the influence of sudden displeasure human thought runs sometimes astray with terrific swiftness. Say

Koitza saw her son already going to the house of that fiend, Tyope, night after night, whereas in reality he had never called there as yet. She fancied that she heard him in conversation with this girl, confiding in her little by little, just as Zashue used, before he and she became man and wife. But what could Okoya tell after all that might prove of harm to her? He was a mere child as yet. At this stage of her reasoning, a cloud rose within her bosom and spread like wildfire. Was it not strange that the discovery of the owl's feathers, the betrayal of that dread secret, almost coincided with Okoya's open relations with the daughter of the man who, she felt sure, was at the bottom of the accusation against her? A ghastly suspicion flashed up and soon became so vivid that no doubt could arise, — her own son must accidentally have discovered the fatal feathers; he himself without intending any harm must have mentioned them to the girl, perhaps even in the presence of her mother.

Say became satisfied that she held the key to her betrayal. The riddle was solved. That solution dissipated all hopes of salvation, for if her own son was to be witness against her in the dreaded hour when the tribal council had to determine for or against her guilt, there could be no doubting his testimony. And Tyope would have that testimony in any case, for if Okoya should deny, Okoya's own betrothed might be brought face to face with him as a witness. Thus she reasoned in much less time than it can be written, and these conclusions overwhelmed her to such a degree that she turned away from her favourite child in bitter passion, with the conviction that her son in whom she had trusted was her destroying angel. She hid her face from him in anger and grief.

Okoya noticed his mother's feelings. Her anger was inexplicable to him, unless it meant disappointment in relation to some of her own supposed dark designs. It made him angrier still, for Say's bitterness against the Koshare was in his opinion only feigned. Persuaded that his mother was false to him, and that she was even harbouring evil designs, he rose abruptly and left the house in silence.

He could no longer refuse to believe that she was planning his destruction. Otherwise, why did she oppose what to him appeared the prelude to a happy future? And why that apparent duplicity on her part, — condemning the Koshare to his face, and, as he thought, being in secret understanding with them? Only one explanation was reasonable, the only one within reach of the Indian mind, — that Say Koitza was in some connection with evil powers which she, for some reason unknown to him, was courting for the purpose of his destruction; in other words, that Say Koitza, his own mother, was a witch!

Nothing more detestable or more dangerous than witchcraft is conceivable to the Indian. To a young and untrained mind like Okoya's the thought of being exposed to danger from such a source is crushing. The boy felt bewildered, dazed. He leaned against the wall of the great house for support, staring at the huge cliffs without seeing them; he looked at people passing to and fro without taking any notice of their presence. He could not even think any more, but merely felt, — felt unutterably miserable.

If only he knew of somebody who might help him! This was his first thought after recovering strength and self-control. Why not speak to Hayoue? The idea was like the recollection of a happy dream, and indeed he had harboured it before. It roused him to such a degree that he tore himself away from the wall against which he had leaned as on a last staff, and straightening himself he walked deliberately toward the upper end of the Rito, where the cave-dwellings of the Water clan were situated.

Hayoue might be at home, still it was more than likely that the Don Juan of the Rito had been spending the last night elsewhere. If at home, so much the better; if not, there was nothing left but to wait until he came. The prospect of waiting and resting was not an unpleasant one for Okoya, who felt exhausted after the shock of disappoint- ment and disgust he had just experienced. As he slowly approached the recess wherein the grottoes of the Water clan lay, he halted for a moment to catch breath, and just then descried Shotaye, who was coming down toward him. The woman had been quite a favourite of his ever since she became so kind to his sick mother. Nevertheless he had always felt afraid of her on account of her reputation as a doubtful character. Now the sight of her made him angry, for she was his mother's friend and a witch also! So he resumed his walk and passed her with a short, sulky *guatzena*. Shotaye noticed his surly manner and looked straight at him, returning the morose greeting with a loud *raua* that sounded almost like a challenge. Then she went on with a smile of scorn and amusement on her lips. She was not afraid of the young fellow, for she attributed his surly ways to sitting up late.

Okoya was glad to get out of the woman's reach, and he did not stop until at the entrance to the caves which Hayoue and his folk occupied. There was no necessity of announcing himself; he merely lifted the curtain of raw- hide that hung over the doorway, and peeped in.

His youthful uncle — so much he saw at a glance — was not in. Another young gentleman of the tribe lay on the floor beside the other members of the family. All were sound asleep yet, and Okoya dropped the curtain quietly and turned toward the brook. On its banks he selected a

spot where, unseen to others, he could look down the valley.
Here he threw himself on the ground to watch, and await
Hayoue's coming.

Although deeply anxious to meet his uncle, Okoya entertained no thought of impatience. He had to wait, that was
all. Beside, his heart was so heavy, so full of grief and
despair, that not even his surroundings could divert him
from gloomy thoughts. The brook murmured and rustled
softly by his side, its waters looked clear and limpid; he
neither heard nor saw them. He only longed to be alone,
completely alone, until his uncle should come. Okoya
had not performed his morning ablutions, but there was no
thought of them; for he was in deep sorrow, and when the
Indian's heart is heavy he is very careful not to wash.

Flat on his stomach, with chin resting on both hands,
indifferent to the peculiar scenery before him, he nevertheless scanned the cliffs as far as they were visible. The
grottoes of Tzitz hanutsh opened right in front of him;
lower down, the entrances of a few of the caves of Kohaio
hanutsh could be seen, for the rocks jutted out like towering pillars. They completely shut out from his gaze the
eastern cave-dwellings of Tzina hanutsh. Farther to the
east, the wall of cliffs swept around to the southeast,
showing the houses of the Eagle clan built against its base,
the caverns of Yakka hanutsh opening along a semicircle
terminating in a sharp point of massive rocks. In that
promontory the port-holes of some of the dwellings of the
Cottonwood people were visible. Beyond, all detail became undistinguishable through the distance, for the north
side of the Rito turned into a dim yellowish wall crowned
by dark pine-timber.

Okoya lay there, scanning, watching every doorway back
and forth the whole length of the view; hours went by;
there were no signs of Hayoue. Yet Okoya did not rise in

angei and pace the ground with impatience, he did not
scratch his head or stamp, he did not even think of swear-
ing, — he simply waited. And his patient waiting proved
of comfort to him, for he gradually cooled off, and freed
from the effects of his violent impressions, began to think
what he could do. Nothing, absolutely nothing, at least
until he had seen Hayoue. To wait for the latter was a
necessity, if it took him the whole day. But to wait in the
same posture for hours was rather tiresome, so he rolled
over on his back, and folding his arms under his head began
to gaze on the skies.

Bright and cloudless as they had appeared at sunrise, a
change had come over them since which attracted even
Okoya's attention. Instead of the usual deep azure, the
heavens had assumed a dingy hue, and long white stream-
ers traversed them like arches. Had the boy looked in
the west he would have seen shredded clouds looming up
behind the mountains, a sure sign of approaching rain.
But he had become fascinated by what was directly
above him, and so he watched with increasing interest
the white arches overhead. Slowly, imperceptibly, they
pushed up, crossing the zenith and approaching the
eastern horizon, toward which the boy's face was turned.
And while they shifted they grew in width and density.
Delicate filaments appeared between and connected bow
with bow, gradually thickening, until the zenith was but
one vault of pale gray. The boy watched this process
with increased eagerness; it caused him to forget his
troubles. He saw that rain — one of the great blessings
for which he and his people had so fervently prayed,
chanted, and danced yesterday — was coming on, and
his heart became glad. The spirits — the Shiuana — he
thought, were kindly disposed toward his people; and
this caused him to wonder what the Shiuana might really

be, and why they acted so and so, and not otherwise. The Shiuana, he had been taught, dwelt in the clouds, and they were good; why, then, was it that from one and the same cloud the beneficial rain descended, which caused the food of mankind to grow, and also the destructive hail and the deadly thunderbolt?[1]

A faint, muttering sound, deep and prolonged, struck his ear. He started, for it was distant thunder. The Shiuana, he believed, had read his thoughts, and they reminded him that their doings were beyond the reach of his mind. Turning away from the sights above, he looked again down the valley. There, at last, came the long-expected Hayoue, slowly, drowsily, like one who has slept rather late than long. Hayoue, indeed, was so sleepy yet that his nephew had to call him thrice. After the third *umo*, however, he glanced around, saw Okoya beckoning to him, and came down to the brook. Yawning and rubbing his eyes he sat down, and Okoya said, —

"Satyumishe, I want to speak to you. Will you listen to my speech?"

Hayoue smiled good-naturedly, but looked rather indifferent or absent-minded as he replied, —

"I will; what is it about? Surely about Mitsha, your girl. Well, she is good," he emphatically added; "but Tyope is not good, not good," he exclaimed, looking up with an expression of strong disgust and blowing through his teeth. It was clear that the young man was no friend to Tyope.

[1] A clear definition of the Shiuana is not easy to give. In a general sense, they might be called the "spirits of the Fetiches." As everything strange, unusual, or inexplicable is attributed to spiritual origin, the numbers of the Shiuana are very great. Even the pictures of the sun-father, of the moon-mother, etc., are Shiuana, in the sense of their supposed spiritual connection with the deified beings they represent.

Okoya moved uneasily, and continued in a muffled tone
of voice,—

"You are not right, nashtio; it is not concerning Mitsha
that I want to speak to you."

"About what else, then?" Hayoue looked up in surprise, as if unable to comprehend how a boy of the age of
Okoya could think of anything else than of some girl.

His brother's son took from his neck the little satchel
containing sacred meal. Without a word he opened it, and
scattered the flour in the usual way to the six regions. Then
he pointed to the clouds and whispered, "The Shiuana are
good," at the same time handing the bag to his uncle.
The latter's astonishment had reached its maximum; the
boy's actions were utterly incomprehensible to him.

Again the sound of distant thunder vibrated from the
west, and the cliffs sighed in return.

"They are calling us," Okoya whispered.

Hayoue became suddenly very sober. He performed
the sacrifice in silence, and then assumed the position of
an earnest and attentive listener.

"Do you like the Koshare?" began Okoya, in a
whisper.

"No. But why do you ask this?"

"Because I don't like them either."

"Is that all you had to tell me? I could have told you
that in their own presence." Hayoue seemed to be disappointed and vexed.

"That is not why I called you, umo," Okoya continued;
"it is because the Koshare know that I dislike them."

"What if they do know it."

"But they might harm me!"

"They cannot. Otherwise I should have been harmed
by them long ago. But I don't care for them."

Okoya shook his head and muttered,—

"I am afraid of the Koshare."

The other shrugged his shoulders.

"I am not," he said. "Men can do harm with their hands and with their weapons; and against those you have your fist and the shield. Those Above" — he pointed at the skies — "can harm us; they can kill us. But men — why, we can defend ourselves."

Okoya felt shocked at words which sounded to him like sacrilegious talk. Timidly and morosely he objected, —

"Don't you know that there are witches!"

"Witches! There are no witches."

Again there was a mutter from the west, a hollow, solemn warning; and the cliffs responded with a plaintive moan. Even incredulous Hayoue started, and Okoya sighed.

"I will tell you why I ask all this," said he, and he went on to explain. Beginning with the incident provoked by Shyuote, he confessed to the suspicions which it had aroused in his mind, and laid the whole process of his reasoning bare before his listener. His speech was picturesque, but not consciously poetic; for the Indian speaks like a child, using figures of speech, not in order to embellish, but because he lacks abstract terms and is compelled to borrow equivalents from comparisons with surrounding nature. Hayoue listened attentively; occasionally, however, he smiled. At last Okoya stopped and looked at his friend in expectation. The latter cast at the boy a humorous glance; he felt manifestly amused by his talk.

"Motātza," he began, "in what you have told me there is not more substance than in the clouds above, when the Shiuana do not dwell in them. It is colour, white colour. It is nothing. You have been painting; the picture is done, but no spirit is there. Shyuote is a lazy, idle brat; he shirks work; but when you say to him, Sit down and eat, then he all at once becomes active. In this way he sneaks

around from house to house. He may have overheard
something said about you and your ways, he may even have
surprised the Koshare while talking among themselves.
But it is quite as likely that the toad has invented the
whole story just in order to anger you, for he always finds
time to sneak, to lounge, and to hatch lies, the lazy, good-
for-nothing eavesdropper! I tell you what it is, that boy
is fit for nothing but a Koshare, and a real good one will
he become."

"But," Okoya rejoined, "if the Delight Makers have
spoken about the yaya and me, there must be some cause
for it."

"Don't you know that these shutzuna always find some
occasion for gossip?" Hayoue cried. "Don't they run
into every house? Don't their women stick their noses
into every bowl, in order to find out what the people cook
and eat? Rest easy, satyumishe, your mother is good, she
has nothing in common with the Koshare."

"But is not the nashtio one of them? Your brother, my
father? Is he like the rest of them?"

Hayoue replied, assuming an important mien, —

"It is true that brother is, and I don't like it; but we
can't change it. It was so ordained long ago, for my father
himself was Koshare. Beside, let me tell you that not all
that the Koshare do is wrong. If there were no Koshare, it
would not be good for the people. They must see that
Those Above assist us when the corn ripens, and inasmuch
as they perform their duties, they are necessary to us. It
is also well that they should bring joy and mirth among
the tribe, but " — he raised his hand and his eyes flashed —
" they must not go beyond their duty. Their leader shall
not presume to be more than the Hotshanyi, who has to
suffer and bear for our sake and for our good. They shall
do their duty and no more. It is not their duty to make

people believe that they are wiser than the chayani and to induce the people to give them bowl after bowl full of meal, feathers, shells, and whatever else may be good and precious. For it is not to the Koshare as a body that all these things are distributed; it is only their naua who gets them, and through him his hanutsh, at the expense of all the other clans. Neither shall the Koshare alone enjoy our makatza, pretending that it pleases Those Above !"

It thundered again, louder and longer than before. Hayoue stopped, and then went on.

"Zashue fails to see all this. He is Koshare, and follows in the tracks of the others like a blind man. But we, the Cuirana, — we see it. I am not a principal, I cannot sit in council and speak, but withal I have noticed these doings for a long time. I tell you, motātza, that if the Delight Makers, the old fiend who rules them, and Tyope are not restrained very soon, there will be sorrow in the tribe; the people will become weak because they will be discontented, and finally the Moshome may come and destroy us all."

"But if the Koshare are so powerful," retorted Okoya, "must I not be on my guard?"

"With some of them, to be sure. Beware of Tyope and of the old rogue; they are base and dangerous men. Avoid Shtiranyi, avoid Ture Tihua, Pesana, and the like of them. But your father, Zashue, and Shiape, your grandfather's brother,— do you believe they would forsake you? Mind, boy, even if the Koshare be against you, you are not lost. There is your umo, Topanashka, and he has great weight with the old men, with the council, and with the people. There is your clan, Tanyi, and in fine I and my people are here too." He uttered these words proudly, looking at his nephew encouragingly. But Okoya was not fully reassured; his doubts were not removed. There was one thing yet that he held in reserve for the last, and that was his dread of witchcraft and the suspicion that such a danger threatened him from his own mother. He resolved to tell his friend all, including the scene of the morning and the conclusions he had drawn from it.

"Hayoue," said he, "you are good and wise, much wiser than I; still, listen to me once more."

Louder and nearer sounded the thunder. Hayoue bent over toward Okoya, a close, attentive, sympathizing listener. The young man related everything, — his relations with Mitsha, how he had quarrelled with his mother, and the conclusions at which he had arrived touching his mother's evil designs and practices. At this point Hayoue began to laugh, and laughed till he coughed.

"And you really believe this !" he cried. But at once he grew very serious and even stern. " Motātza, it is not right in you to think thus of your mother. Say Koitza is good ; she is better than most women at the Tyuonyi, far too good for my brother Zashue, and better than I or you. I know her well, and even if there should be witches, which I do not believe — "

A loud thunderpeal caused the mountains to tremble. Hayoue started, shook his head, and muttered, —

"They call loudly. It may be that there are witches. At all events " — he raised his voice again — " if there are such women, your mother does not belong to them. It is not right, brother, for you to think such things of your mother. You have done her a great wrong, for I tell you again she is good and she is your best friend. Where do you belong? Whose blood is yours? Is it your father's? Are the Water people your people? No, Tanyi is your hanutsh. Your mother's clan are your kindred. Mind, satyumishe, our life is in our blood, and it is the blood of her who gave you life that flows in your veins. When you say aught against your mother, you tarnish your own life."

" But why does she not want me to go with Mitsha? "
Okoya asked, and pouted.

" Don't you see why, satyumishe ? Don't you understand
it ? Say knows Tyope ; she mistrusts him and is even afraid
of him. Mitsha is a good girl, and your mother has nothing against her ; but she is her mother's daughter, and that
mother is Tyope's wife. If Mitsha becomes your wife you
will go and live with her, until Tyame hanutsh has a house
ready for Mitsha. You will even have to stay at the home
of Tyope's wife. Now I cannot say that Hannay, the wife
of Tyope, is really bad ; she is not nearly as bad as he, but
then Hannay is silly and allows him to make her his tool.
Everything that concerns her clan — things that he of course
is not entitled to know — she tattles to him ; and she tells him
everything else that she sees, hears, or imagines. I know it
to be so. Now, your mother is afraid lest through Mitsha's
mother, first Mitsha, afterward through her you, might become entangled in the coils of that sand-viper Tyope. For I
tell you, motātza," — his eyes flashed, and he shook his
clenched fist toward the houses of the Eagle clan, — " that
man is a bad man ; he is bad from head to foot, and he
thinks of nothing but injury to others for the sake of his
own benefit."

" But what has Tyope done? How do you know that he
is such a bad man? "

" That's just it. He never acts openly. Like the badger,
after which he is named, he burrows and burrows in darkness and covers up his ways ; and when the earth caves in
beneath those who walk over his trap and they fall, he is
already far away, and looks as innocent and bland as a
badger on top of the ground. But if you follow him, then
he will turn around and snap at you, like a real typope.
Your mother is right in fearing him ; perhaps not so much
on her account as for your sake. You and Mitsha are both

very young, and that man knows how to entrap such little rabbits."

Okoya could not deny the truth of his uncle's speech. He felt that he had wronged his mother, had misinterpreted her motives; and now he was ashamed of himself. Nevertheless Indian nature is exceedingly wary and suspicious in all important matters, and it struck him that Hayoue was trying to dissuade him from his project of union with Mitsha. Knowing the propensities of his gallant uncle in the matter of women, he began to suspect that the latter might wish to estrange him from the girl or frighten him off in order to step into his shoes. So he assumed an air of quiet indifference and said, —

"I think it is better, after all, not to see Mitsha any more." With this he attempted to rise; but Hayoue held him back, and spoke very earnestly, —

"No; it would not be well. You are fit for each other, and you must come together. I will help you all I can."

"Can you help me?" Okoya exclaimed, delightfully surprised.

"Perhaps I can, perhaps not. I will talk to your mother and get her to be in your favour; but there is one thing you must promise me faithfully, and that is to be very, very careful. When you go to the house of Tyope's wife and you are asked about anything, say nothing; reveal nothing in regard to matters of our clans but what you might shout over the housetops with perfect impunity. Otherwise " — and his voice sounded like an impressive warning — " you may do great injury to the tribe."

"But if Mitsha herself inquires of me?"

"You must be wise, brother, wiser than she is; for women are seldom wise, — only forward, curious, and inquisitive. Wisdom " — and the dandy of the Rito shrugged his shoulders — "is a gift to man, never to woman. When you and Mitsha are together alone, be wise. Don't ask her anything that does not concern you; and if she begins to pry into your matters, you will have a right to say to her, 'I don't pry into your affairs, so don't ask me about those of my people.' I am sure that she will let you alone there-after, for Mitsha is a good girl. Nevertheless, be careful, for it is as certain as that the brook runs through here that they will attempt to draw you out. Tyope will say to his wife, 'Find out this or that from him.' He may even tell her why he wants to know it. The woman goes to her daughter, and bids her ask the boy about such and such a thing. But she is careful not to let out why, and that Tyope is at the bottom of the inquiry. The girl suspects nothing wrong and asks you, and you tell her all you know. In this manner precious things get little by little into evil hands, and the end of it is evil. If you will promise me that you will be very cautious, I will speak to Say Koitza such words that she will feel glad to see you and Mitsha become one."

Okoya seized the hand of his friend, breathed on it, then clasped it with both hands, lifting it up to heaven. He could not utter a word; joy and hope deprived him of the power of speech. Hayoue suffered him to go through this ceremony; he also felt glad.

The storm was drawing nearer; dense clouds hovered over the Rito, but they did not notice them. Louder and louder the thunders rolled, and in quicker succession came the peals; they heeded not. From the heights in the west there was a sound of gushing rain; they paid no attention to it.

Hayoue spoke again, —

"Something I have yet to tell you. Although Mitsha may like you, and even if her mother be in your favour, — perhaps as much for her own sake as on her daughter's account," he added, with a scornful smile, — "it is by no means certain that Tyope will give his consent. If you become his tool, if you let him wield you as a hand wields flint or stone, then he will be in your favour; if not, he will not be. He knows very well how precious Mitsha is, and with the aid of her mother and of that mother's clan he hopes to sell his pretty girl to his own best advantage. Unless you are willing to let him use you to grind his corn as a woman grinds it on the yanyi, you have no chance; he will barter away Mitsha to a Navajo, if thereby he reaches his ends."

Okoya started, horrified. "Is Tyope as bad as that?" he asked.

"Do you recollect Nacaytzusle, the savage stranger boy?" Hayoue inquired in return.

"I do; but he has left us."

"It does not matter; for to that wild wolf he would rather give Mitsha than let her be your wife. There is no danger of my obtaining her," he added, with a grim smile, "for he hates me like a water-mole. True it is that I, too, detest him as I do a spider."

Okoya felt bewildered.

"Why should he give Mitsha to a Moshome?" he timidly inquired. "What would he gain by it?"

"I don't know; and nobody knows, except perhaps the young Navajo, that fiend. But sure it is, and it bodes no good for us at the Tyuonyi."

A violent crash of thunder was followed by a few drops of rain. Hayoue looked up and said, —

"Kaatsh is coming; let us go."

Both rose and walked toward the caves for shelter. On the high mesa above, the wind roared through the timber; in the valley, it was yet quiet. Lightning flashed through the clouds. Hayoue stood still, grasped the arm of his companion, and pointed at the southern heights.

" If you ever go up there," he warned, " be very careful."
Okoya failed to understand, and only stared.

" Be careful," the other insisted, " and if possible never
go alone." He turned, and Okoya followed. What he had
heard and learned went beyond his comprehension.

Ere they could reach the caves a fiery dart shot from the
clouds that shrouded the mountain-crests; it sped across the
sky and buried itself in the forest above the Rito. A clink-
ing and crackling followed, as if a mass of scoria were shattered, then a deafening peal shook the cliffs to the very
foundations. A strong gust of wind swept down the gorge.
It caused the tall pines to shake, and the shrubbery surged
in the blast. In the nooks and angles of the cliffs the wind
whirled, raising clouds of dust and sand. Raindrops began
to fall, large and sparse at first, afterward smaller but thick
and fast. The first rain of the season poured down upon
the Rito de los Frijoles.

CHAPTER VIII.

SHOTAYE had taken no part in the great dance, and no one had missed her. It was known that whenever the Koshare appeared in public she was certain to stay at home. In point of fact she seldom left her cell, unless it was to ascend one of the mesas for the purpose of gathering medicinal heros. Shotaye enjoyed the reputation of being a strange and even mysterious being; and so long as her services were not absolutely required, nobody cared to intrude upon her. Nevertheless, she often received visitors of the male sex. She despised men most thoroughly, but accepted their attentions if profitable.

On the day following the ayash tyucotz Shotaye left her cave in quest of vegetable medicaments. We have seen how she met Okoya, and how they greeted one another. The boy's sullen manner amused her; she attributed his morose ways to the effects of an over-lively night. Onward she went, down to the edge of the brook, then turned to the right up the course of the streamlet. That the skies threatened to become overcast and that rain might overtake her during the day mattered little. Whenever the Indian is bent upon the performance of some task, sunshine or rain, moonlight or snow, are matters of indifference. Shotaye strolled on regardless of things above or below. People were of as little interest to her as the clouds. The latter could do her errand no harm, and that errand every body might know if they chose to follow her.

Wandering up the gorge of the Rito and along its northern limit, the woman soon reached the upper part, where
the cliffs crowd the water's edge, where the southern slopes
become more rugged and the valley terminates. There a
series of gigantic steps, formed by high and beetling rocks,
closes the Rito to the west. Down that mass of ledges the
brook trickles from its source, and a trail, formerly much
used by the Navajos on their raids, creeps up, meandering
over and between crags, ledges, and shelves of bare rock.
This trail was seldom trodden at that time, and then only
by armed men, for it was regarded as dangerous. Notwithstanding the proximity of the settlement at the Rito,
the Navajos — Dinne, or Moshome — lurked here quite
often, and many an unfortunate had lost his life while
ascending the trail alone.

Shotaye was therefore travelling an exceedingly hazardous
road, but she did not think of danger. Many a time before had she clambered up and down this rocky labyrinth,
and while the Dinne fairly swarmed, nothing had ever
happened to her. It is true that she was exceedingly wary,
and had in her innumerable excursions gathered quite as
much knowledge of the tricks of war as the most experienced scout, so that she felt almost intuitively the approach
of danger. She had gradually become imbued with the
idea that she was invulnerable. To-day, therefore, she
moved along this dangerous trail with the greatest apparent *nonchalance*. Furthermore her thoughts so completely
absorbed her that while ascending from the level of the
Rito she unconsciously went on thinking of nothing else
but of what Say Koitza had told her in the cave, and of
the plans for relief which she had begun to devise, or at
least to revolve in her mind.

The trail is not only rough and long, it is very steep in
places : and the woman stopped for rest, sitting on a ledge

of rocks. Below her the vale was no longer visible ; a dark chasm yawned at her feet ; out of it the cliffs of the Tyuonyi rose like the heads of giants.

One more difficult stretch had to be overcome before Shotaye could reach the timber crowning the plateau on the northern cliffs of the Rito. Massive benches or ledges, abrupt and high, seemed to render farther ascent impracticable. But Shotaye kept on after a short stop without the slightest hesitation. The trail wound its way upward. It crept from rocky step to rocky step, led her from crags to narrow bands skirting dizzy cliffs, until she came to a level where the timber of the northern mesa was easily reached. Once in the shade of pines she looked around ; the original object of her expedition returned to her mind, and she scanned with particular care the underbrush in hope of finding there the herbs on which she based the efficacy of her cures. It thundered audibly, but that was nothing to her.

There, close to a juniper-bush, grew one of the coveted plants. She went to it, knelt down, and began to pull it up by the roots.

Suddenly she felt both of her upper arms seized with irresistible power. Her body was jerked backward. Ere she could think of resistance, she was lying on the ground. Not a shriek, however, escaped her mouth, for although surprised, the woman had presence of mind enough to think that either Tyope or some Navajo must have attacked her. In either case it was useless to scream, for in either case she was lost. As soon however as she was able to glance at her captor her worst fears were dispelled.

The man, or being, whatever he might be, loosened his grip and stood erect. He looked down into her face and grinned. That grin did not in the least beautify his already horrible features. The creature was indeed a man, but so disfigured by paint and accoutrements that any one unaccustomed to the appearance of Indian warriors in full dress must necessarily have taken him for some fiend or demon from the nether world. He was of robust build, his muscular chest was naked to the waist, a kilt of deer-hide covered his thighs, and his feet rested on small hoops laid horizontally and tied to them like sandals. Face and body were painted with a black metallic powder; under each eye there was a red dash. Out of this sinister face the eyes gleamed like living coals; and the smile, though intended for a friendly token, appeared more like a beastly leer. A close-fitting cap covered the skull to the ears, giving it the appearance of ghastly baldness. From under this protection coarse locks of black hair protruded.

Shotaye looked up at the monster, and, strange to say, returned his horrid grin with a smile and with encouraging winks. But the man did not move; he only let go her arms. So she rose. Thereupon he touched her right arm with his left hand, pointed at himself with the right, and uttered in a strange dialect, "Tehua." Afterward he pointed at her, adding, "tema quio," and accompanied these words by most significant gestures.

Shotaye did not understand the language, but the signs were clear to her.

"Koitza," she replied, imitating his motions; "Tehua hachshtze;" and with a wink, "amoshko."

The Indian shook his head; he dropped the arm of the woman, made with both hands the motion of stringing a bow, and exclaimed,—

"Uan save." Grasping the war-club that hung from his wrist he struck two or three blows with it at random, repeated the words " uan save," and looked askance.

This was beyond Shotaye's powers of comprehension. She again pointed at herself, saying,—

"Tyuonyi koitza," then in the direction of the Rito,

made the gesture-sign for killing, and looked at the stranger inquiringly and with an anxious face.

Now the Indian understood her. His eyes sparkled; he shook his head emphatically, uttering, —

"Nyo nyo tema, uan save, uan save;" at the same time he pointed to the west and brandished his war-club.

It became clear to the woman that the warrior was on an expedition against the Navajos, and not after the scalps of her own people; but it was equally plain to her that, being on the war-path, any kind of enjoyment was prohibited to him. This was a disappointment, and the strange dialogue came therefore to a stand-still. Each eyed the other in silence. All at once the stranger stepped up to her, and extending his arms to the west, asked, —

"Uan save?"

She shrugged her shoulders in silence.

"Quio," he said now, and grasped her hand; "tupoge," pointing toward the Rito. "Quio," he beckoned her to go with him. "Puye," waving his hand to the north. Lastly he grinned and whispered, "cuinda?"

There was no possibility of misunderstanding the smile and the motions, although the words, of course, were beyond Shotaye's comprehension. In return she pointed to the west again, made the conventional sign for night and sleep, and began to count her fingers. As she bent the eighth digit the Tehua stopped her, held up every finger of the right hand and three of the left, described, as if in confirmation eight times, an arch from east to west, and concluded by pointing to the north, exclaiming very emphatically, —

"Puye!" He looked at her and laughed aloud, as the Indian does when he feels delighted, pressed both hands against his chest, and uttered proudly, —

"Cayamo."

"Shotaye," she eagerly replied.

The black-painted hero burst out in immoderate laughter.

"Shotaye, Shotaye," he repeated, caught hold of one of her hands, caressed his chest with it, and danced about merrily, exclaiming, —

"Cuindae, Cayamo, cuindae, Shotaye, cuinda!" He counted the number eight several times, and then suddenly bent down. One of his sandals had become loose.

These sandals consisted, as mentioned before, of wooden hoops covered by strips of rabbit-skin and tied to the naked foot with bands of the same material. The wearer stood on them as on wheels lying flat on the ground; he was able to walk and even to run at a moderate speed, and the prints which he made, being circular, gave a pursuing enemy no clew to the direction of his going or coming.

While the man was stooping and fastening the leather thongs, Shotaye scanned his appearance thoroughly. She perceived on his back, aside from a bow and the usual quiver filled with war-arrows, a shield. The painting on that shield she examined with particular care. The target was painted white, with a black rim; and in the centre was a green crescent, with four red crosses. Such figures have no heraldic signification; they are but the creation of fancy or taste, and recall the designs of the ancient Teutons which Tacitus describes, "Scuta tantum lectissimis coloribus distinguunt."

Shotaye evidently took an interest in the stranger. He, on the other hand, looked up to her from time to time with a terrific grin that was intended for a sweet smile. As often as he turned his face toward her she sought to decipher his real features, which the war-paint rendered utterly unrecognizable.

At last the sandal was fastened again, and the Tehua stood erect. He waved his hand to the west and north, repeated the words, " Cayamo, cuinda," and placed a finger on his lips. She nodded, raised eight fingers, softly uttered " raua, raua, Shotaye," and pointed to the north also. Thereupon he moved away stealthily ; but before disappearing in the timber, he turned around once more and waved his hand northward. The woman replied with affirmative nods, and after his form had disappeared she also turned to go. Her eyes sparkled ; a gleam of intense satisfaction illumined her features, as with head erect and heedless of the plants she had come to gather, she penetrated deeper into the forest. She now went due east, in a direction opposite to the one the Tehua had taken.

This had been a very remarkable meeting indeed. More than ever, Shotaye believed that she was invulnerable. The Queres of the Rito and the Tehuas, living north of them on the other side of savage mountain-fastnesses, and more than a day's journey distant, were not always on the best of terms. There was no regular intercourse between the tribes, for the speech of one differed from that of the other. Barter and traffic took place at long intervals ; but as not a soul at the Tyuonyi spoke Tehua, and no one at the Puye understood Queres, such attempts at commercial intercourse usually terminated in a fracas, in bloodshed even, and the party offended sought to make things even afterward by waylaying and murdering such of the other side as might chance to wander in the neighbourhood of their abodes. Actual warfare had taken place between the tribes within the time of Shotaye's recollection, and engagements were fought ; one party got worsted and ran home, the other went home, too, and that settled the matter for the time being. It was, therefore, not at all safe for an Indian from the Rito to meet one from the Puye, and *vice versa.* Women

made an exception, inasmuch as they were exposed only to
capture and adoption in the tribe to which their captors belonged. Such compulsory adoption was rendered very easy
by the fact that nearly the same clans existed among all the
Pueblos. But the Eagle clan, for instance, which the Queres
called Tyame hanutsh in their dialect, bore in the Tehua
language the name of Tzedoa.

As soon as Shotaye saw into whose hands she had fallen,
she felt completely reassured. Even if she were carried off
a prisoner, it was no misfortune. When, moreover, she discovered that the stranger had not even such an object in
view, but was after the scalp of some Navajo, she experienced
a feeling of delight. When at last the Indian readily understood her suggestions, and went so far as to indicate a day
when she should come to him at the Puye, her gladness
knew no bounds. In the accidental meeting, all her hopes
for relief had been realized. She was now able to save
herself by flight to the other tribe, but enough time was left
her to provide for the safety of her companion in peril.

She had no hope or thought of becoming the wife of her
new acquaintance. He was probably married ; but marriage,
as we have seen, was no obstacle to temporary outside friend-
ships. She could take refuge at the Puye without hesitation,
and claim the protection of her warrior. In case she afterward felt like tying herself to one man only, there was no
doubt in her mind that a domestic animal of the *genus* husband could easily be found. How often could she have been
married at the Rito, had the men not looked upon her as a
witch !

The friend whom she had now secured among the Tehuas
called himself Cayamo. Thus much she had guessed, and
guessed rightly. But would she be able to recognize him
after his face was washed and the military undress exchanged for that of civil life? Never mind, she had noted

the paintings on his shield, and that was enough. There
are no two shields alike in one village ; and by uttering the
name Cayamo and describing the white escutcheon with a
green crescent and four red crosses — a thing easy for Indian
sign-language — she could not fail to identify him. That
Cayamo would recognize her and acknowledge her acquaintance she did not doubt for a moment. She even
hoped to meet him half way on the trail to the village of his
tribe, provided the Navajos did not kill the hero. While
she sincerely hoped that he would return safe and in possession of many scalps, there was still a possibility of his own
scalp being taken by the enemy. The Navajos were very
cunning, and their arrows were tipped with very sharp flint.
With all her feelings for her knight, and the reliance she
placed on his broad shoulders, heavy neck, strong arms,
and well-turned legs, accidents remained possible. In case
Cayamo should never return to his native village, what
then? Well, he was not the only man among the Tehuas,
and that consoled her.

There seemed to be but one dark point in the otherwise
bright outlook. Would she have time to put her plans in
execution? Would the Koshare, would Tyope, leave her
sufficient respite? Things might have taken place during
and after the dance that changed the face of matters and
precipitated them beyond remedy. In case, for instance,
that the Delight Makers had overturned Say's household as
they were wont to overturn others, and had discovered the
feathers, was not all hope gone? Shotaye suddenly recollected how Okoya had greeted her that morning, — how surly
his glance, how gruff and unfriendly his call. Was that significant? Still, if the secret had been disclosed, there would
surely have been some noise about it the night before. On
the other hand, it might be that the council had the case in
hand and preferred not to make anything public for the

present. What if the council were in deliberation at the very moment, discussing her fate and that of her accomplice? Would it not be safer, instead of returning to the Rito, to follow the tracks of her new friend, Cayamo, and join him on his dangerous errand?

Yes, it would have been safer, provided Cayamo would have tolerated the companionship of a woman. But this he was not allowed to enjoy, and furthermore, what would then become of that accomplice of hers? The latter thought staggered her.

Shotaye was a very strange woman. She was heartless, cold-blooded, merciless, remorseless, in everything that concerned her relations to others. One person only she excepted in her selfish calculations, and that was her accomplice and victim, Say Koitza. Happen what might, she could not forsake Say. She must at all hazards go back to the Tyuonyi, call at her house, and find out from her whether or not anything had occurred that might jeopardize her plans and designs. In case matters were unchanged, she intended to tell her friend the occurrence of the day, giving her at the same time directions for the future.

Shotaye quickened her step, for the road was long. It was not advisable to return by the trail she had taken in coming, for she needed a pretext for running into the abode of Say Koitza as if by chance. At last she noticed the change in the weather and the approaching shower, and thought it a good plan to regulate her gait so as to reach the valley and the big house when the storm broke. She might then seek shelter under her friend's roof and avoid suspicion.

Crashing thunder roared in the high Sierra, and as Shotaye looked around she saw the rain-streaks that swept down on the mesas in advance of the shower. The Sierra de la Jara had vanished in the clouds, and gray fleeces

whirled about the flanks of the Sierra de San Miguel. She
stood on the brink above the eastern end of the Rito, and be
gan to descend over boulders and crags, and through bushes.
Only a part of the valley was visible; in the corn-fields not
a living soul appeared. Faster and faster Shotaye ran, regardless of rocks and shrubbery. The western mountains
were completely shrouded, lightning tore the clouds, thunder
bellowed nearer and stronger. At last she reached the
bottom and turned toward the houses, panting, perspiring,
but untired. As she passed the new house of the Corn
clan, the first angry blast of the storm met her, and she had
to stop. It filled her with lively satisfaction, however, to
see how accurately she had regulated her movements. She
might get into the big house almost unnoticed, for the rain
began to fall.

At the moment when Hayoue and Okoya found shelter
in the caves of the Water clan, Shotaye dashed through
the gangway of the building. A tremendous shower was
falling, and as soon as she entered the court she was
drenched from head to foot, to the great delight of those
who, well protected themselves, were standing in the doorways of their quarters. One single voice called to her
to come in, but she took no notice of it. Blinded by the
torrents of falling water, she groped her way along the walls,
and finally stumbled into the open door of Say Koitza's
home. Not a single thread of her scanty clothing was dry;
her hair, soaked and dripping, clung to her forehead and
cheeks as if glued to the skin; water filled her eyes, nostrils, and ears. She removed the hair from her brow, shook
herself, coughed, sneezed, and looked around. The room
was empty, but in the inner cell a fire crackled on the
hearth; and Say came out. At the sight of her friend she
burst into a hearty laugh, and asked, —

"Where do you come from?"

"Tziro kauash." Shotaye coughed, then in a whisper she inquired, —

"Are you alone?"

Say's brow clouded, and a deadly pang seized her. What meant this query, this call so unusual, so mysterious? In a low, hollow tone she replied, —

"We are alone," and turned back into the kitchen. Her friend's question sounded like a prelude to dismal tidings.

Both women squatted close to the fire. Not a word was spoken. The new-comer was busy drying herself, and the mistress of the house was struck by her rather cheerful looks. Possibly her sad presentiment was wrong. It was almost impossible to talk, except in a very loud tone ; for the rain fairly roared, peals of thunder followed each other in quick succession, flashes of yellow lightning quivered outside of the little port-hole. The room itself was very dark.

How often had the two women sat here years ago in anxious doubt, but hopeful at last ! How often had Say Koitza complained to her friend on this very spot, — complained of her illness, of the sad outlook before her ; and when she began to recuperate how often she told Shotaye about her plans for the future. Now that future had come, and in what shape !

The roaring outside diminished gradually, the thunder sounded more remote. Through the roof of mud and brush rivulets of water began to burst, forming little puddles on the mud floor and dripping on the heads of the two women. Shotaye took no notice of it, but Say moved to avoid the moisture. The roof seemed a sieve, the floor became a lagune.

Shotaye inquired, —

"Have the Koshare been here?"

"They have," the other said, "and they turned every-thing upside down, but found nothing."

Shotaye drew a long breath, exclaiming, —

"Then everything is right, all right; and you are safe!"

But the wife of Zashue Tihua shook her head mournfully. "No, sa tao," she replied, "it cannot save me. I am lost, lost beyond hope."

"Rest easy, sister. Believe me," the medicine-woman assured her, "you are saved; they can do you no harm."

It rained softly in the court-yard; inside of the room it went on, pat, pat, pat, pat, dripping through the ceiling.

Shotaye resumed the conversation.

"Speak, sa tao," she said; "speak, and tell me what you think. Why is it that you still believe that bad men will be able to do you harm? Don't you know, sister, that you are safe from them now, and that they cannot injure you any more?"

Say Koitza shook her head gloomily and replied, pointing to her ear and eye, —

"Sanaya, what the ear hears and the eye sees, the heart must fain believe."

"Then speak to me; tell me, sa uishe, what it is that your ear has heard, your eye has seen, that makes your heart so sad." The woman spoke softly, entreatingly, as if she was soothing a sick child. But the object of her sympathy sighed, and continued, in the same tone of utter despondency, —

"Sister, had you been present at the ayash tyucotz, when all the people danced and sang, your eyes would have seen what the heart could not approve. I saw my son Okoya Tihua, the child of Tanyi hanutsh, dancing beside Mitsha Koitza, the girl from Tyame; and she is the daughter of our base enemy."

"Is that all that causes you trouble, koya?" Shotaye very placidly asked.

"Listen to me further, yaya," Say entreated. "This

morning I took the boy to task for it, and then I found out
that Mitsha is near to him, — nearer than his own mother.
I discovered that he goes to see her, and thus gets to the
house of the woman of whom they say that she is Tyope's
ear and eye, tongue and mouth. What do you say to that,
sa tao ? "

Shotaye smiled. " Have you ever spoken to Mitsha ? "

" Never ! " exclaimed Say. " How could I speak to one
whose mother is a sand-viper, and whose father a carrion
crow ? "

" Is that all ? "

" You know," Say cried, " how mean Tyope is ! If my
child goes to see his child, is it not easy for the young serpent to ask this and that of my son ? Then she will go
and tell the old sand-viper, her mother, who will whisper it
to Tyope himself. Don't you see it, sister ? "

The argument was forcible, and Shotaye felt the truth of
it. The other proceeded, —

" Okoya may have been going with the girl for a long
while ; and I knew nothing of it. Have you found out,
sister," — she leaned forward and looked at her guest
with a very earnest expression, — " how the Koshare have
learned about the owl's feathers in my house ? "

The other shook her head and shrugged her shoulders.

" Neither have I," continued Say ; " but might not
Okoya — " The hand of her friend closed her lips.

" Hush ! " cried the medicine-woman, imperatively ;
" speak not, believe not, think not, such a thing ! Okoya
is good ; I, too, know the boy. He will never do what
you suspect."

But Say was too excited to listen to her. She drew
Shotaye's hand away from her mouth and exclaimed, —

" Remember that it is but a short time that the Koshare
have known about the feathers."

" And remember, you, that Okoya is of your own blood ! "

" He is young, and the makatza has great power over him, for he likes her. When Zashue " — her voice trembled and she turned her face away with a suppressed sigh — " came to me and I went to him, he often told me things about your people, — things that your hanutsh would not have liked, had they known that I knew of them."

" Hush ! I tell you again. Hush, koitza ! " the other commanded. " Hush ! or I will never listen to you any more. You loathe your own flesh, the very entrails that have given birth to the motātza ! I tell you again, Okoya is good. He is far better than his father ! Thus much I know, and know it well." She looked hard at the wife of Zashue, while her lips disdainfully curled. Say cast her eyes to the ground ; she did not care to learn about her husband's outside affairs.

It was very still in the dark room. Even the rain was scarcely heard ; and from the ceiling it dripped in one place only, — the very spot where the owl's feathers had lain buried. It seemed as if the waters from heaven were eager to assist in obliterating every trace of the fatal tuft. Shotaye turned away from her friend indignantly ; the mere thought of a mother accusing her child, and such a son as Okoya, was revolting to her. Say hung her head and pouted ; and yet she felt that Shotaye was right, after all. And then it was so gratifying to hear from Shotaye's own lips how good her son was.

" Sanaya," she asked after a while, timidly, " tell me for what you came."

" No," the other curtly answered.

Say started. " Be not angry with me," she pleaded. " I do not mean anything wrong."

" And yet you slander your best child."

Say Koitza began to sob.

Shotaye continued, angrily, —

"You may well weep! Whoever speaks ill of his own blood, as you do, ought to be sad and shed tears forever. Listen to me, koitza. Okoya is good; he will not betray anybody, and least of all his mother. And hear my words, — Mitsha also is good; as good as her father is bad, as wise as her mother is foolish. Even if Okoya had found the feathers and had told makatza of it, she would keep it to herself, and the secret would lie buried within her heart as deep as if it rested beneath the nethermost rock on which the Tetilla stands. And in the end let me tell you," — she raised her head defiantly and her eyes flashed, — "if Okoya likes the girl and she wants him, they are sure to come together. You cannot prevent it; neither can Tyope, the tapop, the Hotshanyi, — not even the whole tribe! Those on high hold the paths of our lives; they alone can do and undo, make and unmake."

Say wept no more. She was convinced, and lifted her eyes again.

"Mother," — it was Shyuote's voice which called into the outer room from the court-yard, — "mother, come out and look at the fine rainbow." With this he dashed into the inner door and stood there, the very incarnation of dirt. He had been playing at Delight Makers in the mud-puddles outside with some of his comrades, and was covered with splashes of mud from head to foot. Say bounded from her seat and pushed back the forward youngster.

"Who is with you, sanaya?" he inquired, while retreating.

"Nobody, you water-mole! I want to be alone. I have no time to look at your rainbow. Get away!" and she hustled him outside and quickly returned to the kitchen.

But Shyuote, not satisfied with his mother's statement, rushed to the port-hole to see for himself. This Sho· taye had expected; and as soon as his dirty face dark· ened the opening, it received a splash of muddy rain-watei that caused the boy to desist from further prying.

After Say had resumed her seat by the hearth, Shotaye bent toward her and whispered, —

"Mark me, the Shiuana are with us; the rainbow stands in the skies. Those Above know that what I speak to you is the truth." Okoya's mother nodded; she was fully convinced.

The cave-dweller took up the former subject again.

"Do not misunderstand me, sister," she said; "I do not say that it is well that Okoya should go to the house of the girl's mother. There is danger in it. But your son is careful and wise, and Mitsha is good, as good as our mother on high. Therefore don't cross his path; let him go as he pleases; and if Mitsha should come to you, be kind to her, for she deserves it. All this, how-ever," — the tone of her voice changed suddenly, — "is not what I came to see you for. What I have to tell you concerns me and you alone. Keep it precious, as pre-cious as the green stone hidden in the heart of the yaya; and whatever may happen, be silent about it, as silent as the mountain. Keep your lips closed against every-body until the time comes when we must speak."

Say nodded eagerly, and Shotaye was fully satisfied with the mute pledge, for she knew that the woman dared not betray her.

"Believe me," she continued, "your life is safe. You will not, you cannot, be harmed."

Say Koitza looked at her in surprise; she could not realize the truth of these hopeful tidings.

"They found nothing in your house," resumed the other,

" because, I presume, you removed the feathers in time, and in this you were wise. If Tyope says that he saw you holding owl's feathers in your hands, and you have not kept them, who can speak against you at the council? Rest assured of one thing. Tyope is at the bottom of all our troubles, and unless he or somebody else watched you while you buried the hapi at the foot of the beams on which the Koshare go up to their cave, nobody will believe him when he rises against you. Are you sure," she added, "that nobody saw you?"

"They were all up there, so Zashue himself told me."

"Tyope, also?"

"Tyope," Say replied with animation,—"I saw Tyope. He was outside, clinging to the rock on high like a squirrel to a tree. But he could not see me."

"Then, child, you are safe; let them do as they please."

"But if he comes and says, 'I saw Say and Shotaye with black corn, and owl's feathers on it; and I heard them ask of the evil corn to speak to them'?"

" Then everybody will say, 'Shotaye is a witch, Say only her tool; we must punish Shotaye, she must be killed,' and that will be the end of it."

She brought her face so close to that of her friend that the latter, while unable to see her features, clearly felt her breath. The last words of the medicine-woman shocked Say. She stood toward Shotaye almost in the relation of a helpless child, and the thought of seeing her friend exposed to death produced a feeling of dismay and sadness.

"But, sanaya," she asked, "how can they harm you and let me go free? Am I not as guilty as you? What you did, was it not for me, for my good? Why may I not go along if they send you to our mother at Shipapu?"

"Hush, sa uishe," the other retorted. "Do not speak thus. I have led you to do things which those on high do

not like, so I alone must suffer.   Nevertheless " — she laid
her hand on the other's lap — "rest easy; I shall not die."

In her simplicity, Say, when Shotaye mentioned the
probability of her suffering capital punishment, had not
thought of her children and of the consequences that would
arise in case she herself were to share that fate.   She felt
greatly relieved upon hearing the cave-woman speak so
hopefully of her own case, for she bethought herself of those
whom she would leave motherless.   But her curiosity was
raised to the highest pitch.   Eager and anxious to learn
upon what grounds Shotaye based her assurance of safety,
Say nestled close to her side in order not to lose a syllable
of the talk.   It was necessary, for Shotaye proceeded in a
slow solemn whisper, —

"Sister, I shall be accused and you will be accused also.
If you are brought before the council, and they ask you
about our doings, deny everything, say no to everything,
except when the black corn is spoken of.   That you may
confess.   They will inquire of you why we used the evil
cobs.   Answer, and mark well my words, that you did not
understand what I was doing, that you only did what I told
you to do.   Lay all the blame on me."

"But it is not true," the little woman objected.

"Never mind, provided you go free."

"They, then, will kill you!"   Say cried.

"Be not concerned about me; I will save myself."

"How can you?"

"That is my secret; still this I will confide to you;"
her whisper became scarcely audible as she added, "I shall
flee!"

"Whither?" gasped Say in surprise.

"To the Tehuas!   But, sa tao, be silent, as silent as the
stone, as quiet as kohaio when in winter he is asleep.   Whatever you may hear, heed it not; what you may see, do not

notice. Deny everything you can deny, and what you have to confess lay on me. Do as I tell you, sa uishe," she insisted, as Say moved uneasily, " and trust to me for the rest."

Shotaye arose, shook her wet garments, and stepped into the outer room. There she turned around once more, and repeated in a low but impressive voice, —

" Sa tao, trust in me, and believe also that Okoya is good, and Mitsha better yet. Be kind to both and be silent."

She stepped into the court-yard, and Say Koitza remained standing in the doorway.

The rain had ceased ; the sky was clear again, all ablaze with the richest golden hues over the crest of the big houses. It was near sunset. Say watched her friend as she went to the entrance ; and as Shotaye's form vanished in the dark passage Okoya emerged from it, coming toward his mother, slowly, shyly, but with a smile on his countenance. That was surely a good omen, and she anticipated the timid " guatzena " with which he was about to greet her by a warm and pleasant " raua opona."

CHAPTER IX.

THE interview between Okoya and Hayoue, which took place at almost the same time that Shotaye fell in with the Tehua Indian on the mesa, had completely changed the mind of Say Koitza's eldest son, and turned his thoughts into another channel. He saw clearly now to what extent he had been led astray by mere imagination, — to what sinister depths his reasoning had carried him. Since Hayoue's talk, Okoya felt like another man. The world of his thoughts, limited as it was still, appeared now in rosy hues, hope-inspiring and encouraging in spite of all obstacles. These obstacles he saw in their true light, and the last warning of Hayoue had made a deep impression. But obstacles clearly understood are half surmounted already, and "threatened people live long."

It is not good for man to be alone. Okoya had felt the truth of it bitterly. Now that he knew that he was not forsaken, he was filled with strength and vigour. On the whole, an Indian is much less exposed to isolation than a white man, for his clan and, in a wider range, his tribe, stand by him against outside danger; but when that danger arises within the narrow circle of constant surroundings there is imminent peril. Okoya had fancied that such peril threatened his own existence, and that he stood alone and unsupported. Now he saw that in any event he would be neither abandoned nor forsaken, and this imparted to his spirit a degree of buoyancy which he had never experienced before.

When he issued from the cave where both his uncle and he had found shelter, the storm was over, and nature had assumed a different aspect. A heavy shower in the mountains of New Mexico is often followed by illuminations of peculiar beauty. So it happened then. The west, where the sun had already descended behind the mountains, was crossed by a series of arches displaying successively from below upward the most resplendent gold, bright orange, green, and finally deep blue colours. In the eastern skies the storm-king hovered still in a mass of inky clouds above the horizon, but these clouds had receded beyond the graceful cone of the Tetilla, which stood out in front of the dark mass of the storm sharply defined, with a rosy hue cast over every detail of its slopes. The air was of wonderful transparency, and every tint of the brilliant heavens above and in the west seemed to reproduce itself with increased intensity, on the dark, cloudy bank in the east, in the dazzling arch of a magnificent rainbow. The rays of the setting sun no longer penetrated the depths of the vale, they only grazed the moisture-dripping tops of the tallest pines, changing them into pyramids of sparkling light.

Okoya looked at the scenery before him, but its beauty was not what caused him to gaze and to smile. The Indian is quite indifferent to the sights of nature, except from the stand-point of strictest and plainest utilitarianism. The rainbow fascinated the boy, not through its brilliancy and the perfection of the arch, but because the rainbow was in his conception Shiuana, and a messenger from Those Above.[1] Where the ends of the luminous arch appear to rest, a message from heaven is said to be deposited. No more favourable token could have greeted him, for although

[1] In the symbolical paintings of the Pueblos, the rainbow is represented usually as a tri-coloured arch with a head and arms at one end and with feet at the other. It is a female deity.

the message was not for him, since the brilliant bow seemed to stand far off from the Rito, still the Shiuana, the spirits, graced the sky with their presence. They appeared clad in the brightest hues, and what is bright and handsome is to the Indian a harbinger of good.

No wonder, therefore, that the boy greeted his mother with a happy face and a pleasant smile. He had passed Shotaye in the entrance, and his salutation to her was widely different from the gruff notice he had taken of her in the morning. When, afterward, he met his mother's gaze and saw how kindly she looked at him, how warm her invitation to come in sounded, his heart bounded with delight, and he obeyed her summons with a deep sigh of relief. His appearance was not very prepossessing, for between the caves and the big house a number of newly created mud-puddles and rivulets had crossed his path. His scanty clothing was profusely bespattered, and broad cakes of mud clung to the soles of his naked feet. Before entering the house he carelessly shook off and scraped away the heaviest flakes, and then went in and sat down on the bundle of skins. Say Koitza offered him no change of clothing; she did not bring a pair of slippers, warm and dry, for his wet feet. No, she simply went into the kitchen and let him alone. Such is the Indian custom. But in the kitchen she began to move about. She was cooking, and that proved beyond a doubt that everything must be right again. After a while she squatted in the inner doorway and inquired, —

"Where were you while it was raining?"

"With Hayoue."

"How late did he come home?" She laughed; he chimed in and answered, —

"Late enough; I had to wait a long time before he came, and so sleepy was he, — as tired and sleepy as a bear in spring."

"Do you know where he spent the night?" The tone of the conversation sounded easy and pleasant.

"I don't know the name of the makatza," — here Okoya laughed again and his mother caught the contagion, — "but she must belong to Oshatsh. He did not say much, for he was tired from yesterday."

"Was she a short, stumpy girl?"

"I don't know. It must have been the same one with whom he was at the dance. I paid no attention to her."

"It is Haatze; I know her. She is a strong girl and tall."

"Do you think he goes to see her?" Okoya asked.

"It may be, and it may be not. Hayoue goes to every one; he is like a fly, — he sits down everywhere and stops nowhere."

Okoya enjoyed hugely his mother's joke. The latter with some hesitancy continued, —

"Does he also visit Mitsha Koitza?"

Okoya bent down to avoid her glance, then he resolutely replied, —

"No."

"Are you sure of it?"

"I am sure." He cast a furtive glance at his mother.

"Did Mitsha tell you?"

Not in the harsh tone of an inquisitor were these words uttered. Say spoke them softly, gently; and Okoya was comforted. He was moved by the question.

"No," he replied in the same manner; "Hayoue spoke to me about it."

Say felt a decided relief. It was clear to her now where Okoya had spent the day, and how he had spent it. She liked her husband's younger brother and trusted him. Although very fond of the other sex, Hayoue was still honest and trustworthy in everything else. Her son had evidently spoken to his uncle about Mitsha, and in Say's estimation he could not have chosen a better person in whom to confide.   Hayoue, she knew, harboured toward Tyope sentiments akin to her own.   His advice to Okoya must therefore have been sound.   On the other hand she was herself, since the talk with Shotaye, greatly drawn toward Mitsha.   This made her anxious to find out what Hayoue thought of the girl.   So she put the direct question, —

"You spoke with your nashtio about Mitsha?"

"I did."

"What says he of the makatza?"

Had the room been better lighted Say would have seen how flushed Okoya's face became, notwithstanding the tawny colour of his complexion.   The boy saw at once that he had confessed much more than he had intended, — that the secret of his interview of the morning was divulged.   Recede he could not; neither could he conceal his embarrassment.   He began to twist the end of his wrap, and stammered, —

"He says not much."   And then he stared at the doorway with that stolid air which the Indian assumes when he is in trouble.

"Does he speak good or ill?" Say insisted.

"Good," muttered Okoya, casting his eyes to the ground.   The mild, soft smile which played over his mother's features as he uttered the word escaped him. When he raised his eyes again her looks were serious, though not stern.   He was completely bewildered.   What had occurred to cause his mother to speak in this manner?   Had she changed her mind since morning, and why so suddenly?   He had, of course, no thought of attributing to Shotaye and to her influence this surprisingly favourable change, for he did not know the intimate relations existing between her and his mother.   S he remained silent, staring, wrapped in his own musings. His mother looked at him in silence also, but with a half-suppressed smile.

At last she asked,—

"Sa uishe, will you eat?"

"Yes," he replied, considerably relived by this turn in the conversation. He rose and moved briskly toward the entrance to the cooking apartment; but Say held him back.

"Tell me, but tell me the truth; did Hayoue say it was well for you to go with Mitsha?"

Okoya was so embarrassed by this direct query that he could not answer at once. He stood still and hung his head.

"Tell me, child," Say insisted.

"He said"—the words were scarcely audible—"that it was well."

"Did he also say it was good for you to listen to the words of Tyope and his woman?"

Now light began to dawn upon the boy. He felt a presentiment of something favourable. "No," he exclaimed, "he said that I must beware of Tyope and of his koitza; but that Mitsha I could trust."

"Then it is well, sa uishe," replied the mother; "come in and eat."

Okoya could hardly believe his senses. Had his mother really said, "It is well?" Was it possible that she was satisfied and in sympathy with his feeling toward Mitsha? Such was his surprise that he performed his prayers before squatting down to the meal without a thought of the ko-pishtai, to whom he scattered crumbs mechanically. He forgot to eat, and stared like a blind man with eyes wide open, heedless of the food, heedless of everything around him.

"Eat," said Say to him. Twice she repeated the invi·
tation ere he came to himself and reached out for the first
morsel. Aware of his mute astonishment and conscious of
his perplexity, his mother finally asked, —

"What is the matter with you, motātza?"

He merely shook his head and stared.

Very few young Indians in Okoya's condition would have
placed so much stress on their mother's consent or dissent.
All or nearly all of them would simply have left the old
home and would have joined their betrothed at her mother's
house; and only the clan, and not the family, could have
interfered with their action. In the case of Okoya it was
different, and unusual circumstances complicated the matter.
Mitsha's clan was that of Topanashka, his own maternal
grandfather; and if he spoke against the union matters
would be desperate. His mother, therefore, held the key
to the situation, inasmuch as through her both the Eagle
clan, to which Mitsha belonged, and Tanyi hanutsh, his
own consanguine cluster, could be favourably or unfavour-
ably influenced. As things appeared now, all seemed most
promising. Even his mother — who a short time ago had
expressed herself so bitterly against his choice — was now
favourable to it. What could Tyope do under such circumstances? Nothing at all. So the boy reasoned unconsciously; but beside, he felt glad, he felt happy, because
his mother approved of him. He was fond of his mother
at the bottom of his heart, as fond as any Indian can be.

Say Koitza approved his choice. There was no doubt
about it, and still she had not spoken plainly as yet. At
any other time he would have maintained a prudent reserve
and waited his time to inquire. To-day he felt so surprised,
so completely stupefied, that only one course was left him,
and that was to learn her real feelings by asking his mother
directly for an explanation of her inexplicable demeanour.

When, therefore, Say asked again, "What ails you, motātza, why don't you eat?" he turned to her with a heavy sigh, placed both hands on his knees, and replied, —

"I cannot eat until I have asked a question of you. Tell me, yaya, how it is that this morning, when I said to you that I was going with Mitsha Koitza, you grew angry at me, and now you say it is right? Tell me, sanaya, how it comes about that you like the girl in the evening, whereas in the morning she was not precious to you?"

His mother smiled. She sat down beside him, and her face almost touched his own. The glare of the fire illuminated her features, so that their expression became fully visible to him. Then she spoke softly, —

"Umo, have I not often said to you, 'Beware of Tyope'? Is it not so, sa uishe?"

Okoya nodded affirmatively.

"Can you suppose that I should feel easy at heart, if you go to the house where dwells the woman of that man?"

Okoya trembled. This was a discouraging beginning. Had he mistaken his mother's views? In a faltering voice he replied, —

"No."

Say continued, "When for the first time you said, 'Mitsha and I see each other,' I felt afraid. My heart spoke to me and said, Your child is lost; and then sa nashka became angry. This was early in the morning; but afterward, when I was sitting alone here and the Shiuana called loudly above during the storm, it seemed to me as if some kopishtai whispered, 'Mitsha is good, — she is as good as Okoya; she will belong to him, and not to her mother, much less to her father.' And as I was thinking, I heard the kopishtai again, saying to me, 'Okoya is good; he is your child, and Mitsha will become your daughter, for she is of your father's own blood.' And as the kopishtai

thus spoke, the Shiuana thundered louder and more loud.
Then I thought it must be right and good for the motātza
to go to the girl, and I was no longer angry. And then
you came, and I asked you what I wanted to know, and
you told me what Hayoue had said. So it is well, and
thus it shall remain."

The sigh of relief heaved by Okoya at hearing these
words was as sincere as it was deep. He had barely
strength to ask in the meekest manner possible, —

"Then you have nothing against my going to Mitsha?"

"Nothing; I like to see you go, for Mitsha is good
and " — her voice became a whisper — " the Shiuana have
thus disposed it. But " — she spoke louder again — " hear
me, go to Mitsha, and to her alone."

"But I cannot disown her mother and father."

"You need do nothing of the kind unless you wish. Be
pleasant to the man, as behooves you, but be careful.
Never say sanaya is doing this or that, or to-day they speak
so or so at the estufa. If Tyope queries what is your yaya
doing, answer, her usual work. If he inquires about what
is going on in the estufa of Tanyi hanutsh, reply to him,
'Nashtio, I am only a boy, and do not know what the
men talk about.' To Tyope's wife say nothing but what
even Shyuote might hear. To the makatza you can say,
"Let us be together and live for each other and talk as is
right. What concerns your hanutsh shall be hidden from
me, and I will be silent on anything that concerns mine.'
If you will do thus, sa uishe, then you can go to see
Mitsha; and I myself would like to see the girl who is to
become my child."

This was too much for Okoya. He grasped with both
his hands the hand of his mother, carried it to his lips, and
breathed on it. Then he gave back the hand, and said
with an effort,—

"You are good, yaya, and I will do as you say. Hayoue said to me the same things you have."

"Hayoue is a true friend. His tongue is like his heart, and you did right in taking his advice."

A tall figure stepped into the apartment with a shuffling step. His loud greeting, "guatzena," cut off further talk for a moment. Both mother and son, taken by surprise, answered, —

"Raua Ā."

It was Hayoue himself who thus suddenly appeared. He complied with the request to sit down, and afterward with the customary invitation to eat. But he seemed as much surprised as the inmates themselves; for while eating, his glance flitted inquiringly from mother to son, as if he were astonished to see them together. When he had finished, he asked, —

"When will Zashue be here?"

"I do not know," replied Say.

Hayoue turned to his nephew, —

"Okoya, will you let me speak to your yaya alone?" These words he accompanied with a knowing wink at the young man. It amused Okoya to see that his uncle came so decidedly *post festum* in the matter, but he at once rose and went out.

In the court-yard it was still very damp, and hardly anybody was outside of the dwellings; but from the estufas there sounded merry talking, singing, and the beating of drums. Okoya stood a while in the doorway, undecided whether he ought not to go to Mitsha at once. He wavered, but at last the impressions received during the day, especially the warnings about Mitsha's mother, prevailed, and he concluded not to go at this time. He was afraid as yet to cross the threshold of that woman's home. So he crept into the estufa of Tanyi hanutsh, sat down beside the others, and soon joined in the chorus of discordant voices in the everlasting refrain, —

"Ho-ā-ā! Heiti-na! Ho-ā-ā! Heiti-na!"

In the meantime Hayoue had drawn closer to Say in the kitchen, saying, —

"Sister-in-law, I have come to speak to you concerning Okoya."

She motioned to him to remain where he was, and said, half in jest, half in earnest, —

"Stay where you are, I hear you. You talk loud enough for me."

"Rest easy, samān," he replied, with a peal of laughter that fairly shook his tall and slender form. "Have no fear, I am tired out after yesterday. But I must talk to you about the motātza." He patted his knees and looked straight into her face. "Are you aware that your child goes with the child of Tyope?"

"I am," said Say, with a smile.

"What do you think of it?"

"Good," was the simple reply. "And you?"

"Good, yes, in one way, and not good in another."

"What do you think of the girl?" the woman inquired.

"Very, very good!" Hayoue emphatically exclaimed. "But her mother and her father," — he hissed through his teeth and shook his head with every sign of disgust, — "they are very, very bad."

"I think as you do," said Okoya's mother, "and yet I know that the boy is good and the girl is good. Why should they not go together?"

"I say the same, but how comes it that you believe so now?"

"I presume the motātza has told you a different story?" Say suggested, with a smile.

Hayoue nodded.

" I thought differently," she explained, " but now my heart has changed."

" You are right," the young man said approvingly, adding, " but he must avoid the snares which that turkey-buzzard Tyope may set for him, and we must preserve him from them."

" I warned him."

" So have I, and he promised to be wise."

" Had we not better speak to Zashue?" suggested Say Koitza.

Hayoue remained thoughtful for a while ; then he said, —

" I dislike to say aught against my own brother, but in this matter I dislike to speak to him."

"He is Okoya's father," objected Say.

" True, but he is Koshare, and completely under Tyope's influence. Nevertheless do as you like, for you know him better than I do."

" He ought to come soon," Say said, and rose.

She went out. A noise of quarrelling children was approaching the door. Soon she clearly distinguished the voice of Shyuote scolding.

" Come with me, worm ! Go home, frog ! " he yelled, and mournful cries succeeded to his kind invitation. At the same time his young sister, propelled by a violent push of his fist, stumbled into the outer room and grasped the dress of her mother for protection.

" Satyumishe is beating me," whined the little one, glancing anxiously toward the entrance. In the doorway appeared Shyuote himself, a solid lump of mud from head to foot. His black eyes stared out of the dirty coating that covered his face, like living coals. The appearance of his mother put an end to his hostile actions, — he felt uncertain about the manner in which they would be viewed by his parent. Say quickly changed his forebodings into absolute certainty.

"Are you not ashamed of yourself, you big, ugly uak," she scolded, "to beat your poor little sister?"

"She would not come home."

"Neither would you, lazy brat, else you would have been here a long while ago! Do not cry, my heart," — she turned to the weeping child, — "do not weep. He will not hurt you any more, the bad, bad mocking-bird. Weep not." She took the crying child into her arms in order to carry her into the kitchen, but on the way she turned back and called, —

"Shyuote!"

"What do you want," growled the boy, and stumbled after her.

"Do you know where your nashtio is?"

"He is coming."

"Go and tell him to come. Say that Hayoue is here, and that he wants to see him."

"Did I not tell you that he was coming?" muttered the unruly lad. This answer was too much for Hayoue, who until now had been a mere listener. He said in a peculiar tone of command, —

"Will you go or not, you silly, lazy, good-for-nothing whelp! Go at once, or I will lead you where your father is;" and he pretended to rise.

Shyuote had not noticed the presence of his uncle. His sudden appearance upon the scene was to him an unwelcome sight, and he sped away with unusual and commendable alacrity. Hayoue was greatly amused and laughed aloud.

"That urchin," he said, "is more afraid of me than of Zashue and you together. The brat is no good, and will never do for anything but a Koshare. How different is Okoya!"

Say had again squatted near the hearth. She gathered the crying child into her arms. The little girl continued to sob for a while, and at first refused to eat. Finally Say persuaded her to take one of the corn-cakes, and still sobbing, she pushed the greater portion of it gradually into her little mouth. Thus chewing, sobbing, and resting on the lap of her mother, the child forgot all fear, and ultimately forgot herself and fell asleep.

"Umo," Say began again, " I think it is better to speak to Zashue about it. Not that he has anything to do in the matter, but then you know how it is. Sooner or later he must hear of it, and if we tell him first he may perhaps assist us in teaching Okoya and advising him about the future. All the boy needs is counsel, for we cannot prevent him from going to live with the people of Tyame hanutsh with this girl."

" The people of Tyame," Hayoue remarked, " are good. It is only that woman of Tyope's who is bad, and after all she is not all-powerful."

" How would it do," suggested Say, " to call sa nashtio ? "

Hayoue looked at her like one to whom has come a sudden revelation.

" Topanashka, the maseua," he said ; " you are right, koya, this is a wise thought. Nashtio is very wise. He will give us counsel that we can trust, but do you think he is here ? "

" He was in his cell while it rained."

Hayoue rose. " I will go and call him," he said. " He can help us. Zashue listens to the talk of the old man, and what he says goes far with my brother." With this Hayoue, ere Say could interpose a word, went out and left her alone with the sleeping child.

She felt happy. For years past she had not enjoyed the feeling of contentment, of quiet bliss, that filled her now.

It seemed as if the danger that threatened her so direly had vanished. Her thoughts were all with the future of the child whom only a few hours ago she had so bitterly accused. Shotaye had worked wonders.

But it was not the influence of Shotaye alone that produced uch a great change in the mind of Say Koitza. It was he fact that at the same time, and through the unwelcome interruption by Shyuote, the Shiuana — so she believed — had sent her a message confirmatory of the woman's admonition. Say did not, she could not, reason as we should under similar circumstances. The rainbow of whose presence the awkward boy informed her appeared to her, not in the natural order of phenomena, but, in the light of her creed, as a messenger specially sent by one or more of the innumerable spirits which surround man in nature, whose call she had to obey implicitly. This implicit, slavish obedience to signs and tokens of a natural order to which a supernatural origin is assigned, is the Indian's religion. The life of the Indian is therefore merely a succession of religious acts called forth by utterances of what he supposes to be higher powers surrounding him, and accompanying him on every step from the cradle to the grave. The Indian is a child whose life is ruled by a feeling of complete dependence, by a desire to accommodate every action to 'he wills and decrees of countless supernatural beings.

In the eyes of Say Koitza, the whole afternoon appeared how like an uninterrupted chain of dispensations from Those Above. She was, of course, convinced that the rain had come in response to the prayers and ceremonies of yesterday's dance. That same rain had driven Shotaye to shelter under her roof, had given the medicine-woman an opportunity to clear the mind of Say of many a dismal fear, many a distressing apprehension and suspicion. The rainbow, in her eyes, was a token that what the cave-dweller said was true; it was also the messenger through whose agency Okoya, and later on Hayoue, had drifted into her home with cheering tidings. Even Shyuote had arrived at the right moment, in time to be sent after the husband and father. So happy felt Say, that in view of Shyuote's opportune coming, she almost regretted having scolded the boy.

An intense feeling of gratitude toward the powers above filled her heart. Among these powers there are two that appear not so much superior to the rest as more intimately connected with the fate of man, — as more directly influencing his weal and woe. These are the prominent figures of the sun-father and his spouse the moon-mother. It is principally the latter that moves the hearts of men, and with whom mankind is in most constant relations. Say Koitza felt eager to thank the Mother Above for all she had received that day. She went to the recess in the kitchen wall where the yaya, that fabric of snow-white down tied into a graceful bunch of drooping plumage, was carefully stored away, wrapped in a cover of deerskin. She took out the plumage and placed it before her on the floor, scattered sacred meal around it, and whispered a prayer of thanks. Hardly had she replaced it, when the sound of voices approached the outer doorway. It was Zashue and Shyuote, who were coming home together.

Zashue seemed vexed at being called home. He looked around with a scowl, for Hayoue, whom he had expected to meet, was not there.

"Why did you call me, koitza?" he grumbled, "satyumishe is not here. Give me something to eat!" He threw himself down on the floor. Shyuote nestled by his side, proud of being under his father's immediate protection. Zashue said to him, —

"Have you eaten, sa uishe?"

14

" Not yet."

" Why don't you feed Shyuote?" Zashue asked his wife.
'Surely Okoya had his stomach full long ago, whereas this
poor little frog here —"

"This toad, you ought to call him," Say interrupted her
husband, in a tone of indignation. " He has been away
from home all day, as he is wont to be. Besides, when he
came home at last, he beat his little sister. Okoya was
here early, therefore Okoya got what belonged to him."
She placed the food on the floor before her husband, and
proceeded in a dry tone, —

" Hayoue has gone to call sa nashtio. I want the maseua
to hear what we have to say to you."

Zashue was surprised at his wife's manner. She spoke in
a way that betokened more resolution than he was wont to
see her display. But he was in her house, and had to accept the situation. So he fell to eating, careful all the while
to supply his favourite child with the best morsels. At the
close of the meal Hayoue returned, saying, —

" Sa nashtio is coming soon." Turning to his brother he
asked, —

" Where have you been all day, satyumishe?"

" With the naua," was the short reply. " And you?"

" At home ; I felt tired from yesterday."

" And from kenayte !" Zashue taunted, laughing. Say
joined in the laugh.

" I don't ask you where you were last night."

" At home." Say confirmed it.

" Surely?"

" Certainly."

" Then you are better than people say."

" Sh — sh — !" the woman cried, pointing to Shyuote,
" you need not speak thus. Sa uishe," -— she turned to the
boy, — " go to rest."

"I won't!" growled the disobedient child, "I want to hear what you say."

"That is just what you shall not," commanded the woman. "Go out at once. Lie down on the hides."

Even the father became impatient now, for he saw that nothing would be said in the boy's presence. So he ordered him to leave. Slowly and reluctantly Shyuote obeyed; but when his sullen glance accidentally met the eye of Hayoue he accelerated his motions. His uncle was not a favourite of his.

"Well, what do you want? Why did you call me?" This query Zashue negligently addressed to his brother, as if expecting the latter to inform him of the object of the interview. But it was Say Koitza who undertook the task of replying. In earnest and measured tones she said, —

"Umo, we have called and sent for you in order to tell you that Okoya, my child, your son, is going with the girl of Tyope. Now we wish to ascertain what you think of it, and what you have to say."

"Is that all?"

"Okoya is your child as well as mine," Say emphatically stated; "it cannot be immaterial to you whom he selects for his wife."

"I don't bother about that," he yawned. "The motātza is old enough to care for himself. It is his business and yours, koitza. It does not concern me, and still less you," turning to his brother.

"Neither do I take part in it without request from Okoya," answered Hayoue, sharply. "But Okoya has spoken to me about it and begged me to see his mother in his behalf. I have therefore a right to be here and to speak."

"We expect sa nashtio also," the woman remarked.

"Nashtio! Who? Tyope?" Zashue looked at his wife in surprise.

"Tyope!" Say exclaimed, "he shall never cross my threshold. I mean Topanashka; he shall give his speech; him we want and expect."

"In that case you do not need me," replied Zashue, attempting to rise. "I go to my people." Hayoue touched his arm.

"Satyumishe," he said gravely, "it is not well for you to leave us now. We must speak with you more."

"It is none of my business," growled the elder brother.

"And yet you must hear about it, for Mitsha is a daughter of the Koshare."

"She is not Koshare herself, her mother only and Tyame hanutsh are entitled to speak." Zashue was becoming impatient.

"Hachshtze," Say interfered, "I know that you are not fond of Okoya. Still he is good."

"Far better than Shyuote," interjected the younger brother.

She continued, —

"But mark my words; is it right that our child should go to the house where dwells the wife of a man who for a long time past has sought to torment me, who harbours ill-will toward my hanutsh and your hanutsh, and who, notwithstanding that you believe him to be your friend and are more attached to him than you are to your wife and child, is not your friend at all?"

Zashue was visibly impressed by these words of his wife. Was she perhaps aware of the secret motives of the upturning of her household, which he and Tyope had performed yesterday? He could hardly imagine that she could know anything about it, and yet her utterances intimated some occurrence of the past that had opened a wide breach forever between her and Tyope. Might not that occurrence have prompted the latter to his accusation against Say? This was an entirely new idea to him, and, while he felt ashamed of having yielded to Tyope against his own wife, he now began to suspect the real motives which inspired the man in his denunciations. He replied hastily, —

"I am not with Tyope."

"He is your best friend," Hayoue objected.

"That is not true."

"Hachshtze," Say said in a tone of serious reminder, "speak not thus. I know that you and Tyope are good to each other. I know that he gives you advice, and I know too " — her voice rose and grew solemn — " that you have told him many things which neither Tzitz hanutsh nor Tanyi hanutsh like him to know."

"Tyope is wise."

"And he is also very bad," the younger brother exclaimed. This made Zashue angry.

"If he is such a bad man why do you want to throw away Okoya, that jewel," he said with a grin of irony, "on that bad man's daughter? It seems that you have called me in, only in order to slander the best of my brethren. I am Koshare, and will remain Koshare, whether it pleases you, koitza, or not. The motātza here," alluding to Hayoue, "has still less to say about it. He is Cuirana and has his people; I am Koshare and have my people. Okoya may do as he pleases. If he thinks that his father's brother is nearer to him than his father himself, let him believe it forever. Now let me alone; and as to his makatza, do as you please. I will return to my brethren!" He rose angrily and went out.

Hayoue shook his head and looked sad; Say drew a suppressed sigh and stared before her in silence. After a while she rose and fed the fire, and a more vivid glow spread over the room where both sat again motionless, absorbed by their own thoughts.

A shuffling sound was heard outside, a muffled step in the outer room. Then the woman's father entered the kitchen with the usual salutation, spoken in a hoarse voice.

"Guatzena." He sat down near the hearth, where his daughter had placed a deerskin for him.

Holding both hands up to the fire, his quick glance shot from one of those present to the other, scanning the expression of their features. Then he asked quietly, —

"Where is Zashue?"

"He went to the Koshare," Hayoue explained.

"Why did you call me?"

Say answered in a meek, submissive manner, —

"We wished to speak to you, nashtio, for Okoya, my child, has told me something that may be good, although it may also not be good. It is something I like to see, and yet it also makes my heart heavy. He has spoken about it to satyumishe, too," — she nodded at Hayoue, — "before he said anything to me. Therefore Hayoue came to see me, and we thought it would be well to seek your advice. For, umo, you are wise and we are foolish; you are old and we are but children. Therefore listen to our speech kindly, and then open our hearts with your speech as a father should with his children."

The old man was flattered by this address from his daughter, and glanced at Hayoue with the air of one who feels proud of the achievements of his child. The young man, too, bowed in approbation. Topanashka turned to Say, and said in an affable tone, —

"Speak, sa uishe; I am glad to listen."

"Sa nashtio," she began, "Okoya is young, but he is no longer a child. His eyes have seen a girl and that girl has pleased his heart. So he has gone to that girl and may be with her at present. I hold this to be good, umo. What do you think?"

"It is well, and it is good for him and for the tribe," the old man asserted.

"Afterward he came and said, 'Sanaya, I am going with that makatza; does she please you?' I believe that was right also?"

"It was right."

The woman omitted the incident of her quarrel with Okoya as well as her interview with Shotaye, and said, —

"He also went to Hayoue and told him to speak to me for him. Was that right, sa nashtio?"

The old man remained thoughtful for a while, and then declared, —

"It was right."

"Should he not have said to his father, 'sa nashtio, do you speak to the yaya for me'?"

The reply was very positive, —

"No."

"Why not, sa umo?" Hayoue interjected.

"I will explain this to you later on," Topanashka answered. Turning to his daughter again he inquired, —

"Who is the makatza, and to which hanutsh does she belong?"

"She belongs to your people."

"To Tyame? Who is her mother, and what is the name of the girl?"

"She is called Mitsha Koitza; Tyope Tihua is her father, and her mother you know too. Is all that good also?"

The maseua pressed his lips together firmly, energetically, lowered his eyelids, and gazed before him in silence. The others exchanged a rapid glance, and then both looked at the ground, remaining thus in expectation

of the old man's reply. He kept silent for a long while
At last he inquired of the woman, —

"Do you know the child?"

"I have seen her, but have never spoken to her."

"Do you know her?" He turned to Hayoue.

"Why not?" replied Hayoue, with a smile. "I know
everybody who wears a petticoat."

"Have you been to see her?"

"No."

"Never?" Topanashka looked at him suspiciously.

"No!"

"How can you know her, then?"

"As I know all the others, — by meeting them out of
doors, talking, and playing with them. I know them all, —
all!" And the beau of the Rito yawned complacently, and
stretched himself.

"Is she a good girl?" continued Topanashka.

"She is," the youth replied emphatically.

"Does she talk much?"

"No."

"Is she easily angered?"

"That I don't know. I have never teased her."

"Is she a good worker?"

"So they say."

"Good-looking?"

"Raua, raua!" Hayoue exclaimed.

"Tall?"

"Yes."

"Strong?"

"I believe so."

Topanashka became silent again, and both Say and
Hayoue observed the proper decorum by fastening their
glances on the floor in silence. Then the old man raised
his head, and spoke slowly and in solemn tones, —

"It is well; all you have said to me is well, my children. The daughter of my hanutsh is a good girl, she is a handsome girl, she is a strong girl. Therefore she is as a woman ought to be. Okoya is like her; they belong to each other; and it is wise for a son of Tanyi to wed a daughter of Tyame. The body must be as the heart; each must suit the heart and the body of the other, and since the two go with each other it is a sign that they are fitted to live together. But the hearts of men must abide by what Those Above" — he pointed upward — "command, and before we decide we should ascertain how the Shiuana are disposed."

Here Say interrupted him, and suggested, —

"When he was coming to speak to me the rainbow stood in the skies. Is not that a sign that the Shiuana are with my child?"

Topanashka smiled a kind, benignant smile, and said, —

"It is right to think thus, sa uishe, but remember that the rainbow is a messenger to a great many and for many purposes. As long as we have not asked the Shiuana themselves, we cannot say; we do not know whether they approve or not. I shall therefore go to the yaya of our tribe and ask them to pray to Those Above that they may let them know if what we now treat of is good or not. For as long as Pāyatyama himself does not connect the paths of the two young people all our doings are in vain. In the meantime do not hinder Okoya from seeing the girl; and when I come to you with the answer from Those Above, and that answer is favourable, then, Say, go you to the people of the Eagle and say to them, ' My son asks for your daughter in order that your numbers may be increased.' I myself like to see the blood of my children flow in that of mine own."

Hayoue and his sister-in-law looked at each other in

mute admiration at this speech, which to them appeared so wise, so thoroughly appropriate.

Topanashka went on, —

"You have told me that Mitsha is the child of Tyope. That, it is true, is not good. But if Okoya is strong and if Mitsha is true to him what can Tyope do? He belongs to his hanutsh, his daughter to hers; and the people of Tyame have no faith in those of Shyuamo, for they mistrust them. But warn the motātza; tell him to be prudent; for Tyope is cunning, — as cunning as shutzuna and as treacherous as the wildcat, and my grandson is young. But let them go together, for I am glad to see Tyame and Tanyi become one often."

"Ā-ā!" was the admiring and affirmative ejaculation of both his listeners. Every word he had spoken was according to their convictions, and besides, whatever he said was law to them. Hayoue rose, breathed on the hand of the old man, said "tro uashatze, umo," and left. After his departure Topanashka also rose, but before crossing the threshold he whispered to Say, —

"They found nothing?"

"Nothing."

"Was Tyope along?"

"He was."

"In that case they may accuse you as much as they please, they cannot do you any harm."

"But who could have told them?"

"That I do not know and cannot know; but rest easy, you are safe." With these words he left the dwelling and returned to his own abode, where his deaf consort was already asleep. The fire had gone out; it was dark in his humble home; still Topanashka did not go to rest, but sat down in a corner and mused. He felt happy in the thought that Okoya and Mitsha might become united; it caused him pleasure that his grandson should wed a child of his own clan. Still with his strong attachment to the faith, or creed, in which he was born, he would not yield to his own wishes until the will of the higher powers was ascertained. To that end he was resolved to apply to the leading shamans of the tribe. In order, however, that the Shiuana might look favourably upon his request, he determined upon doing penance himself during four consecutive days. Until this was performed he would not even speak to the medicine-men. The self-sacrifice he thus imposed was to be light, and not a formal fast. It limited itself to a much less substantial nourishment, and to a shorter rest during the hours of night.

CHAPTER X.

At the time of which we are speaking, the chief civil officer of the tribe at the Rito, — its tapop, or as he is now called, governor, — was an Indian whose name was Hoshkanyi Tihua.

Hoshkanyi Tihua was a man of small stature; his head was nearly round, or rather pear-shaped, for the lower jaw appeared to be broader than the forehead. The lips were thin and the mouth firmly set, the nose small and aquiline. The eyes had usually a pleasant expression, but when the little man got excited they sparkled in a manner that denoted not merely an irascible temper, but a disposition to become extremely venomous in speech and utterance. Hoshkanyi Tihua was nimble, and a good hunter. He seldom returned from a hunt without a supply of game. On such occasions he was always suitably welcomed by his wife, who suffered him to skin the animal and cut up the body. When that was performed she allowed her husband to go to rest, but not before; for Koay, Hoshkanyi's wife, was not so much his companion in life as his home-tyrant; and however valiant the little fellow might try to appear outside of his home, once under the immediate influence of that home's particular mistress he became as meek as a lamb. Koay was an unusually tall woman for an Indian, — she overtopped her husband by nearly a head; and the result of this anomalous difference in size was that Hoshkanyi felt very much afraid of her. Koay had a temper of her own, besides, which temper she occasionally displayed at the expense of the little tapop's bodily comfort. Among the Pueblo Indians the wife is by no means the slave only of the lord of creation.

Hoshkanyi had somehow or other acquired the reputation of being an experienced warrior. Whether he really deserved that reputation or not was never accurately ascertained. At all events, he was the lucky possessor of one scalp, and that gave him prestige. There is no doubt that he acquired the trophy in a legitimate way; that *is*, he had not stolen it. Once upon a time a war-party of Navajos infested the avenues to the Rito. They succeeded in killing a defenceless Indian, who had wandered from the bottom of the gorge, and whom they found on the mesas somewhere wending his way back to the homes of his tribe. After the fact became known, a party went out to take revenge, and it so happened that there was deep snow, and the murderers could easily be trailed. On the top of what to-day is called the Potrero Viejo the avengers surprised the Navajos fast asleep. It was bitterly cold, and evil tongues affirmed that the Navajo whose scalp Hoshkanyi Tihua brought home had been frozen to death previous to the arrival of the hero from the Tyuonyi. However that may be, our governor returned with one scalp; and he was declared to be manslayer, and henceforth counted among the influential braves of his community.

Hoshkanyi Tihua was by no means silly. He possessed the valuable faculty of keeping his mouth closed and of holding his tongue under circumstances when it would be disadvantageous to him to speak. This faculty had been inculcated after long and earnest training by his great wife. Whenever there was no danger, Hoshkanyi proved very outspoken; but as soon as there was the slightest sign of active opposition he became extremely wise, and shrouded his views in a cloud of dignified gravity.

In addition to these qualities Hoshkanyi was the happy owner of an unlimited amount of personal vanity. His ambition had no definite object, provided some external authority was associated with his person. After having for a long time fulfilled the rather insignificant office of assistant to the governor of the tribe, his ambition at last became gratified with the announcement that after the governor's demise the Hotshanyi, or chief penitent, and his associates had designated him as the incumbent of the office. So Hoshkanyi Tihua rose suddenly to the rank of one of the chief dignitaries of his commonwealth.

The choice thus made by the religious heads of the Queres did not satisfy everybody, but everybody was convinced that Those Above had spoken through the mediums to whose care the relations between mankind and the higher powers were specially committed. Everybody therefore accepted the nomination, and the council confirmed it at once. The majority of the clans opposed Hoshkanyi because he belonged to the Turquoise people, who were rendering themselves obnoxious to many by pretensions which they upheld by means of their number, and by their connection with the leader of the Koshare. The Turquoise clan was beginning to assert in tribal affairs an unusual influence, — one that really amounted to a pressure. Tyame and Tanyi particularly felt this growing power of Shyuamo at the expense of their influence. Of all the less numerous groups, Tzitz hanutsh was almost the only one who took the side of Tanyi under all circumstances, and this was due exclusively to the fact that the marriage of Zashue with Say Koitza bound the two clans together. Topanashka himself was a member of the Eagle clan, and through him the Water clan, feeble in numbers, enjoyed the support not only of Tanyi but also of Tyame hanutsh.

In proposing for the vacant position of tapop a member

of the Turquoise people, the chief penitents had in a measure acted discreetly. They certainly acted very impartially,
or they considered that already one important office, — the
office of maseua, or war-captain, — was held by a member of
one of the most numerous hanutsh, Tyame. It appeared
unwise to them to refuse to as large a cluster as Shyuamo
an adequate representation in the executive powers of the
community. So they chose Hoshkanyi, as a member of the
Turquoise clan, and proposed him for the office of tapop, or
civil chief. That more opposition was not made to this
selection was due to two facts, — first, to the tacit acknowledgment on the part of all that it seemed fair to give Shyuamo a share in the tribal government, and second, to the
equally tacit conviction that Hoshkanyi, while in appearance
a man of determination and perspicacity, was in fact but a
pompous and weak individual, ambitious and vain, and
without the faculty of doing harm. In both these points
public opinion at the Rito was right.

It will be seen from what has been said that there prevailed a strong desire on the part of the chief religious
authorities to preserve a certain equilibrium between the
components of the tribe. That anxiety to maintain an even
balance of power was in itself evidence of danger that this
equilibrium might be disturbed. The great penitents, — or
as they are erroneously called to-day, caciques, — had not
and could not have any clear conception of the condition of
affairs in the government of their people. Men old, even
prematurely old from the effects of the life of constant
abnegation and self-sacrifice to which they had to resign
themselves, excluded from listening to anything that was
or might indicate strife and contention, they knew not what
was going on under cover of apparent harmony. Theoretically and from the stand-point of their duty, which consisted
in praying and suffering for the peace and happiness of the

community, and thus securing these boons by means of more direct intercourse with Those Above, their choice was excellent. Practically, it was the most dangerous step that could have been suggested and carried out.

They did not consider that instead of giving to Shyuamo a legitimate share in the government of the tribe, they virtually gave the Turquoise people a majority. For the latter had already two representatives of great influence. Tyope was delegate to the council, where he represented his clan ; and the Koshare Naua, who also was a member of Shyuamo, not only belonged to the leading councilmen but was one of the religious heads ! By adding Hoshkanyi as tapop it gave the Turquoise clan an unfair preponderance. For while Hoshkanyi was a weak man, — while he was mortally afraid of his inflexibly honest colleague, the maseua Topanashka, he was dependent upon Tyope and upon the chief of the Delight Makers, because both belonged to his clan. He very soon began to display an utter flexibility to the desires of the two last-mentioned individuals, to the disadvantage of those who did not coincide with their views.

This marked preponderance of Shyuamo in tribal affairs aroused apprehensions on the part of the other strong clans; it also caused the greater number of the weaker clusters to gravitate toward the growing element of power held by the Turquoise people. A schism was slowly and imperceptibly preparing itself among the people of the Rito. That schism was not the work of circumstances, it was being systematically prepared by two crafty men, — Tyope and the Koshare Naua.

In working at such a division these two men had in view well-defined objects. Their aim in itself was not absolutely illegitimate, since it foreshadowed what would be an inevitable necessity in the course of time. What rendered their doings reprehensible and positively odious were the means employed to hasten events. Their object was nothing less than to expel a part of the people, for the exclusive benefit of the remainder.

The extent of land that can be cultivated in the gorge of the Rito is small, and the tribe was growing in numbers. The time was sure to come when the crops would no longer be adequate for all. Furthermore, a positive danger threatened the people in their dwellings. The rock, being extremely friable, crumbled constantly; and now and then inhabited caves were falling a prey to the wear and tear of the material in which they had been excavated. As this slow decay was sure to continue, it was logical to expect that room must be found for the houseless outside. Already the Corn clan had been compelled to build a house in the bottom of the valley. All this further tended to curtail the space for agriculture, and rendered a diminution of numbers prospectively imperative.

These facts had been recognized by Tyope, and he had talked with the Koshare Naua about them for some time past. They were the only persons who had thought of them, not so much deploring the necessity arising therefrom in the future as hailing them as welcome pretexts for their immediate personal aims. Neither Tyope nor the Naua had such high ambition as to aspire to a change of the basis of social organization. Neither of them had any conception of government but what was purely tribal, but they both aspired to offices and dignities such as tribal organization alone knows. These seemed unattainable for them as long as there were other powerful clans at the Rito besides their own, whereas in case some of the former were expelled, it would leave vacant and at their disposal the positions which they coveted.

Tyope, for instance, looked forward to the dignity of head

15

war-chief, or maseua; but as long as Topanashka lived he saw no chance for himself. He therefore concocted with the young Navajo the sinister plan of murdering the old man. It was even uncertain, in presence of the two powerful clans of Tanyi and Tyame, whether after the death of Topanashka it would be possible for him to secure the succession. For the chief penitents, who selected officially the new incumbent, while they were in no manner accessible to outside influence, might consider the general tendency of affairs, and for the same reasons that they chose Hoshkanyi Tihua for tapop might determine upon appointing some member of Tanyi or Tyame as maseua. Tyope had foreseen such a contingency, and had therefore suggested to Nacaytzusle the propriety of converting the isolated murder into a butchery of the adult men as far as possible. His suggestion to surprise the Rito while the Koshare were at work in their estufa had a double aim, — in the first place it made it less dangerous for the Navajos, in the second it appointed a time when most of the men of the Turquoise clan were out of reach of an enemy. The blow must then fall upon the males of other clans, for the majority of the Koshare were from the people of Shyuamo. This plan was out of the question since the night when his negotiations with Nacaytzusle had come to such a disastrous termination. But Tyope had laid his wires in other directions also. Seeing that he could not reduce the numbers of the tribe by one fell blow, or that at least his endeavours might not succeed, he was devising in his peculiar underhand way means to create a disunion, and trying to secure for the time of the crisis a commanding position for his own clan.

As he could never have attempted all this alone, he needed an associate, an accomplice. That accomplice he readily found in the old Koshare Naua. In the same manner that Tyope aspired to the position of war-chief, the chief of the Delight Makers was coveting the rank of leading shaman, or medicine-man. Not the dignity of cacique, — for that position entailed too many personal sacrifices, and carried with it a life of seclusion and retirement that presented no redeeming features, — but the office of hishtanyi chayan, or principal medicine-man, was what the Naua desired to obtain. That position did not entail greater priva-tions than the one which the old schemer occupied, but it secured for its incumbent much greater sway over the people, and placed him in the position to exert a degree of influence which was beyond the pale of Koshare magic. The Naua was working toward his end by ways and with means different from those employed by Tyope. His machinations were directed against the religious heads of the tribe, and he persisted in securing for the society of Delight Makers a prominence that lay outside of their real attributes. Therefore Hayoue did not speak amiss when, in his interview with Okoya, he accused the Koshare, and principally their leader, of attempting to usurp functions and rights belonging properly to the main official shamans, and thus secure for themselves undue advantages.

Tyope and the old Naua had found each other, in accordance with the proverb about birds of a feather. Their understanding was perfect, although it had been brought about gradually and without the formality of a conspiracy. Each worked in his own line and with his own means, and neither had any thought of going beyond what the tribal organization could give them. There was no idea of revolutionizing or even reforming the organization. Had one of them entertained such a thought the other would have become his bitterest enemy, for both were deeply imbued with the principles on which rested the existence of the society in which they had been born. All they aspired to was to eliminate a certain number of men or people, in order to secure with greater ease certain advantages. It was the survival of the fittest, as primitive society understands it and as refined society attempts to enact, though with more refined means.

The stumbling-blocks in the path of these intriguers were the chief penitents, — the cacique, or as their titles run, the Hotshanyi, or principal cacique, and his two assistants, the uishtyaka and the shaykatze. These men, selected for the purpose of doing penance for all and thus obtaining readier access to the ear of the immortal ones, were the official keepers of peace among the tribe. For the Indian feels that a house divided against itself cannot stand, and that the maintenance of harmony through a constant appeal to the higher powers is the most important feature in the life of his tribe. To discredit in an underhand way the caciques was the special aim of the Koshare Naua, and to direct the eyes of the people to his own achievements in religious magic, — in one word to place the power of the Koshare and their specific medicine on a higher plane than all that the official penitents might achieve. To do this was a very slow piece of work, and it had to be brought about in such a manner that nobody could suspect his object. But both Tyope and the aged scoundrel were working their plans with the utmost caution, and the religious heads of the tribe had not the slightest suspicion of what was going on against them.

The Tyuonyi, therefore, was quiet on the surface, but there were occasional ripples of that placid brook which earnest and thoughtful observers could not fail to notice. Hayoue, although very young, was one of these observers; but none saw more and penetrated deeper into the real state of affairs than Topanashka. He and the Hishtanyi Chayan, who to some extent was his trusty friend, felt that a tempest was coming. Both saw that the disturbing powers were rooted in the society of the Koshare, that Tyope and the Naua must be the leading spirits. But how and to what ultimate end the machinations were intended escaped their penetration. For the same reason they could not come actively to the relief of the situation, as no overt action had as yet been committed which would justify an official movement against the conspirators.

Topanashka had for several days been keeping the informal fast upon which he had determined for the benefit of his grandson's wooing. It was a warm, pleasant afternoon. Since the rain which followed upon the ayash tyucotz the sky had been blue again as before; the season for daily showers had not yet commenced, and the people were in the corn-patches as busy as possible, improving the bright days in weeding and putting the ground in order. The bottom of the gorge therefore presented an active appearance. Men and women moved about the houses, in and out of the cave-dwellings, and in the fields. From the tasselled corn that grew in these plots a tall figure emerged; it was Topanashka himself, and he directed his steps toward the cliffs at the lower end, where the Turquoise people dwelt. The old man moved as usual with a silent, measured step which would have appeared stately had not his head leaned forward. He was clad in a wrap of unbleached cotton, and a leather belt girded his loins. Around his neck a string of crystals of feldspar was negligently thrown; and a fetich of white alabaster, representing rudely the form of a panther, depended from the necklace hanging upon his breast.

The people of the Turquoise or Shyuamo resided on the lower range of cliffs, and formed the most easterly group of cave-dwellings on the Rito. Here the rocks are no longer absolutely perpendicular; they form steps; and the slope

leading to them is overgrown with shrubbery, except where
erosive action of wind, as well as of water or frost, has
scooped out strange formations in advance of the main
wall. These erosions are mostly regular cones, tent-shaped,
between and behind which open chasms and deep rents
like the one above which, as we recollect, lies the estufa of
the Koshare. Topanashka walked toward the upper part
of the cluster of dwellings of Shyuamo, where the ascending
slope was sparsely covered with brush. In front of one of
the caves sat a woman. She was unusually tall for an
Indian, and neither young nor old. She appeared to be
busy extracting the filaments from shrivelled leaves of the
yucca, which had been dried by roasting, and afterward had
been buried to allow the texture to decay. So engrossed
was the woman by her task that only when the old man
stood by her side, and asked, "Where is the tapop?" did
she notice his presence.

Koay, for it was she, the towering consort of the governor
of the Tyuonyi, did not condescend to reply in words to
the inquiry of the war-captain. She resorted to a lazy
pantomime by gathering her two lips to a snout-like projection and thrusting this protuberance forward in the
direction of the doorway before which she was squatting.
Then she resumed her occupation.

The visitor paid no further attention to the uncivil
woman. He passed in front of her unceremoniously, and
entered the cave. The apartment was like those we have
previously described, with the single difference that it was
better lighted, somewhat larger, and that the household
effects scattered and hung around were of a different character. Implements of warfare, — a bow and a quiver with
arrows, a shield — convex and painted red, with a yellow disk,
and several green lines in the centre, — were suspended from
the wall. The niches contained small vessels of burnt clay

and a few plume-sticks. A low doorway led from this room into another, and beyond that there was even a third cell, so that Hoshkanyi Tihua, the civil chief of the Queres, enjoyed the luxury of occupying three apartments.

Still this was not the dwelling which he commonly inhabited. His wife descended from the Bear clan; and her home, and consequently his also, was higher up the gorge, among the caves belonging to the people of the Bear. But as his father had recently departed this life, and his mother was left alone, she had begged her only son to remain with her until one or the other of her brothers or sisters might be ready to take her in charge, either by moving into her abode or by her going to them. Hoshkanyi, therefore, had temporarily gone to live with his mother, but his portly consort was careful not to let him go alone. They had no children, and she felt constrained to keep an eye upon the little man.

In the room which Topanashka had entered, his executive colleague was sitting on a round piece of wood, a low upright cylinder, whose upper surface was slightly hollowed out. Such were the chairs of the Pueblos in olden times. With the exception of that well-known garment peculiar to Indians and babies, and called breech-clout, the governor's manly form was not concealed by any vestment whatever. But while he evidently thought that at home the necessities of costume might be dispensed with, he had not abandoned the luxuries of ornamentation. He wore on his naked body a necklace of wolves' teeth, ear pendants of black and green stones, and wristbands of red leather. The latter he carried in order to relieve his heart, still heavy under the severe blow that he had experienced through the death of his father.

The tapop was also at work. By means of the well-known fire-drill he was attempting to perforate a diminutive

shell disk and thus transform it into the shell bead so essential to the Indian. So intent was he upon this arduous
task that he failed to notice the coming of Topanashka; and
the latter stood beside him for a little while, an impassive
observer. At last Hoshkanyi Tihua looked up, and the
visitor said to him, —

"Umo, you have sent for me and I have come. But
if you are engaged, or have no time now, I do not mind
returning again."

There was a decided irony in the manner in which the
old man uttered these words, and Hoskanyi felt it. He
rose quickly, gathered a few robes, and spread them on the
ground. In short he was as pleasant and accommodating,
all at once, as he and his wife had been careless in the beginning. Topanashka settled down on the hides, and in
the meantime the woman also entered the room and quite
unceremoniously squatted beside the men. Hoshkanyi
said to her, —

"We have to talk together, the maseua and I." He
fastened on his spouse a look timid and imploring; it was
plain that he did not venture to send her out directly, —
that he was afraid of her. Koay looked at him carelessly,
and said in a very cool manner, —

"I want to hear that talk."

"But I will not allow it," interposed Topanashka; and
his cold, piercing eye rested on the woman's face. She cast
hers to the ground, and he proceeded, —

"As long as you are here, the tapop and I cannot speak."

She lifted her head angrily, with the manifest intention
of rebelling, but as soon as her eyes met the cold, determined glance of the war-chief, she felt a chill, rose, and
left the room. Hoshkanyi Tihua drew a sigh of relief; he
was grateful to his visitor for having so summarily despatched his formidable spouse. Then he said, —

" Umo, I have sent for you because a speech has been spoken here in this house, which belongs to my mother. That speech may be good and it may not be good, and I cared not to tell my thoughts until I had spoken to you, nashtio. The matters of which it treated belong before the council, but I do not know whether to say to you, the nashtio of the Zaashtesh, Call them together, or not." He was manifestly troubled, and fastened an uncertain glance upon the face of the other.

Topanashka very composedly answered, —

" You are as wise as I, umo ; you know what your duties are. Whenever you say to me, Go and call together the council, I shall do it. If you do not tell me to do so, I shall not."

Hoshkanyi moved in his seat ; the reply did not suit him. After some hesitation he continued, —

" I know, father, that you do as the customs of the Zaashtesh require," — he held himself erect with an attempt at pride, for he felt that in the present instance his personality and word represented customs which were law, — " but I do not know that I shall tell you so or not. Do you understand me, umo ? "

" I understand your words, Tapop, but you know that I have only to act, whereas it is your office to speak."

The cool reply exasperated the little man. He retorted sharply, —

" And yet you have often spoken in the council, when your hanutsh wanted something ! "

Topanashka lifted his eyes and gazed fully, calmly, at the other ; he even suppressed a smile.

" Then it is your hanutsh, Shyuamo, that wants something this time ? "

Hoshkanyi felt, as the saying is, very cheap. His secret was out ; and his plan to obtain an expression of opinion from the maseua ere he came to a conclusion himself, a total failure. The latter added in a deprecating way, —

" If you do not know what to do, ask the Hotshanyi. He will give you good advice." This was just what the governor wished to avoid, but he knew that when Topanashka had once expressed his opinion it was useless to attempt to dissuade him.

After an interval of silence the civil chief looked up and said, —

" Come, let us go to the Hotshanyi."

Topanashka thought over this proposal for a moment. " It is well," he at last assented ; " I will go." With this he rose. The governor rose also, but was so embarrassed and excited that he would have run out as he was, in almost complete undress, had not the maseua reminded him by saying,—

"Remember that we are going to the Shiuana," adding, "take some meal along."

"Have you any with you?" inquired Hoshkanyi, with a venomous look. The other responded quietly,—

"I do not need any. You are seeking their advice, not I." That settled the matter.

As both went out, Koay, who had been sitting as close by the doorway as possible, snappishly asked her husband,—

"Where are you going, hachshtze?"

Topanashka took the trouble of satisfying her curiosity by dryly answering,—

"About our own business." The icy look with which he accompanied his retort subdued the woman.

The Hotshanyi, or chief penitent, lived with the people of the Prairie-wolf clan. His abode consisted of two caves on the lower and one on the upper tier. The two officers of the tribe wandered slowly along the cliffs, past the abodes of the Sun clan, Topanashka walking as usual,—erect, with

his head bent slightly forward, — Hoshkanyi with a pompous air, glad to display himself in company with his much
more respected colleague, to whom all the pleasant greetings which the two received on their peregrination were
really directed. When they reached the cave wherein the
cacique resided, Hoshkanyi entered first.

Close to the fireplace, which was one of those primitive
chimneys like the one we have seen in the home of Shotaye,
an old man was seated on the floor. His age was certainly
greater than Topanashka's; he was of middle height, lean
and even emaciated. His eyes were dim, and he received
the greetings of his visitors with an air of indifference or
timidity; it was difficult to determine which. Pointing to
the floor he said, —

"What brings you to my house, children!" and he
coughed a hollow, hectic cough.

The tapop began, —

"We wish — "

"Do not say we," the maseua corrected him, "you wish.
not I."

Hoshkanyi bit his lips and began anew, —

"I and my brother here have come because I want to
ask you something. But if you are at work, grandfather,
then we will go."

"I am not working, sa uishe," said the cacique. "Speak;
I listen. What is it you wish?"

"Can I see the kopishtai?" Hoshkanyi whispered
anxiously.

The eyes of the Hotshanyi brightened. His look suddenly became clear and firm. With surprising alacrity he
rose, as if he had become younger at once. His whole
figure, although bent, attained vigour and elasticity. Before
leaving the cave he looked inquiringly at Topanashka, who
only shook his head and said in a low tone, —

"I have nothing to ask."

The two left the room. The place where Those Above were thought to be accessible to the intercession of man was the cave adjoining, but there was no communication between the two chambers.

Presently the cacique crept back to where they had left Topanashka alone, and Hoshkanyi followed. The former resumed his seat by the hearth, whereas the tapop cowered in front of him. He looked anxiously in the old man's face, and at the same time shot an occasional quick glance over toward the maseua. In a hollow voice the Hotshanyi said,—

"You may speak now, sa uishe; the kopishtai know that you are here."

"Sa umo Hotshanyi," the tapop commenced, "I have listened to a speech. Things have been said to me that concern the tribe." He stopped short and fastened his eyes on the floor.

"This is well," the cacique said encouragingly; "you must hear what the children of Pāyatyama and Sanatyaya are doing; you are their father."

Hoshkanyi sighed, and appeared to be much embarrassed.

"Speak, motātza," urged the old man.

"I don't know what to do," the little man stuttered.

"Have you been asked to do anything?"

"Yes, they have —" He stopped, sighed again, and then proceeded hastily and with an expression of anguish in his face, "Shyuamo hanutsh asks that Tzitz hanutsh — "

The Hotshanyi commanded him to desist.

"Stay, stay, Hoshkanyi Tihua!" he hoarsely exclaimed. "You know that we, the mothers of the tribe, will not listen to anything that divides our children among themselves or that might cause division among them. You ask for advice from me. This advice you shall receive, but

only on things that I can know of and which I dare to
hear. If you speak to me of strife and dispute, I shall not
listen to it. Speak of yourself, not of others."

Topanashka was an attentive listener, but not a muscle in
his face moved; whereas the little tapop was manifestly in
great trouble. He coughed, hemmed and hawed, twisted
his body, moved uneasily in his seat, and at last continued
in a faltering manner, —

"I do not know whether or not I ought to call the
council together."

"Were you asked to do it?"

"Yes."

"Then you must do it; it is your duty," replied the
Hotshanyi. He spoke imperatively, and with remarkable
dignity of manner. Thus the first point was settled. And
the tapop with growing uneasiness proceeded to his next.

"It has been said to me that I should send my brother
here," pointing at Topanashka, "to call together the
fathers. Now is it well to do so, or shall I send the assistant civil chieftain to the men?" Hoshkanyi spoke like a
schoolboy who was delivering a disagreeable message.

The matter in itself seemed of no consequence at all,
but the manner in which the governor spoke and acted
looked extremely suspicious. Both of his listeners became
attentive; the cacique displayed no signs of surprise, but he
looked at the speaker fixedly, and inquired of him, speaking very slowly, —

"Is my brother the maseua willing to go?"

"I have not asked him as yet."

"Then ask him," sternly commanded the old man.

Almost trembling, the tapop turned to Topanashka, who
was sitting immovable, with lips firmly set and sparkling
eyes.

"Will you call the council together, nashtio?"

"No!" exclaimed the maseua.

"You have heard what your brother says," coldly proceeded the cacique; "you know now what you are to do. My brother will not go, and you can only command him if the council orders you to do so. Therefore send the assistant; he is your messenger. Do your duty and nothing else, for it is not good to attempt anything new unless Pāyatyama has so directed." The words were spoken in a tone of solemn warning, and even Topanashka was startled, for never before had he heard the Hotshanyi speak thus. The old man had always been very meek and mild in his utterances, but now his voice sounded almost prophetic. Was he inspired by Those Above? Did the Shiuana speak through him? Was there danger for the tribe?

At all events the conference had come to a close, for the cacique had bent his head, and spoke no more.

"Trouashatze, sa umo," said Topanashka, and left the room. Hoshkanyi followed hurriedly. The cacique took no notice of their departure.

When both men stood outside, Topanashka turned to the tapop coldly, asking, —

"Are you going to call the council?"

"I will," whined the little man.

"For what day?"

"I don't know yet."

"But I want to know," sternly, almost menacingly, insisted the other. "I want to know, for I shall be present!"

"Four days from now," cried Hoshkanyi, trembling.

"What time?"

"I don't know yet. When the moon rises," he added in despair, as the cold, determined gaze of Topanashka met his eye. Without a further word the war-chieftain turned and went off.

Hoshkanyi was utterly annihilated. He had made a total failure, and as he stood there like a child that has just been thoroughly whipped he began to curse the weakness that had caused him to yield to the advice and the demands of Tyope. For it was Tyope who had brought him to act the part in which the unfortunate governor had so disgracefully failed. Tyope, when as representative of the clan Shyuamo he asked the tapop to call together the council for a matter wherein the Turquoise people were interested, had artfully told him that as one of their number it would be better if the maseua would issue the call. He knew very well that this was an innovation; but the deceiver made it apparent that if Topanashka should yield, and commit the desired misstep, the blame would of course fall upon the war-chief, and the civil chief would profit by the other's mistake, and would gain in the opinion of the people at the expense of the maseua.

But Tyope, cunning as he was, had underrated the firmness and perspicacity of Topanashka as much as he had overrated the abilities of Hoshkanyi. As soon as the latter saw the rigidity of his colleague in a matter of duty, he felt completely at sea; he lost sight of everything that Tyope had recommended, tumbled from one mistake to another, and finally exposed himself to grave suspicions. As the popular saying is, he let the cat out of the bag, and made an absolute, miserable fiasco. All this he saw clearly, and he cursed Tyope, and cursed himself for having become his tool. More than that, he trembled when he thought of what Tyope would say, and also what his own energetic wife would call him, and even perhaps do to him, if he went home. For Koay was sure to exact a full report of what had occurred; and to save himself, nothing remained but to tell her lies. This he finally determined upon. But to Tyope he could not lie; to Tyope he must tell the truth:

and then? Hoshkanyi Tihua wended his way home wrapped
in thoughts of a very unsatisfactory nature.

While the governor of the Queres was thus agitated by
unpleasant forebodings, the mind of the war-chief was not
less occupied by gloomy thoughts. Of all the leading men
of the tribe, Topanashka saw perhaps most clearly the sinister machinations of some of the Turquoise people. Still he
had not discovered, and could not even surmise, the real object of their intrigues. Of an intention to divide the tribe
he had no idea. Personal ambition, greed, and thirst for
influence was all he could think of; and he felt sure that
they would not prevail, for to personal ambition the tribal
system afforded little, if any, opportunity. It was manifest
however from what Hoshkanyi had involuntarily divulged,
that the clan Shyuamo intended to press some claim against
the small Water clan, which besides was so distantly located
from the abodes and the lands of the Turquoise that he
could see no just reason for a claim. It was equally impossible for him to imagine the nature of the claim. Quarrels
between clans are always most dangerous for the existence
of a tribe, for disruption and consequent weakening is likely
to result from them. The old man felt the gravest apprehensions; he saw imminent danger for his people; and still
he could not arrive at any conclusion before the threatening
storm had broken. There was no possibility of averting the
peril, for he could not even mention its approach to any
one.

Topanashka was calm and absolutely brave. His life was
nothing to him except as indispensable for the performance
of his duty. He knew long ago that the leaders of the
movement for which the Turquoise people were used as bat-
tering-rams hated him, that he was a thorn in their flesh,
a stone in their crooked paths. If the revelations of Hoshkanyi created deep apprehensions in him, it was out of no

personal fear; in the present instance it was clear that a
trap had been set for the purpose of decoying him into a
false move. It was the first time that anything of the kind
had been attempted; and Topanashka looked upon it as
very serious, not for his individual sake, but because it
showed that it was undertaken jointly with a move that was
sure to bring about internal disturbances, and was probably
a part of that move itself, and because it exhibited a degree
of boldness on the part of the schemers which proved that
their plans were nearly, if not absolutely, mature. A crisis
was near at hand; he saw it, but it could not be prevented.
A deep gloom settled on the heart of the old maseua, and
something like despondency crept over him at times. It
caused him to forget the matter of his grandson's wooing
and his proposed appeal to the Shiuana in behalf of Okoya,
and to look forward to the momentous time, four days hence,
when his mind would become enlightened on the impending danger. All his thoughts were henceforth with the
council and the object for which it was to be held. He
looked forward to it with sadness and even with fear. It
was clear to him that the hour of that council must become
an evil hour in the annals of his people.

CHAPTER XI.

THE four days at the expiration of which the council was to take place were drawing to a close, for it was the night of the fourth, that on which the uuityam was to meet. It was a beautiful night; the full moon shone down into the gorge in its greatest splendour, and only along the cliffs was it possible to walk in the shadow. The air was cool and balmy; not a breeze stirred; and the population of the Rito seemed to enjoy the luminous, still, and refreshing hours that followed upon a warm and busy day. Laughter, singing, shouting, came from the roofs and the vicinity of the houses, as well as from the caves and their approaches. The people felt happy; few if any suspected that a momentous question agitated the minds of some of their number.

Two men were walking along the cliffs toward the group of cave-dwellings which the Prairie-wolf clan inhabited. They hugged the rocks so closely that most of the time their figures disappeared in the inky shadows of projecting or beetling cliffs and pillars. One of these men asked in a low tone, —

" Are you going to the uuityam ? "

" I am," replied the other.

The words were spoken in a tone sufficiently loud to enable any one acquainted with the inhabitants of the Tyuonyi to recognize in the first speaker Tyame Tihua, the delegate or councilman from the Eagle clan, in the other, our old friend Topanashka. After exchanging these few words both continued their walk in silence.

The round chamber in which the meetings of the tribal council were usually held exists to-day as a semicircular indentation in the cliffs, the rudely arched ceiling of which is still covered with a thick coating of soot. The front wall has crumbled long ago. At the time we speak of it was entire, and the apartment formed a nearly circular hall of more than usual size, with a low entrance in front and two small air-holes on each side of the doorway.

As the two men approached the place, they noticed that a number of others were already congregated in front of it, but that no light issued from the interior. It was a sign that the council was not yet assembled, and especially that the religious chiefs had not made their appearance. Those who were present assumed any posture imaginable, provided it gave them comfort. They talked and conversed about very unimportant matters, and laughed and joked. There was no division into separate groups, foreshadowing the drift of opinions and of interests ; for no lobbying was going on. Every one seemed to be as free and easy as in his own home or in the estufa among his companions, and the greatest apparent harmony prevailed. One man only had retired to a rocky recess where he sat aloof from the others in the darkest shadow of the already shadowy spot. It was the old chief of the Delight Makers, the Koshare Naua.

When the last two comers reached the group and offered the usual greeting, the conversation — in which the delegate from Tzitz hanutsh, a short, stout man, and his colleague from Oshatsh had been the loudest participants — came to a sudden stop. The subject of the discussion was not a reason for its abrupt breaking off, for it was merely the all-absorbing topic as to whether two summers ago it had

rained as early as this year. It was out of respect for the
maseua, out of deference to his presence, that the other
clan representatives became silent, all except one. That
one was Tyope, who continued the subject, as if he intended to display greater independence than the rest.
Nevertheless, as no one paid attention to his speech, he felt
at last constrained to drop into silence. Not for a long
time, however, for as if he wished to atone for his lack of
civility he called out to Topanashka, —

"You are late, sa nashtio ! "

"Early enough yet, satyumishe," replied the old man
quietly, and Tyame remarked, —

"Shyuamo dwells nearer to the uuityam than we. The
Turquoise men have everything close at hand, — the tapop,
the place, everything, and everybody. All we have is the
maseua," he added laughing, "and he is very old."

The laughter became general, and Tyope said in a tone
of flattery, —

"Our nashtio is old, but he is still stronger than you,
Tyame. He is also wiser than all of us together. Our
father is very strong, runs like a deer, and his eye is that of
an eagle."

There was something like irony in this speech, but Topanashka took no notice of it. He was looking for the
tapop, a difficult task in the darkness, where a number of
men are grouped in all kinds of postures. Finally he
inquired, —

"Where is Hoshkanyi? "

"Not here," came a reply from several voices.

"And the yaya? "

"Tza yaya," was the negative answer.

"Then we are not too late," said the war-chief, turning
to Tyame. He sat down among the rest, and the talk went
on as before his arrival.

At last the governor came. He offered a short greet‐
ing and received a careless reply. Then he crawled into
the cave, and his assistant followed him. Soon a rustling
noise was heard inside, a grating like that of a drill fol‐
lowed, and everybody outside became silent. The tapop
was starting the council-fire, and he used for the purpose
that venerable implement of primitive times, the fire-drill.
It was a sacred performance, therefore the sudden silence
of all within hearing of the process. Little by little a glim‐
mer of light illuminated the entrance of the cave; the fire
had started, which was a favourable omen. Now the con‐
versation might be resumed, but nobody entered the room.
The fire was burning, and its light shone vividly through
doorway and port-holes, and the men outside were begin‐
ning to move and to yawn, and some had even fallen
asleep, but no one gave a sign of impatience. Stillness
prevailed; it was so late that all noise and bustle had
ceased, and the rippling and rushing of the brook alone
pervaded the night.

Several more men approached from various directions;
their steps were almost inaudible, and when they reached
the company each invariably uttered a hoarse " guatzena, sa
uishe." One by one the new-comers glided into the estufa,
until six of them had entered. Then a metallic sound was
heard within, as if two plates of very hard material were
beaten against each other. All rose at once; those who
had fallen asleep were shaken and pulled until they woke;
and one after another filed into the chamber, Topanashka
being the last. The metallic sound produced by two plates
of basalt had been the call to council.

The interior of the estufa was as brightly illuminated as a
small fire could make it, the smoke of which found egress
through the door and the two air-holes, or rose to the
low ceiling, where it floated like a grayish cloud. The air

was heavy and stifling, and the odour of burning pitch proceeded from the pine wood with which the flames were fed
in the centre of the room.   Close to the fire the tapop had
squatted, with three aged men by his side in the same
posture.   All three wore short, black wraps with red stripes.
We recognize in one of these men, who sit with humble,
downcast looks, the chief penitent, or Hotshanyi ; the other
two are his assistants, the shaykatze and the uishtyaka.
In their immediate neighbourhood sat three others, whose
hair also was turning gray ; but they sat upright and looked
around with freedom and assurance.   Their dress had
nothing particular or distinctive about it, but each carried
on his head feathers of a certain kind.   One, with a tall,
spare figure, an intelligent face, and dark complexion, wore
behind each ear one blue and one yellow feather.   He was
the Hishtanyi Chayan, the principal medicine-man of the
tribe.   Next to him was the Shkuy Chayan, or great shaman
for the hunt, equally tall, slender, and with a thin face and
quick, unsteady glance.   The third, or Shikama Chayan, was
an individual of ordinary looks and coarse features, who was
decorated by a single upright feather.   The leaders of the
societies of the Koshare and Cuirana had squatted among
the central group, while a projection that ran around the
whole room served as a bench, or settee, for the representatives of the clans.

   This arrangement corresponded closely to the degree of
importance of the various officers, or rather to their assumed proximity to the higher powers under whose protection the tribe believed itself to be placed.   The tapop,
as chairman of the meeting, occupied the middle, together
with the principal religious functionaries, — the yaya, or
mothers of the tribe.   On the outer circumference were
placed the nashtio, or fathers, the delegates of the clans.
The Koshare Naua and his colleague of the Cuirana held

an intermediate position. Topanashka, as military head, and the assistant governor, who had neither voice nor vote, sat beside the entrance, guarding it. A lieutenant of the maseua crouched outside to prevent the approach of eavesdroppers.

As soon as the rustling noise occasioned by so many people taking their seats in a small room had subsided, the Hishtanyi Chayan again seized the two basalt plates and caused them to ring. When the metallic sound was heard, everybody became very quiet; and not one of the twenty-three men that composed the meeting moved. All maintained the deepest silence, fastening their eyes on the ground. The shaman scattered sacred meal to the six regions, then he raised his eyes to the ceiling, and finally turned to the three caciques with the formal greeting, " Guatzena, yaya ! " then to the others, with " Guatzena, nashtio ! "

Raising both hands upward, he pronounced the following prayer : —

" Raua Pāyatyama our father, Sanatyaya our mother, Maseua, Oyoyāuā ! You all, the Shiuana all, the Kopishtai all, — all, raua ! Hear what we shall speak, witness all our deeds. Make wise the heart, cunning the ear, bright the eyes, and strong the arm. Give us wisdom and goodness, that our hearts may listen ere we say 'yes,' 'no,' or 'perhaps.' Assist your children, help the Zaashtesh, that they may remain united among themselves, wise, far-seeing, and strong. We call upon you, the Shiuana, the kopishtai ; whisper to us good thoughts and guide us to the right. To you, Pāyatyama, Sanatyaya, Maseua, — to all of you we pray. Raua, raua ! Ho-ā, ho-ā, raua ! "

Again the speaker scattered yellow meal in front of the principal penitent, who only bowed in a dignified manner in response. The remainder of the assembly uttered an affirmative " Ā, ā," and one after the other rose and deposited sacrificial meal before the cacique. When each of them had resumed his seat, the Hishtanyi Chayan turned to the tapop and looked inquiringly.

Hoshkanyi Tihua assumed an air of solemn importance, for he was to play a prominent rôle. He glanced around the circle pompously; but when his eye caught the cold gaze of Topanashka he felt almost a chill, and shrank to natural and more modest proportions. He looked quickly in the direction where Tyope was sitting; but the delegate from Shyuamo hanutsh held his face covered with both hands, and did not notice the pleading look of the little governor. So the latter began in an unsteady tone, —

"Hotshanyi, shaykatze, uishtyaka, and you, the mothers of the tribe, hear me! Hear me also, you who are our fathers," — his voice grew stronger; he was recovering assurance. "I have called you together to listen to what I say." He crowed the last words rather than spoke them.

"My brother, the nashtio of Shyuamo hanutsh," continued he, "has spoken to me and said," — he stopped and shot a glance of inquiry over toward Tyope, but Tyope failed to note it, — "satyumishe has said, 'Tapop, my hanutsh is numerous and has many children, but only very little maize; the motātza and the makatza are many, but of beans there are few, and the field we are tilling is small.'" Hoshkanyi Tihua was manifestly pleased with his own eloquence, for he again looked around the room for marks of admiration. Only the icy look of Topanashka met his gaze, and he proceeded more modestly, —

"My brother from Shyuamo then said to me, 'See here, nashtio Tapop, there are the people from Tzitz; they are the least in numbers on the Tyuonyi, and yet they have as much ground as we; and they raised as much maize and even more beans, for they are higher up than we, and get more water than we. Now, therefore, call them together, all the yaya and the fathers, and say to them, "Shyuamo hanutsh demands from Tzitz hanutsh that it should share its field with us, for where there are two mouths of Shyuamo there is only one of Tzitz; but when Tzitz raises one ear of corn, Shyuamo grows not more than one."'"

He had spoken, and drew a heavy sigh of relief. The most profound silence reigned. Tyope remained with his head bowed and his face covered with both hands. Topanashka sat rigidly immovable, his cold piercing gaze fastened on the tapop. The representative of the Water clan made a very wry face and looked at the fire.

The tapop had yet to perform one duty ere discussion could begin. He turned to the Hotshanyi and addressed him, —

"Sa umo, you and your brethren the shaykatze and the uishtyaka, I address; what do you say to what Shyuamo is asking? Speak, yaya; we are your children; we listen. You are old and wise, we are young and weak."

The old cacique raised his dim eyes to the speaker and replied in a hoarse voice, —

"I thank you, sa uishe, — I thank you for myself and for my brethren here that you have put this question to us. But"—the voice grew more steady and strong—"you know that it is our duty to pray, to fast, and to watch, that peace may rule among the Zaashtesh and that nothing may disturb it. We cannot listen to anything that calls forth two kinds of words, and that may bring strife," — he emphasized strongly the latter word; "we cannot therefore remain. May the Shiuana enlighten your hearts. We shall pray that they will counsel you to do good only."

The old Hotshanyi rose and went toward the doorway. His form was bent, his step faltering. His two associates followed. Not one of those present dared to look at them. None of them noticed the deeply, mournfully significant glance which the cacique, while he crept through the door, exchanged with Topanashka.

The address which the governor had directed to the official penitents was a mere formality, but a formality that could not be dispensed with. It was an act of courtesy toward those who in the tribe as well as in the council represented the higher powers. But as these powers are conceived as being good, it is not allowed to speak in their presence of anything that might, in the remotest manner even, bear evil consequences such as disunion and strife. Therefore the caciques, as soon as they had been informed of the subject, could not stay at the meeting, but had to retire.

This happens at every discussion of a similar nature, and their departure was merely in the ordinary routine of business. Nobody felt shocked or even surprised at it. But everybody, on the other hand, noticed the reply given by the aged Hotshanyi, felt it like some dread warning, — the foreboding of some momentous question of danger to the people. An uneasy feeling crept over many of the assistants who were not, like Tyope and the Koshare Naua, in the secrets of the case. After the departure of the caciques, therefore, the same dead silence prevailed as before.

The tapop broke the silence by turning officially to the principal shaman and asking him, —

"Sa umo yaya, what do you hold concerning the demand of our children from Shyuamo?"

The Chayan raised his face, his eyes sparkled. He gave his reply in a positive tone, —

"I hold it is well, provided Tzitz hanutsh is satisfied." He bent his head again in token that he had said as much as he cared to say for the present.

Hoshkanyi Tihua then interrogated the Shkuy Chayan, who very pointedly answered.—

" It is good."

His colleague, the Shikama Chayan, remained non-com-
mittal, saying, —

" It may be good, it may not be good ; I do not know.
My hanutsh is Shutzuna," — he cast a rapid glance to where
the delegate of the Prairie-wolf people was sitting, — " and
we have enough land for ourselves."

The governor now addressed the same question successively to the Koshare Naua and to the leader of the Cuirana.
The dim eyes of the former began to gleam ; his shrivelled
features assumed a hideous, wolfish expression as he spoke
in a voice trembling yet clear, —

" It is well.   Our brethren deserve what they demand.
If the crops ripen, my children from Shyuamo are those
who pray and fast most of all.   My hanutsh alone counts
more Koshare than all the others together.   If they get
more land they will fast and pray so much the more, and
this they do not for themselves only, but for the benefit of
all who dwell on the Tyuonyi."

The Cuirana Naua, on the other hand, gave a confused
and unsatisfactory reply.   In his opinion it would be well
if both clans could agree.

It was next the turn of the clan delegates to be called up.
They were those most directly interested, but until now
they had, out of deference for their religious leaders, maintained an absolutely passive attitude.   After the Cuirana
Naua had spoken, however, many raised their faces, changed
their positions ; some looked at the tapop with an air of
expectancy, others glanced around, still others seemed to
denote by their demeanour that they were anxious and
eager to speak.   Tyope and Topanashka, alone, did not
change their attitudes.   The former remained with his
head bent and his face covered with both hands ; the latter, who happened almost directly to face Tyope, with

head erect and an expression of calm watchfulness on his features.

It was of course impossible to foretell the general feeling among the members of the council in regard to the demands of the Turquoise people. The Shkuy Chayan and the Koshare Naua had declared themselves favourable to their pretensions, but on the other hand the Hishtanyi Chayan — and his word had greater weight than their speeches — had made a very significant suggestion by reminding the governor in his reply that the matter did not properly come before the tribal council, but should be settled between the two clans directly interested. Hoshkanyi Tihua should have taken the hint; but Hoshkanyi Tihua had not the slightest tact; and besides, as a member of the clan Shyuamo, he felt too much interested in the matter not to be eager to press it at once, however imprudent and out of place such action might be. He was, moreover, utterly unconscious of the fact that he was nothing but a tool which both Tyope and the Naua wielded to further their perfidious designs.

The tapop therefore called upon the delegate of the Sun clan to speak. He dwelt not far from the Turquoise people, and he expressed himself strongly in their favour.

"It is true," said he, "and I know it to be so, that my friends of Shyuamo are hungry. I know it, and it is true also, that the Water people have too much ground. It is right, therefore, for Shyuamo to ask for a share of what they have in excess. How much it shall be, they must settle among themselves."

Everybody did not appear to be satisfied with this; but when the tapop summoned the representative of the Bear clan to give his opinion, the speech of the latter was not only stronger, it was even offensive to the Water people. He accused them of having done wrong in not sharing their fields with the clan of the Turquoise some time before, since it was the duty of those who had too much to divide with those who were poorer. He said that it was wrong on the part of Tzitz to have remained silent when they knew how much Shyuamo did for the tribe, while at the same time they had not enough for their own existence. He charged the tapop, in the name of the council, with delinquency in not having required the Water people to share their superabundance with those of the Turquoise. The delegate of Kohaio was not only aggressive in his speech, but his manner of delivering it was brusque and violent, and created quite a stir; and many of the members cast glances at him which were not of a friendly nature.

It was now the turn of the delegate of the Water people; and much depended upon what he would say, for he was, besides the members from Shyuamo, the party most interested in the proceedings. Kauaitshe, as he was called, was not, unfortunately, the man for the situation. Short and clumsy in figure, extremely good-natured and correspondingly slow in thought and action, he was intellectually heavy and dull. When the demand upon his cian was first formulated, he listened to it like one whom it does not concern, and only gradually came to the conception that the matter was after all of prime importance to him and to those whose interests he had been selected to defend. Kauaitshe was thunderstruck upon arriving at full comprehension; he was bewildered, and would much rather have run away from the council. But that was impossible. He heard the men speak one by one, and — what to him caused most anxiety — he saw the moment approaching when he also would be called upon; and the prospect filled him with dismay. What should he say! What could he say! The injustice intended toward his constituents, the necessity of undertaking a task for which he felt himself incapable, terrified him at first and soon drove him to utter despair; and as all weak and lazy natures, when they see themselves driven to the wall, become frenzied, Kauaitshe, when the tapop turned to him, exploded like a loaded weapon, venting his wrath upon the governor instead of calmly discussing the matter itself. He saw in the governor not only a member of the clan whose plans were detrimental to the interests of his kinsmen, but chiefly the instrument by means of which he was placed in the present difficult position. His face turned dark, then yellow. His eyes glowed like embers. Bounding from his seat, he advanced toward the chairman and hissed, —

"I have heard. Yes," — his voice became louder, — "I have heard enough. Enough!" he screamed. "You want to take from us what is ours! You want to rob us, to steal from my people in order that your people may prosper and we may suffer! That is what you want," and he shook his clenched fist in the face of the tapop. The latter started up like an irate turkey, and screamed, —

"You lie! what we want from you is right! You are only a few people, and you are lazy; whereas we are many and thrifty; you are a liar!"

"Hush! hush!" sounded the voice of the principal shaman, between the shouts and screams of the disputing parties.

"No! no!" shrieked Kauaitshe, "I will not hush. I will speak! I will tell these friends — "

"Water-mole!" yelled the tapop in response; and both the Koshare Naua and Tyope cried at once, —

"We are Shyuamo, not shuatyam." Their voices sounded like the threatening snarls of wild beasts.

"Hush! hush!" the Hishtanyi Chayan now sternly commanded. Rising, he grasped the little governor by the shoulder, pulled him back to his place on the floor, and

warningly raised his hand toward Kauaitshe, whose mouth
one of his colleagues had already closed by force.

"If you hope for light from Those Above," the medicine-
man warned the delegate from Tzitz, "you must not name
in their presence the powers of darkness." To the tapop
he said, —

"Do your duty, but do it as it ought to be done!"

Kauaitshe reeled back to his place, where he sat down in
sullen silence. It happened to him as it always does to
any one who loses his temper at the wrong time and in
the wrong place; after the flurry is over, they find that
they have wasted all their energies, and remain henceforth
incapable of any effort. The delegate of the Water people
was *hors du combat* for the remainder of the evening.

The incident had made an impression on the assembly.
Nearly everybody shared more or less in the excitement.
Now that quiet was restored, apparent calmness seemed to
prevail in their minds again. The men stared as motionless as before; but their faces were dark, and many an
eye displayed a spark of passionate fire. Topanashka had
not moved during the quarrel, and Tyope hid his face in
his hands as before.

Hoshkanyi's voice still trembled as he called upon the
representative of Tanyi hanutsh. The latter replied,—

"There is more land yet at the Tyuonyi; let Shyuamo
increase their ground from some waste tract."

"There is no room for it," growled the Koshare Naua.

"I say there is," defiantly retorted the other.

The delegate of the Prairie-wolf people was not only of
the same opinion as his predecessor, he even mentioned a
tract of waste land that lay east of the cultivated plots,
from which Shyuamo might take what they needed. The
speaker of Tzina hanutsh, however, was of an adverse
opinion. He remarked that it was always better for a

smaller clan to divide their ground with a more powerful one, as in that case larger crops would be raised. As matters stood, he added, only a portion of the land belonging to the Water people was tilled. This the member from Huashpa denied, and reminded him that the Hishtanyi Chayan had suggested that the whole matter should be settled by the two clans privately. Both the Cuirana Naua and Tyame, the delegate of the Eagle clan, could not refrain from expressing their approval in an audible manner by the customary "Ā-ā," and the Shikama Chayan slightly nodded assent.

It was already late, but nobody thought of the hour. On such occasions the Indian can sit up whole nights without ever thinking of rest. Not only was everybody interested, but the excitement, although barely visible on the surface, was rapidly growing; and personal ill-feeling and spite cropped out more and more.

Tyame having expressed himself in favour of the opinion of the delegate from Huashpa hanutsh, the tapop could not refrain from going out of the ordinary routine in order to slight him, and to give the floor to the member from Hiits Hanyi. This flattered the popular delegate, and he accordingly spoke so strongly in favour of the claim presented by Shyuamo that at the close of his speech several voices at once grunted assent. Both parties were growing decidedly bitter.

Tyame noticed the intended slight; so when Hoshkanyi called him up he opened his talk with the remark, —

"One can see that you are Shyuamo."

"That is what I am," the little fellow bragged.

"But you are tapop also," Tyame objected.

"Why do you speak thus? Are you angry that you could not be used for the place?" venomously inquired the governor.

"If I were in your place," retorted the Eagle, "I should do as is customary, and call upon each one in turn."

"You have time enough left to speak against Shyuamo," said the chief of the Delight Makers in a wicked manner.

"That I shall do, most assuredly," exclaimed Tyame. "I am against giving Shyuamo any more ground than they have at present. You have enough for yourselves, for your women, and for all your children. Do more work in the field and do less penance; be shyayak rather than Koshare!" He rose and turned toward Tyope. "Your woman belongs to our hanutsh, and I know that it is not you who feed her; and so you are, all of you. You live from other people's crops!"

Tyope looked up, and his eyes flashed; but in a quiet tone he answered, —

"Your woman is Shyuamo; you know best how it is." The other continued with growing passion, —

"And when your wife was from Tzitz everybody knew that it was not you who supported her, but that she maintained you!"

Loud murmurs arose, and the Shkuy Chayan called Tyame to order, so that Tyope did not have time for a reply to this insulting insinuation.

Of all the clans represented three had yet to express their views. These were the clans of Yakka, of the Panther, and Shyuamo. The delegate of the Corn people was no friend of Tyame's, therefore he spoke directly against what the Eagle had intimated. He emphasized how detrimental it might become for a small cluster to own too much tillable land while a large and important clan was suffering for the lack of vegetable food. With notable shrewdness, he exposed to the meeting the danger for the whole tribe in case one of its principal components should begin to decrease in numbers. He wound up by saying, —

17

"The strong hanutsh are those who maintain the tribe, for they are those who give us the most people that do penance for the welfare of all, be they Koshare or Cuirana. They also have the greatest number of warriors and hunters. If they have nothing to eat, they cannot watch, pray, and fast in honour of Those Above! So the Shiuana and the Kopishtai become dissatisfied with us, and withdraw their protection from their children; and we become lost through suffering those to starve who are most useful." But he omitted altogether the important fact that there was still waste land in the gorge, and that it was far preferable to redeem such tracts than to create dissension.

Still it must be acknowledged that the clearing of timbered expanses, such as those on the eastern end of the valley mostly were, opposed great difficulties to the Indian. At the time when the Rito was settled, the native had only stone implements. To cut down trees, to clear brush even, was a tedious and protracted undertaking when it had to be performed with stone axes and hatchets. Fire was the most effective agent, but fire in such proximity to the dwellings was a dangerous servant. On the western end there was no tillable land beyond the patches of the Water clan. Still, if there had been any disposition on the part of Shyuamo to be reasonable, they would have remained satisfied with extending their field slowly and gradually toward the east; but neither Tyope nor the Naua really wanted more land; what they desired was strife, disunion, an irremediable breach in the tribe.

The Panther clan, whose representative had to speak now, was a cluster which belonged neither to the larger nor to the smaller groups. Occupying, as was the case, a section of the big house, the Panther people were consequently near neighbours of Tanyi, and they sympathized generally with the latter. Their delegate, however, was Koshare, and he leaned not so much toward the Turquoise as toward what seemed to be the desire of the leading Delight Makers, — the Naua and Tyope. He therefore expressed himself bluntly in favour of Tzitz hanutsh giving up a certain quan·tity of land to the clan Shyuamo, without stating his opinion or suggesting in the least how it ought to be done.

Every member of the council, Tyope and Topanashka excepted, had spoken. The majority of votes seemed in favour of the claim represented, but it is not plurality of votes which decides, but unanimity of opinion and con·viction; and finally and in the last instance, the utterances of those who speak in the name of the powers above. The shamans had given their opinions, the Shkuy was manifestly favourable to Shyuamo, but his colleague, the Hishtanyi Chayan, had spoken in a manner that restricted the point at issue to a discussion among the clans directly interested. The Histanyi Chayan was a personage of great authority, and many of those who were on the side of the Turquoise people thought his word to be law in the end. They had shown themselves friendly toward their brethren of Shyu-amo, willing, however, to abide by what the closing discussion would bring to light. That discussion was yet to commence, and the opening was to be the speech of Tyope himself. Much stress also was laid upon what Topanashka would say, for he too was to take part. Some had their misgivings concerning the real object of the move which every one felt certain Tyope and the Koshare Naua had set on foot; and when the tapop summoned Tyope to speak at last, there was something like a subdued flutter among the audience. Many turned their heads in the direction of the speaker, others displayed in their features the marks of unusual attention.

Tyope rose slowly from his seat. He looked around quietly; there was a sardonic smile on his lips. His eyes almost closed; he spoke in a muffled voice, slowly and very distinctly. He was evidently master of his subject, and a natural orator.

"Yaya, nashtio, Tapop, I have heard what you have all said, and it is well, for it is well for each one of you to have spoken his thoughts, in order that the people be pleased and delight come into their hearts. For there are many of us, the fathers of the tribe, and each one has his own thoughts; and thoughts are like faces, never two alike. For this reason did I speak to our father the tapop that he should call in the uuityam, in order that all might hear and that nobody could say afterward, — 'Shyuamo hanutsh has taken from Tzitz hanutsh what belonged to the Water people, and behold we knew nothing about it!' Shyuamo hanutsh " — he raised his voice and glanced around with flashing eyes — " has many people; Shyuamo is strong! But the men of the Turquoise are just! They go about in day-light and speak loudly, and are not like the water that roars at night and drops into silence as soon as oshatsh brightens the world." After this fling at the delegate of the Water clan, Tyope paused a moment; he seemed to wait for a reply, but none came, the explanation of his action in car-rying the matter before the council appearing to satisfy all. "Shyuamo hanutsh," he proceeded, " is great in numbers but weak in strength, for its people have no food for them-selves, and what they raise is barely enough for their koitza, their makatza, and the little ones. They themselves must starve," he cried, " in order that other clans may increase through the children which my men beget with their daughters!"

The most profound silence followed these words. The speaker paused again and looked around as if challenging an answer. He felt very sure of his point.

"We have worked, worked as hard as any one on the

Tyuonyi, but our numbers have grown faster than our crops. Go and look at the field of Shyuamo and you will see how many are the corn-plants, and how large the ears of corn, but the field is too small ! We have not more land than the Turkey people, and not as much as the Water clan ! When during last summer no rain fell, notwithstanding all our fasting, prayer, and sacrifice, when yamunyi dried up and kaname shrivelled, Tzitz hanutsh still had enough to eat, and its men grew fat ! " This hint at the stout representative of the Water clan created great hilarity. Her representative growled, —

" You are not lean either."

Without noticing this interruption, Tyope proceeded, —

" Its women and its children are well ! But we, at the lower end of the cliffs," — he extended his arm to the east, — " starve in order that your daughters and the little ones whom we have begotten to the other clans shall not perish. We had no more than food enough to pray for, to fast for, in order that the Shiuana might not let our brethren be lost." Here the Koshare Naua, as well as the representative of the Panther clan, uttered an audible " Ā-ā ; " and even the Shkuy Chayan nodded. " How many Koshare are there in Tzitz hanutsh? How many in Tanyi? How many in Tyame who would sacrifice themselves for the ripening of fruit? How many in Huashpa? Shyuamo alone has as many Delight Makers as the remainder of the Zaashtesh. One single clan as many as eleven others together ! And " — he drew himself up to his full height and fastened on the delegate of the Water clan a glance of strange fierceness, as he cried — " while your Koshare feed themselves well between the fasts, ours starve to regain strength after they have watched, prayed, and starved ! "

This explosion of bitter reproach was again followed by deep silence. Tyope was indeed a fascinating speaker.

The maseua and the Hishtanyi Chayan were the only ones
whom his oratorical talent could not lead astray. Чe proceeded in a quieter tone, —

"We need more land. Some of our fathers have suggested that we should extend our territory to the eastward
and open the soil there. They mean well; but there is not
enough, and the pines are too near. Shall we go as far as
Cuapa, where there is enough soil, or where the kauaush
descends to the painted cave? Shall we go and live where
the Moshome would surround us and howl about like hungry
wolves? No! Ere we do this we have thought to say to our
brethren, 'Tzitz has more land than it needs; Tzitz is our
brother; and we will ask them, "Satyumishe, give us some
of that of which you have too much, so that we may not be
lost."' But not to the Water people alone did we wish to
speak; no, to all of you, to the yaya nashtio and the tapop,
that you all may know it and assist us in our need. For
rather than starve we shall leave the Tyuonyi and look for
another place. And then," he concluded, "you will become weak and we shall be weak; and the Moshome, the
Tehuas, and the Puyatye will be stronger than the Queres,
for we shall be divided!"

He resumed his seat in token that his speech was ended.
From all sides sounded the affirmative grunt "Ā-ā-ā;" the
Shkuy Chayan and the Cuirana Naua even nodded. Tyope
had spoken very well.

Hoshkanyi Tihua was delighted with the talk of his clan-
brother. Forgetful of his position as chairman he looked
around the circle proudly, as if to say, "He can do it
better than any one of you." The stillness that followed
was suddenly broken by the voice of the Hishtanyi Chayan,
who called out in a dry, business-like manner, —

"Our brother Tyope has spoken well, and all the others
have spoken as their hearts directed them to speak; but my

brother " — he emphasized the *my* — " the maseua has not
yet said what he thinks. My brother is very wise. Let
him open his heart to us."

There was a slight commotion among the assembled parties. The speech of Tyope had so monopolized their attention that none of them had thought of the maseua. Now
they were reminded of his presence through the principal
medicine-man himself, and that reminder acted like a re
proach. The eyes of all, Tyope and the Koshare Naua
excepted, turned toward the doorway, where Topanashka
was quietly sitting. The two men from Shyuamo affected
to pay no further attention to what was going on.

Topanashka Tihua remained sitting. He directed his
sharp, keen glance to the Hishtanyi Chayan, as if to him
alone he condescended to speak. Then he said, —

" I believe as you do, nashtio yaya, but I also believe as
you, Tyope, have spoken." So great was the surprise caused
by this that Tyope lifted his face and looked at the old
man in blank astonishment. Kauaitshe stared at Topanashka like one suddenly aroused by a wondrous piece of
news.

" Tyope is right," continued the maseua; " Shyuamo
has not soil enough. He is also right in saying that
there is not room enough on the Tyuonyi for making
new plantations."

" Ā-ā, " the delegate from the Turquoise interjected.

" It is true our brethren are suffering for want of land
whereon to grow their corn. It is equally true that Tzitz
hanutsh has more land than it needs, and it is well that
Shyuamo should ask for what it wants and not leave the
Zaashtesh forever. Tyope has well spoken."

Nothing can describe the effect of this speech. Even the
chief of the Delight Makers smiled approvingly a hideous,
satanic grin of pleasure. He felt like loving the speaker;

that is, provided the schemer had been capable of liking anybody but himself. The eyes of Tyope sparkled with grim delight. Kauaitshe and Tyame hung their heads, and reckoned themselves lost forever. The maseua continued, still addressing the principal shaman, —

"But you are right also, nashtio yaya, when you say that it is Tzitz hanutsh who shall decide whether or not it wishes to part with some of its fields for the benefit of the Turquoise people." Both Tyope and the Koshare Naua grew very serious at these words. "We cannot compel the Water people to give up any of their soil."

"No," the Shikama Chayan audibly whispered.

"But if Shyuamo hanutsh says to Tzitz hanutsh, 'We will give you such and such things that are precious to you if you give us the land,' and does it, — then I am in favour of compelling Tzitz hanutsh to give it; for it is better thus than that the tribe should be divided and each part go adrift. These are my thoughts, sa nashtio yaya."

The Hishtanyi Chayan actively nodded assent, and all around the circle approving grunts were heard. The old man's speech satisfied the majority of the council, with the sole exception of those who represented the clan Shyuamo; it was now their turn to become excited, and the Koshare was the first one to display his dissatisfaction.

"What shall we give?" he muttered. "We are poor, we have nothing. Why should we give anything for that which does not help the others? It will help us, but only us and nobody else. We give nothing because we have nothing," he hissed at last, and looked at Tyope as if urging him to be firm and not to promise anything under any circumstances. Tyope remained mute; the words of the maseua appeared to leave him unmoved. But Tyame, the man of the Eagles, became incensed at this refusal on the part of the Turquoise people. He shouted to the Koshare Naua, —

"What! you will give nothing? Why are you Koshare, then? Why are you their chief? Do you never receive anything for what you do? You are wealthy, you have green stones, red jewels from the water; you have and you get from the people everything that is precious and makes the heart glad. You alone have more precious things than all the rest of us together!"

"It is not true!" exclaimed Tyope.

"We are poor!" screeched the Koshare Naua.

Kauaitshe now interfered; he had recovered from his stupor and yelled, "You have much, you are wealthy!" Turning against Tyope he shouted to him, —

"Why should we, before all the others, give you the soil that you want? Why should we, before all the others, give it to you for nothing? You are thieves, you are Moshome, shutzuna, tiatiu! No!" He stamped his foot on the ground. "No! we will give you nothing, nothing at all, even if you give us everything that the Koshare have schemed and stolen from the people!"

The commanding voice of the Hishtanyi sounded through the tumult, — "Hush! Hush!" but it was of no avail; passions were aroused, and both sides were embittered in the highest degree.

The delegate from Tanyi jumped up, yelling, "Why do you want the ground from Tzitz alone? Why not our field also;" and he placed himself defiantly in front of Tyope.

The member from Huashpa cried, —

"Are the Water people perhaps to blame for the drought of last year?"

"They are!" screamed the Koshare Naua, rising; "Ta-pop, I want to speak; make order!"

"Silence!" ordered the little governor, but nobody paid any attention.

"Satyumishe Maseua," now shouted the principal sha man, "keep order, the nashtio Koshare wants to speak!"

The tall man rose calmly; he went toward the cluster of wrangling men and grasped Kauaitshe by the shoulder.

"Be quiet," he ordered.

Nobody withstood his determined mien. All became silent. Topanashka leaned back against the wall, his gaze fixed on the Koshare. Everybody was in suspense, in ex- pectation of what the Naua might say. He coughed, and began addressing the leading shaman, —

"Yaya Hishtanyi, you hear that the Water people refuse to give us the land that we so much need. They ask of us that we should give them all we have for a small part of theirs. The motātza from the hanutsh Huashpa has asked whether Tzitz hanutsh is perhaps the cause that the crops failed last year. I say it is the cause of it!"

"How so?" cried Tyame.

"Through Shotaye, their sister," replied the old man, slowly.

It was not silence alone that followed this utterance. A stillness ensued so sudden, so dismal, and so awful that it seemed worse than a grave. Every face grew sinister, every one felt that some dread revelation was coming. Tyope held his head erect, watching the face of the old maseua. Topanashka's features had not moved; he was looking at the Koshare Naua with an air of utter unconcern. The Hishtanyi Chayan, on the contrary, raised his head; and the expression of his features became sharp, like those of an anxious inquisitor. In the eye of the Shkuy Chayan a sinis- ter glow appeared. He also had raised his head and bent the upper part of his body forward. The Shikama Chayan assumed a dark, threatening look. The name of Shotaye had aroused dark suspicions among the medicine-men. Their chief now asked slowly, measuredly, —

"You accuse a woman of having done harm to the tribe?" Henceforward he and his two colleagues were the pivots around which the further proceedings were to revolve. The tapop was forgotten; nobody paid attention to him any longer.

" I do ; I say that Shotaye, the woman belonging to Tzitz hanutsh, has carried destruction to the tribe."

" In what way? "

" In preventing the rain from falling in season."

" And she has succeeded ! " ejaculated Tyope, in a low voice, — so low that it was not heard by all.

The Shkuy Chayan continued the interrogatory. Nobody else uttered a word; not even the Hishtanyi spoke for the present. The latter disliked the woman as much as any of his colleagues; but he mistrusted her accusers as well, and preferred, after having taken the initiatory steps, to remain an attentive listener and observer, leaving it to his associates to proceed with the case. The Shkuy, on the other hand, was eager to develop matters; he had been secretly informed some time ago of what was known concerning the witchcraft proceedings of Shotaye, and he hated the woman more bitterly than any of his colleagues did; and as the charge was the preventing of rain-fall, it very directly affected his own functions, — not more than those of the Hishtanyi, who is ex-officio rain-maker, but quite as much.

For drought not only affects the crops; it exerts quite as baneful an influence upon game ; and game, as food for man, is under the special care of the Shkuy Chayan. He is the great medicine-man of the hunt. Drought artificially produced, as the Indian is convinced it can be through witchcraft, is one of the greatest calamities that can be brought upon a tribe. As a crime, it is worse than murder, for it is an attempt at wholesale though slow extermination The sorcerer or the witch who deliberately attempts to pre vent rain-fall becomes the object of intense hatred on the part of all. The whole cluster of men assembled felt the gravity of the charge. Horror-stricken, they sat in mute silence, awaiting the result of the investigation which the Shkuy Chayan proceeded to carry on.

" How do you know that the aniehna " — he emphasized the untranslatable word of insult, and his voice trembled with passion — " has worked such evil to the people? " The query was directed to the Koshare Naua. The latter turned to Tyope, saying, —

" Speak, satyumishe nashtio." He squatted again.

The eyes of all, Topanashka's excepted, who did not for a moment divert his gaze from the chief of the Delight Makers, were fixed on Tyope. He rose and dryly said, —

" I saw when Shotaye Koitza and Say Koitza, the daughter of our father the maseua," — everybody now looked at the war-chief in astonishment, dismay, or sorrow; but he remained completely impassive, — " who lives in the abodes of Tanyi hanutsh, caused the black corn to answer their questions. And there were owl's feathers along with the corn. It was night, and I could not hear what they said. It was in the beginning of winter; not last winter, but the winter before."

" Is that all? " inquired the Hishtanyi Chayan in turn. It displeased him to hear that Tyope had been eavesdropping in the dark, — the man had no business in the big house at night.

" I know also," continued Tyope, " that Shotaye gathered the feathers herself on the kauash toward the south."

" Did you see her? "

" Yes," boldly asserted Tyope. He lied, for he dared not tell the truth; namely, that the young Navajo was his informant.

"Is that all?" queried the Hishtanyi again.

"After we, the Koshare, had prayed and done penance in our own kaaptsh I at one time went back to the timbers on which we climb up to the cave. At their foot, below the rocks, I found this!"

He drew from beneath his wrap a little bundle, and handed it to the shaman, who examined it closely and gave it to his colleagues, who subjected the object to an equally thorough investigation. Those sitting along the wall bent forward curiously, until at last the bundle was turned over to them also. So it went from hand to hand, each one passing it to the next with sighs and marks of thorough disgust. The bundle was composed of owl's feathers tied to a flake of black obsidian.

"I found a second one," quietly said Tyope, pulling forth a similar bunch. Now the council gave demonstrations not only of amazement but of violent indignation; the shamans and Topanashka alone remained calm. Both bunches were given to the tapop, who placed them on the floor before him.

The Hishtanyi Chayan inquired further, —

"Where did you find the feathers? Say it once more."

"At the foot of the rocks, where we ascend to our estufa on cross-timbers."

"Did you see who put them there?"

"No."

"When do you think they were placed there?"

"While the Koshare were at work in the estufa."

"Do you know more?"

"Nothing more." Tyope sat down, and the interrogatory was over.

It was as still as a grave in the dingy, ill-lighted chamber. No one dared even to look up, for the matter was in the hands of the yaya, and they were still thinking over it. The demands of Shyuamo hanutsh were completely forgotten, the owl's feathers had monopolized the attention and the thoughts of every one in the room.

At last the Hishtanyi Chayan rose. He threw a glance at his colleagues, who understood it, and rose also. Then the great medicine-man spoke in a hollow tone, —

"We will go now. We shall speak to our father the Hotshanyi, that he may help us to consult Those Above. Four days hence we shall know what the Shiuana think, and on the night following " — he turned to the tapop — " we will tell you here what to do. In the meantime," — he uttered these words like a solemn warning, — " hush ! let none of you exchange one word on what we have heard or seen to-night. Let none of you say at home, ' I know of something evil,' or to a friend, ' bad things are going on in the tribe.' Be silent, so that no one suspect the least thing, and that the sentence of the Shiuana be not interfered with. Nasha ! " he concluded, and went toward the exit. Ere leaving the room, however, he turned once more, adding, —

" And you go also. Each one for himself and alone. Let no one of you utter words, but all of you pray and do penance, keep open your ears, wide awake your eye, and closed your lips."

With this the shamans filed out, one after the other. Their muffled steps were heard for a moment as they grated on the bare rock. One by one the other members of the council left the chamber in silence, each wending his way homeward with gloomy thoughts. Dismal anticipations and dread apprehension filled the hearts of every one.

CHAPTER XII.

AT the time when the tribal council of the Queres was holding the stormy session which we have described in the preceding chapter, quite a different scene was taking place at the home of the wife of Tyope. That home, we know, belonged to Hannay, the woman with whom Tyope had consorted after his separation from Shotaye ; and it was also the dwelling in which he resided when other matters did not keep him away. The tie that bound Tyope to his second wife was of rather a sensual nature. Hannay was a very sensual woman, but in addition to this she possessed qualities that made her valuable to her husband. She was extremely inquisitive, listened well, knew how to inquire, and was an active reporter. On her side there was no real affection for Tyope ; but her admiration for his intellectual qualities, so far as she was able to appreciate them, knew no bounds. It amounted almost to awe. Their connection was consequently a partnership rather than anything else, — a partnership based on physical affinities, on mutual interest, and on habit. Of the higher sort of sympathy there was no trace. Neither had room for it among the many occupations which their mode of life and manner of intercourse called forth.

If Tyope was shrewd and cunning, and if he made of his own woman his eye, ear, and mouth, as has been said in one of the previous chapters, Hannay was not a fool. She did not of course understand anything of his plans and schemes, and he never thought it necessary to inform her; but she knew how to manage him whenever anything aroused her curiosity. She contrived to gratify this sometimes in a way that her husband failed to detect, — by drawing from his talk inferences that were exceedingly correct and which he had no thought of furnishing. For Tyope knew his wife's weakness; he knew that if her ears and her eyes were sharp, her tongue was correspondingly swift; and he tried to be as guarded as possible toward her on any topic which he did not wish to become public property. Nevertheless Hannay succeeded in outwitting her husband more than once, and in guessing with considerable accuracy things that he did not regard as belonging within the field of her knowledge. So, for instance, while he had carefully avoided stating to her the object of the council, she nevertheless had put together in her own mind a number of minor points and hints to which he attached no importance, and had thus framed for herself a probable purpose of the meeting that fell not much short of the real truth.

The main desire that occupied Hannay's mind for the present was the union between Okoya and her daughter Mitsha. Okoya had, unknown to himself, no stronger ally than the mother of the girl. The motive that actuated her in this matter was simply the apparent physical fitness of the match and the momentary advantages that she, considering her own age and the loose nature of Indian marriages, might eventually derive from the daily presence of Okoya at her home. In other words, she desired the good-looking youth as much for herself as for her child, and saw nothing wrong in this. From the day when Okoya for the first time trod the roof of her dwelling in order to protect Mitsha, she had set her cap for him. But she knew that there was no love on the part of Tyope for the relatives of Okoya, paternal or maternal, and she was too much afraid of him to venture open consent to a union that might be against his wishes. In her mind Tyope was the only stumbling-block in the path of the two young people; that is, in the way of her own desires.

She had consequently set to work with a great deal of tact and prudence in approaching Tyope about the matter. After a number of preparatory skirmishes, she at last ventured to tell him of it. To her astonishment he took it quite composedly, saying neither yes nor no, and displaying no feeling at all. He saw not the least objection to having Okoya visit her house as often as he might please; in fact, he treated the matter with great indifference. This was a decided relief to her, and she anxiously waited for Okoya's first visit to impress him most favourably regarding not merely herself but her husband.

Tyope indeed did not attach the slightest importance to Okoya personally. The youth had no value for him at present; he did not dislike him; he did not notice him at all. The boy was as unobjectionable to him as any one else whom he did not need for his purposes. But there were points connected with the union that affected Tyope's designs very materially, and these would come out in course of time, although he foresaw them already. In the first place, intermarriage between the clans of Tanyi and Tyame was not favourable to his scheme, which consisted in expelling gradually or violently four clusters, — Tanyi, Tyame, Huashpa, and Tzitz, from the Rito. The last-named cluster he wanted to get rid of on account of Shotaye, whom he feared as much as he hated; the other three he wished to dispossess of their houses, which were the best secured against decay on the Tyuonyi, in order to lodge therein his own relatives and their partisans. Had Okoya aspired to the hand of a daughter of the Turquoise clan,

18

Tyope would have been in favour of his pretensions at once.

On the other hand, Okoya was very young; he might be flexible if properly handled; and in case the boy, whose father was already a Koshare and completely under Tyope's influence, could be induced to join the society of the Delight Makers, it would be a gain fully compensating for the other disadvantages of the situation. One more Koshare in Tanyi, and one who would dwell with Tyame, besides, after marriage, was a gain. It would facilitate the realization of the plan of a disruption of tribal ties by creating disunion among the clans most powerful, after Shyuamo. Tyope did not care for the expulsion of certain special clusters as a whole, provided a certain number and a certain kind of people were removed. But the matter of making a Koshare out of Okoya was a delicate undertaking. His wife had already suggested as much to him, and he had insinuated to her that she might try, cautioning her at the same time against undue precipitation. Finally he left the whole matter in her hands without uttering either assent or dissent, and went about his own more important and much more intricate affairs.

Hannay awaited Okoya with impatience, but the youth had not appeared again. He was afraid of Tyope and also afraid of her. The warnings of his mother and Hayoue he had treasured deeply, and these warnings kept him away from the home of Mitsha. Still he longed to go there. Every evening since the one on which Say encouraged him to go, he had determined to pay the first regular visit, but as often as the time came his courage had abandoned him and he had not gone. And yet he must either go or give up; this he realized plainly. There might be a possibility of some other youth attempting the same, and then he would be too late, perhaps. There was no thought on his part of giving up; he felt committed; and yet he was more afraid of going to call on the maiden than he would have been of encountering some wild beast. Not on Mitsha's account, oh no! He longed to meet her at her own home, but he feared both her parents.

Say Koitza instinctively noticed her son's trouble, and she became apprehensive lest out of timidity he might suffer to escape him what she now more and more regarded as a golden opportunity. At last, on the evening when the council was to meet, a fact that was well known to all, she said to her son, —

" I hear that sa nashtio maseua is going to the uuityam to-night; in that case Tyope will be there also." More she did not say, but Okoya treasured the hint, and made no remark about it, but at once thought that the time had come to pay a visit to the maiden. After the sun had gone down he went out and leaned against the northern wall of the big house, gazing steadily at the dwellings of the Eagle clan. There were too many people about yet for him to attempt the call, and futhermore it was so early that the council could hardly have assembled. By the light of the moon he saw clearly the movements of the people, although it was impossible to recognize individuals at any distance. The boy sat down and waited. From where he rested he could not fail to notice when the delegates of the clans that inhabited the big house left for the council, and that would be the signal for his own starting. His heart beat; he felt happy and yet anxious; hope and doubt both agitated his mind.

One of his comrades stealthily approached Okoya, sat down on the ground beside him, threw one arm around his shoulders, and began to sing loudly. Okoya chimed in, and the two shouted at the top of their untrained voices into the clear still night. Such is the custom in Indian villages.

A third one joined them, finally a fourth. The latter lay down on his stomach, rested his elbows on the ground, his chin in both hands, and sang in company with the others. Soon after, two men issued from the gangway and walked down the valley; at last another went in the same direction. These were the members of the council, and now it was time for Okoya. As soon as the song reached a pause, he stood up, said "sha," and turned to go. One of his companions seized him by the ankles, saying, "It is too early for you to go to see the girls;" and all together added, laughing, "Don't go yet, later on we will all go together."

But Okoya stepped firmly on the arm of him who attempted to hold him back, so that the boy loosened his grip; then he jumped into the passage, where they could not see him. He disliked to have any one notice that he went to see Mitsha. Waiting in the dark passage for a short time, he glided out at last on the side farthest from where the boys were still sitting and singing, crossed the ditch into the high corn, and went through the latter upward until opposite the western end of the building. Crossing the ditch again, he reached the slope that led to the buildings occupied by the people of the Eagle. In order to mislead his comrades, in case they should be on the lookout, he went higher up along the cliffs till he reached the caves of Tzina hanutsh. Here he looked back. The three boys were singing lustily the same monotonous rhyme at the same place where he had left them.

From the rock dwellings of the Turkey people there was a gentle declivity to the houses which the clan Tyame had constructed against the perpendicular wall of the cliffs. Okoya walked rapidly; now that he had started, he longed to reached Mitsha's home. Children still romped before the houses; on the roofs entire families were gathered, loudly talking, laughing, or singing. Some of them had even built small fires and cooked their evening meal in the wonderfully cool and invigourating air. The terrace of the abode whither Okoya directed his steps was deserted, but a ray of light passed through the opening in the front wall. Nothing seemed to stir inside when the boy approached.

Had Okoya glanced at that little opening he might have discerned a woman's face, which looked out of it for a moment and then disappeared within. Had he stepped closer to the wall he might have heard a woman's voice inside calling out in a low tone, — " Mitsha, he is coming ! " But he neither looked nor listened ; he was barely able to think. His feelings overpowered him completely ; wrapped in them he stood still, lost in conflicting sentiments, a human statue flooded by the silvery moonlight.

Somebody coughed within the house, but he did not hear it. Again the face appeared in the small, round air-hole. Okoya had his face turned to the east and away from the wall of the house. At last the spectator within thought that the boy's musings were of a rather long duration, and she called out, —

" Sa uishe, opona ! "

He started and looked toward the dwelling, but saw only two black points peeping through the port-hole. Again the voice spoke, —

" Why don't you come in, motātza ? " Now he became conscious that Hannay was calling him into her home.

His first impulse was to run away, but that was only a passing thought ; and it became clear to him that he had reached the place whither he was going, and furthermore that the women were alone. Without a word of reply he climbed the roof and nimbly down into the apartment. He was still on the ladder when Hannay repeated the invitation, —

" Opona, sa uishe."

His greeting was responded to by a loud and warm
"Raua, raua" from the mother, and a faint, slightly tremu-
lous "Raua ā" from another voice, which from its softness
could only be that of Mitsha. The room was dark, for the
fire was about to go out; but beside the hearth cowered
a female figure who had placed fresh wood on the embers and was fanning them with her breath. It was Mitsha.
At the entrance of the visitor, she quickly stroked back
the hair that streamed over her cheeks and turned her
face half around. But this was for a moment only; as
soon as the wood caught fire and light began to spread
over the room she again blew into the flames with all
her might. It was quite unnecessary, for the fire burned
lustily.

Hannay stood in the middle of the floor, wiping her
mouth with the back of her hand. Stepping up to the boy
she said, —

"You have not been here for a long time, motātza." It
sounded like a friendly reproach. He modestly grasped
her fingers, breathed on her hand, and replied, —

"I could not come."

"You did not want to come," said the woman, smiling.

"I could not," he reiterated.

"You could had you wished, I know it; and I know also
why you did not come." She added, "Well, now you are
here at last, and it is well. Mitsha, give your friend something to eat."

The significant word "friend" fell on fertile soil. It eased
Okoya at once. He sat down closer to the hearth, where
the maiden was very busy in a rather confused manner, her
face turned from him. Still as often as the strands of hair
accidentally parted on the left cheek, she shot quick side-
glances at him. Okoya, balancing himself on his heels,
quietly observed her. It was impossible to devote to her

his whole attention, for her mother had already taken her seat close by him and was claiming his ear. She offered slight attraction to the eye, for her squatting figure was not beautiful. Okoya grew lively, much more lively than he had been on his first visit.

"Why should I not have wanted to see you?" he good-naturedly asked.

"I will tell you," Hannay chuckled; "because you were afraid."

"Afraid?" he cried, "afraid? Of whom?" But within himself he thought the woman was right. Hannay smiled.

"Of Mitsha," she said; adding, "she is naughty and strong." A peal of coarse laughter accompanied this stroke of wit. The girl was embarrassed; she hid her face on her lap. Okoya replied, —

"Mitsha does not bite."

"She certainly will not bite you," the mother answered, causing the maiden to turn her face away.

"Does she bite others?" Okoya asked. Again Hannay laughed aloud, and from the corner whither Mitsha had retreated there sounded something like a suppressed laugh also. It amused her to think that she might bite people. Her mother, however, explained, —

"No, Mitsha does not bite; but if other boys should come to see her she might perhaps strike them. But you, sa uishe," — the woman moved closer to him, — "you, I am sure, she will not send away. Is it not so, Mitsha? Okoya may come to see you, may he not?"

The poor girl was terribly embarrassed by this more than direct question, and Okoya himself hung his head in confusion. He pitied the maiden for having such a mother. As Mitsha gave no answer, Hannay repeated, —

"Speak, sa uishe; will you send this motātza away as you do the others?"

"No," breathed the poor creature thus sorely pressed. A thrill went through the frame of Okoya; he looked up, and his eyes beamed in the reflex of the fire. The woman had watched him with the closest attention, and nothing escaped her notice. Her eyes also sparkled with pleasure, for she felt sure of him.

"Well, why don't you give the motātza some food?" she asked her daughter again. "On your account he has walked the long way from the big house. Is it not so, Okoya?"

"Yes," the boy replied innocently.

Quick as thought Mitsha turned around, and her eyes beamed on him for an instant. He did not notice it, and she forthwith stepped up to the hearth. Even though she lacked evening toilette, Mitsha presented a handsome picture; and her friend became absorbed in contemplation of the lithe, graceful form. She lifted the pot from the fire, placed the customary share of its contents before Okoya, and retired to a corner, whence she soon returned with a piece of dried yucca-preserve, regarded as a great treat by the Indians, because it has a sweet taste. As she was placing the dessert on the floor, the boy extended his hand, and she laid the sweetmeat in it instead of depositing it where she had originally intended. Okoya's hand closed, grasping hers and holding it fast. Mitsha tried to extricate her fingers, but he clutched them in his. Stepping back, she made a lunge at his upper arm which caused him to let go her hand at once. Laughing, she then sat down between him and her mother. The ice was broken.

"You are very strong," Okoya assured her, rubbing the sore limb.

"She is strong, indeed," her mother confirmed; "she can work well, too."

"Have you any green paint?" the girl asked.

" No, but I know a place where it is found. Do you want any? "

" I would like to have some."

" For what do you use the green stone? "

" Next year I want to paint and burn bowls and pots." Mitsha had no thought of the inferences that he would draw from her simple explanation. He interpreted her words as very encouraging for him, not only because the girl understood the art of making pottery, but he drew the conclusion that she was thinking of furnishing a household of her own.

Hannay improved the opportunity to still further praise her child. She said, —

" Mitsha does not only know how to paint; she can also shape the uashtanyi, the atash, and the asa." With this she rose, went to the wall, and began to rummage about in some recess. Okoya had meanwhile taken one of the girl's hands in his playing with her dainty fingers which she suffered him to do.

"See here" the woman cried and turned around. He dropped the girl's hand and Hannay handed something to him.

"Mitsha made this." Then she sat down again.

The object which Okoya had received from her was a little bowl of clay, round, and decorated on its upper rim with four truncated and graded pyramids that rose like prongs at nearly equal intervals. The vessel was neatly finished, smooth, white, and painted with black symbolic designs. There was nothing artistic in it according to our ideas, but it was original and quaint. Okoya gazed at the bowl with genuine admiration, placed it on the floor, and took it up again, holding it so that the light of the fire struck the inside also. He shook his head in astonishment and pleasure. Mitsha moved closer to him. With innocent pride she saw his beaming looks, and heard the admiring exclamations with which he pointed at the various figures painted on the white surface. Then she began to explain to him.

" Lightning," said she, indicating with her finger a sinuous black line that issued from one side of the arches resting on a heavy black dash.

" Cloud," he added, referring to the arches.

" Rain," concluded the maiden, pointing at several black streaks which descended from the figure of the clouds. Both broke out in a hearty laugh. His merriment arose from sincere admiration, hers from equally sincere joy at his approbation of her work. The mother laughed also; it amused her to see how much Okoya praised her daughter's skill. She was overjoyed at seeing the two become more familiar.

Okoya returned to his former position, placing the vessel on the floor with tender care; and Mitsha resumed her sitting posture, only she sat much nearer the boy than before. He still examined the bowl with wonder.

" Who taught you to make such nice things?" he asked at last.

" An old woman from Mokatsh. Look," and she took up the vessel again, pointing to its outside, where near the base she had painted two horned serpents encircling the foot of the bowl.

" Tzitz shruy," she laughed merrily. The youth laughed, so did the women, all three enjoying themselves like big, happy children.

" For whom did you make this?" Okoya now inquired.

" For my father," Mitsha proudly replied.

" What may Tyope want with it?" asked the boy. " I have seen uashtanyi like this, but they stood before the altar and there was meal in them. It was when the Shiuana appeared on the wall. What may sa nashtio use this for?"

"I don't know," Mitsha replied, and her eye turned to her mother timidly askance and with an expression of doubt.

Hannay saw here an excellent pretext to put in a word of her own which she had wished to say long before.

" I will tell you, sa uishe ; I will speak to you as I would to my own child." The artful flattery had its desired effect. Okoya became very attentive ; he moved closer apparently to the mother, — in reality, to the daughter.

" You know Tyope is a Koshare, and I am Koshare too ; and he is very wise, a great man among those who create delight. Now it may be that you know also what we have to do."

" You have to make rain," said the youth ; for such was the common belief among the younger people about the duties of the society.

Hannay and Mitsha looked at each other smiling, the simple-mindedness of the boy amused them.

" You are right," the woman informed him. " After we have prayed, fasted, and done penance, it ought to rain, in order that yamunyi may grow to koatshit, and koatshit ripen to yakka." In these words she artfully shrouded the true objects of the Koshare. It enhanced their importance in the eyes of the uninitiated listener by making him believe that the making of rain was also an attribute of theirs. "See, uak," she proceeded, " on this bowl you see everything painted that produces rain." One after the other she pointed out the various figures. " Here you see the tad- pole, here the frog, here the dragon-fly and the fish ; they, as they stand here, pray for rain ; for some of them cry for it, when the time comes others live in the water, which is fed from the clouds, or they flit above the pools in summer. Here is the cloud and lightning, and " — she turned the vessel bottom side up — " here are the Shiuana themselves," pointing at the two horned serpents. "These live everywhere where Tzitz is running or standing. In this uashtanyi we keep meal in order to do sacrifice at the time when rain ought to fall. The pictures of the Shiuana call the Shiuana themselves! So you see what the Koshare want with this thing."

Okoya's lips had slowly parted in growing astonishment; and Mitsha, to whom the explanation was not altogether new, watched the expression of his features with genuine delight.

"And when you pray and scatter meal out of this," — pointing to the bowl, — "does the rain always come?"

"Always."

"Why, then, did it not rain last summer?"

"That I cannot tell you," said the woman. "Only the Shiuana know. Besides, there are bad people who stop the rain from coming."

"How can they do that?" cried both Okoya and Mitsha in surprise, neither of them having heard as yet of such a thing.

"I must not tell you that," said Hannay, with a mysterious and important air; "you are too young to know it. Tell me, Okoya," — her voice changed with the change of the subject, — "does Shotaye Koitza often come to see your mother?"

This question was highly imprudent. But Hannay was often imprudent. Smart and sly in a certain way, she was equally thoughtless in other matters. The query so sudden, so abrupt, and so uncalled for must, she ought to have foreseen, look extremely suspicious. And yet Okoya was on the point of answering, "She was at our home a few days ago." In time, however, he bethought himself of the warnings she had received, and replied in an unsteady tone, —

"I don't know."

Hannay noticed his embarrassed manner, and saw at a glance that he was forewarned. The "no" of the boy told her "yes." The discovery, however, that Okoya was on his guard was rather disagreeable; it angered her so much that her first impulse was to send him away. But she soon changed her mind. The youth was obedient; and if now he obeyed the counsels of his people, why might he not later on become accustomed to submission to his wife's people also? At all events he was good-natured, and according to Hannay's conceptions, good-natured folk were always silly. That smart but ill-natured persons might also prove extremely silly on occasions was far from her thoughts, and yet the very question she had imprudently put to Okoya was an instance of it.

It did not occur to her that it might yet be problematic whether Okoya would ever become a traitor to his own people. She could not conceive how anybody might be different from her and from Tyope, and of course she had no doubt concerning his ultimate pliability. And she relied also upon the influence Mitsha would exert upon her future husband, taking it for granted that her child had the same low standards as her parents. That child Hannay regarded merely as a resource, — as valuable property, marketable and to be disposed of to the most suitable bidder. In her eyes Okoya appeared as a very desirable one.

She saw that the courtship, if thus it may be called, was advancing most favourably; and thought it proper, now that the ball was in motion, to allow it to roll alone for a short time, — in other words, to leave the house under some pretext, abandoning the young folk to themselves. After her return she intended to sound Okoya again, though in a more skilful manner. So she replaced the bowl in its niche and went toward the ladder. Before ascending it she turned and said. —

" I will be back soon."

The youth smiled, and she gave him a knowing, signifi-cant wink, climbed on the roof and down to the ground, and remained standing outside for a while, until she thought that the young people had forgotten about her. Then she glided noiselessly to the air-hole and peeped in. They still sat by the hearth, examining together some object the na-ture of which she could not discover; and Mitsha was explaining something to the boy. Evidently the girl was showing him another piece of her handiwork. She heard them laugh merrily and innocently. They were like chil-dren at play. Satisfied with the outlook, Hannay crept off to a neighbour's dwelling where the whole family was gathered on the house-top. She took her seat by the old folk and joined in the conversation. That conversation was nothing more nor less than the merest gossip, — Indian gossip, as genuine as any that is spoken in modern society ; with this difference only, that the circle of facts and ideas accessible to the Indian mind is exceedingly narrow, and that the gossip applies itself therefore to a much smaller number of persons and things. But it is as venomous, the backbiting as severe and merciless among Indians as among us ; and there is the same disposition to criticise everything that does not strictly pertain to us and to our favourites, the same propensity to slander the absent and to be of the same opinion as those present so long as they are within hearing distance.

Gossip has a magic power. It fascinates more than any other kind of conversation. It fascinated Hannay, and time rolled on without her noticing it. The night was so beautiful, so still, so placid, and it felt so comfortable out-side on this terrace, whereon the moon shone so brightly, that Hannay sat and sat, listened and talked, until she had forgotten the young folk at home.

Suddenly a dark shadow covered the roof; the change was so abrupt that everybody looked around. What a moment ago was plunged in the silvery bath of the moon's rays was now wrapped in transparent darkness. But the valley below and the slope in front were as softly radiant as before. The moon had disappeared behind one of the cliffs, and the shadow of the rocks was now cast over the houses of the Eagle. It reminded the talkers that it was late, and it also reminded Hannay of her visitor. She clambered hurriedly off and hastened home. Again she looked through the circular vent. It was dark inside, and still. After listening a while she distinguished regular breathings. It was easy to recognize them as those of Mitsha, who was soundly, peacefully asleep. Hannay, as soon as she reached the floor of the apartment, called out, —

"Sa uishe!" No reply.

"Sa uishe!" No answer.

She groped about in the dark until her hands touched the sleeping form. She pulled the girl's dress and shook her by the arm until she sighed and moved, and then asked, —

"Sa uishe, has your father come?"

"No," murmured the still dreaming child.

"Where is Okoya?"

"He has left."

"Will he come again?"

"Oh, yes," breathed Mitsha softly; then she turned over, sighed, and spoke no more.

Hannay was happy. The boy would return! That was all she cared for. She really liked him, for he was so candid, so good, and so simple-minded. With such a son-in-law much was possible, she thought. Okoya could certainly be moulded to become a very useful tool to her as well as to Tyope. The woman felt elated over the results of the evening; she felt sure that notwithstanding one

egregious mistake, of which of course she would be careful
not to speak, her husband would be pleased with her management of affairs. It was long after midnight when that
husband returned to the roof of his wife, and Hannay was
already fast asleep.

Okoya had gone long before Hannay thought of returning. He went home happy, and satisfied that Mitsha
henceforth belonged to him. And yet after all there was a
cloud on his mind, — not a very threatening one, yet a
cloud such as accompanies us everywhere, marring our
perfect happiness whenever we fancy we have attained it.
Mitsha had said to him, while they were alone, —

" If you were only Koshare, the sanaya would give me to
you."

Okoya thereupon imagined that without Hannay's consent he could never obtain the maiden. On the other
hand, the idea of joining the Delight Makers did not at all
suit him. He feared in that case the opposition of his
mother. After he had returned to the estufa and lain down
among the other boys, who were mostly asleep, he revolved
the matter in his mind for a long time without arriving at
any conclusion whatever. Had he been less sincere and
less attached to his mother, such scruples would hardly have
troubled him; had he owned more experience he would
have known that his apprehensions were groundless, and
that Hannay could not, if she wished, prevent him from
becoming Mitsha's husband.

CHAPTER XIII.

When, at the close of the eventful meeting of the council at which the accusation against Shotaye and Say Koitza had fallen like a thunderbolt upon the minds of all present, the principal shamans warned the members of that council to keep strict silence and to fast or pray, that reminder was not to be understood as imposing on them the obligation of rigid penitence. Secrecy alone was obligatory; it remained optional with each how far he would carry his contrition. The three caciques, however, and the chief medicine-men had to retire and begin rigorous penitential ceremonies. Therefore the Hishtanyi Chayan had said that he was going to speak to the leading penitents at once.

Some of the fathers of the tribe, however, took the matter so much to heart that they obeyed the injunction of the great medicine-men literally, and took to sackcloth and ashes as soon as they reached home. Their motives were extremely laudable, but their action was by no means wise. They lost sight of what the shaman had strongly insisted upon; namely, that none of them should, by displaying particular sadness or by dropping mysterious hints, attract attention, and thus lead the people to surmise or suspect something of grave import. The shaman knew the human heart well, at least the hearts of his tribe; but with all his well-intended shrewdness he overlooked the fact that the very recommendations he gave had fallen on too fertile ground, and consequently worked more harm than good.

19

For the majority of the councilmen were so horror-stricken by the disclosures of Tyope and of the Koshare Naua, that they went to do penance with a zeal that could not fail to draw the attention of everybody around them. Thus Kauaitshe, the delegate of the Water clan, and Tyame, he of the Eagles, and several others considered it their duty to fast. Not a word concerning the meeting passed their lips; but when on the following morning each one of them retired to a secluded chamber or sat down in a corner of his room, his arms folded around his knees, speechless, motionless; when he refused to partake of the food which his wife or daughter presented to him, — when he persisted in this at-titude quietly and solemnly, it could not fail to attract atten-tion. The father, brother, or husband fasted! Whenever the Indian does penance it is because he has something heavy on his mind. In the present instance, as it hap-pened immediately after the council, it necessarily led to the inference that at that council momentous questions must have been discussed, and also that these questions had not been solved. Otherwise, why should the councilmen fast?

Penitence, with the Indian, is akin to sacrifice; the body is tormented because the soul is beyond human reach. The fasting is done in order to render the body more accessible to the influence of the mind. Often, too, one fasts in order to weaken the body, in order to free the soul from its thralls and bring it into a closer relation with the powers regarded as supernatural. At all events, fasting and purifications were a sure sign that serious affairs were in process of development, and such proceedings on the part of some of the nashtio could not fail to produce results the opposite of what the shaman had intended.

It would have been different had the yaya alone retired for penitential performances; nobody would have been struck by that, for everybody was accustomed to see them at work, as such voluntary sacrifice on their part is usually called; it was their business. But since the nashtio also, at least in part, performed similar acts, it could not help producing, slowly and gradually but surely, a tremendous amount of gossip and a corresponding number of speculations of a rather gloomy nature.

That gossip was started in the cave-dwellings of Tzina hanutsh. The stout representative of the Water clan had married into that cluster, and lived consequently among them with his wife. He returned home wildly excited; he did not go to rest at all; and when his family awoke they saw him sitting in a corner. As soon as he declined to eat, remaining there in morose silence, they all knew that he was grieving and chastising himself. Everybody thought, "The nashtio of Tzitz since his return from the council is doing penance. What can have happened last night!"

Owing to the custom which compels a man to marry outside of his own clan, the abodes of the women of each clan were frequented by their husbands. They of course belonged to different clans. Their natural confidants were not their wives, still less their children, but their clan-brothers and clan-sisters. During the day that followed the council, a man whose wife was from the Turkey people, but who himself belonged to Shyuamo, went down to the caves of the latter. There he was received with the remark,—

"The nashtio of the Eagles, Tyame, who lives with us, is fasting."

He replied in surprise, "And Kauaitshe is also doing penance."

A third, whose wife belonged to the Bear clan, was within hearing; and he quickly added, "The delegate from Hiitshanyi dwells with Kohaio; he, too, is fasting!" It was strange! People said nothing, but they shook their heads and separated.

Similar things occurred in the houses of the Tanyi. There
the representative of the Bear clan was in retirement. In the
big house news circulated faster than anywhere else on the
Tyuonyi, and in a very short time it became known that not
only the nashtio from Kohaio, but especially that the Hishtanyi Chayan and the Cuirana Naua were secluding themselves. Step by step the news got abroad and went from
clan to clan, while the people compared notes without expressing opinions. At sunset it was known all over the
Rito that since the council at least six of the clan delegates
were fasting, besides the three shamans. When at last
news came that a woman had gone to see the wife of the
chief penitent, and had heard from her that her husband
was working, things began to look not only strange but
portentous.

In an Indian village, gossip about public affairs comes to
a stand-still as soon as the outlook seems very grave. A sullen quiet sets in ; the hanutsh recede from each other, and
only such as are very intimate venture to interchange opinions, and even they only with the utmost caution. For any
event that concerns the welfare of the community is, in the
mind of the aborigine, intimately connected with the doings
of Those Above. And if the Shiuana were to hear an ir-
relevant or unpleasant utterance on the part of their children, things might go wrong. There is, beside, the barrier
between clan and clan, — the mistrust which one connection
feels always more or less strongly toward the others. Instead of the excitement and display of passion that too often
accompany the preliminaries of great events in civilized
communities, and which too often also unduly precipitate
them, among the Indians there is reticence. They do
not run to headquarters for information ; they make no
effort at interviewing the officers ; they simply and sullenly
wait.

This patient waiting, however, is only on the surface. In strictly intimate circles apprehensions are sometimes uttered and opinions exchanged. But this is done in the clan, and rarely in the family.

In the present case it was not reticence alone that pre-vailed. The conviction that great things might be brought to light soon, caused uneasiness rather than anything else. Apprehensions were increased by the fact that only a part of the dignitaries of the tribe were doing penance. The Ko-share Naua was not fasting, neither was Topanashka; and Tyope went about with the utmost unconcern. Members of the clans whose delegates kept secluded became suspi-cious of the fact that their nashtio appealed more particu-larly to the higher powers, and hence that his constituents — such was their conclusion — were in danger of something as yet concealed from the people. Suspicion led to envy, and finally to wrath against such as appeared to be free from the necessity of intercession. Tyope had thrown a firebrand among he tribe, and the fire was smouldering yet. But it was merely a question of time for the flames to burst forth. It was even easy to guess when it must occur, for no such fast can last longer than four days. At their expiration, if not before, all doubts must be dispelled. With this abso-lute certainty the people rested, not content, but submitting to the inevitable.

Only two men among the Queres knew the whole truth of the matter, and these were Tyope and the old Koshare Naua. They watched with apparent calmness, but with the greatest attention, the approach of the storm which they had pre-pared. Everything went on to their hearts' content. They did not need to do penance, for their sinister plans were advancing satisfactorily.

And a third at the Rito, although unknown to them, also began to see the truth gradually with a distinctness that was fearful, that was crushing to him. That man was the head war-chief, Topanashka Tihua. A series of logical deductions brought him to ravel step by step the game that was being played. He saw now why Tzitz hanutsh had been made to bear the first assault. It was on account of Shotaye. But as the demand was put, it involved ultimately the question of residence, and consequently an expulsion of the Water people. This could never have been merely on account of one woman and in order to get rid of her, since it was so easy to put Shotaye out of the way by the mere accusation of witchcraft. That accusation itself appeared to the old man to be a mere pretext and nothing else. To expel the small Water clan alone was not their object either. His daughter, the child of Tanyi, was also implicated, and with this thought came a flash of light. Not one clan alone, but several, were to be removed, and as he now saw plainly, mostly the clans occupying houses which were not exposed to the dangers which threatened the cave-dwellers from the crumbling rock. Tzitz had only served as an entering-wedge for their design that the house-dwellers should make room for the others. The more Topanashka thought over it, the more he felt convinced that he was right. And the stronger his convictions the more he saw that the plans of the two fiends, Tyope and the Naua, were likely to succeed. They were bad men, they were dangerous men; but they certainly had a pair of very subtle minds.

Was it possible to defeat their object? Other men, differently constituted from Topanashka, might have come to the conclusion that it was best to leave the Rito with their people at once, without any further wrangling, and make room peaceably. To this he could never consent. None of his relatives or their friends should be sacrificed to the intrigues of the Turquoise people. Rather than yield he was firmly determined that the Turquoise people themselves should go. But only after they had done their worst. It was true, as Tyope had said, that a division of the tribe entailed a dangerous weakening of both fragments; but then if it must be, what else could be done? Still he was in hopes that the Shiuana would not consent to a separation, and in his firm belief in the goodness of Those Above he resolved, when the time came, to do his utmost for the preservation of peace and unity. But it was a crushing weight to him. Not a soul had he with whom to communicate, for his lips were sealed; not one whom he might enlighten and prepare for the hour of the crisis. And he felt unconsciously that he was the pillar on which rested the safety of his people, — he and the Shiuana! The feeling was no source of pride; it was a terrible load, which he longed in vain to share with some one else. Topanashka did not attempt to do penance externally; he was too shrewd for that; but he prayed as much as any one, — prayed for light from above, for the immense courage to keep silent, to hope, and to wait.

The news that Kauaitshe, the delegate from Tzitz hanutsh, was fasting had reached the cave-dwellings of his cluster late in the afternoon. Zashue had carried it thither, communicating the intelligence secretly to his mother and sister. They were speaking of it, the old woman with apprehensions, and Zashue in his usual frivolous manner, when Hayoue entered.

"Do you know," said he, "that the nashtio of Tyame is doing penance?"

"So does ours," remarked Zashue, growing serious. He began to see matters in a different light.

"What may this all be about?" wondered the younger brother.

The elder brother shrugged his shoulders, sighed, and rubbed his eyes; and all four kept silent.

"Is it perhaps from the uuityam?" asked Hayoue; and his mother exclaimed,—

"Surely it is."

"Then something must have occurred," continued Hayoue; and with a side-glance at his brother, "I wonder if Tyope is fasting also?"

Zashue denied it positively, and added, "The Naua is out of doors."

"In that case it is our people again who have to suffer." His passion was aroused; he cried, rather than spoke "The Shyuamo never suffer anything. Who knows but the shuatyam, Tyope, and the old one have again done something to harm us!" Ere Zashue could reply to this sally the young man had left the cave.

When Hayoue stood outside he noticed Shotaye sitting on her doorstep.

"Guatzena, samām," he called over to her.

"Raua A," the woman answered, extending her hand toward him as if she wished to give him something.

He went over to her, took the object, and looked at it. It was the rattle of a snake.

"Where did you get this?" he asked.

"I found it above, where a rattlesnake had been eaten. Do you want it?"

He shook the rattle and inquired, —

" Will you give it to me?"

" Yes."

" It is well; and now I will tell you something that you don't know yet. Our father, Kauaitshe, is fasting."

" He is right," Shotaye remarked; " it will make him leaner."

Both laughed, but Hayoue said with greater earnestness, " Tyame is doing penance also.

" Then he is with his woman from Shyuamo," flippantly

observed Shotaye; "it will make Turquoises cheaper." She turned away with an indifferent air. Her careless manner struck the young man, and when he saw that she would not speak, but only gazed at the sky, he went off with the present he had received. He felt differently; he took the matter very seriously. He directed his steps toward the tall building where it might be possible to ascertain something else. Hayoue was afraid of the Turquoise people and their designs.

Shotaye was far from indifferent to the piece of news which Hayoue had brought to her. But neither was she surprised. She expected as much. It was therefore easy for her to appear perfectly calm and unconcerned. She was fully convinced that her case had been the subject of last night's discussion in the council, but the fact that the delegates were doing penance proved that the matter was still pending, and that no conclusion had been reached. There was consequently time before her still, and the reprieve amounted to about four days. She had time to reflect and to prepare her course of action. The sooner she was alone and left to her own musings the better, and that was why she turned away so abruptly from the young man. Hayoue drew from her manner the inference that the woman busied herself with thoughts entirely foreign to his own, and did not wish to be disturbed. But as soon as he turned to go she watched him through one corner of her eye. When he was far enough away, she rose, and slowly crept back into her dwelling.

We need not follow the train of thought that occupied Shotaye.

It was in the main the same that had filled her mind during the last week. One thing was certain, she was not silly enough to fast. She would not commit such a blunder. Neither would she call on Say Koitza. She regarded her companion in danger as sufficiently advised, and felt sure that the wife of Zashue was prepared for any event. Why then disturb her? It might only lead her into committing some disastrous blunder. Without Shotaye's direct knowledge Say was sure to do nothing at all, and that was the best for both. For the present, all that could be done was to remain absolutely quiet and to wait.

Hayoue, on the other hand, was not so philosophical. As he strolled down the valley, his mind was deeply agitated. It seemed clear to him that a grave question had been propounded at the council, and it could only have originated through some deviltry on the part of the evil spirits of the Turquoise clan, Tyope and the old Naua. This made him very angry, and he vowed within himself that when the time came he would take a very active part in the proceedings.

He would rather have commenced the fray at once by slaughtering Tyope and his accomplice ; but then, it was not altogether the thing to do. Neither would it do to go about and inquire at random. Nothing was left to him but to have patience and wait.

Waiting, however, did not interfere with his disposition to talk. With a nature as outspoken as that of Hayoue, it was impossible to wait without saying something to somebody about it. But to whom? At home he could not speak, for there was Zashue, and he was never impartial when any one of the Koshare was concerned. Okoya would be far preferable, and he determined upon looking him up. His nephew was not in the big house, and Hayoue went out to the corn-patches. The Indian goes to his field frequently, not in order to work, but simply to lounge, to seek company, or to watch the growing crops. Okoya was in his father's plot, sitting comfortably among the corn ; but it was not the plantation that occupied his thoughts, they were with Mitsha ; and he pondered over what she had told him the night before, and how he might succeed in making her his beyond cavil. Looking up accidentally he discerned the form of his uncle coming toward him, and his face brightened. He motioned Hayoue to come, and this time Hayoue was eager to meet Okoya.

The uncle wore a gloomy face, and the nephew noticed it at once. But he thought that if his friend intended to confide in him he would do so spontaneously. He had not long to wait. Hayoue sat down alongside of him and began, —

"Do you know where sa umo is, — the maseua?"

"He is at home, I think. At least he was there when I went away."

"Is he doing penance?"

Okoya stared at Hayoue in astonishment.

"No, he ate with us. Why should he fast?"

"Do you know," Hayoue continued to inquire, "that the nashtio of Tzitz and the nashtio of Tyame are fasting?"

"I did not, but I know that the Hishtanyi Chayan is at work."

Hayoue extended his neck and pricked up his ears. "What," said he, "the yaya also?"

"Indeed, the Cuirana Naua also. Did not you know it? You are a nice Cuirana."

The uncle shook his head.

"That is bad, very bad indeed," muttered he. Okoya was perplexed. At last his curiosity overcame all diffidence and he asked, —

"What is it, satyumishe nashtio? Do you know of anything evil?"

Hayoue looked at him and said, —

"Okoya, you and I are alike. When your heart is heavy you come to me and say, 'My heart is sad; help me to make it light again;' and when I feel sorrow I go to you

and tell you of it. When you came to me up there " —
he pointed to the west — " it was dark in your heart. To-
day it is night in mine."

The speech both astonished and pleased the boy. He
felt pride in the elder's confidence, but was too modest to
express it. So he merely replied, —

" Nashtio, I am very young, and you are much wiser than
I. How can I speak so that your heart may be relieved?
You know how I must speak, and when you tell me I will
try and do it."

He gazed into Hayoue's features with a timid, doubting
look ; he could hardly conceive that his uncle really needed
advice from him.

It was Hayoue's turn to sigh to-day. Slowly he said, —

" Last night the uuityam was together, and to-day the
yaya and the nashtio are fasting."

Okoya innocently asked, —

" Why do they fast? "

" That is just what I want to know," Hayoue impatiently
exclaimed, " but surely it bodes nothing good."

" Why should the wise men want something that is evil? "
said the other, in surprise.

" You are young, motātza, you are like a child, else you
would not ask such a question. The wise men are doing
penance, not because they intend harm, but in order to
prevent the people from being harmed. Do you understand me now? "

It began to dawn on Okoya's mind ; still he had not fully
grasped his uncle's meaning.

" Who is going to do evil things to us? Are there
Moshome about? "

Hayoue was struck by the remark. He had not thought
of this possibility. It might be that the older men had
learned something of the approach or presence of Navajos.

A few moments of reflection, however, convinced him of the utter improbability of the suggestion. If there were danger of this the warriors, to whom he belonged, — that is, the special group of war magicians, — would have been the first to be informed of it; and they would all be now in the estufa preparing themselves for duty, and the maseua first of all. Instead of it the old man was up and about as usual. No, it could not be; and he accordingly said, —

"It may be that some sneaking wolf is lurking about, but I do not believe it. See here, satyumishe, I belong to those who know of war, and I should certainly have heard if there were any signs of the Dinne. And our father the maseua would not have remained about the big house. No, umo, it is not on account of the Moshome that the yaya and nashtio take no food."

"But if there are no Moshome about, whence could there come danger to us?"

"From there;" and Hayoue pointed to distant cliffs where some of the cave-dwellings of Shyuamo were visible at the diminutive openings in the rock.

"Why from there?"

"From Shyuamo hanutsh."

"What can Shyuamo want to do harm for?"

Hayoue grew really impatient.

"You think of nothing else but your girl," he grumbled. "Have you forgotten already what I told you of Tyope and of that old sand-viper, the Naua?"

It thundered in the distance; a shower was falling south of the Rito, and its thunder sounded like low, subterranean mutterings. Hayoue called out, —

"Do you hear the Shiuana? They remind you of what I said."

The parts were reversed. It was now the uncle who

reminded the nephew of the voices from the higher world. Okoya hung his head.

"Listen to me," continued Hayoue; "I know that you do not like it that I speak against Tyope, but I am right nevertheless. He is a bad man and a base man; he only looks at what he desires and to the welfare of his hanutsh. Toward others he is ill-disposed; and his companion is worse yet, the old fiend."

"Yes, but what can they gain by doing evil to others?" Okoya asked.

"I don't know."

"How can I know it, then? I am much younger, much less wise than you."

Hayoue saw the candour of the boy and it troubled him. It was true; Okoya was too young yet, too inexperienced; he could not fully understand what Hayoue was suspecting, and could not give him any light or advice. It was useless to press him any further. But one thing Hayoue had achieved, at all events. He had enjoyed an opportunity to vent his feelings in full confidence, and that alone afforded him some relief. After musing a while he spoke again, —

"Let it be what it may, I tell you this much, brother: be careful, and now especially. Speak to nobody of what I have told you; and should you go to see Mitsha, keep your ears open and your mouth shut. I cannot find anybody to speak to except you and the maseua, but our father I dare not ask, for when the others are fasting Topanashka's lips are closed until the time comes to act. Meanwhile, brother, we must wait. I am going back to the katityam, for it is not good to run about and pry. Nobody knows anything but the yaya and the nashtio, and these do not speak to us." With these words he rose and left Okoya alone.

Much as the latter was attached to his father's brother, he was still glad to see him go. The sinister hints which

Hayoue had dropped were as good as incomprehensible to him. That the Zaashtesh could be damaged through some of its own people he could not conceive ; still he believed it, for Hayoue had said so and it must be true. But it was equally true that Okoya's thoughts were with his own affairs exclusively, and his uncle's talk affected him mainly on that score. It increased his already uneasy feelings. The fear that Mitsha would be given him only on condition that he became Koshare was now stronger than ever, and his prospects appeared still further complicated in the light of Hayoue's disclosures. Nevertheless, nothing was absolutely certain so far ; and he could not precipitate matters. In his case, too, there was nothing left but to wait.

The shower, which was sending floods of moisture into the valleys farther south, only grazed the Rito, sending a short and light rain upon its growing crops. It surprised Zashue upon his return to the big house, and drove him to shelter at his own, that is, his wife's home. He did not really care to go there, for since the time when he and Tyope had searched the rooms, Zashue had kept rather away from his spouse.

He did not suspect her any longer; but the very conviction on his part that she was innocent, and that consequently he had wronged her, kept him away from her presence. The weaker a man is, the less he likes to acknowledge guilt. He feels ashamed of himself, but will not acknowledge it. The Indian in this respect is as tough as other people, if not tougher. To beg pardon for an offence committed is to him a very difficult task. He is a child, and children rarely make atonement unless compelled. They conceal their guilt, and so does the Indian. If he has wronged any one, the redman persists in acting as if nothing had happened, or he pouts, or avoids the party offended. Zashue did not pout, but he avoided his wife's dwelling as much as possible, and felt embarrassed when there, or as had been the case a few days ago, when the matter of Okoya's wooing was discussed, he availed himself of the first pretext to take leave. To-day it was different; he had to go there for shelter. Say received him in her usual way, almost without a word, but with a look that was at once friendly, searching, and unsteady. It was dark in the inner room, and Zashue failed to notice his wife's glance.

Say also had heard of the fasts and penitence to which some of the officers of the tribe had submitted; and she rightly surmised that the accusation against Shotaye, and against herself perhaps, had at last been made, and was the cause of such unusual proceedings. But Shotaye had judged her well when she decided upon not troubling Say with a visit. It was unnecessary, for Say took everything calmly and with perfect composure. The positive assurance of Shotaye that she was safe, and still more the words of her father to the same effect, had completely reassured the woman. She looked forward to coming events with anxious curiosity rather than with apprehension. Still as her husband unexpectedly entered her dwelling, she could not resist the temptation to sound him, and to find out, if possible, what he thought about affairs. While kneading the corn-cakes she therefore asked, in a quiet, cool manner, —

"Hachshtze, do you know that the nashtio are fasting?"

"All of them?"

"I don't know," she replied, going on with her work, "and yet I know this much, — that sa nashtio does not fast He ate with us and is going about as usual."

"What may it all mean?" he inquired of her.

She shrugged her shoulders, and asked, —

"Does Tyope do penance?"

In view of the intimate relations existing between Tyope and Zashue this was a very natural question, and yet it stung Zashue. He interpreted it as a covert thrust. But as he bethought himself of the charges which Hayoue had uttered against the delegate from Shyuamo, a whole series of ideas rose within him so suddenly, and so far from pleasant or comforting to himself, that he forgot the conversation and inclined his head in thought.

Say Koitza was too much absorbed by her work to notice the change in her husband's manner at once. After a few moments of silence she reiterated her question. Zashue appeared to wake up; he started, saying, —

"I don't know; but why do you ask this?"

The woman realized that her inquiry might have been imprudent, but with great assurance explained, —

"Because he is nashtio, and a great one at that. Shyuamo is a strong hanutsh, and what it wants will be done. It alone can do more than Tzitz and Tanyi together."

The quick, bold, apparently unpremeditated reply relieved Zashue of an undefined feeling of suspicion that had arisen within him. During his moment of thoughtfulness he had been led from the accusations of Hayoue against Tyope unconsciously to the accusation which Tyope had launched before against Shotaye and his own wife. Quick as lightning it flashed upon his mind that that accusation had perhaps been formulated again, and this time officially before the council. And if Say were innocent, as he still believed, why did she inquire about him who was the originator of it? He did not attribute her query to a guilty conscience, for the Indian has but a very dim notion about human conscience, if he thinks of it at all. He would have gone further and have seen in the utterance of his wife the evidence of some positive knowledge. Did Say know anything about the real object of the stormy visit

20

which he and Tyope paid to her home during the dance of
the ayash tyucotz? Her ready reply to his mistrustful inquiry had allayed suspicions as to her guilt for the time
being, but on the other hand he felt strong misgivings that
she had found out something, either of what the Koshare
said or thought concerning her, or about the attempt which
Tyope and he had failed in. One thing, however, grew to
be more and more certain in his judgment; namely, that a
charge proffered against Shotaye was probably the cause of
the extraordinary fastings going on among the tribal heads.
More he could not surmise, still less find out. But he
determined upon being very guarded toward his wife
hereafter. Say, on her side, had a similar feeling toward
him. The breach which social customs already established
between man and wife was gradually but surely widening.

Still they continued to talk quietly. No one seeing them
together in the dingy kitchen would have suspected a lack
of harmony, or discontent, much less the sinister preoccu-
pations lurking in the heart of each. Both felt that it was
useless, that they must abide their time, avoid imprudent
words and queries, conceal from each other their misgivings, and wait

CHAPTER XIV.

MORE than eight days had elapsed since the one on which Shotaye had pledged her new friend, the Tehua warrior, to meet him at the homes of his tribe. She had not redeemed that pledge. In appearance she was unfaithful to Cayamo, as her knight was called; and yet her lack of compliance with her promise was not intentional. She calculated that her case would have come up by that time; and until this occurred, the energetic woman had no intention of leaving the Rito, much less of forsaking her friend Say Koitza. Now that her case had been delayed, the eight days had grown to nearly ten. The chayani and the caciques were fasting still, as well as some of the clan delegates.

Twelve days had passed, and it was the last day of official penance. That evening something was sure to occur to relieve the situation. So everybody thought at the Tyuonyi; so Shotaye thought herself. But she felt more than usually excited and worn out. It was not fear; it was the natural longing of a soul replete with energy and activity to see a matter ended that kept her in suspense. In regard to Say Koitza she felt perfectly reassured; the woman had not shown herself at her cave, and must feel quiet, cautious, and careful.

When the sun rose on the fourth day, it found Shotaye just about to take her morning meal. That was soon over, for there was no coffee, no hot rolls, no butter. It consisted merely of cold corn-cakes. When she had satisfied her appetite, she rose, shook the crumbs from her wrap, and went out. She had made a full toilet; that is, she had rubbed her face with her moistened hands and dried it with a deerskin, whereby a little more dust was added to her cheeks. She felt *pro forma* clean.

It was yet so early that hardly any one showed himself out of doors. The sun peeped up behind the volcanic heights in the east, casting a glow over the summits and crests that rise above the Rio Grande in that direction. The Tetilla stood out boldly, crowning the black ridges with its slender, graceful cone.

Shotaye strolled down the Rito. A few people were about; but regardless of these and what they might think or say, she wandered along past the dwellings of the Eagle clan. What if Tyope should see her? "Let him see me," she thought; "let him become convinced that I know nothing, that I rest easy, without any suspicion whatever of the dreadful fate he has prepared for me. Later on he may find out that his former wife is more than a match for him."

She went on and on, and passed the big house. A few men stood on the roofs, gazing motionless in the direction where the sun rose like a mass of melted ore. Farther she went, always down stream, quietly and with the greatest apparent unconcern. A girl from Yakka hanutsh greeted her in a friendly voice; she returned the greeting cheerfully. The cliffs wherein Oshatsh, Shutzuna, and lastly Shyuamo resided were to her left as she passed the grove where Okoya and Shyuote had had their first discussion. Here she turned to the north, in the direction of the spot where she had met the Tehua Indian. Even on this upward trail, rocky as it was and overgrown with shrubbery, her form was plainly distinguishable from below. But Shotaye scorned to conceal herself, she walked without haste or

hurry; her errand was perfectly legitimate and everybody
might see her undertake it.

Everybody might indeed witness her doings as far as these
could be seen. She simply took a walk on the mesa of the
Bird, Ziro kauash. She hoped also to gather some useful
plants, — such as the shkoa, a spinach-like vegetable; as-
clepias; apotz, a fever-medicine of the genus *artemesia*, and
many other medicinal herbs known to the Indian and used by
him. For it had sprinkled if not rained every day of late,
and last night's rain was still visible in the drops that covered the leaves. The ground was soft, and her step left
plainly distinguishable tracks. Not only might every one
see her; she almost invited people to follow her on her
wanderings. Tyope, the Koshare Naua, the Chayani, might
trail and spy out her movements as much and as long as
they pleased, step by step if they wished; for the real object
of her stroll they would never be able to guess.

After reaching the top of the plateau, Shotaye sat down
on a protruding rock, from which she might look over the
whole valley beneath. She cared little for this; her main
object was to rest and to think. What she now undertook
was a step preliminary to the last act. A trail almost indis-
tinguishable, so little was it used of late, led from the Rito
to the north, where the Tehuas dwelt in caves in the rock
which they name Puye. This trail was the object of
Shotaye's search. We know of her intention to take refuge
among the northern tribe of village Indians, but she had
meanwhile determined upon something else. She not only
wanted to go but had determined upon returning! Yes,
she would return, though not alone. With armed men
from the Puye she intended to return in the stillness of
the night. She would hide her companions at the approaches to the Tyuonyi, and lie in wait for Tyope and
the old Delight Maker, for the Chayani also if possible.

The Tehuas would reap many scalps; she would have had her revenge; and the deed could be so performed as to make those at the Rito believe that the Navajos were the perpetrators. This was her plan, and she did not feel the slightest scruple or compunction. For years she had been, among her own people, the butt of numberless insults and mortifications. Now it had gone so far that her life even was in imminent peril. Ere this should be lost, she would prove to her enemies that she was alive, and terribly alive !

To reconnoitre the ground, to study every detail of it, to store her memory with everything that might be useful or valuable in the lay of the land, was what she had come for now. After she felt thoroughly rested she rose, and continued her walk. Where she had been sitting, the trail was plain, for there it descended into the gorge. So she only noticed the place and then went into the shrubbery to seek for plants. She gathered a few leaves of the dark-green shiutui, sauntered from juniper-bush to juniper-bush, glanced from time to time upward into the tops of pines to see whether they bore edible nuts of the kind now called piñons, or threw stones at the noisy birds that fluttered about.

Again she came upon the trail, and her trained eye could follow it for some distance until it disappeared in the timber. So far she felt sure of her impressions for the future and turned away to the right, penetrating deeper into the forest. She could find her way even at night, for the moon shone still. Besides, once acquainted with the spot whence she had to start, it mattered little whether there was any path or not. The Indian needs only two points to guide himself, — the place of departure and the spot where he wants to arrive. Moreover, for her flight it was better not to follow the trail at all. She felt sure of meeting some one of the Tehuas in the vicinity of the Puye.

The topographical details attracted the woman's attention much more than the path. She studied them carefully, pretending to hunt for plants. Unconsciously she went farther and farther, regardless of time, for it was yet early. The surface of the Ziro kauash is slightly undulated, as well as the mesa to the south of the Tyuonyi; the timber is relatively sparse; the pines are grouped together at intervals; and juniper and cedar bushes cover it uniformly like an extensive, irregular plantation.

Such is the topography of the mesas west of the Rio Grande, from the Rito until one is beyond, and opposite to San Ildefonso. They are traversed and cut by deep ravines and cañons, which run generally from west to east, emptying their waters after storms into the valley of the river through narrow gaps, or terminating before reaching the stream against a towering wall of volcanic rock. Ere Shotaye noticed it, the shrubbery had begun to grow thinner, until she noticed in front something like a vacant space, indicating a gap; beyond that gap there was timber again. This told her that she had reached the brink of the first cañon north of the Rito.

In these solitudes game is not by any means so plentiful as might be supposed. This is particularly the case in the vicinity of Indian settlements. The merciless methods of communal hunting either exterminate or frighten away most of the larger animals. Roaming tribes send parties of men, hunters or warriors, long distances away; and these not only slaughter but frighten the deer, the mountain sheep, and the mountain goat, driving them into regions less accessible to man. The turkey alone, that noble bird, with its dark, iridescent plumage, remains everywhere; and Shotaye had already heard their loud cackling and calling before she entered the high timber. Several gobblers as well as hens had run away on her approach; at last they rose into the

air one after the other, flapping their wings until they settled down on a tall piñon that was visible from where the
woman stood.   There were four birds on the tree.   With
necks extended and eyelids alternately opening and shutting,
they peered down on her, ready to soar away at the least
suspicious motion.   Shotaye could not resist glancing at
them.   It seemed as if something was creeping up the tree
very slowly.   Like a grayish streak, a long body flattened
itself against the trunk.   Shotaye grew attentive, and the
more so as the suspicious object all at once disappeared
below the nethermost branches.   The turkeys themselves
were so occupied with the appearance of the woman that
they lost thought of everything else.   One of them, a gobbler, braced himself up, his breast bulged out, his head and
neck drawn in ; then quickly thrusting them forward, sent
out a loud cackle.   At this moment the pine-branches were
violently tossed about.   With noisy flapping of their wings
the hens rose into the air ; their companion flapped his
wings but once or twice, and disappeared in the tree-top.
For a moment the twigs and branches rustled and rattled ;
then all was still.   A panther had surprised them and secured one for his breakfast.   A long distance off might be
heard the cackling of another gobbler ; the forest was full
of turkeys.

Shotaye burst out laughing.   The panther had done well.
He had enough to satisfy his appetite, besides, and there
was no danger of her being attacked.   The American panther is not dangerous to man ; but he carries a mouthful of
very sharp teeth, and his claws are long ; he is a powerful
animal, agile and large.   Nobody can foretell what might
happen in case he should be ill-humoured.   The woman
began to scan the landscape around ; it was a clear space,
and she could see the bushes from their tops down to the
ground.   The base of one of these bushes attracted her

attention. Almost level with the soil, something black appeared beneath its branches. As she examined it more closely she saw that it was not really black, but of a grayish brown, like the colour of the soil. It was neither a plant nor was it a part of the earth itself, nor a stone. It might be some animal. The more she looked the more she became satisfied that it was neither animal's skin nor fur. The object was hairless. Only the skin of a human being could appear so smooth. Her first impulse was to hide; but before she could execute her purpose the object moved slightly, and something white appeared above the black. It was disk-like, and on it there was some object of a red colour. The eyes of Shotaye sparkled; she abandoned all thoughts of concealment or of flight, and fastened her gaze on the strange thing beneath the shrub. It became clearer and clearer to her that it was a human form, and that on its back was a white shield decorated with red. That shield she knew to be Cayamo's.

But what could Cayamo be doing here? Or was it perhaps not he, but some Navajo who had vanquished the proud warrior and was carrying home his weapons in triumph? The latter appeared rather improbable, and yet who could tell? At all events the man was alive, for he had moved. It was equally certain that he had not seen her. In order to clear up all doubt Shotaye looked around for shelter, and saw near by a bush that afforded a scanty hiding-place. She glided to it noiselessly; and changing her position, got nearer to him, and was even able to see more of his body and dress. The first glance satisfied her that he was not a Navajo, but a village Indian, and indeed her friend Cayamo.

Every trace of fear disappeared. Shotaye left the shelter of the bush and stepped up toward him rather noisily, at the same time calling his name. He did not reply; and as she came nearer, the regular breathing and the heaving of his chest showed the cause of his silence ; the great warrior from the Puye was fast asleep ! Under different circumstances she would have left him and quietly retired, but now she could not; the opportunity was too favourable, matters too threatening for her. She must be recognized by him once more, must show to him that she still counted on his pledge, on his friendship, his protection. Yet she did not wake him, but went close to his prostrate form and bent over it, even holding her breath for a while.

He slept profoundly. The war-paint on his face was sorely blurred; the campaign had not improved his appearance,—the face with closed eyes resembled a lump of dirt rather than a human head, his kilt was tattered, and his legs covered with scars and scratches. The circular sandals, much dilapidated, were tied to the belt; and close to them was another object, which Shotaye began to examine attentively, while her eyes flashed at the sight of it. It was a piece of human skin covered with gore and straight hair partly plaited. Her heart began to pulsate proudly and in delight, for she saw that Cayamo had secured a scalp, the scalp of a Navajo! Cayamo was a great warrior! Shotaye was careful not to touch the trophy, for no woman is allowed to handle the sacred token until after its taking has been duly celebrated in the great dance of the tribe. But lest the hero might wake up prematurely and notice her presence in too close proximity to the repulsive laurels which he had won, Shotaye quietly withdrew and sat down at some distance from him, where he could easily see her, and quietly awaited his rising from the slumbers of fatigue.

In point of fact it was not proper for her to remain so close to him. The scalp-crowned warrior must keep aloof from the other sex until he has been purified and has

danced. Shotaye relied upon the extraordinary circum‑
stances, and upon his interpretation of her presence as
having run after him, to obtain his forgiveness. Further‑
more they were alone ; and a few moments spent in the
practice of sign-language could not, she trusted, deprive the
scalp of the magic qualities attributed to it. Had it been a
warrior from the Rito she would have left him long ago.

Cayamo was manifestly tired, for he slept hard. The
sun stood close to the zenith, and still he dozed. The
luminary of day did not only illuminate, but its heat was
scorching ; the shadows under cover of which Cayamo had
retreated were moving gradually, and the unkempt head of
the hero became exposed to the most direct rays. The
heat began to disturb him : he groaned, stretched himself,
moved uneasily, and attempted to turn over. In this he
bent his shield, and the hard leather struck him in the ribs.
Cayamo woke up ! He opened his eyes and yawned,
closed them again, then opened the lids a second time,
when his look became suddenly a stare of surprise. Light‑
ning-like he rose to a sitting posture, and grasped the bow
as well as his war-club. In this position he stared at the
woman, who smiled, winking and placing a finger on her lips.
As soon as she whispered " Shotaye," the threatening flash in
his eye vanished ; he dropped both weapons and threw his
features into a repulsive, hideous grin intended for a soft
smile. Then he rose. It was very plain that he felt over‑
joyed, and that he would fain have expressed his delight to
the woman through some clumsy caress, but he restrained
his feelings and became serious.

Extending his arm to the west, he shook his head in
a warning manner, pointed to himself, made the sign in‑
dicating the act of men coming, and said, " Uan save ; "
then he waved his hand northward, afterward at the sun;
and finally he pointed at Shotaye, uttering, —

"Uiye tha, ' two days ! ' "

She could not fully comprehend. Until better informed she drew the conclusion that the Navajos were in pursuit of him, but more she failed to understand. To ascertain his meaning she pointed at him, then at herself, raised four of her fingers, and asked, —

"Tehua?"

Cayamo shook his head, counted two on his fingers, accompanying the gestures with the words, —

"Tema quio Puye," pointing to the north at the same time. Now her doubts were cleared. Shotaye saw that two days hence she would be expected among the Tehuas. She nodded eagerly and rose. If the Navajos, as she rightly concluded, were on her warrior's trail, it was unsafe for both of them to remain here long ; but neither could she insinuate to Cayamo that she would like to go with him at once. To her surprise the man bent down and with his fingers drew a line on the ground which ran in the direction where the cave-dwellings of the Tehuas were situated. The woman bent over him with great curiosity.

"Tupoge," said Cayamo, indicating the southern end of the line and looking askance. Shotaye nodded that she understood, and he slowly moved his fingers along the line to the north, uttering, —

"Tema quio."

The northern terminus of the streak he designated as Puye. Finally he made a mark across the middle of the line, saying very positively, —

"Uiye tha Shotaye Teanyi." These words he accompanied successively with the signs for the number two, for male Indian, and for the meeting of two persons.

Nothing could be clearer. Two days hence Shotaye was to leave the Rito for the Puye ; and as Cayamo himself would be unable to meet her, owing to the ceremonies which he had to perform in honour of the scalp, some male friend of his, called Teayni, would meet her half-way and conduct her safely to the abode of his people. With a radiant face the woman nodded assent, and made other gestures expressive of delight and agreement. Cayamo took advantage of his cowering posture to fasten the war-sandals to his naked feet, and then rose and took the trail towards the north, but Shotaye held him back in token of misgivings. He understood her motive, but pointed to his circular foot-gear and smiled. It was clear that he trusted to the round tracks left by that contrivance for safety. So he went on toward the brink of the gorge that lay before them. As soon as his form had sunk below it, Shotaye also turned, this time in the direction of the Rito.

Everything was right at last! She felt safe, completely safe; for the road was clear to her, and furthermore Cayamo, of whose attachment she was now fully convinced, would provide for a guide during the second half of the journey, which was utterly unknown to her. Everything was moving to her fullest satisfaction, provided she could escape from the Rito.

In regard to that matter she had scarcely any doubt, unless — and this thought came to her while she was wending her way slowly homeward — some one should have followed her and witnessed the strange meeting between her and Cayamo. In that case everything might be lost. But there were not the slightest marks of human presence about. Nature, even, seemed to slumber in the heat of the day; an occasional lizard rustled through the dried twigs and fallen pine needles, a crow sat on a dry limb, and high up in the air an eagle soared below the mares' tails that streamed over the sky. It would have been very disagreeable, to say the least, if one or other of the Navajos who were in pursuit of Cayamo should cross her path; but of this she had little fear. She was already too near the Rito for that. Soon the gorge opened at her feet, showing a placid, lovely picture, — the little valley down below, huge pines raising their dark columns by the side of light-green corn-patches, and the tall pile of the big houses looming up like an enormous round tower. But Shotaye was not affected by scenery. Walking along the brink to the west she at last reached the upper end, where twelve days ago she had ascended, and where the brook, swollen by late rains, now gushed down the ledges in a series of murmuring cascades. Here she began her descent, and as the sun disappeared behind threatening clouds over the western mountains, she entered her home again. Shotaye had spent nearly the whole day on the mesa, had spent it profitably, and was — so she fancied — in complete security as regarded her ultimate designs.

And yet had the woman, after taking leave of the strange Indian and after the latter had gone out of sight, peered into the shadow of the pines on one of which the panther had so nimbly captured the unsuspecting turkey, she might have noticed something that would have greatly modified her ideas on this point. For behind one of them there stood, all the while she and the Tehua were carrying on their pantomime, a human figure intently watching them. Pressed against the trunk of a tree there was, motionless, quiet, calm, not a common spy, but a cool observer of her doings, whose presence was accidental, but who not only watched but at the same time judged and passed sentence on her actions.

A short time after Shotaye had set out on her walk, Topanashka Tihua also started in the same direction. With all the self-control he had maintained, inward agitation and sorrow nearly overcame him. The nearer the hour came when the momentous question that was going

to shake the existence of the tribe to its very foundations
would be taken in hand, the more conscious he became that
he was carrying a terrible load, and that upon his action depended nearly everything. The feeling of responsibility was
crushing. He had, of course, ascertained nothing new;
neither had he thought of making notes of what met his
gaze. But on this last day he felt the necessity of being
alone ere the dread moment came. Others could not help;
he was alone with his thoughts, and yet, as he did no fasting, not alone in the proper use of the word. On that last
day, therefore, he resolved upon retiring to some solitude.
It would attract no undue attention, and he would have
done according to the spirit of the shaman's instructions.
After leaving the Rito he climbed to the northern mesa,
and instead of resting on its brink as Shotaye had, he
strolled into the timber perfectly at random, hardly conscious whither he directed his steps, and content to be for
once alone with his dismal thoughts.

However much he speculated and reflected upon the
matter, he drew not the slightest comfort from it. The
main factor he lacked; namely, a knowledge of the judgment
which Those Above would render. This the chayani alone
knew, and they alone would proclaim it at the council. If
the case of Shotaye only had been before the meeting, his
position would have been very simple. All he had to
do was to kill her if found guilty, and he was ready to do
this at any time. He did not especially hate the woman,
and all he cared for in such an event was to perform his
duty. In regard to his daughter Say he no longer entertained any apprehension. Matters, however, had degen-
erated into a venomous contention between two clans,
amounting almost to a schism in the tribe. If now the
Chayani in the name of the Shiuana proclaimed that
Shyuamo was right, and the others, his own clan included,

resisted, what then? He had to obey, he had to execute what Those Above decreed; for that purpose was he called maseua, like him who bears the same name and is the most active among all the deities on high. What the Shiuana determined was right always.

The old man sat down under a tree and attempted to ponder over this little query of " always." But he did it in vain. It was a problem perhaps not beyond the reach of his intelligence, if it had been properly cultivated, but far beyond the limits which training and custom had set to the working powers of that intelligence. He staggered from doubt to doubt, and finally gave it up. No other conclusion could he reach than to wait. But waiting alone gives no light, does not comfort, gives neither strength nor wisdom. Strength and wisdom, so the Indian believes, are gifts from above, and can be obtained by prayer. Topanashka came to the conclusion that he would pray. He picked up a stone, and was searching his memory for one of the many formulas that the Indian has in his rituals, when a faint pattering sound attracted his attention.

It was as if something glided through brushwood. He forgot to pray, and listened. Now it sounded again, at a greater distance from him. Only some animal could have produced the noise; a human being would either have come up to him if a friend, or kept absolutely still if a foe. He looked and looked, and at last caught a glimpse of the panther's yellowish fur gliding along the ground. When a cat glides stealthily she is on the hunt. His curiosity was fully aroused; he longed to see what the animal was hunting and how he would succeed. Furthermore the panther is in the eyes of the Pueblo Indian the symbol of the greatest physical power. A feeling overcame the old man as if this symbol was presenting itself to him at the very time when he needed the greatest moral strength himself: and the

animal appeared like a living fetich, a hint from Those
Above. He followed the movements of the puma eagerly.
The tree where the turkeys sat stood near; he had heard
their gobblings long ago without paying any attention to
them. But now they explained the movements of the
gigantic cat; he was creeping up to the birds. The puma
approached the tree noiselessly; at its foot he laid down his
head, and raised his tail, sweeping the ground with nervous
force. Now the beast of prey began to climb the trunk of
the pine carefully and noiselessly. He reached the lower
branches and disappeared within their maze. Then followed his spring; and the turkeys flew away, all but one.
With a tremendous leap the cat broke through the tree-top
and down on the ground, with the wriggling bird in his
jaws, and trotted off howling.

Topanashka had witnessed the performance with interest and with genuine pleasure. He admired the strength
and the swiftness of the animal hunter. Unconsciously his
thought turned back to the intended prayer, and he earnestly addressed it now to Those Above, that they might give
to his heart the strength which the panther had shown in
his limbs. Placing two sticks on the ground before him
and a stone over them, he rose to go. But another sight
met his eyes, and he stood still as if rooted to the soil, gazed
and gazed. His eyes opened wide, then his expression
became dark and almost fierce.

On the clear space beyond the pines on which the puma
had caught his prey, a woman sat near a cedar-bush; and in
the shade of the bush a man rested. The first glance convinced Topanashka that the man wore paint, and carried
the accoutrements and weapons of a warrior. It was not a
warrior from the Rito; he was positive it could not be.
Nor was it a Navajo. He undoubtedly belonged to some
foreign tribe of village Indians, in all probability to the

Tehuas. What was he here for? And what business had the woman in his company? Indians in war-paint do not associate with women. Topanashka strained his eyes, and recognized to his astonishment and dismay the woman Shotaye.

He could not contain himself any longer. Like a shadow he moved forward and hid behind the trunk of a pine, whence he could see more and better. From there he witnessed the strange pantomime of Shotaye and Cayamo. He was too far off to hear the words, but the gestures spoke plainly enough. As they pointed and gesticulated to the west, north, and south, he thought that they were planning some murderous surprise for the Queres, — that Shotaye was betraying her own people and conspiring with an enemy of her own stock. Fierce wrath filled his heart. Yes, Tyope's charge was true; the woman was a witch, and had Topanashka been armed he would have sought to kill her on the spot. But though he had no weapons, his hand clutched a stone, raised it from the ground, and held it in readiness. The interview ended, the Tehua disappeared, and Shotaye went in the direction of the Rito. Topanashka felt tempted to follow her at once, to overtake her if possible and secure her person, or even to execute summary justice; but she was sure not to escape him. She had evidently not noticed his presence and had gone back to her den in the cliffs in complete security. There, on this very evening, he would seize her, drag her before the uuityam, disclose her shameless and dangerous plots, and doom her to the horrible death she deserved to suffer.

Whither was her accomplice, the Tehua, going meanwhile? He was probably returning to his people to report, and to lead back those in whose company he intended to carry out the projected assault. The old man could not stop him, being himself unarmed : but he could follow at a distance, cautiously and without exposing himself to danger. For it was possible that the hellish plot had developed much further, and that the warriors from the north were lurking already near by to pounce upon the Queres at daybreak. It was not only from the instinct of the old warrior scout, it was out of a sense of duty as head war-chief that he determined at once upon following the Tehua. As soon as Shotaye, too, was out of sight, he went over to the spot where the interview had taken place and examined the soil carefully. The round impression made by a war-sandal struck his eye; it proved to him beyond any possibility of doubt that his inferences were correct. The old man straightened himself to his full height. His piercing glance went in the direction whither the Tehua had gone. He bent forward again and followed the same line toward the north.

The sun had just set over the Rito. It disappeared behind dense clouds; a storm was gathering in the west. Its wings were spreading like tentacles; they pushed on to meet the moon, whose light was just rising in the east as a dim whitish arch. The orb itself still remained below the horizon. Gusts of wind whirled up the gorge from the east at intervals, causing the pines to sigh, the willows and poplars to rustle. The corn whispered and tinkled. The usual bustle prevailed about the houses and in front of the caves.

Before the grotto where the council was to meet that night, men were standing, sitting, or lounging. They were the delegates who had come to listen at last to the oracle which was to be revealed to them through the mouth of the great shaman. Their number was not yet complete; the Tapop, Tyope, the Koshare Naua were there, but neither the Caciques nor the Chayani nor the Maseua had put in an appearance. Everybody was silent, hardly a word was heard from time to time, seldom a whisper. The men were in part exhausted by long penitence, but mostly depressed as if some nightmare was still weighing upon them. The obligation to be silent imposed by the medicine-man was yet in force.

One by one those who were lacking came. The medicine-men appeared at last, and only the yaya and the maseua were missing. The tapop, prompted by a wink of the Hishtanyi Chayan, went into the cave and prepared the council-fire. It burned well, but nobody came.

Distant thunder rolled through the clouds; lightning flashed from them in fiery red tongues. The wind continued to blow in gusts, but at long intervals only. Between gust and gust it grew dismally, anxiously, still. The singing, shouting, laughing of the people had almost ceased. Now the wind again whirled up the valley stronger than before, and as its noise ceased, a plaintive sound, a distant howling, floated on the air. It waxed in strength and power till it rose into the night shrill and heart-rending. The men listened in surprise. Sobs, cries, shrieks, from time to time a piercing scream, were the dismal sounds that struck upon their ears. All came from the large building; it was a lament by many voices, the sad, soul-rending lament over the dead!

Breathlessly they listened. Hurried footsteps rushed toward them, several men came running up the slope. When the foremost of them reached the group he asked, panting, —

"Where is the tapop?"

Hoshkanyi Tihua stepped forward and inquired, —

"What has happened? What do you want?"

"Our father the maseua," gasped the man, "is dead! He was killed on the Ziro kauash!"

"Who killed him?" demanded the principal chayan, placing himself in front of the speaker.

The Indian raised his arm on high; from it depended a circular object. As the pale light of the rising moon fell on it, it was plainly distinguishable as a circular war-sandal!

CHAPTER XV.

"DID you find that?" asked the shaman.

"Yes, I found it. I and Hayash Tihua together."

"Where?"

"On the kauash, on the trail that leads to the north."

"Who killed sa nashtio?" the chayan further inquired. He alone carried on the investigation; Hoshkanyi Tihua had mingled with the rest again, and stood there silent and speechless over the terrible news. Neither did any of the others utter a single word, but from time to time one or the other shook his head and sighed deeply.

"We don't know," replied the Indian, "for we did not find anything else."

"Have you looked for more?" emphasized the medicine-man.

The other hung his head as if he felt the reproach. "No," he said in a low tone.

"Why not?"

"Because we were afraid that other Tehuas might be around."

"How do you know that the people from the north have killed our nashtio?"

"Because the Moshome Dinne never wear such." He pointed to the sandal, which he had handed to the tapop.

"Did the shoe lie where our father died?"

"No, we found it closer to the Tyuonyi."

A flutter went through the group, — a movement of surprise and of terror. Many persons had collected, and the steps of more were heard coming up. In the valley the wind sighed. Louder than its plaintive moaning sounded the howling wail that continued in the great house with undiminished power. The Hishtanyi continued, —

"How did the shuatyam kill our father?" His voice trembled as he uttered these words.

"With arrows."

"Have you brought them along?"

"Yes."

"How many?"

"One."

"Where is the corpse?"

"At the house of Tanyi hanutsh."

The shaman turned around. "Tyame," he called to the delegate of the Eagle clan, "do your duty. And you, too, Tapop."

The group was about to disperse when the Shikama Chayan called back the men who had brought the news. All stood still and listened.

"Is the head entire?" asked the medicine-man.

"The scalp is not on it."

A murmur of indignation arose. The chayan turned away and walked slowly along the foot of the cliffs toward his dwelling. Every one set out for the great house, talking together excitedly, but in low voices. The tapop, Tyame, and the two men who had found the body took the lead. The Hishtanyi Chayan and the Shkuy Chayan came last.

The nearer they came to the great building, the louder and more dismal sounded the lamentations.

The storm was approaching with threatening speed. One dense mass of inky clouds shrouded the west. From time to time it seemed to open, and sheets of fire would fill

the gap. To this threatening sky the death-wail ascended
tremulously and plaintively, like a timid appeal for redress.
In response the heavens shot angry lightning and thunder-
peals. The cliffs on the Tyuonyi trembled, and re-echoed
the voices from above, which seemed to tell feeble humanity
below, " We come ! "

It was long before sunset when the old war-chief of the
Queres, after having thoroughly examined the spot where
the interview between Shotaye and the Tehua Indian took
place, began to follow on the tracks of the latter. He was
undertaking a difficult, an extremely dangerous task. It is
not easy for a man well provided with weapons to pursue
an armed Indian, but to attempt it unarmed is foolhardi-
ness. The Indian is most dangerous when retreating, for
then he enjoys the best opportunities to display his main
tactics in warfare, which are hiding and patient lurking.
He has every opportunity to prepare his favourite ambush,
and woe unto him who runs after an Indian on the retreat,
unless the pursuer is thoroughly prepared and well acquainted with the war-tricks of the redman. The annals
of western warfare give sad evidence of the disastrous results. The mountaineers among the Indian tribes are those
who are best skilled in the murderous hide-and-seek game.
Indians of the plains have less occasion to cultivate it.

Topanashka Tihua was aware that if he followed the
Tehua he was risking his own life. But it was not the first
time he had attempted such dangerous undertakings, and so
far he had never failed. With the configuration of the ground
and the landmarks in vegetation and scenery he was far
better acquainted than the Tehua. Furthermore, he enjoyed the material advantage that the latter could not have
noticed him. Everything depended on ascertaining unseen
as much as possible about the enemy's movements.

From some of Shotaye's gesticulations the maseua had concluded that the Tehua would proceed on the old trail leading from the Rito to the Puye, or at least keep himself very near that trail. He was confirmed in it by the direction which the friend of the woman took after leaving her. Topanashka maintained, therefore, the same course, going slowly and with the greatest caution. He kept on the alert for the least noise that struck him as suspicious, or for which he could not at once account.

In consequence of the heat of the day, the forest was remarkably still. Not a breeze sighed through the tops of the pines, for the wind that blows toward a coming storm and heralds its approach rises later in the day. The distant gobbling of turkeys was a sound that awakened no suspicions, the more so as it grew fainter and fainter, receding in the direction of the higher crests and peaks. Neither were the numerous crows a source of uneasiness to him. On every clearing these birds gravely promenaded by half-dozens together, and his cautious gliding across such exposed places did not in the least discommode the dusky company. As soon as Topanashka came in sight of the trail again he kept near it, but to its left, gliding from tree to tree or creeping across clear expanses from shrub to shrub. He therefore moved more slowly than the Tehua whom he was pursuing.

In this manner he had advanced for quite a while, always keeping an eye on the trail to his right, when he caught sight of a suspicious object lying directly in the path, where the latter was barely more than a faint streak across the thin grass that grows sometimes on the plateaus in bunches. At once the old man stopped, cowered behind a juniper, and waited.

A novice on the war-path, or an inexperienced white man, would have gone to examine the strange object more closely,

but the old scout takes such unexpected finds in the light
of serious warning. Nothing appears more suspicious to
him than something which seems to have been accidentally
dropped on a trail over which hostile Indians are retreating.
He forthwith thinks of a decoy, and is careful not to approach. For Topanashka it was doubly significant, for had
the object purposely been placed there, it led to the disagreeable inference that the Tehua was aware of his pursuit.
In that case he was sure to lie in wait for him, and upon
nearer approach he could expect an arrow-shot without
the least doubt. That shot might miss him, but at all
events the lurking enemy would find out that his pursuer
was an unarmed man, and that there was no danger in
attacking him openly. Then the situation would become
desperate.

Still, as the old man had always kept to the right of the
trail, it was possible that the enemy had not so far noticed
him. But somewhere in the neighbourhood of the suspicious object that enemy must be hidden; of that he felt
sure. It was a very serious moment, for any awkward
movement or the least noise might bring about his destruction. Under such circumstances many a one sends a short
prayer to Heaven for assistance in his hour of need. Not
so the Indian ; he has only formulas and ritualistic performances, and there was no time to remember the former or
to think of the latter. Topanashka strained his eyes to the
utmost to find out the nature of the suspicious object that
lay not far from his hiding-place, but he could arrive at no
satisfactory result. It appeared to be round, like a flat
disk ; but of what material it was made and for what purpose it had been manufactured, he could not discover. At
last it flashed upon him that it might be one of the circular
war-sandals of the Tehua, whose tracks he had noticed from
time to time, which the owner might have taken off and

deposited here. There was no doubt that the enemy must be close at hand.

Topanashka had no thought of turning back. Flight was very difficult, since he did not know where the foe lurked. To wait was the only thing to be done, — wait until night came, and then improve the darkness to return to the Rito in safety. But what of the all-important council-meeting, at which he was compelled to assist? Crouched behind the juniper-bush, cautiously peering out from behind it now and then, the old warrior pondered over the situation. At last he saw what to do.

Slowly extending his feet and legs backward, he little by little succeeded in laying himself flat on his stomach. He had noticed that not far behind him there was another and much taller bush. Toward this bush he crept, but like a crawfish, feet foremost. Had his enemy stood otherwise than in a line with the first shelter which Topanashka had made use of, he would surely have sent an arrow during this retrograde performance. He continued to crawfish until the tall bush was between him and the smaller one. Once covered by the former, he raised his head and looked around.

A peculiar stillness reigned. Not a breeze stirred, the sun was blazing hot, notwithstanding the long, trailing clouds that traversed the sky.

" Kuawk, kuawk, kuawk ! " sounded the cries of several crows, as they flew from a neighbouring tree. They went in the very direction where Topanashka suspected the Tehua to be, and alighted on a piñon in that neighbourhood. The old man glanced, not at the birds, but at the trunk above which the crows were sitting. It was not thick enough to conceal the body of a man, and about it the ground was bare. If there had been anybody hiding there, the cunning and mistrustful birds would never have alighted.

The maseua took this into consideration, and began to doubt the correctness of his former conclusions. Yet it was wiser not to attempt a close examination of the sandal; such curiosity might still lead to fatal results.

Like an old fox, Topanashka determined to circumvent the dangerous spot, by describing a wide arc around it. He would thus meet the trail farther north, and be able to judge from signs there whether or not the Tehua was close upon the Rito. First he would have to crawl backward until he was at a sufficient distance to be out of sight altogether.

This movement he began to execute in his usual slow and deliberate manner, crawfishing until he felt sure that he could not be seen from the point where the crows had taken their position. Once during his retreat the birds fluttered upward, croaking, but alighted again on the same spot. Something must have disturbed them.

Topanashka arose, straightened himself, and moved ahead as noiselessly as possible. He maintained a course parallel to the trail.

The old man considered himself now as being in the country of the enemy and on hostile ground. For whereas he was in reality not far from the Rito, still, possibly, he had an enemy in his rear. It is the custom of a warrior of high rank in the esoteric cluster of the war magicians, ere the trailing of an enemy begins, to pronounce a short prayer, and Topanashka had neglected it. His indignation at the discovery of Shotaye's misdeed was the cause of this neglect. Now it came to his mind.

"Kuawk, kuawk, kuawk!"

A crow flew overhead. It came from the tree where the others had been sitting, or at least from that direction.

To the Indian the crow is a bird of ill omen. Its discordant voice is, next to the cry of the owl, regarded as the most dismal forewarning. The use of its plumage in magic is strongly condemned. Was it not strange that those harbingers of misfortune so persistently followed him, and that their repulsive croaking always interrupted his thoughts? Topanashka resolved to make good on the spot what he had omitted, and ere he moved, to pray.

In place of the formula which the warrior recites when he is on the track of an enemy, Topanashka selected another one, spoken upon entering dangerous ground where enemies may be lurking. It seemed to him that the latter was better adapted to the occasion, since he was unarmed and therefore unable to fight in case of necessity. He still carried with him the same fetich, a rude alabaster figure of the panther, which we saw dangling from his necklace on the day he went to visit the tapop. But the necklace he had left at home this time, and he carried the amulet in a leather satchel concealed under his wrap. He took out the wallet and removed the fetich from it. To the back of the figure was fastened a small arrow-head, on the sides a turquoise and a few shells were tied with strings of yucca fibre.

The old man squatted on the ground, took from the same satchel a pinch of sacred meal, and scattered it to the six regions. Then he whispered, —

" Ā-ā. Nashtio, Shiuana, Kopishtai! Make me precious this day, even if the land be full of enemies. Let not my life be threatened by them. Protect me from them. Let none of the Moshome go across this line," he drew a line in the sand with the arrow-point, " give me protection from them! Mokatsh, Tyame, Shiuana, shield my heart from the enemy."

While pronouncing the latter words he drew three more lines, breathed on the fetich, placed it in the satchel again, and rose. He felt strengthened, for he had performed his duty toward the Shiuana, had satisfied Those Above.

"Kuawk, kuawk, kuawk!" The crow soared back over his head. The ugly, ill-voiced bird! Topanashka's eyelids twitched angrily; he was amazed.

He resumed his walk, or rather his cautious, gliding gait, his head bent forward, all his faculties strained to see, to hear, and to detect. Frequently he would stop, hide himself, and listen. All was quiet around him, for even the crows kept silent or were heard in the distance only.

The glare of the sunlight was less vivid, the afternoon was on the wane. The late hour was not alone the cause of the diminution of light; the sun was shrouded by heavy masses of clouds. With the waning daylight it grew cooler, a faint breeze being wafted over from the Rio Grande.

The old man rightly supposed that he was approaching the trail again and would soon strike it. The cañon near which he had surprised Shotaye and her ally lay some distance in his rear and to the right, for the old trail crosses it at its upper end, and the cañon bends to the north. Topanashka intended to reach this upper terminus. He expected in case other Tehuas should be about, that they would be hidden in that vicinity. He wanted to strike the path first, and survey it, if from a distance only, then keep on again in a line parallel to its course until it crossed the ravine. Afterward he would go back to the Tyuonyi, if possible, with the sandal as corroborative evidence.

He almost chided himself now for not having picked up the foot-gear. The more he reflected, the more he became convinced that his suspicions about some ambush having been prepared by means of the sandal were groundless. The crows especially seemed to be a sure sign of it. That bird is very bold, but also very sly; and had a warrior or any human being been in concealment, would never have selected his vicinity for a place of comfortable rest. Had they not flown away as soon as he approached their roosting-place? And yet he moved very slowly and noiselessly.

But why did the crows so persistently follow him? What signified their restlessness, their loud and repeated cries? It boded nothing good. The black pursuivants either fore-told or intended evil. Were they real crows?

The Indian is so imbued with the notion of sorcery that any animal that behaves unusually appears to him either as a human being changed into an animal, or some spirit which has assumed the form for a purpose. That purpose is either good or bad. Owls, crows, and turkey-buzzards, also the coyote, are regarded as forms assumed by evil spirits, or by men under the influence of evil charms. The more Topanashka reflected upon the conduct of the birds, the more superstitious he became concerning them. They cer-tainly meant harm. Either they sought to allure him into danger, or they indicated the presence of imminent peril.

Whatever that danger might be and wherever it might lurk, the man thought of nothing but to do his duty under all circumstances. He was, after all, glad that he had not taken up the sandal. It had brought him as far as he was now, and he considered it his duty to go to the bitter end, and find out everything if possible. That he exposed him-self more than was really necessary did not enter his mind. He failed to consider that if he were killed, nobody would be able to give timely warning at the Rito, and that the very search for him might expose his people to the danger which he was striving to avert. Death had little terror for him; it was nothing but the end of all pain and trouble.

As soon as Topanashka believed that he had come again into proximity of the path, he resumed his previous methods of locomotion; that is, he began to crawl on hands and feet. The timber was of greater density here, for it was nearer the foot of the mountains.

In proportion as the trees become taller and as they stand closer together, the ground below is freer from shrubbery, and may be scanned from a certain distance with greater ease. Nevertheless the soil is more rocky, ledges crop out on the surface, isolated blocks appear, boulders, and sometimes low, dyke-like protuberances

When Topanashka felt certain of the proximity of the trail, he scanned the ground very carefully. It was still flat, notwithstanding some rocky patches. The shade was deep, and as far as the eye reached, nothing moved; nothing suspicious was seen, nay, nothing that bore life, except the sombre vegetation. The wind increased in force; the pines faintly murmured from time to time; a blast penetrated beneath them to the surface of the soil, chasing the dry needles in fitful whirls or playing with the tall bunch-grasses that were growing profusely here.

If any man was about he certainly kept outside the range of vision. So the old man reasoned, and he began to creep toward a place where the smoothness of the rocks indicated the wear and tear of human feet. It was the only trace of the trail, and barely visible. As he approached the place he knew that he must be seen, but he relied upon the fact that a man lying flat on the ground is very difficult to hit. An arrow could scarcely strike him, and in no case could the wound be other than slight, for the shot must come from a distance, as there was, he felt certain, no one near by.

He glided like a snake, or rather like a huge lizard, which crawls over obstacles, and whose body adapts itself to depressions instead of crossing or bridging them over. His cautious progress scarcely caused a leaf to rustle or a stone to rattle, and these noises were perceptible only in the vicinity of where they were produced. So he pushed himself gradually close up to a ledge, which, while of indifferent height, still protected his body somewhat. On this ledge he expected to notice scratches which indicated that the trail passed over it.

It was as he suspected, — the rock was slightly worn by human feet; but of fresh tracks there could of course be no trace here, for only long and constant wear and tear, and not an occasional hurried tread, can leave marks behind. But Topanashka noticed a few fragments of rock and little bits of stone that lay alongside the old worn-out channel. Without lifting his head, he extended his arm, grasped some of the fragments, and began to examine them.

Loose rocks or stones that have been lying on the ground undisturbed for some time, always have their lower surface moist, while the upper dries rapidly. When the yellowish tufa of these regions becomes wet, it changes colour and grows of a darker hue. Topanashka had noticed that some among the stones which he was examining were darker than the others. The Indian, when he examines anything, looks at it very carefully. One of the fragments was darker on the surface; of this he felt sure, as when he removed them he was careful to keep them as they lay. Below, the piece had its natural colour, that of dry stone. He assured himself that the darker shade really proceeded from humidity; it was still moist. The fragment, therefore, must have been turned over; and that, too, a very short time ago. Only a large animal or a man could have done this. He looked closely to see whether there were any scratches indicative of the passage of deer-hoofs or bear-claws, but there were none except those that appeared so large as to show plainly from a distance. There was every likelihood, therefore, that some human being had but very lately moved the stones, and not only since the rain of last night but since the surface had had time to dry again; that is, in the course of the afternoon.

22

He moved his body forward where he could examine the soil alongside the ledge. The grass was nowhere bent and broken, still that was no sufficient indication. There at last was a plain human track, the impression of a naked foot with its toe-marks to the north, and the impression was fresh! But the Tehua walked on round sandals. Had he not lost one of them? It was very uncomfortable walking on one of the circular disks only. Topanashka rose on hands and feet and crept farther, regardless of what might be behind him. His eyes were directed northward and he relied upon his ear to warn him of danger in the rear.

The trail lay before him quite distinct for a short distance. Close to it some grasses were bent, and on the sandy place near by there was a print as if from a small hoop, but the impression was old and partly blurred. In vain did the old warrior search for other marks; the rain had obliterated everything except this faint trace that might originally have been plainer because deeper. It looked as if the wearer of the sandal had stepped on the grass-bunch with the fore part of his foot, slipped back lightly, and thus pressed the hind part of the hoop deeper into the soil. In that case some trace of the heel-print might still be found. And indeed a very slight concavity appeared behind the impression of the sandal. The heel was turned from the north, consequently the man was going to, not coming from the Rito. The tracks were surely old ones.

Everything was plain now. The Tehua had lost one of his sandals and was returning on his bare feet. But why should he leave it? Why did he not take it along? Even that Topanashka could easily explain. People from the Rito frequently roamed over the northern mesa, close to the Tyuonyi. He might have noticed the presence of some of them, and have fled in haste, leaving his foot-gear behind.

Most likely the ties or thongs had given way, and he had no time to mend them. That was an evidence also that the man was alone, else he would not have fled with such precipitation. Neither was he in this vicinity any longer. Topanashka felt that his task was done; he could not gain anything by proceeding farther.

" Kuawk, kuawk, kuawk ! " sounded overhead. A crow had been sitting quietly on the tree above him, but now it flew off again, the unlucky bird ! Its cry startled the old man, and he raised his head to look after the herald of evil, following him with his eye. All was still. Then he rose to his knees.

A sharp humming twang, a hissing sound, and a thud followed in lightning-like succession. Topanashka bends over, and at the same time tumbles forward on his face. There he lies, the left cheek and shoulder on the ground. The left arm, with which he has sought to support the body, has slipped; and it now lies fully extended partly below the head, the prostrate head. The chest is heaving painfully, as if under extraordinary pressure. Face and neck are colouring; the lips part; the throat makes a convulsive effort to swallow. The eyes are starting; they denote suffocation and terrible pain. The legs twitch; they seem struggling to come to the rescue of the body's upper half.

From the back of the old man there protrudes an arrow-shaft. It has pierced it close to the spine, between it and the right shoulder-blade, penetrating into the lungs, where it now stabs and smarts.

From a distant tree-top there sounds the hoarse "kuawk, kuawk" of the crow. Otherwise all is still.

The wounded man coughs; with the cough blood comes to his lips, — light red blood. The thighs begin to struggle as if formication was going on in the muscles. It is an impotent movement, and yet is done consciously; for the trunk of the body, which was beginning more and more to yield, now begins to turn clumsily backward; the left hand clutches the soil; the arm is trying to heave, to lift. But the weight is too heavy, the shaft inside too firmly and too deeply rooted. Nevertheless the hips succeed in rising; the trunk follows; then it tumbles over on the back, contracts with a moan of pain and suffering, and lies there trembling with spasmodic shivers.

Topanashka has made this superhuman effort for a purpose. He feels that his wound is severe, that his strength is gone; his senses are darkened and his thoughts confused. Still there is a spark of life left, and that spark demands that he should attempt to see whence came the arrow that so terribly lacerates his breast. But as he has fallen over heavily, the point of the arrow has been pressed deeper. Flint — an arrow-head of flint with notched edges — tears; the muscles do not close about the intruder. The blood flows into the chest; it fills the lungs; he suffocates. Yet all consciousness has not vanished, although pain and oppression overwhelm the physical instruments of consciousness, and deprive the will of its connection with its tools. The will longs to see him who has destroyed its abode, but it no longer controls the shattered tissues; the nerves shiver like the broken springs of clockwork ere they come to a stand-still forever. The eye still distinguishes light occasionally, but it cannot see any longer.

Weaker and weaker become the breathings. On both sides of the mouth a fold begins to form over the blood that has curdled and dried; new fillets stream to the lips from within. The legs still twitch convulsively.

Now a stream of blood gushes from the open mouth; wave after wave rushes up with such swiftness that bubbles and froth form between the lips and remain there. A chill pervades the whole body; it is the last nervous tremor; the lower jaw hangs down, showing with fearful distinctness the folds, the ghastly folds, of death.

All is still. Through the tops of the pines comes a humming sound like a chant, a last lay to the brave and dutiful man. Still, stark, and stiff he lies in his gore. His career is ended; his soul has gone to rest.

And thus all remained quiet for a short time. Then the grass was waved and shaken in the direction to which the old man had turned his back in the last hapless moment. The grass seemed to grow, to suddenly rise; and a figure appeared which had been lying flat behind a projecting rocky ledge. As this figure straightened itself, bunches of grass dropped from its back to the ground. It was the figure of a man.

But it is not the Tehua Indian who stands there motionless, with bow half drawn and an arrow in readiness, who gazes over to the corpse to see whether it is really a corpse, or whether it will need a second shaft to despatch it forever. The man is of middle height, raw-boned and spare. Shaggy hair bristles from under the strands that surround his head like a turban. He wears nothing but a kilt of deerskin; from his shoulders hangs a quiver; a flint knife depends from the belt. This man is no village Indian, notwithstanding that dark paint on his body. It is one of the hereditary foes of the sedentary aborigines, — a Navajo!

He is eying the dead body suspiciously. If it is surely dead the second arrow may be saved. Those glassy eyes; that sallow face; and the fold, the ghastly fold that runs on both sides of the mouth, of that mouth filled with blood now clotting, — they show that life is gone.

Still the savage keeps his bow well in hand, as with head and neck extended he steals forward slowly, mistrustfully approaching his victim. When he is close to the body his eyes sparkle with delight and pride, and his face gleams with the triumph of some hellish spirit.

He touches the corpse. It is warm, but surely lifeless. He grasps at the wrap; it is of no value to him, although made of cotton. Beneath, however, there must be something that attracts his attention, for he quickly tears off the scanty dress and fumbles about the chest of the victim. A horrible grin of delight distorts his features, already hideously begrimed, for he has found the little bag and takes from it the fetich of the dead man. That fetich is a prize, for with it the magic power that was subservient to the victim while alive now becomes the victor's. He handles the amulet carefully, almost tenderly, breathes on it, and puts it back into the bag. Then he detaches his stone knife, grasps it with the right hand, and with the left clutches the gray hair of the dead man and with a sudden jerk pulls the head up. Then he begins to cut the scalp with his shaggy knife-blade of flint.

A faint whistling sound, as of some one hissing near him, is heard; and ere he looks up a male voice by his side has said, —

"That is good, very good!" The words are spoken in the Dinne language.

The murderer looks up, staying his work of mutilation. By his side there stands another Navajo, dressed, painted, and armed like himself.

A short time after he had risen from his hiding-place and was stealing over toward the body of his victim, this other Navajo had appeared in sight. He watched from the distance his companion's proceedings, and as he recognized that he was busying himself with some dead body, approached rapidly, though without the least noise. He discovered the dead, stood still, fastened a piercing glance on the prostrate form, and heaved a great sigh of relief. Notwithstanding the paint on his face it was easy to see how delighted he was at the sight. He again advanced, not unlike a cat which is afraid to go too near another that is playing with a mouse, for fear of being scratched or bitten by her. But when unobserved he had reached the Navajo, he could not withhold a joyful exclamation that startled and interrupted the murderer. He asked, —

"Dost thou know who that is?"

The other shrugged his shoulders.

"That is Topanashka, the strong and wise warrior. That is very, very good!"

Navajo number two looked closely at the corpse; then he grasped the hair again and resumed the cutting. Number one touched his arm.

"Why do you do this?" he asked.

The other chuckled.

"Dost thou not see it, Nacaytzusle," said he; "the people of the houses know that we only take a lock of the hair. If now they find the body and see that this" — he pointed to the skin — "is gone, they will think it is one of those up here" — waving his hand to the north — "that has done it."

Nacaytzusle, for he was indeed the second Navajo, nodded approvingly and suffered the other to go on.

Cutting, scraping, tearing, and pulling, he at last succeeded in making a deep incision around the skull. Blood flowed over his fingers and hands. Then he grasped the gray hair, planted himself with both feet on the neck, and pulled until the scalp was wrenched off and dangled in his fist. Over the bare skull numberless fillets of blood began to trickle, at once changing the face and neck of the dead into a red mass. Then he turned to the other, nodded, and said, —

"It is well."

Nacaytzusle turned his eyes upon the dead, and replied in a hoarse voice, —

"It is well."

He scanned the surroundings suspiciously.

"Thou hast done well, very well," he said to the murderer. "Thou art strong and cunning. This one " — he touched the body with his toes — "was strong and wise also, but now he is so no longer. Now," he hissed, "we can go down into the Tu Atzissi and get what we want."

"What dost thou mean, Nacaytzusle?" inquired the victorious Navajo.

"Go thou back to the hogan," whispered Nacaytzusle to him, "and tell the men to be there," pointing southwestward, "four days from now. I will be there and will speak to them."

The other nodded.

"Let us go," said he.

They moved off in silence without casting another glance at the dead. Their direction was southwest. They carefully avoided making the least noise ; they spied and peered cautiously in every direction, shy, suspicious. Thus they vanished in the forest like wolves sneaking through timber.

Evening had set in. Stronger blew the wind, and the top of the pines shook occasionally with a solemn rushing sound that resembled distant thunder. The breeze swayed the grass, the blades nodded and bowed beside the remains of the brave man as if they were asking his forgiveness for the bloody deed of which they had been the innocent witnesses. A crow came up, flapping her wings, and alighted on a tree which stood near the corpse, and peered down upon the body. Then she croaked hoarsely, jumped to a lower limb, and peered again. Thus the bird continued to descend from one branch to another, croaking and

chuckling as it were to herself. At last she fluttered
down to the ground, a few paces from the body, peeped
slyly over to where it lay, and walked toward it with slow,
stately steps and eager nods. But something rattled in the
distance; the bird's head turned to the east, and as quick
as lightning she rose in the air and flew off with a loud,
angry, " kuawk, kuawk, kuawk ! "

Two men are coming toward the spot. They are Indians from Tyuonyi who came up in the course of the
afternoon with bows and arrows. They perceive the body,
and the blood on it and around it. Both stand still, terrified at the sight. At last one of them exclaims, —

" It is one from the Zaashtesh ! "

They run together to the spot, heedless of the danger
which may yet be lurking about. They bend over the
dead, then look at each other speechless, confused. At last
they find words, and exclaim simultaneously, —

" It is our father, Topanashka Tihua ! "

" It is sa nashtio maseua ! "

Both men are young yet, they weep. Their sorrow is so
great, in presence of the loss sustained by them and by
all, that they forget all caution. Had the Navajos been
about still, two more of the house-dwellers would have
fallen.

They attempt to decide what is to be done; their
thoughts become confused, for the terrible discovery dis-
tracts them. Little by little they become conscious that it is
impossible to leave the body here, a prey to the wolves and
carrion crows; that it must be brought home, down into the
valley where he was so beloved, so worshipped almost, by
everybody. Nothing else can be done.

With sighs and sobs, stifled groans and tears, the body
is raised up, one supporting the head, the other the feet.
Thus they drag and carry it along on the old trail to the

Rito. Blood clings to their hands and to their dress. Never mind. Is it not the blood of a good man, and may not with that blood some of his good qualities perhaps pass into them? Not a word is spoken, not even when they lay down the corpse to rest themselves a while. In such moments they stand motionless, one by the mutilated head, the other at the feet. They look neither at each other nor at it, for if they should attempt it tears would be sure to come to their eyes. Without a word they lift up the body again, tenderly as if it were a child's, and on they go, slowly, painfully, and silently.

It is night now, and the forest is more full of life. The dread voices of the darkness are heard around them; coyotes howl and whine; in the distance owls hiss and shriek and flit from tree to tree, as the panting men approach. They think not of danger, not even of those who so ruthlessly slaughtered their great and good maseua; on they go as fast as the heavy load permits and as their heavy hearts afford them strength.

Now one of them stumbles and falls, and as he rises he notices that the object over which he has tripped is still clinging to his foot. He cannot see what it is, but grasping it, discovers a round war-sandal, over which he has stumbled, whose thongs have remained between his toes. This discovery he communicates to his companion. With fresh vigour they resume their dismal march. It is dark, so dark that nothing more can be seen; nothing more is heard save distant thunder and the discordant voices of the night in the forest. Slowly and silently they proceed homeward with their gory but precious burden.

CHAPTER XVI.

LAMENTATIONS over a dead body are everywhere a sad and
sickening performance to witness and to hear. Among the
aborigines of New Mexico — among the sedentary tribes at
least — the official death-wail is carried on for four days.
The number four plays a conspicuous rôle in the lives of
those people. And it is natural that it should. Four are
the cardinal points, four the seasons, four times five digits
depend from hands and feet. The Queres has not even a
distinct term for finger or for toe. He designates the
former as one above the hand, the latter as one above the
foot. Four days the redman fasts or does penance; four
days he mourns, for that is the time required by the soul
to travel from the place where it has been liberated from
the thralls of earthly life to the place of eternal felicity. At
the time of which we are speaking, the body was still
cremated, and with it everything that made up the personal
effects of the deceased.[1] If a man, his clothes, his weapons,
his loom, in case he had practised the art of weaving, were
burned; if a woman, the cooking utensils were "killed;"

[1] I borrow these facts from Spanish sources. Both Castañeda and
Mota Padilla mention cremation as being practised in the sixteenth
century by the Pueblos. The latter author even gives a detailed
description. Withal, the fact that the Pueblos also buried the body
is more than abundantly established. Both modes of burial were
resorted to, and contemporaneously even, according to the nature of
the country and soil. There is comparatively little soil at the Rito.
The mourning ceremonies, etc., I have witnessed myself.

that is, either perforated at the bottom or broken over the funeral pyre and afterward consumed. In this manner the deceased was accompanied by his worldly goods, in the shape of smoke and steam, through that air in which the soul travelled toward Shipapu, in the far-distant mythical North. The road must be long to Shipapu, else it would not require four entire days to reach it; and there are neither eating-places nor half-way houses on the way, where the dead may stop for refreshments. Therefore the survivors placed on the spot where the body had rested for the last time an effigy of the dead, a wooden carving, and covered it with a piece of cloth; while by the side of this effigy they deposited food and water, in order that neither cold, hunger, nor thirst might cause the travelling spirit to suffer. But the road is not only long, it is also dangerous; evil spirits lie in wait for the deceased to capture him if possible, and hamper his ultimate felicity. To protect himself against them a small war-club is added to the other necessaries, and to render the journey safe beyond a doubt a magic circle is drawn, encompassing the statuette with a circle of cruciform marks, imitating the footprints of the shashka, or road-runner. As these crosses point in all four directions, it is supposed that evil spirits will become bewildered and unable to pursue the soul in its transit. At the end of the fourth day, with many prayers and ceremonies, the circle is obliterated, and the other objects, including the effigy, are taken away by the shamans to be disposed of in a manner known to them alone.

During the period of official mourning the loud wail was carried on incessantly, or at least at frequent intervals; fasting was practised; the women wept, sobbed, screamed, and yelled. Both sexes gathered daily around the place where the effigy lay, praying loudly for the safe journey and arrival at Shipapu of the defunct. The women alone shed

tears on such occasions, the men only stared with a gloomy
face and thoughtful mien. They recalled and remem.
bered the dead. What the great master of historical
composition has said of the ancient Germans may be
applied here also: "Feminis lugere honestum est, viris
meminisse."

In the humble abode where Topanashka Tihua had dwelt
with his deaf old wife, and where his bloody remains had
rested previous to being borne to the funeral pyre, his
effigy lay covered by the handsomest piece of cotton cloth
that could be found among the homes of the Rito, and a
quaintly painted and decorated specimen of pottery contained the drinking-water for his soul. It was dusky in the
room, for the window as well as the hatchway afforded little
light. Subdued voices sounded from the apartment, monotonous recitals, which the loud refrain, "Heiti-na, Heiti-na,"
at times interrupted. The poor deaf widow sat with tearful
eyes in a corner; her lips moved, but no sound came from
them; only, when the leader of the choir broke out with
appropriate gesticulations, she chimed in loudly. When at
such a signal the other women present began to tear their
hair, she did the same, and shouted at the top of her voice
like the others, "Heiti-na, Heiti-na!"

Group after group of mourners visited the room, until
both clans, Tanyi and Tyame, had performed their duty.
Hannay, too, had made her appearance; she had shed
tears like a rain-cloud, had howled and whined more than
any one else. Her grief was surely assumed, for when
Tyope asked her in the evening she told him everything in
detail that she had noticed, — how this one had looked,
how such and such a one had yelled, — plainly showing
that the flood of tears had in no manner impeded her
faculties of perception, the sighs and sobs around her in no
manner deafened her attentive ear. Tyope listened with

apparent indifference, and said nothing. She attended to
the weeping part, he not so much to the duty of pious
recollection as to that of deep thinking over the new phase
which matters had entered upon in consequence of the
bloody event.

For this sudden death of the maseua was for his designs
a most fortunate occurrence. The only man who in the
prospective strife between the clans might have taken an
attitude dangerous, perhaps disastrous, to his purposes, was
now dead; and the office which that man held had become
vacant. There was but one individual left in the tribe who
might yet prove a stumbling-block to him; that was the
Hishtanyi Chayan. But the great medicine-man was not so
much a man of action as a man of words, and the force of
his oracular utterances Tyope hoped to destroy through the
powerful speeches of the Koshare Naua and the strong
medicine of the Shkuy Chayan. The plans of Tyope had
been immensely furthered by the terrible accident; they had
advanced so much that he felt it indispensable to modify
them to some extent. Terror and dismay were great at
the Rito, and the council had been adjourned *sine die.*
There could be no thought of a fresh accusation against
Shotaye until the four days of official mourning were past,
and the campaign against the enemy, which the bloody
outrage imperatively called for.

The murder by the Tehuas, as Tyope and the others
believed, of the principal war-chief of the tribe, at a time
when the two tribes were without any communication with
each other, was too great an outrage not to demand immediate revenge. The murder could not have been the result
of a misunderstanding or accident, else the scalp would not
have been taken by the murderer. It was premeditated,
an act of deliberate hostility, a declaration of war on the
part of the Tehuas. The dead man's scalp had certainly

wandered over to the caves of the northern tribe ; it was
certainly paraded there in the solemn scalp-dance by which
the Tehuas, beyond all doubt, publicly honoured and rewarded the murderer.

Tyope knew that the Queres were of one mind and that
the official mourning alone kept them from replying to this
act of unjustifiable hostility by an attack upon the Puye,
but he also knew that as soon as the four days were past a
campaign against the Tehuas would be set on foot. The
Hishtanyi Chayan had retired to work, and that meant war !
He and the Shikama Chayan fasted and mourned together ;
their mourning was not only on account of the great loss
suffered by the tribe in the person of the deceased ; they
bewailed a loss of power. That power had gone over into
the enemy's ranks with the scalp of the murdered man.

Although the death of Topanashka was for Tyope an
event of incalculable benefit, he had exhibited tokens of
regret and sorrow. His manner was dignified ; he did not
mourn in any extravagant fashion, but conducted himself
so that nobody could suspect the death of the old man to
be anything else than a source of regret to him. Furthermore, he intended by his own example to foster the idea
among his tribal brethren that the outrage was so grave
that it demanded immediate and prompt redress. The
carrying out of this redress was of the greatest importance
to him. The sooner it was executed the better it would
suit his plans.

During the last interview of Tyope with the young Navajo, the latter had charged him with having asked the
Dinne to kill the old maseua during an incursion which his
tribe were to make into the valley of the Rito. It was true
that Tyope had suggested it, but he had not told the Navajo all that he designed through this act of treachery.
His object was not merely to rid himself of the person of

Topanashka; he sought an opportunity of becoming the ostensible saviour of his tribe in the hour of need. If the Dinne had made the premeditated onslaught, he would, after he had given them time to perform the murder, have appeared upon the scene, driven off the assailants, and thus recommended himself to the people for the vacant position of war-chief. The game was a double one on his part; first he was to betray his kinsfolk to the Navajos, and secondly to turn against the Navajos in defense of the betrayed ones. Tyope realized that it was a very dangerous game, and he had therefore desisted and even gone so far as to repel the young Navajo at the risk of his own life.

As matters stood, all had gone far better than he ever hoped for. Without complicity on his part, Topanashka had been put out of his way; and the office coveted by Tyope was vacant. An important military enterprise was to follow at once. Tyope intended to go on this campaign at all hazards, in order to distinguish himself as much as possible. This he was able to do, for he possessed all the physical qualities necessary for a powerful Indian warrior, and he was very crafty, cunning, bold and experienced. He belonged to the society of war magicians, and held in his possession most of the charms and fetiches used for securing invincibility. There was no doubt in his mind that he would return from the war-path crowned with glory and with scalps, provided he was not killed. Should he return alive, then the time would come for him to set the Koshare Naua to work to secure him the desired position. Once made maseua he would resume his former plans, push the case against Shotaye to the bitter end, and try to divide the tribe. For the present the two objects had to be set aside. The expedition against the Tehuas must take the lead of everything else.

While Tyope was prompted, by the grief and mourning

that prevailed, to display fresh activity and resort to new
intrigues; while at the same time his wife improved the
occasion for her customary prying, listening, and gossip, —
their daughter, Mitsha, on the other hand, really mourned
sincerely and grieved bitterly. She mourned for the dead
with the candour of a child and the feeling of a woman.
When she, too, had gone to the house of the dead to pray,
her tears flowed abundantly; and they were genuine. The
girl did not weep merely on account of the deceased, for
she could not know his real worth and merits; she grieved
quite as much on Okoya's account. The boy had been to
see her every evening of late. He was there on the night
when the corpse was brought home, and they heard the wail
and rushed out on the roof. At that moment Hannay had
returned, full to the brim with the dismal news. Okoya forgot everything and returned home, and Mitsha went back
to the room and wept. While her mother proceeded in
her account with noisy volubility, Mitsha cried; for Okoya
had often spoken of his grandfather, telling her how wise.
strong, and good sa umo maseua was. She felt that the
young man looked up to him as to an ideal, and she wept
quite as much because of her feeling for Okoya as for the
murdered main-stay of her people.

While she thus mourned from the bottom of her heart,
the thought came to her how she would feel in case her
father was brought home in the same way. Mitsha was a
good child, and Tyope had always treated her not only
with affection but with kindness. He gave her many precious things, as the Indian calls the bright-coloured pebbles, shell beads, base turquoises, crystals, etc., with which
he decorates his body. He liked to see his daughter shine
among the daughters of the tribe. With him it was specu-
lation, not affection; but Mitsha knew nothing of this, and
felt that in case her parent should ever be borne back to

this house dead, and placed on the floor before her covered with gore, she must feel just as Okoya felt now. And yet the dead man was only his grandparent. No, it was not possible for him to be as sad as she would be in case Tyope should meet with such a fate. And then she wondered whether the whole tribe would regret her father's death as much as they regretted the loss of Topanashka. Something within her told that it would not. She had already noticed that Tyope was not liked; but why, she knew not. Okoya himself had intimated as much. She knew that the boy shunned her father; and her attachment to Okoya had become so deep that his utterances began to modify her feelings toward her own parents.

If she would sorrow and grieve for her father's loss, if Okoya was mourning over his grandfather's demise, how must the child of the murdered man, of such a man as Topanashka, feel? His only child was a woman like herself. A true woman always feels for her sex and sympathizes with other women's grief; and besides, that woman was the mother of the youth who had won her heart. Okoya had told her a great deal about his mother, — how good she was and how content she was to see him and her become one. The girl was anxious to know his mother, but a visit to a prospective mother-in-law is by no means an unimportant step. If it is accompanied by a present it bears the character of an official acceptance of courtship. That step Mitsha was afraid as yet to take; it was too early; there were too many contingencies in the way.

Still she longed to go to Say Koitza now. But visits of condolence are not in vogue among Indians as long as there is loud mourning, except at the house where the mourning is going on. How much Mitsha would have given to be permitted to go to Say, sit down quietly in a corner, and modestly and without speaking a word, weep in her company.

At the same time she felt another longing. Since the night of the murder Okoya had of course not been to see her, and she naturally longed to meet him also in this hour of sadness and trial. Once when she had gone to the brook for water, Zashue had crossed her path; but he looked so dark and frowning that she did not venture even to greet him.

It was the last day of mourning, and nearly everybody at the Rito who could or ought had paid his respects to the dead. The Chayani of lesser rank alone returned from time to time to perform specially strong incantations in aid of the still travelling soul. Mitsha had gone down to the brook to get water. It occurred only once a day during these days, for the people of Tyame fasted, taking but one frugal meal daily. Everybody was very careful also not to wash, and Mitsha herself was as unkempt as any one else of her clan.

Bearing the huashtanyi on her head, she was returning, when as she passed the corner of the big house her eyes discovered a man standing with his back turned to her, gazing at the cliffs. He seemed to face the dwellings of the Eagle clan. As the girl approached, the noise of her step caused him to turn, and she recognized Okoya.

The youth stepped up to her; his eyes were hollow, and now they became moist. He attempted to control himself, to restrain the tears that were coming to his eyes at the sight of her; but he sobbed convulsively. When she saw it tears came to her eyes at once. The two children stood there, he struggling to hide his grief, for it was unmanly to weep, and yet he was young and could not control his feelings; she, as a woman, feeling at liberty to weep. She wept, but silently and modestly. It grieved her to see him shed tears.

He, too, felt for her; but it was soothing to his own grief

that Mitsha mourned. He too was longing to meet her; the four days of separation had been very long to him.

"He was so good," Okoya at last succeeded in saying Fresh tears came to his eyes.

Mitsha merely nodded and covered her face with a cor-ner of her wrap.

"Have you been to him?" he asked.

She nodded; Okoya continued, —

"To-morrow I will come again."

Eager nods, mingled with sobs and accompanied by rub-bing of the eyes, were her reply. The nodding proved that his call would be very, very welcome. She uncovered her face, her eyes beamed through tears, and she smiled. As sincerely as she felt her grief, the announcement that he would return as soon as the mourning-time was over made her happy, and her features expressed it. She went her way quietly, Okoya following her with his eyes.

He longed to say to her, "Come with me, and let us go together to my mother; she weeps so much." But it could not be; it was useless to mention it. About his mother Okoya felt deeply concerned, for she did not bear her grief as the others bore theirs. She was not noisy like the rest. Utterly oblivious of her daily task, she neither cooked nor baked nor cared for anything. Her husband and children had to go hungry, while she sat in a corner sobbing and weeping. It was indeed a blessing for her that she was able to weep; otherwise her reason might have given way under the terrible and crushing blow. With the loss of her father she felt as if lost forever, as if her only support, her only hope, had gone. The past came back to her, not like an ugly dream, but as a fearful reality threatening sure destruc-tion. Between her and the accusation which she felt cer-tain had been fulminated against her before the council, there stood henceforth no one, and at the end of the mourning she expected to be dragged before the council at once and condemned to death! And what sort of death? Exposed to public wrath as a witch, bound and gagged, tied to a tree, with the rough bark lacerating her breast, and then beaten, beaten to a jelly, rib broken after rib, limb after limb, until the soul left the body's wreck under the curses of bystanders. Oh, if she could only die now a swift, an honourable death like that of her father!

If she could only have seen Shotaye! She expected the cave-woman surely to come down to cheer her up. She felt a longing for her friend, a desire to see her, to hear her voice. But day after day ran on, night after night followed, and Shotaye did not come. It did not surprise her that Shotaye did not appear on the first day, but on the evening of the second she began to tremble. When the night of the third came, her apprehensions became distressing. On the fourth, Shotaye must surely come; expectation, and finally disappointment, almost tortured to death the poor woman, for Shotaye came not.

Everything seemed to conspire to render her hopelessly miserable. She lost sight of her surroundings, grew speechless, and almost devoid of feeling. The others explained her state as one of profound and very natural grief, and let her alone. But it was uncomfortable in the house when the mistress took no notice of anything, and did not even provide the most necessary things, not even drinking-water. Therefore Zashue, as well as Okoya, preferred to go out of doors, there to await the termination of the disagreeable period of mourning at the end of which they confidently expected Say to return to her normal condition.

After he had separated from Mitsha, Okoya sauntered, without really knowing whither, up the gorge and down the northern side of the cultivated plots. He gradually neared the cliffs, and found himself beyond the dwellings of the

Water clan, and therefore beyond the uppermost caves that were inhabited. The gorge, narrow and covered mostly with underbrush and pines, afforded to his sight but a single conspicuous object, and toward this he turned at once.

To his right lay some caves that had been long ago forsaken, and whose front wall had partly crumbled. Below the short slope leading up to them are the traces of an old round estufa. A plain concavity in the ground indicates its site to-day. At the time when Okoya strolled about, the roofing alone was destroyed, and part of the interior was filled with blocks of stone that had tumbled from the cliffs, crushing the roof. Okoya, from where he stood, had the interior of the ruin open before him, and he saw in it, partly sitting and partly reclining, the figure of his friend Hayoue. It was a welcome discovery.

He had not met Hayoue since the death of his grandfather, for the brother of Zashue had avoided the great house and its inmates on purpose. He mourned earnestly and sincerely, and wished to be alone with his thoughts. But Okoya was not disposed to let him alone. He knew that if his uncle spoke to any one he would speak to him, and that if he felt indisposed to enter into any conversation he would say so at once. Hayoue was very outspoken.

The boy jumped down from block to block noisily, for he wanted to attract his uncle's attention beforehand. The latter looked up. As soon as he saw who the disturber of his musings was, he waved his hand, beckoning him to come. Okoya obeyed with alacrity, for he saw that Hayoue felt disposed to talk. Throwing himself down beside him he waited patiently until the other saw fit to open the conversation. They both remained for a while in silence, until Hayoue heaved a deep sigh and said, —

"Does Zashue, my brother, mourn also?"

"Not as we do," replied Okoya; "yet he is sad."

"It is well. He is right to feel sad. Sad for himself, for you, for all of us."

"Sa umo was so good," whispered the boy, and tears came to him again; but he controlled his feelings and swallowed his sobs. He did not wish the other to see him weep.

"Indeed sa umo maseua was good," Hayoue emphasized, "better than any of us, truer than any of us! None of us at the Tyuonyi is as strong and wise as he was."

"How could the Moshome kill him, if he was such a great warrior," Okoya naïvely inquired.

"See, satyumishe, he was struck from behind. In this way a Moshome may kill a bear, and so yai shruy destroys the strongest mokatsh. Sa umo had no weapons, neither bow nor arrow nor club. He did not suppose that there were any Moshome lurking about as tiatui lies in wait for the deer. Had sa nashtio gone south or toward the west, he would have carried what was right, but over there," — he pointed northward, — "who would have believed the people over there to be so mean as these shuatyam of Tehuas now prove to be? Destruction come upon them!" He spoke very excitedly, his eyes flashed, and he gnashed his teeth. Shaking his clenched fist at the north, he hissed, "And destruction will come upon them soon! We shall go to Kapo and come back with many scalps. We will not get one only, and crawl back, as shutzuna does after he has stolen a turkey. We shall go soon, very soon!"

Okoya yielded to the excitement which the latter part of his friend's speech bespoke. His eyes sparkled also, and his chest heaved at the mention of blood.

"Satyumishe," he exclaimed, "let us go, I and you together. Let us go and get what may please our father's heart!"

Hayoue looked at him; it was an earnest and significant look.

"You are right, brother. You are wise and you are good. You also know how to hit with an arrow, but you are not uakanyi."

"But I shall be one, if I go with you," boldly uttered the boy.

His uncle shook his head, and smiled.

"Don't you know, sa uishe, that every one cannot go with the warriors, when they go on the war-path? Every one cannot say, 'I am going,' and then go as he pleases and when he pleases. Every one cannot think, 'I am strong and wise, and I will follow the enemy.' If the Shiuana do not help him, the strongest is weak, and the wisest is a child before the foe. See, satyumishe, I am as good a uakanyi as any one, but I do not know whether, when the Hishtanyi Chayan says in the uuityam which men shall go and take from the Tehuas what is proper, I may go with them. Perhaps I shall have to stay, and some other one will go in my stead."

"Must not all go?" Okoya asked; he was astonished

"Every one must go whom the maseua chooses." With a sad expression he added, "Our maseua is no more, and ere the Hotshanyi has spoken to the yaya and nashtio, and said to them, 'such and such a one shall be maseua,' it is the Hishtanyi Chayan who decides who shall go and who shall stay at home."

His nephew comprehended; he nodded and inquired, —

"Does not the Hishtanyi Chayan fast and do penance now?"

"Our nashtio yaya," Hayoue replied with an important and mysterious mien, "has much work at present"

"Do you know what he is working?" naïvely asked Okoya.

"He is with Those Above."

The reply closed the conversation on that subject. Okoya changed the topic, asking, —

"Satyumishe, you are not much older than I. How comes it that you are uakanyi already?"

Hayoue felt quite flattered. He was indeed very young for a war magician, and he felt not a little pride on account of it. Assuming a self-satisfied and important air, he turned to his nephew with the query, —

"When you go out hunting, what is the first thing you do?"

"I take my bow and arrow and leave the house," readily answered the boy.

"This is not what I ask for," growled Hayoue. "What kind of work do you do ere you rise to the kauash?"

The boy understood at last.

"I place the stone, and speak to Those Above."

"If before you go hunting you do not speak to them, are you lucky?"

"No," Okoya mumbled. He recalled the unlucky turkey-hunt of some time ago, when he had forgotten to say his prayers before starting, of which we have spoken in the first chapter.

"Why have you no luck?" Hayoue further asked.

"Because the Shiuana are not satisfied," replied the other. His uncle nodded.

"Are you a hunter?" he asked.

"Not yet, I am only learning."

"Why do you learn?"

"In order to know."

"When you once know, what can you do then?"

"I can — " Okoya was embarrassed. "I can make the Shiuana help me."

"That is it!" Hayoue exclaimed. "If the Shiuana do

not help, you can do nothing ; no matter how swift you run,
how far you see, and how sure your aim is. But of the
Shiuana there are many, as many as grains of sand on the
shore of the great river below here, and when we do not
know them we cannot speak to them and beg for assistance. Just as there are Shiuana who assist the hunter, there
are those who help us, that we may strike the enemy and
take away from him what makes him strong, that it may
strengthen us. Look at Tyame, the nashtio of Tzitz hanutsh ; he is swift and strong, but he knows not how to call
to Those Above and around to help him take the scalp of
the Moshome. We must be wise, and listen to what those
speak who know how to address the Shiuana, and what to
give them. We must learn in order to act. I have learned,
and thus I have become uakanyi. And he who will soon
be where in time we also shall find rest, — he taught me
many things. He was good and wise, very good, our father
the maseua," he added, sighing deeply.

"Will you help me to learn and become uakanyi ? "
Okoya turned to him now with flashing eyes.

" I will, surely I will. You shall become one of us. But
you know, brother, that you must be silent and keep your
tongue tied. You must not say to this or that one, ' I am
learning, I have learned such and such things, for I am
going to become uakanyi.' "

Okoya of course assented. Then he asked, —

" I am not uakanyi, and can the Hishtanyi Chayan tell me
to go along too with the men to strike the Tehuas ? "

"Certainly, for there are not many of us, and in the
Zaashtesh all must stand up for each, and each for all. But
when many go on the war-path there are always some of us
with them in order that the Shiuana be in our favour."

" Do the Shiuana help the Tehuas also ? For the Tehuas
are people like ourselves, are they not ? "

"They are indeed Zaashtesh, like the Queres. But I do not know how the Shiuana feel toward them. Old men who knew told me that the Moshome Tehua prayed to Those Above and around us, and that they call them Ohua. Whether they are the same as ours I cannot tell; but I cannot believe them to be; for the kopishtai who dwell over there must be good to their people, whereas the kopishtai here are good to us. Only those who hold in their hands the paths of our lives help those who do right and give them what is due, wherever and whoever they be."

"How soon shall we go against the Tehuas?"

"The Yaya Chayan and the uishtyaka perhaps alone know that. As soon as the Hishtanyi has done his work he will call the uuityam, and then those shall go that must. Perhaps I may go, perhaps not. It may be that both of us will be sent along. But we will go soon," he fiercely muttered, "soon, to take from the Tehuas what is precious to the heart of our father, who now goes toward Shipapu."

Okoya felt wildly excited and could barely restrain himself. Thirst for revenge joined the intense wish to become a warrior. But Hayoue's placed a damper on his enthusiasm, else he might have left that night alone, with bow and arrow and a stone knife, to hover about the Puye until some luckless Tehua fell into his hands. He saw, however, that nothing could be done without the consent and support of the higher powers, and that he must curb his martial ardour and abide by the decisions of Those Above. The present topic of conversation being exhausted, both sat in silence for a while, each following his own train of thoughts. Okoya was the first to speak again.

"Does your hanutsh mourn?"

"The women have gone to weep with the dead," replied Hayoue. "I too am mourning," he added sorrowfully;

"but I mourn as is becoming to a man. Crying and weeping belong only to women."

" I have cried," whispered Okoya timidly, as he looked at his friend with a doubting glance. He was ashamed of the confession, and yet could not restrain himself from making it. Hayoue shrugged his shoulders.

" You are young, satyumishe, and your heart is young. It is like the heart of a girl. When you have seen many dead men and many dying, you will do as I do, — you will not cry any more." He coughed, and his face twitched nervously; with all his affectation of stoicism he had to struggle against tears. In order to suppress them completely he spoke very loudly at once, —

" Tzitz hanutsh has nothing to do with the dead, and yet the women lament and its men think over the loss that the tribe has sustained. I tell you, Okoya, we have lost much; we are like children without their mother, like a drove of turkeys whose gobbler tiatui or mokatsh have killed. Now," — his eyes flashed again and he gnashed his teeth, — " now Tyope and the old Naua are uppermost. Just wait until the men have returned from the war-path, and you will see. Evil is coming to us. Did you notice, satyumishe, on the night when they carried sa nashtio maseua back to the Tyuonyi how angry the Shiuana were; how the lightning flamed through the clouds and killed the trees on the mesa? I tell you, brother, evil is coming to our people, for a good man has gone from us to Shipapu, but the bad ones have been spared."

Okoya shuddered involuntarily. He recollected well that awful night. Never before had a storm raged on the Rito with such fury. Frightful had been the roar of the thunder, prolonged like some tremendous subterranean noise. Incessant lightning had for hours converted night into day, and many were the lofty pines that had been shattered or consumed by the fiery bolts from above. The wind, which seldom does any damage at such places, had swept through the gorge and over the mesas with tremendous force, and lastly the peaceful, lovely brook, swollen by the waters that gushed from the mountains in torrents, as well as by the rain falling in sheets, had waxed into a roaring, turbid stream. It had flooded the fields, destroying crops and spreading masses of rocky débris over the tillable soil. Yes, the heavens had come upon the Rito in their full wrath, as swift and terrible avengers. Both of them remembered well that awful night, and dropped into moody silence at the dismal recollection.

"Are there any other bad men at the Tyuonyi?" Okoya asked; but low, as if he were afraid of the answer.

"There may be others," Hayoue muttered, "but those two are certainly the worst."

Okoya felt disappointed; Tyope, he saw, must indeed be a bad creature.

"Do you know whether Tyope is mourning?" asked his uncle.

"I have not seen him," grumbled the other.

"I am sure he will look as if his mother had died," scolded Hayoue. "He is a great liar, worse than a Navajo. He puts on a good face and keeps the bad one inside. I would like to know what the Shiuana think of that bad man."

"Have we any bad women among us?" Okoya said, to change the conversation.

"Hannay is bad!" his uncle cried.

A pang went through the heart of the other youth. His prospective father and mother in-law appeared really a pair of exquisite scoundrels.

"Are there any others?"

"I don't know. still I have heard," Hayoue looked

about as if afraid of some eavesdropper, — " what I tell you now is only for yourself, — that Shotaye is bad, very bad! After being Tyope's wife for a while, I should not be surprised if — "

" Does she speak to those that can do us harm? " Okoya interrupted in a timid whisper.

" It may be. There is no doubt but she is a harlot; I know it myself, and every man on the Tyuonyi knows it. Other women are also spoken of, but nobody says it aloud. It is not right to speak thus of people when we do not know positively. I have not seen Shotaye since our father died. She is mourning perhaps, for her cave is shut and the deerskin hangs over the doorway. She is likely to be inside in quiet until the trouble is over and the men can go to her again."

Okoya rose to go.

" Are you coming along? " he asked his uncle.

Hayoue shook his head; he still wished to remain alone.

" It may be," he said, " that we shall have to leave in two days against the Tehuas, and I shall remain so that I may be ready when the tapop calls upon us. You rely upon it, satyumishe, we shall go soon, and when it so happens that we both must go you shall come with me that I may teach you how the scalp is taken."

Thus dismissed, Okoya sauntered back down the valley.

When opposite the caves of the Water clan he furtively glanced over to the one inhabited by Shotaye. The deerskin, as Hayoue had stated, hung over the opening, and no smoke issued from the hole that served as vent and smoke-escape. The woman must be mourning very deeply, or else she was gone. She did not often enter his thoughts, and yet he wished Shotaye might come now and see his mother. He was convinced, without knowing why, that his mother would have been glad to see her.

At all events the dismal period of mourning was drawing rapidly to a close, and with it official sadness would vanish. He could hardly await the morrow. On that day he hoped that the question would be decided when the great work of revenge should commence and whether he would be permitted to take part in it. The words of his uncle had opened an entirely new perspective to Okoya. To become uakanyi was now his aim, his intense ambition. As warrior, and as successful warrior, he confidently expected that no one would dare refuse him Mitsha. This hope overcame the grief he had harboured during the days that elapsed, for that grief belonged to the past ; and as the past now appeared to him, it seemed only a stepping-stone to a proud and happy future.

CHAPTER XVII.

OKOYA had been correct in his surmise that Shotaye was
gone. In vain Say Koitza pined ; her friend had left never
to return.

When the news of Topanashka's death reached her, which
it did on the very night of the occurrence, she saw at a
glance that henceforth her presence among the Queres was
an impossibility, for she knew that the deceased was the
only one who could interpose himself between Say Koitza
and her enemies, and thus wield an influence indirectly favourable to herself. She recognized that henceforth Tyope
was free to act as he pleased in the matter, for the medicine-
men would be on his side. And she saw that the days of
mourning that were sure to follow afforded her a capital
opportunity for leaving the Rito unobserved, and executing
her flight to the Tehuas of the Puye.

Shotaye could not believe that Cayamo was the slayer of
Topanashka. Her warrior from the north was in too great
a hurry to get out of the way of pursuing Navajos. He
was too anxious to save the scalp he had taken. Even in
case Topanashka had overtaken him, which seemed impossible, the Tehua would have avoided rather than attacked
the unarmed old man. And if the maseua surprised their
interview and followed her knight, the latter had too much
vantage-ground to be ever overtaken by his aged and unarmed pursuer. The fact that the sandal had been found,
Shotaye interpreted as evidence of Cayamo's precipitate

flight. From her stand-point she reached the very correct
conclusion that the Navajos who followed in Cayamo's
tracks, and not the Tehua, must have killed the father of
her friend Say.

But she saw that her people would fall into error as to
the manner of Topanashka's death. She saw that they
could not have reached a different conclusion, and also
that the error must call forth extraordinary measures of
revenge. She heard enough and saw enough, during the
commotion prevailing at the Rito when the dead body was
brought in, to become convinced that as soon as the
mourning ceremonies were over the Queres would take
the war-path against the supposed murderers of their war-
chief. She took care not to disabuse the minds of any of
her tribal brethren, and said nothing, but felt glad at the
opportunity which the proposed campaign would give her
for revenge.

Flight to the Tehuas was not only very easy, it could be
executed under circumstances that would give her among
the other tribe a position of considerable importance. It
was almost needless to avail herself of the understanding
with Cayamo; she had far more important things to communicate. By informing the Tehuas of the movement on
foot against them, she appeared as a deserter from the
enemy, as a timely friend. If afterward, as she confidently
believed, Tyope should come up with the warriors against
the Tehuas, he would find everything prepared for a disastrous reception. Matters looked exceedingly promising for
her plans.

For all that, she did not forget Say Koitza; but she had
been to some extent forewarned, and as soon as Say heard
of Shotaye's absence she must suspect the truth. After all,
Say was in no real danger. Until the campaign was over,
there was no time to think of her case, and during that

24

campaign Shotaye would provide for the Queres such a rough handling that no thoughts of witchcraft trials would trouble them for some time to come. For there should be mourning, sadness, grief, howling, and gnashing of teeth on the Rito on a very large scale.

Still she did not lose sight of the possibility that her absence might be noticed at an early day, and might arouse suspicion. It was possible, though not at all likely. As long as people mourned, nobody would care for her. After the official mourning was over the council would be convened and the campaign announced. Thereupon all the men who had to take part would have to retire for the customary fasts and purifications, and the Yaya and the Chayani would have to work heavily. Her home was not likely to be visited by any one for a number of days, and when the warriors of the Queres were on the march nobody would call them back because she had disappeared from the Rito.

Perfectly at rest in regard to her own future, reassured as to the fate of Say Koitza, Shotaye had, on the night of the second day after the murder of Topanashka, left her home and climbed to the northern mesa without meeting any obstacle. When the sun rose, she found herself quite near the place which Cayamo, as far as she understood, had designated as the spot where his friend Teanyi would wait for her. Unacquainted with the real distance that separates the Rito from the cave-dwellings above Santa Clara, she had underrated it; and it was only at noon, after she had spent hours walking through the pine timber and in fruitless waiting, that a man stepped up to her from behind a tree and called out, —

"Teanyi!" Then he added, "Cayamo," and inquired, "Shotaye?"

He was the looked-for and longed-for delegate; and

when the sun stood at its height, the two were travelling toward the Puye together.

Shotaye attempted to convey the idea to her companion that the Queres were upon the point of moving upon the Tehuas in force. Her excited gesticulations and broken sentences only succeeded in making him believe that she was herself the object of lively pursuit by a considerable number of men. Therefore when the pair reached the isolated, castle-like rock called Puye, which dominates the country far around, and along the base of which the dwellings of the Tehuas were excavated in friable white pumice-stone, in the same manner as are those of the Rito, Teanyi left her standing before the entrance to his own cave-home, went in, and called his wife to take care of the new-comer while he ran to the tuyo, as the governor is called among the Tehuas. The wife of Teanyi had not been informed of the nature of Shotaye's call, and as she took her into her quarters she eyed her curiously and suspiciously, for it was probably the first time she had seen a human being that spoke a language different from her own. She gave her no food, but waited her husband's return. Shotaye, on her side, cast the quick glance of her lively eyes at everything. From time to time she attempted a word of conversation; she smiled and gesticulated, but the only response was a shaking of the head and facial expressions that denoted suspicion rather than friendship.

Teanyi had informed the tuyo that he had met a woman from the Rito de los Frijoles and had taken her to his home, or rather to that of his wife; that the woman was gesticulating in an unintelligible manner; and that all he could surmise was that there might be Queres approaching the Puye with hostile intentions. He said nothing about Cayamo and his relations toward Shotaye, for Cayamo had enjoined absolute secrecy.

The governor of the Tehuas was a different man from the pompous little tapop of the Queres. The latter would at once have called the council and done everything to surround the event and his own person with as much noise as possible. Not so the tuyo of the Puye. He only said, " I will go with you," and went to the room of Teanyi's wife to see Shotaye and investigate for himself.

The gesticulations began again, and the woman used every effort to make herself understood. The governor did his best to understand her, but no progress was made toward comprehension. She even followed Cayamo's precedent in drawing a line on the floor from north to south, designating the southern end as Tupoge, the northern end as Puye, for thus much she had kept in memory. Then she pointed out on that line the spot where Topanashka had been killed, and said, " Uan save," and made the gesture-sign for killing. Lastly she tried to convey the idea that the Queres were in arms against the Tehuas.

The governor displayed much coolness, and paid close attention during this strange and almost comic interview. He thought he understood that a man from the Rito, probably called Topanashka, had been murdered by the Dinnes on the trail leading to the Puye from the south. He also thought that the Queres were on the war-path to avenge the murder. In what manner this was connected with the excited state of the woman he could not clearly see, unless she was perhaps the widow of the murdered man. In that event she might have become insane from fright and despair ! Her violent gesticulations and the expression of passion and agitation on her features confirmed his suspicion that Shotaye was distracted.

A growing coldness in his manner at last showed the woman what sort of an impression she had been creating, and she felt very uneasy. Not that her life became endangered thereby; on the contrary, the Indian is very considerate and charitable toward such unfortunates. But from the moment that the Tehuas were convinced of her insanity they would attach no longer any importance to her warnings, and a precious lapse of time that should be improved for immediate preparations for defence was irretrievably lost. The Queres might be allowed to approach, and their onslaught would find the Tehuas utterly unprepared. If only Cayamo had been present! But he dared not approach a woman now, for he was at work purifying himself and fasting, in anticipation of the great day when the scalp which he had taken would be feasted over, danced over, prayed at, and sung to. Shotaye found herself in a most painful situation. She noticed how complacently the tuyo smiled, the more she attempted to insist. At last he turned to Teanyi and said a few words to the latter. Teanyi shook his head, and Shotaye followed the discussion that ensued between the two men with eager eyes and ears.

It soon became clear to her that they were of different opinions, and that each one persisted in his own. Finally Teanyi spoke alone, and for quite a while in a low voice; and the governor listened attentively and with growing interest. Though Teanyi's voice was muffled, Shotaye still overheard the word Cayamo several times. Straining her sense of hearing, she caught the words tupoge, tema quio, finally Shotaye also. The tuyo listened, smiled, winked slyly, and at last laughed aloud. At the same time he turned his face to her and nodded most pleasantly; thereupon he said a few words to Teanyi aloud, and the latter turned to his family, which had little by little congregated in the room, and repeated, as appeared to Shotaye, his statements. At the close of his talk all broke out in a joyful laugh. The housewife, who until then had rather frowned at the visitor, now smiled and nodded too, repeating the words. —

"Not Queres; Tehua woman, wife of Cayamo."

All laughed, and the governor exclaimed, —

"It is well."

The case was clear to all. Cayamo, on his expedition to secure scalps, had picked up a sweetheart. Food was placed before Shotaye, and the woman caressed her, inviting her to eat.

In the mean time, one of the boys had left the room. Shotaye was still eating when he returned in company with an elderly man of low stature, whose greeting was answered with the usual reply.

This man cowered down among the rest, and listened with the closest attention to a long speech of the governor. At the close of it he sat for a while scrutinizing the woman's appearance, but when she looked up at him he addressed her in her own dialect, and with the words, —

"Where do you come from?"

A heavy load fell from Shotaye's heart. The ice was broken; henceforth she could explain herself in her own tongue, and inform the Tehuas of everything that was so important to them, so momentous to her. But her first impression, on hearing her tongue spoken by one who was certainly not of her stock, was almost one of fright. People who spoke more than one language were excessively rare at those times; and those who happened to learn the speech of another tribe kept it secret, as Tyope, for instance, concealed his knowledge of the Navajo language from the people of the Rito. The knowledge of more than one tongue was a suspicious and therefore a dangerous gift. The man who now conversed with Shotaye in the Queres dialect was not a native of the Puye. He belonged to the linguistic group of the Tehuas, but to the southern branch, the Tanos, who inhabited several villages west of the Rio Grande and in the country where the city of Santa Fé now stands. Between the Tanos and the Queres there was limited commercial intercourse, for the Tanos claimed the veins of turquoise that abound on the heights near some of their villages, and the Queres went thither at rare intervals to trade for the gems which they were unable to obtain by force.

Through this rare and limited traffic the Tano had become acquainted with some of the men of the Rito, and many years ago had even accompanied them to their home in the mountain gorge. Such visits were literally great affairs at the time, and they lasted long. Extensive formalities were required to ascertain first how far the Shiuana appeared favourable to the new-comer, and how he should make himself understood to them. The medicine-men had to make strenuous efforts in behalf of the visitor. Equally long formalities preceded his departure, and our Tano had in this manner, between reception, residence, and leave-taking, spent more than a year at the Rito de los Frijoles. During that time he had acquired a knowledge of the Queres language, and spoke it therefore not fluently, but still intelligibly.

As Shotaye had appeared excited and agitated as long as she felt helpless in matters of speech, so now she became free, easy, and above all, calm and clear in her utterances, when she could make herself understood. The Tano began to question her in a methodical, and even in an argumentative manner. He spoke slowly and brokenly; but she understood him, and he comprehended fully her replies, for they were given to the same categoric way. Each of her sentences he translated into Tehua, turning to the tuyo at the end of every one of her answers. Shotaye told him everything, with the exception of the matter of the owl's feathers, for these would have been as dangerous among the Tehuas as among the Queres.

She explained the misunderstanding that lay at the bottom of the hostility displayed by the Queres, and finally she insisted that there was no time to clear up that misunderstanding; and since the Queres were already on the march, she urged speedy preparation to repel the assault. She strained the truth on the latter point, but the tuyo forgave her this manifest exaggeration. He knew that there must be at least five days' delay before the prospective campaign. The further the woman proceeded in her exposition of facts, the more she observed, through her quick and scrutinizing glance, that her listeners became deeply interested, and that thoroughly startled, they at last displayed marks of indignation. That indignation, it was plain, was against the Queres; and Shotaye felt that she had gained her point. The breach between the tribes was now widened to such an extent that it could never be healed. At the close of the interrogatory, which had frequently been interrupted by exclamations of surprise and anger, the mistress of the house caressed Shotaye, calling her sister. The tuyo, however, merely nodded to her kindly, uttered in a commanding tone a few words to those present, and went out to attend to his duties of convening the council. But the Tano Indian remained with Shotaye until late in the night. He pretended to keep her company, and to contribute toward dispelling the feeling of loneliness that might overcome her in the midst of people with whom she could not converse. But in reality he remained as a spy, to cross-examine in a covert way. Shotaye was wary, and not one contradiction, not one misstatement, could he detect during their talk. Then he went where the council had gathered, reporting that according to his conviction the woman was not only sincere, but exceedingly well-informed.

It would be superfluous to enter into details concerning

the proceedings of the council. Its composition and the formalities were in the main similar to those of the council of the Queres. One point was earnestly discussed, — the propriety of sending a messenger to the Queres to clear up, if possible, the misunderstanding. But the thought was finally discarded, on the ground that it was not the Tehuas who should make overtures of peace, — because they were absolutely innocent, — but the Queres, for it was they who, ere proceeding to hostile demonstrations, should have called on the Tehuas for explanation. Had the two tribes been on friendly terms, it might have been different; but there existed a breach between them already, and if the Queres chose to still further widen it, the Tehuas felt ready for any emergency. It was resolved to prepare for war at once, to call to arms the entire male population, send ahead the necessary spies, and thus prepared, to wait. With this the matter went into the hands of the great medicine-man and the head war-chief. The former was almost an equivalent to the Hishtanyi Chayan among the Queres, the latter the exact equivalent of the maseua.

The castle-like rock of the Puye, along whose base the numerous cave-dwellings are burrowed out of a very friable and almost snow-white tufa, is situated about ten miles west of the Rio Grande, and not two miles south of the picturesque cañon of Santa Clara. The cliff is over one half mile long, and it dominates the mesa on which it stands. For many miles there are groves of timber surrounding the foot of the high and rugged slope that leads up to the cave-dwellings. While the Queres at the Rito dwelt at the bottom of a secluded gorge, the Tehuas occupied a picturesque citadel rising from a high and level plateau. Northeast of the Puye, and separated from it by the cañon of Santa Clara, there rises a similar rock, equally bold and striking, and higher still, but not as extensive. This is called by the Tehuas, Shu Finne. Its lower rim is also perforated by cave-dwellings, and these were inhabited by a portion of the same tribe. During the night runners were sent to the Shu Finne, calling upon its people for assistance; and videttes were placed on the mountains and on the little mesa capping the cliff. The Tehuas were more numerous than the Queres of the Rito, and might well wait calmly and with dignity until the latter either sought to negotiate or broke out in unjustifiable warfare.

The five days which, as the tuyo had correctly inferred, would be spent by the people of the Tyuonyi in mourning and in warlike preparations, passed; and no messenger of peace came to the Tehuas. The Queres remained in perfect confidence that those whom they intended to surprise were in absolute ignorance of any evil intentions on their part. But when the night of the fifth day had shrouded the landscape in purple darkness, Tehua warriors began to stream down the slopes from the cliff and its cave-dwellings. The deepest silence was observed, instructions having been given beforehand, and the bands of armed men moved noiselessly forward. The plan was not to await the attack at home, but to advance into the more timbered country south of the barren mesa where the cliff rises, and to surprise the enemy on their approach. From reports of spies it was known that no Queres were as yet scouring the heights north of the Rito; and the Tehuas, moving swiftly, were able to place themselves in ambush in the rocky wilderness where, later on, their descendants built and inhabited the now ruined village of the Pueblo of the Bird. One half day's journey would bring the Queres easily to that point, where they certainly would not expect to be met by armed foes. There is water in the vicinity. and the ground is broken with pine groves. It could be foretold with reasonable certainty that the enemy would move in the direction of this place, for it is the straightest course, though not the easiest, from the Rito northward. In this region the Tehua hosts spread out, scouts preceding even as far as the Ziro kauash. The Queres might come, for everything was as ready as Shotaye's fondest hopes could have wished.

During these warlike preparations Shotaye found ample time and opportunity to become initiated into the life of her new home. The old interpreter proved a very useful guide, and she improved his willingness to talk and to ad-vise. He informed her that Cayamo was free, and that as soon as the story of their meeting had become known among the people of the Puye, everybody began to look upon her as his future wife. Shortly before the beginning of the cam-paign, the time of his retirement expired; the ceremonies on the scalp matter had to be postponed on account of the all-important measures of war, and Cayamo was able to pre-sent himself to his future spouse in the natural colour of his skin and in his usual costume. Their meeting was not in the least sentimental. Both laughed aloud and joyfully; they exchanged gestures and signs plainly indicat-ing their future duties and probable results. Those pres-ent laughed in token of approval and applause. At a hint from Teanyi's wife, Shotaye placed some corn-cakes before Cayamo. He ate a few morsels, the courtship formalities were fulfilled, and the bridegroom returned to his duty as a warrior.

The Tano had informed the woman that Cayamo belonged to the clan of the Sun. In return she communicated that the Water people were her kindred. What the Queres called Tzitz hanutsh the Tehuas named P'ho doa, and the members of the clan P'ho were therefore officially requested to take their new sister in charge. Some of the old men of the cluster came over to the dwellings of the Turquoise clan, where the wife of Teanyi lived. In their company came several women, who escorted Shotaye to her new quarters. On the way to the caves of P'ho doa one of the women lightly touched Shotaye's breast, then her own, and whispered, —

"Oyike P'ho."

It was her name, and Shotaye communicated her own in reply. The woman shook her head, whispering, —

"Nyo Shotaye, nyo Tema, 'not Shotaye, not Queres.' Tehua quio." Then she grasped her hand and breathed into Shotaye's ear, —

"Aua P'ho Quio."

Shotaye easily understood the meaning of this confidential communication. With her change of abode her name was to change also. Henceforth she was to be a Tehua woman, and Aua P'ho Quio was to be her name.

The Tano continued his visits as heretofore. He plied the woman with questions, sometimes of the most complex nature. His conduct in this respect was characteristic of the suspicious nature of the Indian generally. The leaders of the Tehuas mistrusted Shotaye still, notwithstanding her clear and positive talk ; and they had instructed the Tano to keep her company and to probe her sincerity and veracity still further. But she was more than a match for all of them. She saw through the maze of the very confused and bewildering interrogatory, and her replies were such as to absolutely confirm the Tehuas in the good opinion they had conceived of her. Whatever the interpreter reported to the tuyo that was of any value to the military operations impending, was immediately communicated to the war-chief through a special runner, for that functionary was in the field already with his men.

Shotaye made use of her conversations with the Tano Indian to direct the attention of the Tehuas toward Tyope.

She described him as the leading warrior and the most influential man on the Rito, as the pivot around which everything revolved and on whose life much would depend. But she was artful enough not to depict Tyope as a bad man, lest the Tehuas might infer her real purpose. She spoke of him as a man dangerous through his good qualities, and as a formidable adversary. In short her words produced such an effect that the governor himself came to interrogate her on the subject, and even caused the war-chief to return from the field on the fourth day, and had him visit Shotaye in company with the interpreter and secure a detailed and accurate description of this dangerous individual. Then they went to the medicine-man and consulted him about the propriety of taking Shotaye along into the field, that she might point out the great warrior who, so they had become convinced, must be killed at all hazards in order to insure success. On the evening of the sixth day, therefore, Shotaye wandered over to Tzirege in company with the commander himself.

Shortly after their arrival among the group of warriors where the war-chief had taken his position, runners came from the south with news that they had detected several Queres in full war-paint creeping northward from the brink of the Rito. These runners were at once ordered back, with strict injunctions to the scouts not to impede the enemy's movements, but to suffer them to advance. The Tehuas were quite scattered, particularly in the front, as is usually the case with bodies of Indians on the war-path. The main bodies concealed themselves between the Tzirege and a deep and broad ravine farther south, called to-day Cañada Ancha. They kept in the woods toward the mountains, expecting their foes to approach on a line closer to the river. The plan was to allow the Queres to come up undisturbed as far as the north side of the Cañada. As the men from the Rito advanced, the Tehua scouts were to close in from the rear and follow them cautiously, until the enemies were all gathered on the desired spot, with the woods to their left and rugged, barren cliffs and peaks to their right. Then the trap would be sprung; and if the Queres took to those bleak fastnesses for defence it would be easy to surround them, cut them off from water, and thus exterminate them completely.

Night had fallen when another message came, to the effect that the numbers of the enemy were increasing, and beginning to spread over the timber in small groups. The war-chief sent a messenger to the Puye, and after midnight the great medicine-man of war appeared in person. The shaman was, like all the others, painted black; a tall plume taken from an eagle rose behind each ear; the left hand carried a rattle; and a little drum was suspended from his shoulder. As soon as he arrived, one of the warriors retired to a spot which was almost hedged in by several bushy cedar-trees. There he built a fire, and as soon as it burned he covered it in such a manner that only a thin film of smoke arose from it. To this smouldering heap the shaman proceeded alone and sat down. There he spent the night, muttering incantations and prayers, shaking his rattle, and striking the drum softly from time to time.

The sounds that proceeded from his discordant music were so faint that they could be heard only in close prox-imity. They were besides the only human sound in this wilderness. Animal voices occasionally disturbed the quietness of the night. Nobody would have supposed that between the Rito and the mesas opposite San Ildefonso of to-day several hundred Indian warriors were hidden, patiently waiting or slowly moving forward. It was a quiet, still night, cool, as the nights mostly are in the rainy season, and dark. The sky was partly overcast; but the clouds did not drift, they formed and dissolved overhead ; and the stars appeared and disappeared alternately as the nebulous fleeces disclosed or shrouded them. Behind the mountain, thunder-clouds rested, and occasional flashes of lightning illuminated the crests, and faint thunder muttered in the distance. It had no threatening sound, and the lightning did not seem like prophetic writing on the sombre clouds. It was a pleasant night and an excellent one for Indian warfare.

The scouts of the Tehuas had reported in the last instance that the bulk of the war-party from the Rito must now be on the move, for no fresh additions were coming up from the gorge. So careless and unconcerned were the Queres, so absolutely sure of the enemy's ignorance of their designs, that they never thought of sending scouts to the upper end of the northern mesa. From there a few Tehuas had comfortably observed everything that happened in the gorge during the day, and as evening came they could report even the numbers of the warriors who took part in the campaign. As soon as these warriors were all on the Ziro kauash, the Tehua spies, after warning those behind them, crept cautiously into the rear of the advancing foe.

All the able-bodied men from the Tyuonyi had not been permitted to join the expedition. Hayoue was not among them, neither was Okoya. It was a sad disappointment to the boy, and yet was he not staying at home in defence of his mother and of Mitsha? Say Koitza had ceased to weep, but the persistent neglect which she thought she suffered from Shotaye grieved her. At last she asked Okoya whether he had seen anything of the cave-woman. His reply, that he thought she had gone, explained everything. She recollected the confident words that Shotaye had spoken to her, and concluded that the woman had carried out her plan of taking refuge with the Tehuas. That

quelled her apprehensions and allayed her fears. Shotaye
knew what she was and had to do; and Shotaye — of this
Say felt convinced — was true to her. In order to be quite
sure of the fact, however, she strolled up to the cave in the
course of an afternoon. The rooms were empty, and Say
turned back. One of Shotaye's neighbours stopped her to
ask where the medicine-woman might be. Say carelessly
replied that she was probably on the heights above, gathering herbs. The wily fugitive had left her household as if
she were about to return soon. With the exception of the
mother of Okoya nobody noticed her absence. She was
known to disappear occasionally for several days; and furthermore, the excitement and bustle incident upon the prospective expedition against the Tehuas engaged everybody's
attention.

Say Koitza could not help wondering whether Shotaye
would inform the Tehuas of the impending attack. Perhaps she might, perhaps not. At all events she felt relieved
upon hearing that neither her son nor her husband nor
even Hayoue were to go with the warriors. The enterprise
aroused within her vague apprehensions; why, she could not
tell. But it pleased her to learn that Tyope was going,—
going as the leader, the war-captain of the party.

Tyope had worked incessantly and with brilliant results.
The Shkuy Chayan and the Koshare Naua had succeeded
in so inveigling the principal shaman that he ordered that
all the men from the Water clan, and those from Shyuamo
with few exceptions, should stay at home for the protection
of the women and children. That included Hayoue, of
whose abilities and popularity Tyope was afraid, and saved
the Turquoise people from the casualties of war. Tyope
went so far as to praise Hayoue in the council, suggesting
that the young man should be intrusted with authority as
war-chief *ad interim*. The suggestion was carried out at

once, and afterward the Hishtanyi Chayan appointed Tyope
as commander-in-chief of the forces marching out. He
himself accompanied the body of warriors as adviser and
spiritual guide to the captain. Nothing could suit Tyope
better. The man was old and not very strong, and people
are often killed in war.

After sunset the medicine-man made his appearance on
the northern mesa and performed his incantations. Tyope
and most of the others breathed on their war-fetiches, and
then group after group stealthily moved onward. The plan,
which had been communicated to every one in its main
points, consisted in reaching before sunrise the very ground
which the Tehuas had selected for their operations; passing the following day in the woods of that vicinity in concealment, and creeping up to the Puye the following night;
then, after sunrise, when the Tehuas would begin to scatter, unarmed and unsuspecting, pouncing upon them and
making a general slaughter. Tyope had under his direction more than two hundred men, and they extended over
a wide front. About twenty experienced warriors, mostly
uakanyi, glided in advance as scouts. Behind them came
at a suitable distance either single warriors or small bands.
The main body came last. It was divided into several
groups. Near the centre were Tyope and the shaman.

Every one knew that his duty for the present consisted in
searching for traces of the enemy without exposing himself
to discovery. Should a single Tehua be observed, and it
became possible for a scout to overpower and kill him without noise, he might do it. In case a number of foes were
noticed, the spy was to give quiet warning to the man nearest to him, that one to those in his rear; and they were to
send a runner to inform Tyope. In the mean time all were
to halt until orders came to move in a new direction. For
Tyope, although he did not in the least suspect that the

25

Tehuas were forewarned, and still less on the alert so close by the Rito, used every possible precaution in order that the surprise might be complete and the blow as crushing as possible.

It was dark in the timber, and the main body of the Queres approached the brink of the first cañon north of the Rito while the advance were cautiously descending into the bottom and the scouts were already farther on. Tyope and the medicine-man were standing a short distance from the descent of the south side and listening to the news which a runner had just brought in from the front.

"Are you sure you have noticed a man?" the Chayan asked in a whisper.

"I am sure of it. He crouched at the foot of a juniper-bush," replied the messenger, positively.

"Has he seen you?" demanded Tyope.

"I believe not."

"When you left was he there still?"

"I could not see any more of him."

"How far is it from here? Where stands the tree?" the Chayan asked.

"It is on the other side of the ravine, near the border to the left."

Tyope pondered a while ; then he said to the shaman, —

"Nashtio yaya, I think we should go more toward the east. What do you say?"

"It is well," muttered the medicine-man.

"Satyumishe," Tyope said to the runner, "go and tell the men to go along the ravine toward the Rio Grande until the trees become smaller. Thence they may go to the north again, but slowly and carefully. Ziua," he called to one of the bystanders, "go and tell those toward the left to come where I stand. Ohotika," calling another, "run to the right and command those there to wait until we join them."

The runners left in the directions indicated.

The information which had just been conveyed to Tyope was most disagreeable. The presence of one human being at the time and place indicated looked very suspicious. If the man had seen his warriors he would certainly run home and give the alarm. All Tyope could do now was to keep as close as possible to the Rio Grande, push up parallel with the river as cautiously as possible, and thus sneak beyond the enemy, in case, as he still could not believe, the latter were in anything like a considerable force. He would thus eventually place himself between them and their village.

After a while the warriors from the left came on hastily, stumbling through the darkness. All together now went down in an easterly direction, where the right wing, if this term can be used, was halting. Thence Tyope despatched runners ahead to inquire whether everything was quiet in front, to repeat the order of slow marching, and to direct them to halt on the northern brink of the Cañada Ancha.

When the runners left, the march was resumed in the usual scattering manner, as if all were skirmishers. Tyope and the shaman remained together. Neither uttered a word. The commander looked up to the stars from time to time. They were peeping out more and more, for the clouds were dispersing. Only from the southwest distant thunder sounded and lightning flashed occasionally. A shower was falling in that direction.

It was past midnight when the main body came up with the advance guard after crossing the Cañada Ancha. Tyope found everything in order, and he directed a farther advance. Tyope was angry. The circuit which he had felt obliged to make made a serious delay, and there was danger that with the early sunrise of the summer months he might be behind to such an extent as to be unable to reach the cover of the

woods in time. If the Tehuas were informed of his approach
they would either prepare for his coming at the Puye — and
the result of an open attack would be to say the least extremely doubtful, — or they would come out in force, and
desultory fighting would ensue. In this those who were
nearest water and supplies always had the advantage. His
idea of striking a sudden blow appeared very much endangered by the presence of Tehuas in the forest. He thought
and thought without arriving at any satisfactory conclusion.
Return to the Rito he could not, for such a retreat was worse
than disaster. Neither could he decide alone; the Hishtanyi
Chayan was by his side and he had to consult him. So he
stood still and turned to the shaman, saying, —

"Nashtio yaya, the night will soon be over, and the sun
may come out from behind the mountain in the east."

"Ko," grunted the medicine-man.

"It is far yet to the houses of the Moshome Tehua."

The Chayan stood still.

"Sa uishe nashtio," said he, "the Shiuana direct us to go
on a different road. I saw an owl fly toward the moon.
Let us go away from the river into the kote to rest and to
hide until the sun goes down again and we may go farther
toward the katityam of the enemy."

This was just as Tyope wanted. He disliked the idea of
passing a day concealed under cliffs and crags where a torrid
sun shone, and where there was water only in the river beneath and at a great depth. But he wanted to be sure of
what Those Above intended, so he asked again, —

"Yaya Chayan, do the Shiuana" — he emphasized the
term — "say that we should go to the west?"

"The spirits say that we should go where there is shade
and water! Let us go to the mountains; there we shall
find both."

"They are right!" Tyope exclaimed. "I believe it is

better to stay there until the sun has risen. I will send word to the men to turn to the left, and we will sleep in the shade of the trees until the time comes to advance."

"You are right, brother," the Chayan assented; "do as you have said."

The two men had lagged behind the others during this conversation. Tyope imitated the cry of an owl. Soon several warriors came up to him. He directed them to go to the front, to the right, and to the left, and give orders that all should move to the westward a short distance, far enough to reach high timber. Then all should halt and prepare to pass the night. He himself moved a short distance only in that direction, in company with the shaman, and selected a spot where the mesa was covered with the usual underbrush and where taller trees already began to appear. Here he lay down to rest with eyes wide open, ready for any emergency. Not far away the medicine-man found a secluded spot where he sat down without fire, oc-casionally touching the drum and reciting his prayers and incantations. They were the same as those which the shaman of the Tehuas was directing to Those Above at the same time and not far from him, but in a different tongue, for the success of his people and the destruction of those for whom the Hishtanyi Chayan was praying.

The decision of Tyope to penetrate into the forest to the west brought the Queres into the very position which the Tehuas desired. The scouts of the latter had obeyed punc-tually and diligently the orders which they had received, fol-lowing step by step the advancing foe and reporting to headquarters any notable move. They possessed the im-mense advantage of knowing every movement the Queres made from the very beginning, and were thus able to ob-serve them unseen. As soon as Tyope had concentrated his forces on the northern brink of the Cañada Ancha, the main

body of the Tehuas receded slightly to the west. As soon
as the Queres began to ascend in that direction, the retrograde movement of the others continued in the centre;
whereas the left wing spread out, and the right slightly advanced to the east along the brink of the ravine. The
scouts were called in with all haste and reinforced, especially the body that faced the Queres in the north. At the
time Tyope lay down to rest, his forces were surrounded
everywhere except on the east. Everything was ready for the
Tehuas to begin their attack upon the unsuspecting foe at
daybreak.

CHAPTER XVIII.

THE change from night to daylight in New Mexico is by no means sudden. Darkness yields slowly to the illumination streaming from the east; and when the moon is shining, one remains in doubt for quite a while whether the growing brightness is due to the mistress of night or to the lord of day.

Nowhere is this more perceptible than on high plateaus covered by sparse timber. Suddenly awaking, one is in doubt at first whether it is sunrise or the full moon that illuminates the landscape. The shadows are weakened, but objects are not much more distinct; a glow pervades the air rather than a positive light.

When the Indian is on the war-path he sleeps but little, and never long. He prefers the day to the night for rest, as he can conceal his movements better in the darkness. Tyope had halted his little army just before daybreak because he felt afraid of going any farther, and because he had arrived close to the place where he desired to remain during the day without exposing his forces to the chance of discovery. None of his men slept; none of them dozed, even. They had all been warned of the possible presence of foes, and although there seemed not the slightest evidence of those foes being aware of their coming, yet the mere apprehension caused uneasiness. There was therefore increased watchfulness on their part.

Every one among the Queres was looking forward with anxiety to the hour when there would be sufficient light to

investigate the situation more closely.   The sky had cleared ;
the air became cooler, and the morning star shone brightly, in
spite of the luminous crescent of a waning moon.   The Hishtanyi Chayan was sitting at the same place where he had retired a few hours before, but he no longer prayed ; he stared
motionless.   Tyope lay on his back behind a juniper-bush.
He was watching the sky and the approach of dawn.   A
number of warriors had lain down in the vicinity, awaiting
the signal to move.

One of these had placed himself in such a position that
he could glance at the forest, which loomed up before him
like a mass of dense shadows with rays of moonlight between.   He peered into that maze of darkness and light for
hours.   But nothing appeared in it worthy of note.   So the
Queres warrior turned around on his back in order to
change position.   He saw the moon rise to the zenith and
the corona borealis disappear below the western horizon.
He noticed also how the stars grew dimmer and dimmer,
how the shadows commenced to wane.   Finally he fixed his
gaze on the east.

Owing to the shrubbery it was not possible to see distinctly, yet anything lying on the ground could be discerned.
From the place where he lay, the Queres Indian looked
through a lane bordered on both sides by bushes of cedar
and juniper.   At the end of that lane he discovered a dark
spot.   That spot disappeared while he was still gazing at it.
He strained his eyes to find the spot again, but it had really
vanished.

The man from the Rito became suspicious.   Again he
looked, but the spot or object, whatever it might be, had
gone out of sight altogether.   He crawled over to the man
nearest him, told him what had occurred, and returned to
his post.   The dark speck or thing had not reappeared ; but
on the right side of the gallery formed by the trees it seemed

as if, somewhat nearer to his own position, something black became apparent and disappeared in an instant. The scout strained both ear and eye. Nothing could be heard, and nothing else of a suspicious character met his gaze.

Meanwhile his companion had crept over to where Tyope was lying, and had reported to the commander the strange apparition. Tyope turned over so as to face the east and said, —

"It is well."

He also began to scan the network of shadows and illuminated patches extending in that direction. The Indian who had spoken to him went back to his post, but very soon returned, whispering, —

"Somebody has crossed over from one tree to another."

"Where?" Tyope asked in a subdued voice.

"There," replied the scout, pointing with his hand toward a group of bushes.

"It is well," said the leader; "go back and keep your eyes open."

The Indian crawled off. Tyope rose to his knees, seized two branches of the tree behind which he had been reclining, and bent them asunder. In this manner he was able to overlook the ground to the east at a greater height than before. The light had increased, but it would have been impossible to discern any object at a distance.

Daylight was growing on the waning night. Had Tyope stood up and looked toward the east, he would have seen the dark, sinuous line which the mountains east of Santa Fé trace along that part of the horizon. Their uppermost snow-fields were beginning to glisten in the light streaming up from beyond.

On Tyope's left a rustling sound was heard; he turned around. One of his men was cautiously approaching.

"There are Moshome in front of us."

"I know it," replied the commander. "How many have you seen?"

"Two."

"And you saw them clearly?"

"Yes, but they sneaked off."

"Did they seem to come toward us?"

"They crept behind a juniper, and after that I could see nothing more."

"Do the others know it?"

"Not yet. Shall I tell them?"

"Go tell them. Afterward return here to me."

Tyope felt embarrassed. It was clear to him that several Tehuas were lurking in the direction whence he had come, and that they were moving toward him. It indicated that their numbers were strong enough to engage him. That looked very, very ominous! If he only knew how matters stood elsewhere, and whether the enemy had shown himself at other points! Tyope grew very uneasy.

Tactics in Indian warfare reduce themselves to a game of hide-and-seek. He who must show himself first is sure of suffering the greater loss. Tyope knew that in case the Tehuas had actually surrounded him they had the greater advantage at their disposal. They might wait much longer than he and his men. They might even wait for days, keeping the Queres penned up in uncertainty, and then break out as soon as the latter were sufficiently exhausted.

The same scout approached again. He crawled like a mole.

"Nashtio," he whispered, "there are Moshome to the left of us."

"Many?" Tyope inquired hastily.

"Six of them have been noticed."

That was exceedingly alarming. He directed the man to stay on the spot, while he glided through the bushes to where the Hishtanyi Chayan had spent the night. The medicine-man was awake, and looked at the captain in astonishment. Tyope placed a finger on his lips and shook his head. The shaman asked, —

"Sa uishe, what is it?"

"Tzatze raua! Tzatze raua!" Tyope exclaimed in a low tone. "The Tehuas are sneaking about us like shutzuna. There are many of them, and they come up from the east. What shall we do, yaya? Speak."

"Tzatze raua," the shaman repeated, shaking his head. "As you say, the Moshome come up behind us?"

"I thought," Tyope suggested, "of sending word to the men in front to come back, and as soon as we could see anything, striking the enemies in our rear. What do you think of it, sa nashtio?"

"Many will go to Shipapu to-day," the Chayan muttered.

"What shall I do? Speak!" Tyope insisted. The last words of the shaman frightened him.

The Chayan gave no immediate reply, but sat musing in a manner indicating that his thoughts were with Those Above. At last he raised his head and replied, —

"We must wait until the sun stands in the sky."

Tyope suppressed a sigh. However much he attributed this answer of the shaman to inspiration from those on high, it appeared to him dangerous. Tyope felt very uneasy, but he was no coward. In case the worst had really happened, if the Tehuas had anticipated and surrounded him, he still inclined to the conviction that concentration of his forces and a rapid onslaught on the foes in his rear would not only save him, but secure a reasonable number of coveted trophies. If this could be speedily effected, the less important would be his loss in attaining it; for as long as the light was faint and dim, the enemy's missiles could not be discharged with certain aim. He had hoped that the Chayan would assent to this suggestion. Now on the contrary, the oracle spoke in a manner that plainly indicated that the Shiuana ordered him to wait until daylight. It was sure destruction, he felt it; but the Shiuana spoke through the medium of the old man, and the Shiuana were of course right. He could not complain or even grumble.

But he might at least prepare everything in advance, so that as soon as the medicine-man gave the signal, his favourite move might be executed with a promptness and alacrity that would surprise the enemy. So Tyope crept back to the juniper-bush in whose neighbourhood his men were grouped.

Dawn was coming on, and the shadows were beginning to assume definite shapes and directions. Tyope sighed when he noticed the approach of sunlight; precious time was being irretrievably lost.

He relieved the warrior whom he had left at his post. The latter whispered to him that nothing suspicious had turned up. Suddenly Tyope started and pressed his ear to the ground; then he darted up, rising to his knees, and listened, straining every nerve, his head turned to the southwest.

In that direction arose loud yells. They were followed by piercing cries. Soon the sounds mingled, so as to create a noise like that which a struggle between men and wolves might produce. These sounds told Tyope that a severe engagement had commenced in that direction. At the same time it struck him that the main body of the Tehuas were probably south and east of his forces, and that consequently by moving swiftly westward he could interpose himself between the Tehuas and their homes, cut off their warriors from their village, and secure complete triumph. But before he could order such a change of tactics he ought to know something definite from the quarter where the fight had begun. To send a runner seemed unadvisable, for he thought it unsafe to lessen the forces around him, if only by a man. Several of his companions had approached, startled by the sudden noise. He motioned them to return to their posts.

The noise of the battle diminished; then it broke out anew and sounded nearer. It seemed to extend to the east. In the west and north everything remained quiet; the enemy appeared to be entirely southwest and east of the little army which Tyope commanded. He felt relieved, and a grim satisfaction crept over his mind. He thought, surely the Tehuas have committed a grave mistake.

If only his people would report to him! Now at last! The bushes rattled, and a man stepped up. In a tone of intense agitation he said, —

"Where is the war-chief?"

"I am here," replied Tyope in a muffled voice, motioning the warrior to lie down. The latter either failed to notice the gesture or misunderstood it, and walked on upright. Something whizzed through the branches of the shrubs; the messenger bent as if suddenly folded up; he grasped at his stomach with his hand, and tumbled to the ground. Tyope stood by his side in the twinkling of an eye. The shaft of an arrow was sticking in his body, and in vain did the wounded man try to pluck it out. Regardless of the horrible pain the unfortunate one was suffering, bent upon catching the drift of his message before the soul could escape the tortured body, Tyope almost lay down on the groaning man.

"What news do you bring? Speak!" he hissed into his ear.

The wounded warrior moaned, moaned again. Tyope grew wild.

"Speak !" he growled, and shook him by the shoulder so rudely that the other screamed.

"The Moshome," he gasped, "they — they — have come on to us." A chill went through his body; he lay there gasping, incapable of speech.

Tyope was frenzied; he again shook the dying man ruthlessly.

"Where have they attacked?" he roared.

"West."

"Have they killed any of our people?"

"I — don't — know," breathed the poor fellow. His head was swaying; it rolled back and forth on the ground. Tyope could not obtain any further reply. So he crawled back and left him to die. The Moor had done his duty; the Moor might go to Shipapu.

Tyope had been so eager to secure from the dying man any information the latter might still be able to impart, that he paid no immediate attention to the noise and uproar which had arisen in his own vicinity. Almost at the very moment when the Queres warrior was mortally wounded, one of Tyope's companions despatched one of his arrows at a Tehua whom he had distinctly seen in front. This shot he accompanied by a loud yell. The foe replied to the challenge in the same manner; arrows whizzed and hissed through the air, crossing each other and tearing through the shrubbery or penetrating the trunks of trees with dull thuds. The fight had begun here too, but little if any damage was done as yet by either side. Most of the arrows were shot at random, and both parties whooped and yelled. Their purpose was manifestly to frighten the adversary by creating an exaggerated impression of their own numbers and strength.

All this did not make an unfavourable impression upon Tyope. On the contrary, as soon as he saw that the engagement had broken out in his rear also, he felt a thrill of pleasure and changed his plans at once. He believed now, in presence of the attacks made by the Tehuas, that the latter had indeed placed all their men between him and the Rito, and that consequently the road to the Puye lay open, and he could rush up, capture the women and children, and hold them for ransom. But he must move swiftly and energetically, leaving the fight to go on as best it might. By advancing with a part of his forces, first to the west and then straight to the north, Tyope might execute his plan of leaving enough men behind to make a desperate stand against the Tehuas here. Without the consent of the Hishtanyi Chayan, however, he felt unauthorized to adopt decisive measures. So he again crept over to the shaman and communicated his plans to him. To his delight the old man rose and said, —

" It is well. Let us go."

It was daylight now, and everything could be plainly seen. The extended skirmishing went on with less ardour than before, neither party pressing the other very closely.

Tyope glided back to one of his men. An arrow well directed struck the ground very near. Whispering into his ear the change of programme, Tyope took off his shield, turned it toward the enemy, and rose on his right knee. Fastened to the left arm and resting on the ground with its lower rim, the shield covered the kneeling man almost completely. The left hand held the bow, and the weapon slightly protruded from behind the protecting target. Tyope then pushed his body forward from behind the bush where he had been crouching.

Hardly was the shield visible when its owner felt a sudden blow against it, and the point of an arrow came through the hide. The shot must have come from a short distance, or it would not have pierced the shield. Ere Tyope discovered whence it came, his companion had discharged his bow, and with a loud whoop hurled himself forward, where he fell headlong behind a little tree. Wild yells sounded from the Tehuas, and several of their warriors rushed up to the spot; branches rattled and bushes shook as the men brushed past them. Tyope had an arrow ready, and he despatched it at one of his foes. He pulled another from the quiver without looking to see whether the first had struck a mark or not, darted up, and with a shout bounded ahead to encounter the enemy. A shot grazed his right hand, scratching the wrist and causing him to drop his arrow. For a time the arm was numb, but Tyope heeded it not. Where the man who had stood beside him had fallen, a number of warriors from both sides were wrangling. A Queres lay dead on the dead body of a Tehua whose scalp he had intended to secure. Two of his brethren were defending his corpse against half a dozen Tehuas. Tyope's right wrist had been paralyzed by the arrow-shot, but he raised his arm and flung the war-club that dangled from it against the head of the nearest foe. The blow was too feeble, and Tyope grabbed the man's hair. Arrows whizzed and shrieked past the fighting group; shrill yells and wild howling sounded from every quarter. The contending parties exchanged insulting cries and abusive words in both languages.

The Tehua whom Tyope had grabbed by the hair made desperate lunges at him from below with a sharply pointed arrow. He succeeded in slightly wounding him in several places. Tyope kicked him in the abdomen, causing him to double up at once. Regardless of the pain in the right hand Tyope succeeded in grasping the war-club at last. With it he directed several blows at the head of the enemy, but they were so weak that only at the third stroke did the Tehua fall. At this juncture an arrow grazed Tyope's tem-

ple. He looked up, and saw that he had been very imprudent in yielding so far to ardour and excitement as to mingle
with his men in a strife for the possession of a single scalp,
and thus expose unduly his own person. He began to
think of withdrawal into the neighbourhood of the Hishtanyi Chayan, but it was not easy to extricate himself.
Warding off a blow aimed at his skull, with his shield he
pushed it into the face of the new assailant with sufficient
force to cause the man to stagger. Then he shouted a few
words to his own men, turned around, and rushed back to
his tree, where he fell down at full length, exhausted and
bleeding. The other Queres, two in number, followed his
example, and the Tehuas did not pursue. The result was
so far favourable to the Queres that they lost but one man
and the Tehuas two; but the scalp of the dead man from
the Rito remained with the enemy.

When Tyope had recovered his breath, he sneaked back
to where he had left the shaman. As he approached the
spot he heard the medicine-man singing and beating his
drum. It was a very good sign to see the shaman at work
with such enthusiasm; still Tyope must disturb him.

"Sa nashtio," he cried, "we must go."

" Heiti-na ! Heiti-na ! " shouted the praying shaman,
drumming incessantly. He was in ecstasies. His uplifted
eyes sparkled; he paid no attention to what was around
him.

" Sa nashtio yaya," Tyope anxiously insisted.

" Do not disturb me, let me alone ! Heiti-na ! Heiti-na !"
cried the Hishtanyi Chayan aloud.

Tyope was in despair. Arrow after arrow was flying past
him, rending twigs and shattering branches. The Tehuas
shot faster than the Queres. They must have a large supply of missiles. Every shot was accompanied by triumphant yells; the enemy was growing bolder.

26

Again the leader tried to rouse the medicine-man to decisive action, but the latter only shook his head in an irritated manner and proceeded with his song louder and
louder. At last he dropped his drum, jumped to his feet,
and began to dance and to stamp, shaking his rattle and
wildly yelling, —

"Raua, raua! Ho-ā-ā, Heiti-na! Ho-ā-ā, Heiti-na!"
Then he stood still, and looked around as if aroused from
a dream. At the sight of Tyope he remembered, and
spoke, panting still, —

"It is well. They are good, Those Above! We will do
as you said!" Heedless of missiles he walked on into the
forest. Tyope heaved a great sigh of relief.

A small whistle made of bone depended from Tyope's
neck. He raised it to his lips and blew a shrill, piercing
blast. The warriors in his neighbourhood turned their
faces toward him. He beckoned to one of them to approach. To this man he gave directions in a low tone.
They were to the effect that they should offer the most
determined resistance to the enemy, while at the same time
they were to retire gradually but slowly from the actual
position, as if yielding to pressure. Their sturdy resistance
was to cover the movements of the main body.

Tyope now stealthily crept away from the line of the
fight. Soon he met a group of his people who, outside of
the range of missiles, were waiting to be called into action.
He sent the majority of them to the front to reinforce
the others. Two runners were despatched to the south
and southwest with orders. With the remainder he set
out slowly, penetrating deeper into the timber. He thus
collected, one after another, the various groups into a
fairly compact body, always sending a few men back to
reinforce the fighting portions. Over one hundred men
were now engaged with the Tehuas. The remainder

moved, as Tyope confidently hoped, upon the cave-dwellings of the unprotected Puye by a detour which would
enable the Queres to avoid the rather exposed site of
Tzirege.

A tremendous noise from the south indicated that a hand-
to-hand encounter was going on there. The noise lasted
but a short time, then it subsided. Shortly afterward a
warrior rushed panting up to Tyope.

"Nashtio," he said, "the Moshome have taken five
scalps."

"Where?" Tyope snorted.

"There;" he pointed southward.

"And we?"

"Three."

"Have the people gone back?"

"A little."

"It is well. Tell the men to come still farther this way,
but very slowly."

He ordered five of his own men to go back with the runner to replace the five whom the Tehuas had killed. With
the rest he pushed forward. He kept beside the Hishtanyi
Chayan, and both walked almost at the head of their little
troupe. Only a few scouts preceded them, so completely
safe did Tyope feel about the west and northwest.

The action in the rear seemed to lag. A wild uproar
broke out in the southwest but no messenger came with evil
tidings. The Queres maintained themselves. All was well.

The engagement had lasted two hours already, and it
might continue in this way for hours more without coming
to a crisis in the mean time. Tyope would creep up to the
women and children of the Tehuas. In case the rear-guard
should be ultimately destroyed by the enemy it mattered
little, for by capturing the non-combatants the Queres still
remained masters of the situation. Tyope was explaining

all this to the Hishtanyi Chayan; and the two, in consequence of their conversation, had remained behind the foremost skirmish-line. The shaman was listening, and from
time to time grunting assent to Tyope's explanations.

Suddenly the shrubbery in front rattled, and moved violently, as though deer were endeavouring to tear through
it at full speed. At the same time there arose in that
very west which had been so still, and close upon the two
men, a fearful war-whoop uttered by many voices. Like
wildfire this threatening howl spread to the west; it seemed
to run along an arc of a circle from the northwest to the
south. The warriors in front came running back in dismay.
Many of them were already wounded. One reached the
spot where the commander and the shaman were standing
spell-bound. There he fell to the ground headlong, blood
flowing from his mouth. His body had been shot through
and through.

However great his surprise at that completely unexpected
attack, and however disastrous it must be to all his plans,
Tyope not only did not lose his head, but rather seemed to
grow cool and self-possessed, and an expression of sinister
quiet settled on his features. Yet he was internally far from
being at ease or hopeful. He blew his whistle. Without
regard to his office the old shaman crouched behind a shrub,
where, placing his shield before him, he listened and spied.
The medicine-man had imitated Tyope's example; the magician was now turned into a warrior !

The signal given by the war-chief was heard by very few
only, for the yells of the Tehuas drowned every other noise.
The enemy this time rushed up without any preliminary skirmishing, and the surprise was so sudden that the Queres were
running back in every direction with their foes in close pursuit. They had no time to gather or to hide. Ere Tyope
knew it, his men were far away in his rear, as well as a num-

ber of his enemies also. To his left he noticed one of his tribe lying on the ground dead, and a Tehua standing with both feet on his back, cutting and jerking at the scalp of the dead man. Tyope was alone, for the medicine-man had fled. The Tehua was so intent upon securing the trophy that he had not seen Tyope, and he could easily have killed him. But hurried footsteps, many voices, and the shaking of bushes in front showed plainly that quite a numerous body of Tehuas was rapidly coming toward him. His own life was too precious in this hour of terrible need to permit exposure for the sake of killing one enemy, so he turned about softly on his knees. The Tehua still did not pay any attention to him, and now the temptation was too great; he quickly placed an arrow on the string and sent the shaft, thanks to the short distance, between the ribs of the unsuspecting foe. Then with a yell of triumph and defiance he darted off in the direction whither his men had scattered.

He had been noticed by some of the Tehuas who were coming up from the west, and without delay they followed in pursuit. But it was not easy to overtake a man like Tyope when fleeing for life. The powerful onslaught of the Tehuas had scattered the Queres in such a manner that friend and foe were intermingled in the forest, and it was not safe for the pursuers to shoot at the fugitives, who were only occasionally visible between tree-trunks and bushes, for the arrow might have struck a friend.

Tyope ran so fast that he soon left his pursuers far behind him. When he noticed that their shouting sounded more distant, he stopped, crouched under a bush that grew near the foot of a large tree, and listened and peered again. He was breathless from the rapid flight, and his heart throbbed so violently at first that he could not clearly distinguish sound from sound. At last he grew quiet, and now heard

the din that seemed to fill the entire forest in every direction except the north. It was nearest toward the east and
south, and there the fight seemed to concentrate. Above
the shouting, yelling, whooping, sounded the piercing war-
whistle. There could be no thought of still winning anything like success, for the day was irretrievably, disastrously
lost. To save as many of the survivors as possible was all
that could be done. Tyope would have raved, had it been
of any avail. This terrible failure, he saw clearly, ruined his
prospects forever. He wished to die, and despair began
for the first time in his life to fill his heart.

The noise of the battle was now approaching rapidly from
the east and south. The Tehuas were forcing his men into
a confused mass; it was no longer an action, it was becoming a slaughter, a butchery of the vanquished. Tyope felt
as if chills and fever were alternately running through him;
his people were without head, for the Hishtanyi Chayan was
useless as a leader. He must try to get through, and as it
was impossible to force a passage, he determined to steal
through at all hazards.

A number of Tehuas had passed without seeing him, in
their eagerness to reach the slaughter-pen into which the
timbered plateau above the Cañada Ancha was converted.
Tyope improved the opportunity to slip from one tree to
another, toward where the greatest uproar was heard. Voices
sounded quite near, and he cowered down between two
cedars. The voices came nearer, and the more he listened
the more he became convinced that his own tongue was
spoken. He was on the point of rising and going up to
the parties who spoke Queres, for they must be friends.
He distinctly heard his name. He looked, and looked
anxiously, for he preferred to find out who they were ere
addressing them. As they came closer he thought he
recognized a woman's voice.

Nearer and nearer came the voices, and at last a group of men stood out between the trees. They were warriors of the Tehuas, and in their midst was a woman. She was speaking to one of them in the language of the Rito, and all around her seemed to be attentively listening. He stared at her, — stared, his eye-balls starting from their sockets, his face colouring and then becoming almost black. Had any one seen Tyope at that moment he must have taken him for some baffled and terrified demon from the nether world.

He felt neither indignation nor passion. His heart stood still; so wonderful was the discovery he was making that he was benumbed, body and soul! For that woman who so confidently stood in the midst of the enemies of her tribe, and who spoke to them with an air of assurance bordering upon authority, uttering his own name time and again, was Shotaye!

Once more his passion came back, and delirious with rage and frenzied with fury he lifted the bow with the ready arrow. But so monstrous was the sight to his eyes that his hand dropped paralyzed, and he was unable to speed the shaft. He stood disarmed, and stared, gaping like a fiend in despair who does not venture to oppose his master. He understood now the connection of events, the unexpected ambush. He saw that it could not have happened otherwise. He saw it clearly, to his shame! The woman whom he had persecuted for years, and whom he was certain that he should destroy utterly at the end of this campaign, had outwitted him and destroyed his plans and hopes forever. Then let her suffer for it! He raised his bow, dropped it again and stared. It was not pity that fettered his otherwise ruthless hand; it was superstitious fear. That Shotaye could have divined all his secret moves and could have saved herself at the right moment filled him with aston ishment and gradually with invincible dread. She was no common witch! Such wonderful insight, such clear perception of the means to save herself and at the same time destroy him, were not human. Rage and passion disappeared; a chill went through his frame and his lower jaw hung down like that of a corpse, as he stared motionless, powerless to act and unable to move.

A change came over Tyope, — a change so sudden and so complete that he was henceforth another man. Hope, ambition, revenge, vanished from his thoughts, and with them all energy left him. The appearance of that woman crushed him utterly. Shotaye appeared to him by the side of the great war shaman of his enemies like some fiend, to be sure, but a fiend of so much higher rank than his own that it was futile to cope with her. The Indian believes in evil spirits, but even they are subjected to the power of deities of a higher order beneficial to mankind. As such a shuatyam the woman appeared to Tyope, — as one whom the Shiuana had directed to accomplish his ruin. Those Above, not Shotaye, not the Tehuas, had vanquished him; and against them it was useless to strive.

With a ghastly look of terror on his countenance, his eyes staring in uncontrollable fright, Tyope slowly receded. Mentally crushed, shivering and shuddering, he at last turned about and fled.

The conviction that he was henceforth utterly powerless had seized upon him. Like an utter coward, unmindful of his rank and duties, and bent only upon saving his life, Tyope ran and ran until he found himself in the midst of the slaughter. He had mechanically warded off some arrows which the enemy had shot at his rapidly approaching figure; but he passed in among friends and foes, heedless of both, until his mad career was stayed by the brink of the Cañada Ancha. In the course of the massacre the Queres had succeeded in breaking partly through the enemy, and gathering on the south, thus securing a line of retreat, or at least escape from the bloody trap. Tyope had reached that point without knowing well whither he was fleeing. The sight of the ravine at his feet stopped him; he looked around absent-mindedly at first, then little by little self-control returned.

A man came up to him. He was covered with blood. A drum was suspended from his shoulder. It was the Hishtanyi Chayan.

"How is everything?" Tyope gasped.

"Where have you been?" the shaman asked in a tone of stern reproach.

"I was cut off and had to hide," Tyope flared up; the manner of the questioner irritated him, and with his anger a portion of his former energy seemed to return.

"Do you not know that the war-chief should carry the life of his men upon his own heart, and care for them more than for himself? That he should not hunt for scalps in the rear of the enemy, as shutzuna follows a herd of buffaloes to eat a fallen calf?" the Chayan hissed.

"And you," Tyope roared, "do you not know that you should speak the truth to the people? Not say that the Shiuana are good, that they say it is well, while the kopishtai and the shuatyam go over to the enemy together to help him! You are a liar! You lie like a Dinne; you are foolish like a prairie dog when shutzuna plays before him!" It was Tyope's last effort at passion. He nearly cried from rage as he brandished his war-club in the face of the shaman. The latter remained calm and spoke not a word, merely fastening on the maddened, raving man a cold, stern glance. Heedless of his threats and insults he commanded, —

"Hush, Tyope, hush! If the evil ones are about us it is because they have followed along from the Tyuonyi! Hush,

I say, do your duty at last. At the Tyuonyi, if we ever get there, we shall see further."

At this moment several Queres burst from the timber. One of them cried to Tyope, —

"Nashtio, the Moshome are too strong, they are coming to kill you and all of us. We must away into the karitya!" And with this he leaped from the brink. He had selected a spot where the rim was precipitous for a short distance. Over he went! A cry of anguish and of helpless despair was heard; then followed a series of thuds, as though a heavy body were falling from step to step. From the depths below a faint moaning arose. Then all was still. The din and noise of the battle was drawing nearer and nearer; soon more of the Queres rushed out and would in their precipitate flight have followed the example of their comrade had not others coming up behind them held them back Regardless of the danger, they clustered together on the brink, and gazed at the shattered, mangled, gory mass beneath, which was once the body of one of their companions. The words of the shaman fell upon Tyope like another blow from above. They cowed him. To avoid the gaze which the old man fastened upon him still, he turned to fly, no longer a warrior, no longer the commander. He was partly imbecile and absolutely cowed. He trembled, but the shaman seized his arm and restrained him. Pointing to the men he said, —

"Save these if you can."

Tyope obeyed, for he had no longer a will of his own. He cast a vacant glance about, but arrows whistled from the timber; the Tehuas were coming. Panic-stricken, the Queres ran along the brink to look for a descent. There was no stopping them, no possibility of restoring order; every one looked out for himself. Tyope cast a pleading glance at the old man by his side, and the Chayan felt that he must henceforth do what was yet to be done. Seeing the Queres clambering down into the gorge in wild haste, and that others were still rushing out of the thickets, he caught Tyope by the shoulder and drew him along, saying in a milder tone, —

"Follow me, sa uishe." He pitied the crest-fallen man.

Henceforth it was the medicine-man who assumed the lead, Tyope gathering energy enough to act as his lieutenant. The shaman was but a mediocre warrior; still in this dismal hour he was the only salvation of the remaining Queres.

Not one half of their number succeeded in reaching the bottom of the Cañada Ancha and taking shelter in the groves of tall pines that dot the vale. It was an anxious time for those who had already found safety behind trees, when they saw the stragglers rush down the rugged slope and tear through the thickets, followed by the Tehuas, who crowded along the brink in greatly superior numbers, yelling, shooting arrows, and waving triumphantly the many, many scalps they had taken. A few of their skirmishers descended some distance, but the main pursuit was stayed by strict orders from the Tehua war-chief. As soon as the first group of fugitives, among them Hishtanyi and Tyope, had reached the bottom of the Cañada, the shaman arrested their farther flight, prevailing upon them to make a stand.

Their position was temporarily a good one. No approach was possible without exposing the assailant to arrow-shots, whereas the defenders were thoroughly protected.

As their numbers increased by accessions from those who had also been able to extricate themselves, their courage returned, and they willingly remained until the time came when the shaman, and Tyope by his command, should direct farther retreat. The leaders of the Tehuas saw this and desisted from an attempt at complete extermination. It would have cost them dearly, and would only have increased the number of their trophies. So the Tehuas remained above the gorge, displaying a threatening front, while in reality the majority of them returned home, and with them Shotaye.

Great was the exultation of the woman when she saw the triumph of her new friends over her own people. She was proud of this result of her craftiness and her skill. When, the engagement over, she scanned the field, looking at the dead and searching for Tyope among them in vain, her disappointment was fearful. Corpse after corpse she scrutinized, turning over the ghastly bodies, peering into the lifeless features, raising the mutilated heads to see more closely, more distinctly. In vain; Tyope was not among them, Tyope had escaped. Her revenge was sterile; it had fallen on the least guilty. She, too, felt that a higher hand must have interfered and made her triumph next to worth-less. As she scanned the bloody, distorted features of the men of her tribe, in the expectation of gloating over those of him against whom she had schemed, she recognized more than one of whose company she had agreeable recol-lections, more than one whom in her cold-blooded, calcu-lating way, she had made her tool for a time. Something like regret arose within her, — regret at her treason. She went back to the Puye with a sting in her heart forever. Outwardly she led a contented life as the consort of Ca yamo, and the Tehuas looked upon her as a useful accession, if not as one who had at one time become the saviour of their tribe; but she could never think of the Rito nor hear it mentioned without feeling a pang. It was remorse, but she did not know it. Never again was she seen by any of her former people.

The position in which the Queres had taken refuge was tenable only for a short time, because the Cañada Ancha has no permanent water-supply. There were a few pools, however, containing remnants of the rain that had lately fallen. But that was not enough. To abandon the groves, in which they felt comparatively safe in presence of the foe, would have been reckless; so the Queres remained during the whole day, while the Tehuas kept guard over them, observing their movements from the cover of the timber on the mesa. As night set in, the Hishtanyi Chayan ordered a slow, noiseless retreat down the Cañada toward the Rio Grande. Tyope passively did what the shaman told him; he had no longer a will of his own. He who had always judged others from the stand-point of their usefulness to him as his tools, was now reduced mentally to be a blind instrument of the man of whom he expected to rid himself on this very campaign. All of Tyope's authority was gone; the men did not reproach him, did not scorn; they simply ignored him, except when he spoke in the name and by direction of the Hishtanyi Chayan. The latter saw more and more the mental downfall of the war-chief, and took pity on him, making him his lieutenant When morning dawned, the little troop halted on the Ziro kauash. They had made a long detour, and now were in dread lest the Tehuas had prepared an ambush near home. Tyope himself was still further concerned. He who had boldly attempted to carry out the most daring schemes, was afraid of returning to his people, now that these schemes had failed. He feared, like a child, reproach and punishment. The spirit of the man was utterly crushed.

When a war-party returns, it never enters the village directly, but halts at some distance and sends a messenger to inform the people of its approach. The Queres halted on the Ziro kauash, and some of them scoured the woods, but no trace of the enemy appeared. The dreaded ambush had not been laid : the Tehuas had certainly returned con-

tent with victory and their trophies. A runner was sent to
the Rito, and the men waited and waited. Even the Hishtanyi Chayan became startled at the long delay. Tyope
squatted at the foot of a tree; he was thinking of the
reception that might be in reserve for him. Everything
manly and strong had left his heart; nothing of it remained
but a languidly putrid core, whose former fermentation had
produced the effervescence that took the shape of energy,
shrewdness, and daring.

At last toward evening a man approached the silent
group. He came, accompanied by the runner, and every
one recognized the features of Kauaitshe, the delegate from
the Water clan. He went straight to Tyope; and the latter
looked at him timidly, almost tremblingly. Kauaitshe's
face looked sad and mournful, but not wrathful. He grasped
the hand of Tyope, breathed on it, lifted it upward with
both his hands, and said in a tone of intense sorrow, —

"Satyumishe, Those Above are not kind to us."

A terrible pang flashed through Tyope's heart, for he had
experienced how little the Shiuana liked him.

Kauaitshe continued in a low voice, — artless, but the
more impressive for its natural sadness, —

"While you went to strike the Tehuas with our men, the
Moshome Dinne came upon us."

A shriek of dismay, of terror, issued from every one present, Tyope excepted. He only groaned, and sinking shrivelled, pressed down his chest against his knees, as if suffering
intense physical pain. He recalled his intrigues with the
young Navajo. This last blow to the tribe was his work
also.

In a monotonous voice the messenger of evil tidings
proceeded, —

"My hanutsh is no more. Tanyi hanutsh is dispersed,
scattered, fleeing through the timber. Of Mokatsh hanutsh

only one girl has remained alive. Of Tyame a few women,
but your wife, satyumishe, is dead; your child Mitsha the
Moshome have carried away, or else she hides in the timber
and starves. The great house is empty, and fire comes out
from its roof. Your people can have the field of Tzitz
hanutsh," he added with trembling voice; "we need it
no longer. But your clan has land enough now, for many
of the men of Shyuamo have gone over to Shipapu!" He
dropped Tyope's hand, wiped away the tears that were
forcing themselves to his eyes, and stood in silence. Not
one of the by-standers moved; the Hishtanyi Chayan lifted
his eyes to the sky, Tyope stared vacantly. He seemed to
stagger. The delegate from the Water clan grasped his
hand again, and said, —

"Come and see how the Shiuana have visited the
Tyuonyi."

CHAPTER XIX.

IT is contrary to the custom of the Indians for a war-party
to enter their village at once upon returning. For at least
one day the warriors must wait at some distance from the
pueblo. They are provided with the necessaries of life, and
afterward are conducted to the village in triumph. In the
present case all these formalities were neglected, but not
through spite or disapproval; the terrible visitation which
the Rito had suffered changed everything; the survivors of
the Queres were anxious to have their numbers increased
by the returning warriors.

Mechanically Tyope accompanied his guide. The warriors followed in sullen silence, the Hishtanyi Chayan alone
holding his head erect. The visitation from above affected
him least of all. No one asked about the details of the
Navajos' attack, but all feared the moment when their valley
homes should come in sight. As they neared the brink of
the gorge many lagged behind.

Tyope was filled with thoughts of the most dismal nature.
He felt wretched, crushed, almost distracted! The news
brought by Kauaitshe weighed him down in a manner that
allowed neither hope or quietude. His plans had become
realized, but how? The loss of his wife he hardly felt, so
much the more did he regret Mitsha's disappearance. But
far above all this loomed up the terrible consequences, less
of the defeat than of the blow which the Navajos, following
the instructions he had once given Nacaytzusle, had struck
during his absence. He had done most toward bringing

about the expedition to the Puye; therefore he had led the flower of the tribe into perdition. During his absence and that of the majority of its defenders the Navajos had executed the fatal surprise. He had often been reproached with his intimacy with the young Dinne, and while the savage remained at the Rito everybody knew that the boy was a favourite of his. What else could the caciques, the leading shamans, infer but that the savage had been able to select his time, and that he, Tyope, had betrayed the tribe to the Dinne? And the worst of it was, it was true! He had at one time suggested the plan and had abandoned it afterward as too dangerous. He had suggested it with the view of furthering his personal ends. Now its execution took place when he least expected it, and when the very event which he had prepared for his benefit struck the most crushing blow he could ever have imagined possible for him to have suffered.

Had Tyope returned from the campaign victorious, it might have been different; but now the Shiuana bore down upon him with crushing power; there was no hope nor thought of his ever rising again. The best he could expect was to be set aside forever as a broken, useless unfortunate.

But the Koshare still remained, and they would not forsake him in the hour of need. The Naua, if alive, would certainly not permit his utter ruin. The two conspirators had prevailed upon the Hishtanyi so that only a few of the Delight Makers accompanied the war-party. Of these, two or three had escaped. How had the majority fared, — that majority which remained at the Rito for prudence's sake? Tyope dared not ask questions; he went along mutely as if in a dream.

The Hishtanyi Chayan stopped Kauaitshe, and asked him, —

27

" Have any of my brethren the yaya suffered ? "

Tyope's heart throbbed, and he turned his face away, so fearful was he of the reply.

" The Shkuy Chayan," replied Kauaitshe, in his simple manner, " is dead. An arrow entered his eye."

Tyope shivered ; misfortune crowded upon misfortune. He could no longer resist inquiring. Panting, he asked, —

" Is our father the Naua still alive ? "

" He lives and mourns. After you were gone with the people, he retired to the place in the cliffs with the Koshare ; and when the Moshome came, nearly all the men were up there."

Tyope's head was swimming. Everything he had prepared for the destruction of others and the security of his own tools had come about as he had schemed, but the results had been fatal to him and his. The Shiuana allowed him to apparently succeed in everything, but they reserved for themselves the final results. It was terrible ; all was lost ; he was forever undone.

Still if the Koshare had been at their estufa, they were out of harm's way.

" Satyumishe," he asked, faltering, " have many of my brethren perished ? "

" Nearly all," was the plain answer. " When the Dinne came upon us, the Koshare rushed out after bows and arrows ; but the Moshome met them before they could reach the houses, and killed many before they could get into the cave."

The poor man had to cling to a tree for support; then he slipped down along its trunk to the ground.

" I am very tired," he murmured. It was not fatigue, however ; it was the ghastly tidings which were poured on his head, so slowly, so surely, with such deadly effect. Kauaitshe looked at him with genuine pity. The Hishtanyi said nothing; he was in his thoughts with Those Above, and hardly listened to the conversation. Kauaitshe extended his hand to Tyope.

"We are not far from the brink," said he, kindly; "come, satyumishe, a few steps only, and you may rest, and I will tell you all, — how the attack came, and how Hayoue saved the Zaashtesh from being all driven into the woods. Hayoue is a mighty warrior; he is wise and very strong. As soon as our mourning is over, the Hotshanyi will make him maseua in place of our father Topanashka. The Shiuana have left us Hayoue; had he gone with you not one of us would be alive."

Even that! Hayoue! Hayoue, whom Tyope had left behind in order to deprive him of all opportunity to distinguish himself! Hayoue had reaped laurels, whereas he had harvested only shame, disgrace, destruction. Hayoue was a great warrior. He had averted a part at least of the disaster which Tyope had secretly prepared for the tribe. The hand of Those Above weighed heavily upon him; all he cared for henceforth, all he could hope for, was not to suffer the rightful doom which he had intended for Shotaye.

That Kauaitshe, the poor simple man whom he so disdainfully rebuked at the council, had been selected to communicate to Tyope all this crushing news, the latter did not interpret as an intentional cruelty. The Indian is not malicious. He will insult and exult over the vanquished foe in the heat of passion; but he will take the scalp and keep it very carefully, respect it, and to a certain extent the memory of the slain. But to sneer at and taunt a fallen adversary in the hour of sadness, and in the condition in which Tyope was, is not the Indian's way. That was not what made Tyope suffer. What overpowered his faculties, darkened his mind, and deprived him of energy for all time to come, were the results that crowded upon him so wonderfully, so completely at variance with his own intentions. And yet they were strictly the consequences of what he had schemed and done. Everything he had thought of and planned had taken place, but the results did not coincide with his expectations. Those Above alone could have directed the course of events; they were against his doings; he was a doomed man.

The reader will forgive a digression. We will leave Tyope and his companions on the brink of the Rito, and abandon them for a while to their sombre thoughts; nay, we will leave the Rito even, and transport ourselves to our own day. I desire to relate a story, an Indian folk-lore tale of modern origin, which is authentic in so far that it was told me by an Indian friend years ago at the village of Cochiti, where the descendants of those who once upon a time inhabited the caves on the Rito de los Frijoles now live. My object in rehearsing this tale is to explain something I have neglected; namely, the real conception underlying the custom of taking the scalp of an enemy.

The Indian friend of whom I am speaking, and whose home I inhabited for quite a while, came over to the little dingy room I was occupying one winter evening. The fire was burning in a chimney not much better than the one Shotaye possessed at the Tyuonyi. He squatted down on his folded blanket, rolled a cigarette, and looked at me wistfully. I felt that he was disposed for a long talk, and returned his glance with one of eager expectation. Casting his eyes to the ground, he asked me, —

" You know that the Navajos have done us much harm ? "

" Yes, you and your brother Shtiranyi have told me so."

He curled his lip at the reference to his brother's knowledge, and said sneeringly, —

"Shtiranyi is young; he does not know much."

"Still he told me a great deal about the wars you had with the Moshome Dinne."

"Did he ever tell you of the hard times the people of Cochiti suffered three generations ago?"

"Never."

"He knows nothing of them. He is too young. I," — he assumed an air of solemn importance, — "I will tell you something; something true, something that you can believe; for the old men, those from a long time ago, tell it, and what they say is so. The Mexicans never hear of it, and to the Americans we don't tell such things, for they think they are too smart, and laugh at what we say."

"Is the story really true?" I inquired, for I saw that something interesting was coming.

"As true as if I had seen it myself. But I was not born when it happened. Cochiti was larger then, a big village, twice as big as it is to-day. But the Navajos were very powerful. They attacked us in the daytime in the fields. They killed the men who went to gather firewood, and they stole our cattle. At night they would come to the Zaashtesh and carry off the women and the girls. There lived at the time a young koitza who had recently married, and she liked her husband. One evening after dark this woman went to the corral. There the Moshome seized her, closed her mouth with their hands, dragged her from the village, tied and gagged her, and placed her on a horse; then they rode off as fast as they could, far, far away to the northwest and the hogans of their people. The young woman cried bitterly, but it availed her nothing; she had to live with one of the Navajos, had to cook for him and work his corn-patch like other women. Soon the koitza saw that it was useless to weep, so she put on a contented look in the daytime, while at night she was thinking and scheming how she might escape from the enemy. Women are sometimes wiser than we are ourselves. Is it not so, sa ukinyi?"

"Certainly."

"It was springtime when she was captured. She suffered summer to pass, worked well, and appeared satisfied. The Moshome began to trust and even to like her. It began to turn cool; the time came when the piñons are ready for gathering, and the captive thought of flight. One morning she said to a young woman of the Navajos, 'Let us go and gather piñon!' Both women went to work and prepared food for several days, then they went out into the timber far away until they came to a place where there were many piñon-trees. There they gathered nuts, and placed them on the blankets; and as noontime came on, and it became warm, the young Navajo woman grew sleepy. So the koitza from Cochiti said, 'Sister, lay your head on my lap, I will cleanse your hair.' As the other was lying thus and the Queres woman cleansed her head, she fell asleep. Thereupon the captive took a large stone, crushed her skull with it, and killed her. Was not that very wise?"

"Indeed," I uttered, but thought to myself that the action was not very praiseworthy from our point of view.

"Then our koitza took a knife, scalped the dead, and concealed the scalp under her skirt. It was now toward evening. All at once the woman heard a voice calling to her, 'Sister!' She was frightened, and looked about, but saw nobody. She lay down. Again a voice spoke close to her, 'Sister, stay here no longer, they are uneasy!' Nothing was to be seen, and the woman began to feel afraid. For the third time the same voice said, 'Do not fear, sister; it is I, the ahtzeta, which speaks to thee. Go now, for the men

are saddling their horses to look for us.' The captive gathered hastily as much food as she could carry with ease ; and
as the sun went down the scalp spoke again, ' It is time to
go, for my people are on their way hither, and it is far to
Cochiti.' So she ran and ran all the night long, and always straight toward our pueblo. Toward morning she felt
tired, and the scalp spoke, ' Lie down to rest, it is far yet to
your people.' She slept, but soon woke again feeling fresh
and bright. Then the ahtzeta said to her, ' Let us go now,
for soon the Dinne will be where you took me and where I
became yours.' On she ran, eating piñons as she went.
At noon the scalp was heard to say, ' My men have found
the place, and are searching for your tracks. You must go
faster.' When the sun set the ahtzeta spoke again, ' Run,
sister, they have found the trail and follow it on horseback.'
Thus she went all night long, and the nearer she came to
Cochiti the more the scalp urged her to quicken her speed,
for the Navajos were coming nearer and nearer. You
know," asked he, " where the sand-hills are, a little this
side of Cuapa ? "

I assented ; that whole track is nothing but sand and
drift, but which particular hills he meant I could not of
course imagine. Still, the Indian knows every foot of the
country, and he supposed that I, having been over the trail
two or three times, recollected every detail of it as well as
he did himself.

" You know also that there are junipers right there."

Such was indeed the case. Not only there, but all over
the country.

" Well, there, about two leagues from Cochiti, the scalp
spoke, ' Sister, they are quite near ; hide yourself.' The
woman looked around, but she saw no other hiding-place
except the junipers. You know them, they are to the left
of the trail."

I nodded of course. There are a great many to the left of the trail.

"Then the scalp told her, 'Crawl into a rabbit-hole under the tree.' You know the hole, don't you?"

I said yes to this query also. Around Cochiti there are perhaps hundreds of rabbit-burrows; and it might have been one of those, although after a full century a rabbit's hole is not supposed to be apparent. The narrator was satisfied, nevertheless, for I had assented.

"It is well; but as the woman looked at that hole she was frightened and replied, 'It is too small.' 'Creep into it,' ordered the scalp. 'I cannot even get my head into it,' objected the koitza from Cochiti. 'Creep in quick, they come!' the scalp cried. The woman tried, and the opening became larger and larger. First she found room for her head, afterward for her shoulders; lastly her whole body was inside. As soon as she was within, the hole closed again and appeared as small as before. Was not that wonderful?"

I thought it was strange indeed, exceedingly wonderful. I could not refrain from asking my friend, —

"But was it really so?"

"So the old men are telling, those from many years ago. It must be true. Therefore don't disturb me in my speech, and listen. The Navajos came on. They saw that the tracks stopped. They jumped from their horses, and the woman heard them go about searching, complaining, howling, scolding. At last they mounted their horses again and rode off. When all was quiet the scalp spoke, 'Sister, they have gone; get out now and let us return to your people.' With this the hole opened; the woman crept out and ran and ran as fast as she could. When she reached the Cañada de la Peralta, the scalp spoke for the last time, saying to her, 'Sister, now you are safe; henceforth I shall speak no more.'

And so it was. On the other side of the ravine stood her own husband. He recognized her at once. They went together to the houses, where she lived for many years."

He paused and looked at me, scanning my face to see the impression made by his tale. Then he continued, —

"You see now, sa uishe, how the scalp saved her to whom it belonged. Therefore we take ahtzeta, for as long as the spirit is not at Shipapu it follows him who has taken the scalp, and serves and helps him. And the strength, wisdom, and knowledge of him whose scalp has been taken, hereafter belong to the man who took it; they increase his power and make the tribe more powerful."

The appearance of the Rito from above presented at first sight nothing startling. From the tall building thin films of smoke arose, but no flames were visible. The house of the Corn clan seemed inhabited, for people stood on its roof. As the returning warriors grouped themselves on the brink to look down into the valley, those below stood still, gazing at them. Then they broke out into a plaintive wail; the women tore their hair, shrieked, screamed, and wept. The men above gazed and listened in silence. Very few men were seen in the vale. The tribe of the Queres seemed divided into two parties, the women lamenting below, the men, like dark, blood-stained statues, standing high above them, posted on yellowish rocks among the shrubbery.

Kauaitshe told Tyope to rest, and he willingly complied. His figure appeared less conspicuous when he sat down. Around the two the others gathered, except the Hishtanyi, who was slowly descending the slope alone, eager to hear the story of the people's misfortunes. Kauaitshe began, —

"It was yesterday, and the sun had not yet come up." He heaved a deep sigh. "All the Koshare were in the estufa over there," he pointed at the cliffs to his right; "the makatza and our koitza were grinding corn; many also had gone to the brook to wash away sadness and grief. Most of them, mainly those of Tanyi, Huashpa, and our women, bathed higher up beyond the fields; some farther down. Shotaye was not among them; nobody knows what has become of her."

Tyope twitched nervously. He knew where the woman had gone.

"Hayoue," the man from Tzitz proceeded, "was the only one who carried weapons. He had gone out very early with Okoya, the youth from Tanyi who is his brother's child. They had started while it was yet night, following the tshinaya up to the top of the rocks. As soon as it became light they noticed tracks and heard sounds that told them that there were Moshome about. They went around by the south, and as it began to dawn they stood there;" he pointed to a spot on the southern mesa directly opposite the big house and facing the latter. "That saved us," he cried; "if Hayoue had not stood there to watch, we should all have died!"

Tyope could not help contrasting the watchfulness of Hayoue with his own supercilious negligence. Yes indeed, it was all over with him; he was good for nothing any more.

"I was in the katityam," Kauaitshe went on, "when I heard the yells of the savages in the corn below. They had concealed themselves there over night, and as soon as the people came forth from their homes unarmed, not thinking of any danger, they rushed upon them and into the big house. I grasped uishtyak and the club, and ran for the stream. There everybody was screaming; some were running this way, others fled that way, but none could get back to the cliffs. none into the houses, for the Moshome stood between them and their homes. They fled toward the south into the kote as a mountain sheep runs from the panther. But as tyame shoots down upon a hind, so the enemies flew after them, scattering them in every direction. All this happened so quickly, brother, that I was not half way down when it was over, and a few of the Dinne rushed up to kill me. They were going to the caves to slaughter the people. I ran back and hid myself, and as they came up I shot at one of them so that he died. The Cuirana Naua killed another; the others ran away. We took their ahtzeta and kept guard over the caves, but for what? There was nobody left of Tzitz hanutsh except a few old women and Ciay Tihua, the little boy. Go down we could not, for below was such a noise, — such fighting, struggling, shouting, and wailing! The Moshome tore the firebrands from the hearths, set fire to the beams, dragged the cloth and the hides into the court-yard and burned them there. Fire came out of the big house, and great was the smoke and black! In the smoke we could see how the shuatyam were dancing on the roofs, and how they threw the dead down upon the ground so that their bodies rattled and the blood spurted and spattered everywhere. Satyumishe, it was sad, very sad; but I could not help, nor could the Naua, for we were alone. Still I have one scalp," he added with simple satisfaction. "Hayoue has many, many! How many have you brought home?"

Tyope cast his eyes to the ground.

"None," he breathed; he could not conceal his contrition and shame. Kauaitshe made no remark. He was not malicious.

"From the great house they ran into that of Tyame hanutsh. There they killed your wife."

"And Mitsha, my daughter?" Tyope asked at last.

"Mitsha was at the brook, and fled with the others. Na·

caytzusle, the fiend, was after her to catch her, but he caught
her not. Hayoue told us afterward that Okoya Tihua killed
the savage just as he had overtaken the girl. Okoya is strong
and good ; he will become a great warrior, like sa umo the
maseua. That is, if he still live."

At last a ray of light seemed to penetrate the darkness
that shrouded Tyope's heart. Nacaytzusle was dead ! The
dangerous accomplice, the only one who might have told
about Tyope's attempted conspiracy with the Navajos, was
forever silenced. He felt relieved also to think that Mitsha
had not become a prey to the savage, and it pleased him to
hear Okoya praised. If the youth had still been at the Rito
he might have become a support for him.

"Where is Okoya?" he anxiously inquired.

"In the mountains or dead," was the reply. "When the
women fled up to the mesa, Hayoue and Okoya ran to meet
them. But the Moshome were too many, and the two became separated. Okoya killed the shuatyam, the Navajo
boy. He went close to him and struck him with his club
till he died. So Hayoue says. Hayoue remained behind ;
he kept back the Dinne and then came down through the
enemy — how I do not know — and protected the katityam, helping the Koshare. All the Moshome who entered
the house of the Eagles — twelve of them — were killed inside ; their scalps are with us. And when the others saw it
they ran out of the big house ; but Hayoue and the men followed and killed nine ere they could hide on the Kauash."

"So you have taken many ahtzeta?" one of the bystanders
asked.

Kauaitshe began to count, "Eleven — two — twelve —
nine ; thirty-four," he concluded, adding, "without those
that Okoya may have if he be alive."

An exclamation of admiration and a grunt of satisfaction
sounded from the lips of those present. But they became

silent and sad again at once, for they, the warriors, had only eight or nine all told.

Kauaitshe's pride and exultation could not last long. He bethought himself of the losses, and continued in a tone of sadness, —

"But we have lost many, many. Nearly one hundred of our people have gone over to Shipapu, and twice as many are now in the woods, hungry and forlorn, or the Moshome have taken them with them. Luckily, they are mostly women. Hardly more than twenty of the men can have died, for it may be that Okoya is still alive. Of these, sixteen were Koshare; and the Shkuy Chayan is no more." He cast a glance of sincere pity at Tyope. The latter said nothing, and all the others stared in mournful silence.

The lamentations below had gone on uninterruptedly. Corpses might be seen lying on the roofs, others partly hanging down over the walls. Two men were carrying a dead body toward the caves of the Turquoise people. In the distance a group was seen dragging another corpse up the gorge. Below the house of Yakka hanutsh there stood a group of men, their faces turned toward the brink of the mesa.

The nashtio of the Water clan rose, and pointed at the group.

"There stand Hayoue, the Shikama Chayan, the three Yaya, the Hotshanyi, Shaykatze, and Uishtyaka; and see, the Hishtanyi Chayan is down on the Tyuonyi already, and goes up to them. Let us go now, and " — he turned to Tyope — "you, brother, tell us what you have achieved and how you all have fared. We cannot receive you as it behooves us; there is too much mourning on the Tyuonyi. The Shiuana have punished us so that we cannot be merry and glad. Therefore I have been sent to ·eceive you, for the men are

few in the vale and " — he looked around as if counting the
bystanders — " of those that went out to avenge the death
of our father not many have come back either."

In dreary silence they began to move downward. Not a
shout, not a whoop, heralded their coming ; not a scalp was
waved on high in triumph. In dead silence those below
watched the sombre forms as they descended slowly, clambering over rocks, rustling through bushes, and coming
nearer and nearer. From the caves issued plaintive wails ;
from the big house moans and subdued crying ascended, —
the lament over the dead on the Rito.

More than a week has elapsed since the return of the discomfited war-party to their desolate and ravished homes.
It is August, and the rains have fallen abundantly. What
little was left of the growing crops, what the torrent has not
destroyed and the Navajos did not lay waste, looks promising. But this remainder is slight, and there is anxiety lest
the surviving inhabitants may starve in the dreary winter.
The formalities of mourning have therefore been performed
hastily and superficially. The remaining Koshare have
retired into the round grotto, there to fast and to pray for
the safe maturity of the scanty crops. But Tyope is not
among them. His accomplice, the Naua, has forsaken him.
He, too, has become convinced that everything is lost for
them, and he has thrown away Tyope like a blunt and useless tool. Hereafter the Naua attends strictly to his official
duties, and to nothing beyond his duties. For the Shkuy
Chayan is dead, the Shikama Chayan has no love for him,
and the old Hishtanyi, who has seen more of the real nature
of events than any on the Rito, went over to the cave of the
old sinner and spake to him a few words. The " old sinner "
comprehended ; he has gone back to his duties and attends
to them exclusively.

Afterward the Chayan called upon the chief penitent, or Hotshanyi, and spoke to him long and earnestly; after him to the shaykatze and the uishtyaka; lastly with all three yaya together. Then the yaya went into retirement, all three in the same place. They are fasting, doing penance, mercilessly mortifying themselves, in order that Those Above may forgive the tribe and suffer it to prosper again.

All this has taken place in silence and secret, and nothing has come to the surface. The only thing that has become public is a general council, not merely of the delegates of clans with the yaya, but of the tribe. Hayoue assisted, with Zashue his brother. Tyope was present also, but he said nothing, and nobody requested him to speak. He was not outlawed; no punishment was dealt to him; he was simply suffered to remain on that lower level to which he had naturally dropped.

The principal question agitating the council was the nomination of a maseua, or head war-chief. The caciques intimated that Hayoue would be their choice, and all concurred in the selection. But Hayoue positively declined, insisting that his clan had virtually ceased to exist on the Rito, and that it was his duty to follow his people in their distress. Zashue also spoke to the same effect. His wife Say Koitza and his children had disappeared, even to the little girl, whose brains were still clinging to the walls of the big house, against which the enemy had dashed her head. However much the people insisted, Hayoue remained firm in his resolve to go after the fugitives and to save them if possible. Most of the people thought them lost, dead, or captives; but both young men were of the opinion that there were too many of them, and that at least some must have escaped. It was consequently the duty of the two youngest survivors to trace them if possible.

The Hishtanyi Chayan was the first to accede to Hayoue's

demands, but conditionally. He insisted that when their
duties were fulfilled Hayoue and his brother should return
to the Rito with the rescued. But Hayoue refused to consent even to this. The grounds given by him were obvious,
though hard to listen to. In case they found a few, he
promised to return; but should there be many yet alive he
was determined upon founding a new settlement. He reproached the council bitterly for having allowed the lack
of arable soil to have been taken as a pretext for de-
priving his own small clan of its allotment in order to give
it to a larger one. That small clan should not come back
and again be in the way of the others. "Tzitz hanutsh,"
said he in closing, alluding to his own performances, "has
saved the tribe; it has done its duty. Now we will go and
see whether our brethren and sisters are still alive; and in
case we find them, seek for another spot where there will be
sufficient room for all."

Every one present did not understand these words; but
the members of the council knew to what the young man
was alluding, and they bowed their heads in shame. Even
the Hishtanyi Chayan felt the reproach, for he knew that it
was partly his fault, since had he followed the hint dropped
by Topanashka, and his own first impressions, all might have
taken a different turn. He did not therefore insist any
longer, and did not even think it advisable to invoke the
will of Those Above in aid of his personal desire. His silence determined the people of the Rito, for they took it
for granted that the higher powers approved of Hayoue's
resolution to leave.

It may seem strange that the Chayan did not insist upon
consulting the Shiuana first, for Hayoue would have been
compelled to abide by their final decision. Here the question arises how far the Indian shaman is sincere in his
oracular utterances, — how much of his decisions is hon-

est error, and how much of his official acts may be deception or mere jugglery.

In most cases of importance the shaman is honest. He really believes that what he says is the echo from a higher world. This firm belief is the fruit of training; and the voices he hears, the sights he sees when alone with Those Above are the products of honest hallucination. His training and the long and painful discipline he undergoes in rising from degree of knowledge to degree of knowledge, the constant privations and bodily and mental tortures, prepare him for a dreamy state in which he becomes thoroughly convinced that he really is a medium. As such he speaks in council, and he is most thoroughly satisfied that what he says is the truth. Of course there are among them some who are rogues, who profit by the credulity of others, and who even invent tricks in order to fasten their authority upon the people in an illegitimate manner. These tricks themselves are not performed in the majority of cases as conscious sleight of hand. They may have been such at their inception, but their origin has been forgotten by subsequent generations, and nothing has remained but the bare wonderful, inexplicable fact of their performance. Thus they have become in course of time hallowed; and the shaman who causes lightning to flash through a dark room, or corn to grow and mature in the course of one day, honestly believes in the supernatural origin of the trick. Such men are often very punctilious, and while they will go to the direst extremity in what they regard as their duties and privileges, will with equal scruple avoid going a single step beyond. Imbued with an idea that they are the mouth-pieces of Those Above, they listen anxiously to everything that is striking and strange, and attribute to inspiration forcible arguments as well as their own speeches and actions. So it was with the Hishtanyi Chayan. The refusal of Hayoue

28

to accept an honourable charge struck him as being an expression of the will of the Shiuana, against which it was his
duty not to protest. When the young man brought forward
such strong arguments he was still further confirmed in his
belief, and bowed to the inevitable in respectful silence.

At the close of the council the Koshare retired to the
estufa, the caciques followed their example, and the Chayan came next. But before he withdrew into privacy,
the great medicine-man had a long talk with Hayoue,
his object being to strengthen the tie which united the
young man with the people of the Rito, and to engage him
not to forsake altogether the abode of the spirits of his
tribe. Hayoue made no definite promise beyond what he
had already pledged himself to at the general meeting.

Hayoue and Zashue had taken leave of the invisible
ones as well as of the inhabitants of the Tyuonyi, and
ascended to the brink of the southern mesa above the
Rito. Here they turned around to look back upon the
home to which neither of them was any longer strongly
attached. The sun was setting, and they wished to improve the night, for fear that Navajos might still be prowling about on the mesas. At the bottom of the gorge
there was little life, compared with the bustle that prevailed in former days. On the plateau the evening breeze
fanned the trees; in the east, distant lightning played about
sombre clouds.

"The corn-plant is good," Zashue remarked to his
brother; "the Zaashtesh will not starve this winter. We
have called loudly to Those Above."

"It is well," said the other in a tone of authority, which
since his achievements he was wont to assume toward his
elder brother; "when the Koshare perform their duty
they are precious to the people."

"Without the Cuirana," the elder replied, "the sprout-

ing corn cannot grow." Zashue had conceived a very
high opinion of Hayoue, and his weaker mind gladly
leaned upon the strong will of the youth. Hayoue started;
it was as if a sudden thought struck him. "Look, see
how good the Shiuana are! We are leaving the Tyuonyi;
and behold, if we find our people there can be no lack
of food wherever we dwell. I am Cuirana, you are Koshare. I pray and fast for the growing corn, you do the
same for the ripening of the grain. It will be well."

"If Shyuote is alive he will help me." Zashue uttered
these words timidly.

"Okoya will help me;" Hayoue spoke with great
assurance. "In that case we shall be four already. How
often have I told you, satyumishe, that Okoya is good.
He is a man; I saw it when he struck Nacaytzusle, the
young Moshome."

The elder brother said nothing. He acknowledged the
wrong he had done his eldest child. In case Say Koitza,
in case Shyuote were still alive, it would be owing to that
elder son of his. And his wife, Say Koitza, he longed
for now as never before. For her sake he had left everything, — his home, his field. Willingly he abandoned his
whole past in order to find her. He regretted all that
he had done in that past, — his suspicions, his neglect, his
carelessness to her. The fearful visitations of the latter
days had changed him completely.

All these thoughts he gathered in one exclamation, —

"If we only find them!"

"Let us go and search," said Hayoue, turning to go.
His brother followed him into the woods.

Henceforth we shall have to follow the two adventurers,
for a while at least. Therefore we also must take leave
of the Rito de los Frijoles. Of its inhabitants nothing
striking can hereafter be told. They lived and died in

the seclusion of their valley gorge, and neither the Tehuas nor the Navajos molested them in the years following. Tyope continued to vegetate, anxiously taking care to give no occasion for recalling his former conduct. The Naua soon died. The subsequent fate of the tribe is faintly delineated by dim historical traditions, stating that they gradually emigrated from the Rito in various bands, which little by little, in course of time, built the villages inhabited by the Queres Indians of to-day. Long before the advent of the Spaniards, in the sixteenth century of our era, the Rito was deserted and forgotten. The big house, the houses of the Eagles and of the Corn clan, are now reduced to mere heaps of rubbish, overgrown by cactus and bunches of low grass. Most of the cave-dwellings have crumbled also. But the Rito always remains a beautiful spot, lovely in its solitude, picturesque and grand. About its ruins there hovers a charm which binds man to the place where untold centuries ago man lived, loved, suffered, and died as present generations live, suffer, and die in the course of human history.

CHAPTER XX.

SUNSHINE and showers! A dingy blue sky is traversed by white, fleecy, clouds, long mares' tails, on whose border giant thunder-clouds loom up, sometimes drifting majestically along the horizon, or crowding upward to spread, dissolve, and disappear in the zenith.

It is the rainy season in New Mexico, with its sporadic showers, its peculiar sunlight, moments of scorching heat, and blasts of cool winds, with thunder overhead. To the right and left rain falls in streaks, but without sultriness, and with no danger from violent wind-storms or cyclones. We are in the beginning of the month of September. It is warm, but not oppressive, and the spot from which we view the scenery around is high, open, and commands a wide extent of country.

We stand on a barren plateau. Lava-blocks are scattered about in confusion, while tall arborescent cacti rise between them like skeletons, and bunches of grass point upward here and there. North of us the mesa expands in monotonous risings and swellings to the foot of a tall, exceedingly graceful cone, whose slopes are dotted with bushes of cedar and juniper. Beyond it are dark humps, denoting by their shape that they are extinct craters. In the distance, west of that beautiful cone, which to-day is called, and very appropriately, the Tetilla, the sinuous profile of a mountain-chain just peeps over the bleak line formed by the mesa and its various corrugations. Nestling within its bosom rests the Rito de los Frijoles.

In the south, dense thunder-clouds overhang massive peaks. Only the base of the Sierra de Sandia, of the Old Placeres, and the numerous ranges beyond, is visible, for a heavy shower falls in that direction. In the east a plain sweeps into view, dotted by black specks looming up from a reddish soil. This plain rises gently to the eastward, and abuts against a tall mountain-range whose summits also are shrouded in massive clouds.

We stand on the bleak and wide mesa that interposes itself between the town of Santa Fé and the valley of the Rio Grande. Not a living object, with the exception of wasps and beetles, can be seen; everything appears dull and dead. The thunder roars in the distance.

And yet there is life of a higher order. Two ravens stalk about in an earnest, dignified manner. The birds look exceedingly and comically serious. Their plumage glistens in the subdued light of the sun. They look out for themselves, and care nothing for the remainder of creation. So deeply are they imbued with a sentiment of their own exceptional position in the realm of nature, that they pay no attention to another phase of life that shows itself near by, though not conspicuously.

Over the surface of the mesa are seen here and there almost imperceptible elevations destitute of vegetation. In these slight swellings, apertures are visible. Out of the latter the head of a small animal occasionally protrudes, disappears again, or rises displaying a pair of shovel-like front teeth. Then a worm-like body pushes up from below, and a yellowish figure, half squirrel, half marmot, stands erect on the hillock, and utters a sharp, squealing bark. This barking is answered from a neighbouring protuberance. From each hillock one of these little animals crawls down; and meeting one another half-way, they stand up facing each other, scratch and bite

for a moment, then separate and return to their re-
spective cave-dwellings. Other similar creatures wriggle
about in the vicinity; the shrill barking sounds far and
near. A colony of so-called prairie dogs dwells in the
neighbourhood.

To this exhibition of animal life the ravens pay no
attention whatever. It is beneath their notice; their aims
are of a higher order than those of beings who live upon
roots and who burrow for their abode. They live on
prey that is far above the simple products of animal
industry. Carrion is what they aspire to. Therefore they
aspire with a lofty mien, prying and peering in every
direction for something fallen. They are not far from
the eastern brink of the mesa, where the volcanic flow
breaks off suddenly in short, abrupt palisades. Who knows
what their keen eyes may have espied along that brink?

Another actor appears upon the scene, a prairie wolf,
or coyote; consequently a rival, a competitor of the
ravens; for he is in the same business. But he belongs
to a higher order; for while the ravens are scavengers,
the coyote is a hunter as well. He would even prey
upon the birds themselves. As he approaches, with tail
drooping and ears erect, and stops to sniff the air and
glance about slyly, the ravens hop off sidewise away from
the dangerous neighbour. Still they are loath to go, for
the wolf may discover something the leavings of which
they may perhaps enjoy. But the coyote lies down,
with his head between his forepaws, and in this attitude
pushes his body forward, almost imperceptibly. Such
motions are very suspicious; the scavengers flap their
wings, rise into the air, and soar away to some more
secure spot.

The coyote, however, seems in no wise disappointed at
the departure of the ravens. He pays no attention to

their flight, but moves on toward the lava-blocks that
indicate the rim of the plateau. There he has noticed
something; an object that lies motionless like a corpse.
It may be a corpse, and therefore something to prey
upon. Nearer the coyote glides. The object is long
or elongated. Its colour is lighter than that of the lava-
blocks surrounding it, but its farther end is dark. Now
that end moves, and the head of an Indian, a village
Indian of New Mexico, looms up above the boulders.
The coyote has seen enough, for the man is alive, and
not carrion. Away the beast trots, with drooping tail
and ears.

The Indian, who has been lying there with his face
turned to the east, rises to his knees and faces about.
His features are those of a man on the threshold of
mature age. We know this man! We have seen him
before! And yet it cannot be, for how thin, how wan,
how hollow the cheeks, how sunken the eyes! The face,
notwithstanding the red paint, appears sallow. Still it
is an old acquaintance, although since we saw him last
he has sadly changed. Now he turns his face to the
south, and we catch a glimpse of his profile. It is Zashue
Tihua, the Indian from the Rito de los Frijoles, husband
of Say Koitza, and father to Okoya and Shyuote.

What is he doing here? It is now more than three
weeks since he and his brother Hayoue took leave of the
Tyuonyi in order to search for their lost people. They
went forth into that limited, yet for the Indian immensely
vast, world to-day called central New Mexico. In a month
a travelling Indian may easily be hundreds of miles away if
unimpeded in his march. But we find him here, barely a
day's journey from the Rito. A strong man cannot have
spent all this time in going such a little distance. He must
have wandered far, strayed back and forth, up and down.

perhaps into the western mountains, where the Navajos lurk, — the bad men who frightened his wife and children away from their homes, or who perhaps captured or killed them. Or he may have gone to the south, where the black cloud is hanging, and where it thunders, and the rain-streaks hang like long black veils of mourning. He has perchance tramped down the Rio Grande valley, through sand, by groves of poplar-trees, and where the sand-storms howl and wail. Now he comes back, unrequited for all his labour and sufferings, for those whom he sought are not with him !

His gaze was not directed to the north when the wolf espied him, but to the east. He may be on the homeward stretch, but he has not given up all hope. His eyes look for those whom he has lost; he is loath to give up the search, loath to return alone to the home which the enemy has soiled with the lifeblood of his youngest child. He is changed in appearance, lean, and with hollow burning eyes he gazes at the clouds as if there he might find his missing wife and children.

As he kneels and gazes, another Indian rises from amidst the shaggy blocks of lava a short distance off, stands up, and then sits down upon a rock. He turns his head to the east. He too is gaunt and thin, his features are pale, and his eyes lie deep in their sockets. On his back hangs a shield ; but it is soiled, beaten, and perforated. To his arm is fastened a war-club, and the quiver on his back is half-filled with newly made arrows. As this Indian turns his face to the north we recognize him also. It is Hayoue, Hayoue as emaciated and careworn as his brother Zashue. They are alone. Neither has found anything yet.

Zashue rises to go where his brother is sitting. As the latter perceives him he points with his arm to the east. There at the farthest end of the plain, at the foot of the high cloud-veiled mountains, a long row of foot-hills recedes in an angle. To this angle Hayoue is pointing. An untrained eye would have seen nothing but cedar-clad hills and the lower end of slopes dark and frowning, above which seething clouds occasionally disclose higher folds of mountains whose tops are shrouded in mist. But Zashue has no untrained eye; he gazes and gazes; at last he turns around to his brother with an approving nod and says, —

"Fire."

"Puyatye Zaashtesh," Hayoue replies; and each looks at the other inquiringly.

Where we might have seen but the usual dim haze veiling distant objects, they have discovered a bluish tint capping the hills like a pale streak. It denotes the presence of smoke, therefore fire. Not a burning forest, for there is no high timber on that range of foot-hills, but smoke arising from a place where people are dwelling. The roaming mountain Indians, the Apaches or Navajos, settle nowhere permanently. The smoke has not been produced by their straggling camp-fires; it indicates the location of a permanent village. Those village Indians that dwell east of the Rio Grande are Tanos, and the Queres call them Puyatye. There must be a Tano village in that corner far away where the bluish film hovers. Hayoue is right, a Puyatye Zaashtesh stands where to-day lies the capital of New Mexico, — the old Spanish settlement of Santa Fé.

The brothers cast their eyes to the ground; both seem to be in doubt, Zashue is the first to speak.

"Do you suppose that our people might be at that Zaashtesh?"

Hayoue shrugged his shoulders.

"It may be, I don't know."

"Will it be safe for us to go to the Puyatye?" the other inquired doubtfully.

The younger sighs and answers, —

"They have never done wrong to us."

"Still they speak the tongue of the people of Karo."

"It is true, but they live nearer to us."

"But they are Tehuas too, like the people of the north, and — "

Hayoue interrupts him, saying, —

"Our folk have gone to them as often as they wished buffalo-hides, and the Puyatye have received them well, giving them what was right. Why should they now be hard toward us?"

"Still if the Tehuas have gone to see them, saying, 'The Queres from the Tyuonyi came to strike us like Moshome over night; look and see that they do not hurt you also,' and now we come with shield, bow, and arrow, what can the Puyatye think other than that we are Moshome Queres?"

Hayoue feels the weight of this observation; he casts his eye to the ground and remains silent. Zashue continues, —

"It is true that the Moshome Dinne cannot have killed all our people. This we found out on the Rātye," pointing to the Sierra de San Miguel; "ere I killed the old man to take ahtzeta from him, he lifted all of his fingers four times and pointed over here. Do you not think, satyumishe, that he meant to tell me thereby that forty of our people escaped and fled to Hanyi?"

"I do; and that is the reason why I believe we shall find them in Hashyuko," — the eastern corner, the Queres name for the place where Santa Fé stands, — replied the other, very positively. "Behold, satyumishe, we have searched everywhere we could, have followed every trail we could follow. Nearly all the tracks were those of our people, of that I am sure, and how far have we not gone after them? Ten days at least we were in the mountains on the tracks of the Moshome Dinne. We fought them and took ahtzeta. At

last we learned that many of our women and children had
been taken by those shuatyam and that we never any more
could obtain them, also that Okoya was probably not still
alive.   Then we went south and saw tracks, — small tracks
of children, larger ones of women, and a few that were those
of men.   We went toward Cuame until we could not see
the tracks because it had rained, and the rain had washed
them away.   To go farther was useless, for whither should
we go?"

"There are other Zaashtesh farther down the Rio Grande,
so the Naua told me," replied Zashue; "but these dwell far,
far away," — he waved his hand to the south, — "where it
is very warm and where there are a great many Moshome."

"Those are too far off," Hayoue said, shaking his head;
"our people did not go so far without resting.   We must
have overtaken them, for we rested not."

The elder brother nodded; he was fully conscious that
they had never rested on the journey.   He felt it now.

"Therefore, brother," Hayoue went on, "I believe that
those whom we look for are there," pointing to the east.
"In the Sierra del Valle are only those whom the Moshome
have captured; the others must have turned back along the
river, crossing it to go to the Puyatye; for there are no
Moshome over here, and if the Puyatye speak like the Tehuas, their hearts are different and more like ours.   I think
we should go to the Zaashtesh yonder, at the foot of the big
kote where the snow is hanging.   If we do not find them
there, then I think we should go farther, as far as where the
buffaloes are feeding.   There are villages there, too, I have
been told, and there our people will be.   If we once know
which of them are alive and free, we shall also know those
who are among the Moshome, and can see what to do for
them."

"It strikes me," Zashue still objected, "that if the koitza

and the little ones were on this side of the river we must have seen their tracks."

" But it rains, brother," Hayoue replied, looking up at the sky. "The Shiuana send us rain every night and often during the day, and it washes away the footprints. Besides, we have merely followed the river thus far, and our people may have turned inland. There is so much sand on the banks that the rain destroys all foot-marks."

Zashue looked up ; a thought had struck him like a flash.

" Have you seen the ravine below here ? " He pointed to the south. "How would it do for us to look there ? The ravine comes from the river."

"You are right," Hayoue assented, rising and moving slowly on. The strong young man was tired, almost exhausted from endless roaming, searching, spying, and from hunger and thirst combined. Zashue took a more southeasterly direction, so that both struck the brink of the ravine at some distance apart.

From the brink they looked down into a deep cleft, at the bottom of which the little Rio de Santa Fé winds its course toward the Rio Grande. This cleft is the gorge which to-day is called Cañon de las Bocas. South of it the plateaus continue with barren undulations and whitish hills. They rise gradually to the base of a sombre mountain cluster, the bulk of which was wrapped in clouds, as well as the huge mass of the Sandia chain to its right. Still farther to the right the Rio Grande valley opened. Sand-whirls chased along that valley to meet a shower which was sending rain-streaks into it. A cloud had meanwhile gathered over the heads of the wanderers, thunder reverberated, and the rain-drops began to fall. The men paid no attention ; they gazed down at the little torrent beneath, at the groups of poplar-trees on its banks, and at the scattered patches of open ground along its course. Their desire was to descend into the gorge to search for traces of those whom they longed for.

The descent was impracticable from where they had stopped. A rim of vertical cliffs of lava and trap formed the upper border of the cleft. Suddenly Hayoue exclaimed, —

"Umo, they are not down here, or we should see them from above. Let us go farther, where there are no rocks, and where the stream enters the gorge. If our people have come through here we must find their tracks at the outlet."

"It is well," replied Zashue.

The shower drizzled out; its main force was spent on the southern plateaus, and cool gusts of wind blew across to the north side. When the brothers had clambered down the rugged slope covered with scattered lava-blocks to the sandy nook where now stands the hamlet of the "Ciénéquilla," clouds had again lifted over Hashyuko, and on the slope of the high Sierra the bluish cloudlet swam clear and distinct.

Much water ran in the bed of the river at the mouth of the Bocas, and there was no hope of finding any tracks there.

The men staggered up and down, and at last Zashue stood still, bent over, and appeared to examine something. Then he called aloud, —

"Come over here!" With this he raised something from the ground. Hayoue went over to him, and both looked at the object carefully. It was a piece of cloth made of cotton dyed black, of the size of a hand, torn off but recently, and soiled by mud and moisture. Hayoue nodded; the find pleased him.

"That is from our women," said he.

"The women from the Puyatye," Zashue said doubtingly, "wear skirts like our koitza."

"It is so, but the women from Hashyuko do not go so far from their homes now. Nothing is ripe, — neither cactus, figs, nor yucca fruit. What should they come out here for? When do our women ever go so far from the Zaashtesh?"

"Shotaye used to go farther," objected the elder.

"Shotaye," Hayoue muttered, "Shotaye was — you know what she was! There is none like her in the world. What she may be doing in case she is alive, nobody can tell."

"I wish I knew her to be with Say Koitza now," Zashue sighed.

"Shotaye is dead," his brother asserted. "But I believe that this rag is from our people, and you were right in coming hither. Look!" pointing to the entrance of the Bocas, "they came through there and from the west. Even if we find no trace of them I still believe that they went to Hashyuko and that we shall find them there. Let us go ere it is too late!"

The last words were uttered in such a positive tone that Zashue yielded, and followed his brother, who since their discovery again moved with vigorous strides. Since the last evening neither of them had eaten anything, and their meal then had been scanty enough. The discovery had infused new strength into their exhausted bodies, and the brothers walked on, side by side, as if they were well fed and thoroughly rested. Zashue still remained in doubt; he would rather have made further researches. He knew from the talk of old men that the Tanos inhabited villages farther south, and it was possible that the fugitives, afraid of the dispositions of the Puyatye that lived closer to the Tehuas, had avoided them in order to take refuge at a greater distance from the people of the Puye. But above all, Zashue felt strong misgivings in regard to the reception which he and his brother, both armed as they were, might find at Hashyuko.

Under different circumstances he would have gone to the Tanos without any fear, and would have entered the village as a guest. Now, since the Queres of the Rito and the Tehuas had come to blows, it was possible that the latter had informed their relatives in the southeast of what occured, and thus made them suspicious of the Queres. He and his brother carried the implements of war, but they were not in war-paint. That looked very suspicious, and they might be taken for spies; and as soon as they should be noticed some of the Tanos might lie in wait for them with evil intentions. If on the other hand Hayoue was right, then all would be right. But he could not agree with his brother on that point. A certain instinct told him that the fugitives had wandered south instead of east. Nevertheless he yielded willingly to the superior energy and determination of Hayoue. Zashue was a weak man, and glad to lean upon a stronger arm, a more determined will.

Hayoue on his part was fully convinced of the correctness of his views. He had no thought of danger. He reflected, and Zashue had overlooked this important point, that, in case the Tehuas notified the Tanos of recent occurrences, they would not fail to boast of their signal triumph, and to represent the defeat of the Queres as akin to complete destruction. Therefore in what light could he and his brother appear to the people of Hashyuko than as fugitives from a tribe well nigh exterminated? Fugitives of that class are always, even by savages, received and treated as guests. Finally, should it come to blows, Hayoue was ready for them also, to give as well as take.

The distance which separated the two men from their place of destination was about twelve English miles. The plain between the upper, or eastern mouth of the Cañon of the Bocas and the foot of the Santa Fé mountain-range rises gradually, and in even but extensive undulations. It

is closed to the north by a broad sandy ridge, which skirts
the northern bank of the little Santa Fé stream. That ridge
extends from the east, where Santa Fé stands, to the volcanic mesa through which the cleft of the Bocas meanders
in the west; and the plain lies south of it, dipping in that
direction as well as to the west also. Several ravines with
sloping borders run through it from east to west; the nearest one south of the Santa Fé river is called Arroyo Hondo. These gorges or channels are dry except in the rainy
season, when torrents of water gush down them for a few
hours after some exceedingly violent shower in the mountains. The vegetation of the plain consists mainly of
bunch-grass, juniper, and tall, arborescent cacti.

Hayoue took the direction to the northeast, keeping between the Santa Fé Creek on their left and the Arroyo
Hondo on the right. As often happens during the afternoon, the sky had begun to clear; and as evening approached, the tall Santa Fé Sierra shone out majestically,
free from clouds, the top of " Baldy " covered with snow.
The high timber on the lower ridges appeared distinct,
and the folds of the mountain-sides clothed in vivid green
alternated with black yet luminous shadows. A cool wind
blew from the south in gusts, and the wanderers hastened
their steps lest night should overtake them ere they could
reach the village, now distinguishable below the blue cloud
of smoke as a reddish protuberance on a bleak hill.

Zashue stood still, and beckoned his brother to do the
same and listen. From the direction they were going came
faint cries; the brothers looked at each other.

" There are Puyatye over there," said Hayoue.

" Ko ! " assented Zashue, then as if making a discovery
he added, " They are hunting rabbits and hares."

" You are right, surely they hunt rabbits," said Hayoue,
his eyes brightening at the suggestion.

"What shall we do?" Zashue asked.

"We will go to them at once," said the other. "That is very good, very good for us indeed, for if they hunt rabbits all their yaya and nashtio will be there too."

One of the broad swellings which traverse the Santa Fé plain lay between the young men and the place whence the sounds came ; it concealed the hunters from their gaze, but the manner in which the cries seemed to shift proved that they were swiftly moving to and fro. Zashue felt greatly relieved, for his explanation that the Tanos might be on a general hunt for rabbits was probably true, and it was a very good sign. The rabbit-hunt is usually a prelude to solemn dances, therefore it was not likely that the Tanos suspected danger or had any knowledge of events at the Puye.

The great rabbit-hunt, still practised by all the Pueblos several times during each year, is a communal undertaking, a religious ceremony, in which not only the men take part, but the women and children also. The object is to obtain the skins which the chief penitents use for some sacramental purpose. It is also a feast and a day of rejoicing and merriment for the whole village. The hunt is under the direction of the principal war captain, and the leading dignitaries share the sport. Long prayers around a fire which is started outside of the pueblo opens the performance. The game is hunted and killed with clubs, and a lively and sometimes amusing rivalry is displayed by both sexes in securing the rabbits, which often gives rise to very ludicrous scenes. Sometimes the hunt is continued for several days in succession.

When the brothers reached the crest of the undulation, they witnessed sights that to a stranger would have been nearly incomprehensible. Men, women, and children were running back and forth in every direction, no longer chasing game, but playing, laughing, romping, with loud and boisterous talk. Small groups were already going home loaded with game, others with empty hands, to the great amusement and merciless jeering of the successful hunters. Among the former were men dressed in the costume of women, while with the lucky ones women in male attire paraded proudly. It was an animated picture spread over a wide expanse, but it was moving back to the village in the east; and when the Indians from the Rito stood still to observe, there remained in their immediate vicinity only a few men in female garb. Beyond them stood a group of five or six persons, laughing and jesting.

Over the broad plain there rested a mild, subdued glow of pleasant twilight; the highest summits of the Sierra glistened in fiery hues.

Hayoue stepped up boldly, his brother keeping alongside watchfully. He was ready, not to flee, but to hide, and use the bow in case of necessity. They were noticed by those standing nearest. The men in women's garb were busy breaking twigs and branches, or cutting them off with stone implements. At the sight of strangers, they suspended work and stared. Hayoue laid aside his bow and quiver, and extended his right hand, calling out, —

" Queres Tyuonyi ! "

No answer came. Zashue could not control his mirth at the sight of the men in such guise ; he broke out in a ringing laugh, pointed at them, and shouted, " Puyatye ! " then to himself with the exclamation, " Koshare ! "

The salutations called forth no reply. The Tanos continued to stare. It was not merely astonishment which caused them to remain motionless ; there was quite as much embarrassment on their part. For these men in women's wraps had had to assume the costumes as a punishment, because they had allowed women to outwit or out-hunt them in the joint pursuit of the same animal. Whenever a man and a woman, during one of these ceremonial hunts, chase the same rabbit, and the woman succeeds in slaying it, then her male competitor must exchange his dress for that of the successful woman, who in turn proudly, amidst applause and jeerings, assumes the garb of the male. The man thereafter has to go on hunting until he kills a rabbit himself, and can by offering it to the woman reclaim his clothing. All are not lucky enough to succeed, and it happens sometimes that the hunt is over before their efforts are successful. Such unfortunates are required to gathei a load of firewood as big as they can carry, and bring it to the house of the woman holding their clothes in pledge Thereupon the dresses are exchanged, and the night passes in the usual childish amusements for the many, in religious rites for the religious functionaries.

The men first seen by the brothers betrayed by theii dress and occupation that they belonged to the unlucky ones. They saw at a glance that the new-comers were village Indians; they also recognized from their behaviour that they came with friendly intentions. This increased their embarrassment, for they knew, or at least supposed, that the strangers would see at once the cause of their strange appearance. So great was their uneasiness, that one of them crouched behind a bush to hide.

Meanwhile all the Tehuas, who had been standing some distance off, came running up, with the exception of one, who was seen going toward the pueblo at full speed. The others held their wooden clubs ready, in case of trouble. Hayoue advanced toward them in his usual unconcerned way, and saluted them with —

" Guatzena, Puyatye ! "

Zashue had remained behind, keeping an eye on the weapons which both of them had laid on the ground.

The Tanos whispered and whispered. They evidently

guessed at the meaning of Hayoue's words, for one of them stepped up, and replied with the usual compliment in Tehua, —

"Senggerehu."

Each grasped the other's hand.   Hayoue uttered " Que-res," and pointing to the west, " Tyuonyi."

To this speech the other replied by pointing at himself and at his comrades with the word " Tano ; " then at the village, which was still dimly visible in the twilight, " Oga P' Hoge."[1]   Thereupon he made the gesture-sign for sleep, and breathed on Hayoue's hand.   The latter responded to the compliment and gave Zashue a signal to come nearer.   When Zashue rejoined the group they all greeted the Queres in the same manner, and the one who was still holding Hayoue's hand began to pull him along, urging him to go to the village with them.   The adventurers from the Rito felt that they might be welcome.   Zashue even made an eccentric, clownish jump, exclaiming, —

"Koshare raua ! Raua Koshare ! "

Boisterous laughter broke out.   One of the Tanos threw his arm around Zashue's neck, shouting at the top of his voice, —

" Hiuonde tema kosare ! "   He pressed him to his breast, whispering, —

" Oga P' Hoge Pare ! "

No mistake was possible ; the Tano was a brother, a Koshare like Zashue, and delighted to meet another from the far-distant west.   More and more lively the men became on both sides ; clumsy attempts at explanation were made ;

---

[1] " Oga P' Hoge " is the name given to Santa Fé by the Tehuas of Santa Clara.   The Tehuas of San Juan call it " Cua P' Hoge," the place or village of the shell beads, or of the shells (Olivilla) from which they make the beads which they so highly prize.   In the six- teenth century that pueblo was already deserted.

words, signs, gestures passed between them, while walking briskly on; and all were merry and in good spirits.

It was night. Behind the gigantic wall of mountains in the east a whitish glare arose, the light of the rising moon. The group had reached the banks of the Rio de Santa Fé, near where now stands the church of Nuestra Señora de Guadalupe. Before them lay a dusky wilderness, abutting against steep hills. On the highest of those, which overlooks the present town in the north, a terraced mound could be distinguished, and from its sides luminous points twinkled in ruddy light. The thumping of drums, shrill flutes, and an undefined noise rhythmic in its character, in which human voices and numerous rattles were confusedly mingled, issued from a quarter above which a glow arose like that of a fire burning within. That irregular pile was the pueblo of Oga P' Hoge; it stood where Fort Marcy was subsequently erected by the United States troops.

The moon had risen and rested on the higher crests of the mountains. Its light penetrated the basin in which now the town of Santa Fé extends, on both banks of the little stream and south of it. When to-day the moon thus stands over the heights, and looks down the turrets and cupolas of the capitol, hospitals and seminaries glisten in phosphorescent light, and the towers of the cathedral loom up solemnly, casting on the ground before it jet-black shadows. Over elegant dwellings, over modest flat roofs of adobe houses, over military buildings, institutes for the education of those of all races and creeds, the moonlight rest peacefully. Brilliant music sounds in the plaza from the heights; in the northwest a spark rushes down in serpentine windings nearer and nearer, — the approaching railway train! From the south a shrill whistle is heard, — another iron horse sweeping up with people and news from the outside world. Shade-trees rustle in the evening breeze, and their leaves dance, alternately plunged in silvery brightness and transparent night.

To-day the heights of Fort Marcy are deserted, bleak by daylight, pale and yet frowning when shines the moon. Since the seventeenth century life has sprung up at its base. At the time when Hayoue and Zashue lived, life was above, and looked down upon a wilderness beneath. To-day the hills are wild. Formerly juniper-bushes, cedar, and cactus alone peopled the banks of the river, growing along the rills and on the drift-heaps formed by the torrent.

The group of men, with Hayoue and Zashue in their midst, halted on the south bank. This did not suit Zashue; it struck him as rather unfriendly or at least as suspicious. Their companions were evidently waiting for orders, ere they crossed the river.

A man came splashing through the water and called out something, which the Queres of course did not understand. At once all conversation ceased, and the Tanos became silent and grave. The new-comer spoke first; he spoke rapidly and in a low voice, then grasped Hayoue's hand to breathe on it, and held it fast. Zashue's hands as well had been seized by two Tanos. His bow and quiver had been removed from him under some friendly pretext. They were disarmed. Then all moved on, forded the stream, and took a trail that led directly to the foot of the hill where stood the pueblo. All sounds of merriment above were hushed, nothing moved but the men and the night wind rustling through the shrubbery. At the foot of the high hill other Indians came up; these were armed, and they followed the group.

All this looked ominous. They were no longer treated as guests; they were prisoners! Zashue was not so much surprised as Hayoue, for he had always mistrusted. Hayoue inwardly raved. He reproached himself for not having lis-

tened to his brother's warnings, for having allowed his rash-
ness, his conceit, his over-confidence, to prevail to such an
extent as to fall into a trap which he felt sure the Tanos
had artfully laid and cunningly sprung upon them. Still all
his indignation and rage were of no avail. Even if he were
able to free himself from the grasp of his guards, and to escape the arrow-shots that would be aimed at the fugitive, he
saw no chance for him in the relentless chase that would
follow. All advantages would be on the side of the Tanos,
who knew the country, whereas he was a total stranger.
Nothing was left him but to resign himself to his fate and
to await the course of events. It was hard for the proud,
self-glorious young warrior; it was not only hard but if he
took into consideration his overbearing manner toward
Zashue, a punishment justly merited. Hayoue hung his
head, crestfallen and in bitter wrath.

At last some one came down the steep hill, muttered a
few words, and the ascent began. Nobody turned back to
glance at the moonlit expanse that was unfolding itself more
and more beneath. A dismal yelping sounded from below,
the voice of a coyote from the banks of the stream. The
wolf had followed the returning hunters. He licked the
blood trickling from the dead game and called his comrades. Other voices answered in the neighbourhood; from
various parts of the basin the barking died away in a mournful, dismal wail mingled with shrieks, sobs, and fiendish
laughter. It rose from the depths, filling the air, re-echoing
from the hills, and changing its modulations, a horrible
chorus of moans and groans alternating with exclamations
of hellish triumph. A shiver passed through both the prisoners; their entrance into Oga P' Hoge took place with
dismal prognostications.

The pueblo was built in the shape of a rectangle. The
north and east sides of it formed a continuous structure;

narrow alleys separated them from the south and the west sides, and between the two there was also an alley of entrance and exit. Through the latter therefore, on the southwest corner, the Tanos entered an open space like a large court-yard, surrounded by the terraced buildings composing the village.

At the approach of the group, human forms had appeared on the flat roofs and peered down upon the prisoners with curious eyes. As soon as the captives entered the square, the number of spectators increased; they came out from the interior, from lower stories, down from the upper tier, men, women, and children. They descended into the square, and the whole population of the village, about four hundred souls, gathered around the strangers and their guard. All the able-bodied men were not among them. A dozen videttes were distributed on the flat roofs, and nearly fifty warriors, hastily armed and equipped, had scattered at some distance from the buildings along the hills throughout the basin, to intercept a possible flight, as well as to guard approaches in case the two prisoners should be merely advance scouts of a larger body of enemies. Of all this Hayoue and Zashue knew nothing, of course; but they noticed that the throng about them was not friendly, that an ominous silence prevailed. Hardly a whisper was heard; a few women only gesticulated wildly.

The Tanos dropped the hands of their captives, but they remained around them still. For a long while they were left to stand; nobody brought them food, nobody offered them water to allay their thirst. The whispering grew louder; it sounded like murmured threats.

At last the hands of the strangers were again seized and they were led across the square to the northeastern corner. The throng opened in front of them as they advanced, closing in behind, and all following like children after a procession. Some ran along the walls, eager to be near and on hand when the strangers came up. Their curiosity was soon gratified, for the square was small. At the foot of one of the notched beams another halt was made. Two of the guards climbed up and exchanged a few words with an Indian sitting on the roof. Then Hayoue was signalled to follow. A Tano came behind him; after him Zashue, and then two armed men. The crowd had meanwhile closed up against the wall, pressing eye and ear against the air-holes, out of which the firelight shone. Nobody attempted to climb the roof, but all remained below, a moving, wrangling crowd of people illuminated by the placid light of the moon.

Another delay occurred on the roof. The wanderers heard loud talking beneath their feet, and concluded that the council sat in a room below, and that they would be led before that august body. There was some consolation in this fact, for it showed at least that they would not be slaughtered at once. But how should they defend themselves? Nobody understood their language, any more than they understood that of the Tanos! The situation seemed desperate. Hayoue, as well as Zashue, felt helpless; but they had to submit to the inevitable. After all, death would put an end to everything; it is beautiful at Shipapu, — there is constant dancing and singing; the girls are always young and the women never too old.

Hayoue's hand was again grasped by one of the guards, and he was motioned to descend into the apartment below. Zashue had to follow. They found themselves in a long room, whose whitewashed walls 'reflected the light of a small fire burning on a rude hearth. Close to the hearth sat a man whom the prisoners at once supposed to be the puyo, or governor. By his side sat another, a small figure, somewhat wrinkled. He wore nothing but a breech-clout of buckskin, for it was summer. Several aged men were gathered in the neighbourhood of the fire. Although none of them wore either ornaments or badges, it was easy to surmise that they were the principal shamans. Along the wall sat, lounged, or squatted the clan delegates, so that all in all there were present about eighteen persons, including the prisoners. Outside, the faces and eyes of listeners appeared from time to time through the air-holes.

The man whom the two Queres rightly took to be the civil chief, motioned them, adding, "Sit down."

They obeyed, and remained sitting with downcast looks. The councilmen glanced at them furtively from time to time. None of them spoke. At last a whisper was heard, and now a voice said in the Queres dialect, —

"Whither are you going?"

Hayoue started, and stared about in the room, looking for the man who in this foreign country spoke his own language. When he finally discovered that it was the small old man sitting by the side of the governor, he gaped at him with lips parted, and an expression akin to fright. He had acquired a dim knowledge of the fact that it might be possible for one man to know more than one language, but he had never met such a prodigy as yet. After the first surprise was over, he still stared at the speaker with inquisitive glances, eager to see whether it was possible to speak two dialects with one and the same tongue. Zashue was less startled. He knew that there were people who had learned a speech different from the one to which they were born. Therefore he replied to the query, —

"We are searching for our women, our daughters, and our children."

"Why do you look for them here? We have them not," said the old man.

"Because we have hunted for them everywhere else and have not found them."

"Are you alone?" continued his interlocutor.

"I and my brother are alone," Zashue asserted.

"Why did your koitza and makatza leave you?"

"The Moshome drove them off."

"The Moshome?" The inquisitor criticised his words.

Hayoue had recovered from his surprise. He interjected in a loud, blunt voice, —

"While the men went out to strike the Tehuas, the Moshome Dinne came upon us. We were only a few, and the shuatyam laid waste our corn, and killed many women. Many more, however, fled; we do not know whither. These we have gone out to find; we are looking for them this day here among you, but you have taken us captives. You have treated us, not as it is customary between the Zaashtesh, but as the Moshome are wont to do when strangers come to their hogans." He looked down again, angry. Zashue endeavoured to give him a warning sign, but Hayoue saw it not.

The old man smiled. Afterward he translated to the Tanos what had been said. His communication excited considerable attention. At the close of his speech, one of the medicine-men replied in a few words. The interpreter turned again to the Queres, asking, —

"Why did the people of the Tyuonyi come upon our brethren in the north by night, like shutzuna? The men from the Puye had done them no harm."

"No harm?" Hayoue broke out. "Did they not murder the best, the bravest, the wisest man, our father the maseua? Was it not enough? If you do not call that a bad, a base deed, then you and all of you are as bad and as base as the Tehuas."

The old man's features remained placid. He replied in a quiet tone, but his manner was cool and measured. —

"I know that you believe that the Tehuas killed your maseua. I know it well; for Shotaye, who now is called Aua P'ho Quio, and who lives with Cayamo in the homes at the Puye, came to warn the Tehuas that the Queres were coming over against them. But it is not true. It was not our brethren from the north, it was the Moshome Dinne." He uttered the name with marked emphasis. "They killed the maseua of your tribe."

We recognize in the interpreter the same old man who served the Tehuas in their first interviews with Shotaye. The Tehuas had despatched him to the Tanos, in order to inform the latter of their signal triumph, and to put them on their guard against the Queres. It was a lucky hour for Hayoue and Zashue, especially for the former, when the old man reached the Tanos.

The two adventurers were thunderstruck. Speechless, with heads bowed, they sat in utter amazement at what they were being told. Everything was so completely new to them, and yet it explained so much, that they were unable to collect their minds at once. The Tanos saw their confusion. What the interpreter told them of the replies of the prisoners had already created much interest, and now their embarrassed state attracted still greater attention. The interpreter, therefore, was prompted to further question them.

"When the Queres moved against the Tehuas, were you along?"

"No," Zashue replied sullenly.

"Have many of your people returned from the north?"

"Enough to hold their own against all who speak your language," Hayoue retorted.

The old man blinked; he had put an imprudent question. After a short pause, he asked again, —

"Why did you alone go out to seek for your people?"

" Because," Hayoue indignantly retorted, " the others had to remain at home to protect the weak ones, in case the Moshome Tehua came for the leavings of the Moshome Dinne." He accompanied these already insulting words with looks of defiance, glancing around with eyes flashing, and lips scornfully curled. His wrath was raised to the highest pitch ; he could not control himself.

Fortunately for him the Tanos did not understand his words, and the interpreter was shrewd enough to see that the young man thought himself justly angry, and withheld his insulting speech ιrom his listeners. He comprehended the position of the strangers, and understood what their feelings must be. He had no doubt in regard to their sincerity and truthfulness. An important point which he realized was the present weakened condition of the Queres tribe. He turned to the meeting and spoke long and earnestly. His speech was followed with the closest atten-tion, and Zashue, who felt more composed than his younger brother, noticed that the words fell on ready ears. A short discussion followed, in which every one participated in turn ; at last all seemed unanimous, and the interpreter, avoiding Hayoue, who sat with eyes gleaming like a loaded electric battery ready to send off flying and burning sparks, turned to Zashue with the query, —

" Have you any trace of your people ? "

Zashue related everything in a simple and truthful man-ner, — how they came to the determination to visit the vil-lage, with the intention in case there should be none of the fugitives here to turn southward and continue their search among the southern pueblos. Every word he said was after-ward translated to the council ; the tuyo delivered a short address ; and the interpreter spoke to the two young men in a solemn, dignified manner, as follows : —

" It is well ! My brethren say that you are welcome

They also say that you should forgive them for having suspected you. The people on the Tyuonyi wronged those at the Puye, and that was not good! But now, since the hand of Those Above has stricken the Queres, we will no longer be Moshome, but brethren, and will forget what has come between us. Are we not all one, we who wear the hair in sidelocks, — one from the beginning; and have we not all come forth at the same place? You are welcome!"

The speaker paused, glancing at the governor. The latter rose, went over to Zashue, took his hand, breathed on it, and lifted it upward. He did the same to Hayoue; then he returned to his seat and gave a sign to the interpreter, who went on, —

"Those whom you long for are not here. But it may be that as you say, brother," — he directed these words to Zashue — "they went to our people farther south. In a few days I will have to go thither, and will be your guide. Meanwhile eat the food and drink the water offered you by those who speak a tongue different from yours, but whose hearts are like your heart, and who like you pray to Those Above. He who dwells up there is our father and your father; she who has her home on high is our mother and your mother. Therefore the mothers and fathers of the Tanos say to you through me that it is well that you should stay here. Be welcome!"

Involuntarily Zashue uttered a deeply felt " Hoä " of relief. Hayoue nodded, and sighed as if breathing freer again. The great medicine-man arose, scattered sacred meal, and uttered a prayer to which all the others listened in deep silence. Then he went to greet the strangers in the customary manner. One by one the others followed, — the second medicine-man, the other chief officials, finally the delegates of the clans. Every one grasped their hands and went through the same ceremonies. The council was ended, and to every one's satisfaction.

Last came the old interpreter, and greeted them, saying, —

"I am Chang Doa, what you call Mokatsh hanutsh, 'panther clan.' Where do you belong?"

"Tzitz hanutsh," Zashue quickly responded.

The old man turned to one of the delegates.

"Father," he called to him in his language, "our sons belong to your people. Will you take them with you, or shall they go to the summer cacique?"

The other reflected a short while, then he replied, —

"The summer cacique is busy; let the brethren come with me. I will lead them to the homes of P'ho Doa."

News of the happy result of the council had already spread outside. When the prisoners of a few hours ago, now transformed into honoured guests, stepped down into the square, every one looked at them pleasantly. The throng dispersed, but many followed them into the houses of the Water clan, where they were treated to the primitive food of those times. Soon they retired to rest on simple couches, there to forget the hardships and dangers they had suffered during the day.

Outside, the deepest silence reigned. The pueblo on the steep hill and the desert plain below shone in the rays of the moon, peacefully, as though they too would slumber. From the thickets along the little stream arose a faint twitter; louder and louder it sounded, and rose heavenward in full, melodious strains, soaring on high through the stillness of the night; it was the mocking-birds' greeting to the hour of rest.

CHAPTER XXI.

AUTUMN in New Mexico, as well as in many other parts of the world, is the most beautiful time of the year. The rains are over, and vegetation is refreshed and has developed. Yellow flowers cover the slopes of the higher ranges; the summits are crowned with glistening snow again; the days are pleasant and the nights calm, clear, and wonderfully cool. Nature in autumn seems to display its greatest charms to allure mankind into placid submission to the approach of rigid winter.

Autumn has come, and the two adventurers of whose reception we have spoken in the last chapter are still guests, kindly treated and waiting for the guide to give the signal of departure for the south. A few days the old man had said, — in a few days he would himself go to the southern pueblos of his tribe. But upon the rabbit-hunts there followed ceremonial dances which lasted for days, and Hayoue and Zashue could not leave until they were over. Then it required several days to rest and to perform certain rites, and Zashue and Hayoue could not leave on that account. Furthermore, Zashue being Koshare, the Kosare of the Tanos held him back for certain performances of their own, and Hayoue could not or would not start alone. Afterward, Hayoue being Cuirana, the Cuirana held something in store for him, and Zashue did not care to start without his brother. And when all that was finished the old man was not ready; and so they are waiting and waiting, and autumn

is here in all its beauty, and Hayoue and Zashue, Zashue au
well as Hayoue, begin to chafe; but it is of no avail; they
must wait.

While they are thus waiting until it pleases their friend to
start, we shall precede them to that south which is their
objective point, in order to anticipate if possible the cravings of the two adventurous young men. They may overtake us there, perhaps when we least expect it.

About thirty miles south of Santa Fé, the southern rim of
the so-called Basin of Galisteo is bounded by a low and
shaggy ridge running from east to west, whose crest is
formed of trap-dyke sharply though irregularly dentated.
In Spanish this ridge and another similar one which trav-
erses the plain several miles north of it, running parallel to
the former, is called very appropriately El Creston, for if
seen from a distance and edgewise it strikingly resembles
the crest of an antique helmet. The plain of Galisteo expands between *crestones*, and on the edges of it stand several villages of the Tanos. Of the Galisteo Basin a Spanish
report from the sixteenth century says : "There they have
no stream ; neither are there any running brooks nor any
springs which the people could use."

The mountain clusters of the Real de Dolores and Sierra
de San Francisco, and beyond these the high Sandia chain,
divide the Galisteo country from the valley of the Rio
Grande in the west. To the south there extends a dreary
plain as far as the salt marshes of the Manzano ; eastward
spread the wooded slopes of the plateau ; above the Pecos
border upon the basin. To the north the plain rises gradually, traversed only by the northern *creston*, until it merges
into the plain of Santa Fé.

On the southwestern corner of the Galisteo Basin a broad
channel discharges its waters into it, passing between the

San Francisco range and the mountains of Dolores. The channel is arid. Mountain torrents rush through it only in the season of thunder-storms, and they have burrowed and ploughed through its surface, scarring it with deep furrows and shifting waterfalls. Near the mouth of the pass and at no great distance from the plain, one of these arroyos has cut through an ancient village, exposing on both banks the lower walls and rooms of its buildings, visible on the surface only as irregular lines and quadrangles of rubbish. The village must have been quite large for an Indian settlement, since seven rectangles with wing-like additions can still be traced. This village in ruins is called to-day the Pueblo Largo, and the name is not inappropriate.

At the time of which we speak, the Pueblo Largo was inhabited, and in as high a state of prosperity as Indian pueblos ever attain unto. It contained, as the ruins attest, nearly fifteen hundred people of the Tanos tribe. Its name was Hishi. The name is well known to-day to the remnants of the Tanos, for they have piously preserved the recollections of their former abodes.

Hishi is not on a beautiful site. It lies in a wide ditch rather than in a valley. No view opens from it, and sombre mountains loom up in close proximity both to the north and west. In the rear of the village, the soil rises gradually to a low series of ridges, from the top of which, at some distance from Hishi, the eye ranges far off toward the plains and the basin of the salt lakes. These ridges are convenient posts of observation. Scouts placed there can descry the approach of hostile Apaches. The latter roam up and down the plains, following the immense herds of buffalo, and prey upon the village Indians whenever the latter present any opportunity for a successful surprise.

The buffalo himself not infrequently comes to graze within a short distance of Hishi. South of the present ruins lies the buffalo spring. When the dark masses of this greatest of American quadrupeds are descried from the heights above the village, the Tanos go out with bow and arrow; and woe to the straggling steer or calf that lags behind. Like the wolf, the Indian rarely attacked any but isolated animals. Only when a communal hunt was organized, and a whole village sallied forth to make war upon the mighty king of the prairies, — only then, previous to the introduction of fire-arms, could the redman venture to assault even a small herd or the rear-guard of a numerous column.

September is drawing to a close, and the autumnal sky is as cloudless and as pure over Hishi as it is over most of the other portions of New Mexico. But in the hollow where the village is situated the sun is scorching, as Hishi lies much lower than the "corner in the east" and lower than the Rito. The chaparro flowers, in dense masses of deep yellow, carpet the earth; and the dark pine forests on the mountain-slopes stare, while yellow streaks sweep up among the dusky timber. In the distance we catch a glimpse of the eastern slope of the Sandia range glistening in the bright yellow hue of the flowers that cover miles of its slanting surface.

On the ridges south of Hishi human figures stand. They are scattered, watching and spying attentively. They are videttes, — outposts, placed to scan the plains and the slopes of the mountains, lest some enemy sneak up and pounce upon the defenceless village. For at the time of which we are speaking the Tanos, or Hishi, are not only defenceless, but singularly unsuspecting and heedless of danger. They would be at the mercy of an enemy, were it not for these guards and scouts, who watch and pry, straining every organ of perception that their people at home may be without care while singing, praying, and making merry

Is not the dance now going on at the village danced, prayed, and sung for their benefit also?

Whenever these outposts turn toward their pueblo they see clouds of dust rising from it, hear loud rhythmic shouting, whoops and yells, beating of drums, and the shrill sounds of flutes. A haze seems to cover the tall and long terraced buildings quite distinct from the vertical columns of sand-whirls that drift over the plain of Galisteo, in calm weather rising above the horizon like thin films of smoke.

It is a great day at Hishi. A dance is performed, songs are sung, and prayers and sacrifices are offered that shall be powerful with Those Above. The people make merry over the fruits of the soil that have now matured. They are grateful, and they wish to be precious to the higher powers in years to come. The great harvest dance is performed to-day. A long procession perambulates the long village. The Koshare trot ahead. They are the same black and white goblins with whom we are already acquainted, but their bodies are decorated now with ripe fruit, with small squashes and ears of corn, all strung to cords of fibre or buckskin, and hung over their shoulders like wreaths. Wild sunflowers adorn their heads. They are followed by the Cuirana, whose bodies are daubed over with bluish clay. Then the general public tramp along. The procession is divided into four sections, the faces of all being painted *ad libitum*. The first detachment is led by an old man whose snow-white hair supports a wreath of yellow blossoms. He is the so-called summer cacique.

The winter cacique leads on the second group. Behind each ear he wears a tall plume from the wings of the eagle, and around his neck are strung rows upon rows of sacred shell beads, turquoises, and gaudy pebbles. The third is preceded by the great shaman of the hunt. His dress is a tight-fitting suit of buckskin; long fringes depend from his sleeves, and the front and shoulders of his jacket are profusely embroidered with porcupine-quills. A small plumelet of eagle-down dances over his head. The last section is led by the highest shaman. His head is also decorated with yellow flowers, and a green and a yellow plume stand erect behind each ear. The war shaman is not to be seen; the spirits of strife have nothing to do with the feast of peace. The war captain and his assistants accompany the procession to keep order and clear the way.

This long, long pageant winds on, meandering through the pueblo to the sound of drums, of flutes, and of monotonous chants; the white satyrs go ahead, then follow the blue ones, then come in single file the men, vigorously stamping, and behind each a woman, tripping lightly.

Every man is loaded with fruit of some kind, and carries corn and squashes also in each hand. Every woman or girl bears on her head a basket of willows or yucca filled with corn-cakes, yucca preserve, and other delicacies, products of the vegetable kingdom. It is a procession of baskets filing through Hishi, solemn and sober, and in the main extremely monotonous. At intervals the Koshare break ranks to cut a few capers, but to-day the Delight Makers of the Tehuas are remarkably decent, for they are those, par excellence, who say grace. Since their labours have been rewarded, and the crops are now ripe, and the people have sufficient food, they are merry in the prospects of an easy winter, and there is no need of any artificial delight-making.

The procession has passed through the entire village and returned to one of its main squares. The end of the pageant is still on the march when the Koshare break ranks again and cluster in the centre of the square. From every side bystanders come up with fruits, scattering them over the ground where the Delight Makers are waiting; and when the soil is well covered with squash, corn, and other vegetables, the white satyrs begin to dance with the most serious faces, singing and lifting their hands to the skies. Gradually the whole of the offering is crushed, and at last pounded into the earth by the feet of the dancing clowns. The earth has brought forth the necessaries of life to man; now man, in token of gratitude, returns a tribute to the earth.

As soon as this part of the ceremony is over, there arises a great shout from all sides. Ears of corn, gourds, cakes of corn meal, pieces of dried preserve, ripe fruits of the yucca, are thrown up into the air; the baskets are emptied, and bystanders run home to replenish them. Whoever can catch anything proceeds to devour it at once. The whole tribe displays its gratitude by throwing heavenward the food which heaven has enabled it to raise. Man intercepts and enjoys it after the will and the deed have satisfied the invisible powers on high.

The usual mass of spectators are gathered on the roofs and along the walls of the houses. When the noisy distribution of offerings begins, many run to get their share. But it is not those who are most eager that are most considered; it seems that the bulk of the food thrown into the air is showering down upon a row of houses on whose terraces stands a group of men, women, and children who seem no part of the inhabitants of Hishi, manifesting this not so much in dress as from their distant and timid deportment. All of them are very poorly clad, the children mostly naked; and yet here and there a girl among them wears a new hide, and some old woman a new white cotton wrap. Their pieces of clothing appear like new mendings on old rags, or like a substantial shawl thrown over scanty vestments. The older members of this peculiar group look down upon the merry spectacle below with grave and melancholy eyes; the younger would fain be merry also, but sadness lurks in their smiles. The children alone yield fully to the excitement and happiness of the hour. As the gifts fall down from above the older ones do not attempt to seize them ; the girls and younger women gather what they can and place them carefully in a heap. What the children do not succeed in devouring at once is taken away from them and placed with the rest. They are improving the opportunity to lay in stores, and the Tanos lend them a willing hand. Spectators below turn over to them what has fallen to their share, others place what they have secured with the little hoard the strangers are accumulating. For these people, so poorly clad and looking so needy, must be strangers in the village of Hishi. Strangers, yes ; but strangers in need ; and could there be any sacrifice, any offering, more agreeable to those on high than the feeding of people whom they allow to live by thrusting them on the charity of fellow-beings? These strangers are after all but children of the same spiritual parents from the upper world, and as such they are brothers, sisters, and relatives.

That the strangers are village Indians can easily be seen. It is proved by the cut of the hair, and by the rags which still protect their bodies from absolute nakedness. But the tongue they speak is different from that spoken by the people of Hishi. To us, however, it is not new. We have heard that dialect before. It is the Queres language, the language of the Rito. The strangers are the lost ones whom Hayoue and Zashue have sought so anxiously and with so much suffering, and for the sake of whom they have exposed their lives a hundred times perhaps, in vain. Zashue was right, the fugitives had turned south from the Bocas ; and had Hayoue been less self-sufficient they would have found them ere now.

Still we miss among that little band of Queres fugitives those with whom we have become more closely acquainted.

In vain we look for Say Koitza, for Mitsha, for Okoya. Can it be true, as Hayoue surmised, that his bosom friend, Zashue's eldest son, is dead?

The throwing about of fruit has ceased; the dance is resumed, and new figures may appear. Everybody hushes, and fastens his gaze on the performance.

The dancers have formed a wide ring. Men and women hold each other by the hands, and dance in a circle around the place which has been covered with objects of sacrifice. One after the other, the Koshare, the Cuirana, after them each one of the four sections, step within the circle, stamping down the fruits spread out there. Two or three of the Delight Makers improve the occasion to cut some of their usual capers, and the spectators laugh to their heart's content. Laughter is contagious, it captures even the melancholy group of Queres; the old among them smile, the young chuckle, the children shout and yell from sheer delight. One boy in particular is very conspicuous from the intense interest he takes in everything the Koshare are doing. He is about ten years of age. A dirty breechclout constitutes his only vestment, but a necklace of multicoloured pebbles adorns his neck; and as often as a Koshare grimaces, or makes an extraordinary gesture, or displays his tongue to the public, this boy jumps up, screams and shouts, and screeches in delirious joy. His whole heart is with the Koshare; he imitates their movements, improves on their gestures to such a degree that those around him smile, exchanging winks of approval as if saying, " He will be a good one."

The head of a girl slowly rises through a hatchway; and as her face turns toward us, we recognize the soft, beaming eyes of Mitsha Koitza. The maiden looks thinner, her features sharper. She remains standing on the notched beam serving as a ladder, and calls out, —

" Shyuote ! "

No reply is made to the call. The din and noise of the dance drown her voice, and all are so occupied by the sights that none pay any attention to her. The youngster who has been devoting all his time to the pranks of the Delight Makers jumps forward in his enthusiasm, and would have tumbled sheer over the low parapet encircling the roof had not one of the men standing near grasped his hair and pulled him back. It saved the boy's life, but the urchin is highly displeased at the informal manner in which he is re-strained. He screams and struggles to free himself. Again the voice of the maiden is heard; this time it is louder and the tone commanding.

" Shyuote ! "

" She is calling you, uak," the man says who has saved the brat.

" I won't go," retorts our old friend Shyuote, for he it is who attempts to play at Koshare here.

" Shyuote, come to sanaya ! " again calls the maiden.

The mention of his mother creates a stir among the by-standers. They forget the dance and turn toward Mitsha. Shyuote still refuses to obey, but the others push him for-cibly to the hatchway. Several of the women approach Mitsha, and one inquires of her in a subdued voice, —

" How goes it below? "

The girl's eyes fill with tears. At last she whispers, —

" It goes — to Shipapu." She turns around and disap-pears beneath, sobbing. Shyuote is sent after her.

The people stand and shake their heads. The news wanders from lip to lip, " She is dying." All the pleasure, every interest in the performance, has vanished. Indiffer-ent to the celebration, the Queres hang their heads in sad-ness ; yet no complaint is heard, not a tear glistens in those mournful eyes. She is only dying, not dead.

But who is dying? The query cannot be answered up here. Let us go down and follow Mitsha.

In the dingy room of an Indian home, where light and air penetrate through a single diminutive air-hole, sit and crouch half a dozen people. They surround at some distance a human being whose head rests on a bundle of skins, the body on a buffalo-robe. The knees are drawn up, and cotton mantles cover the lower extremities. The chest, scantily covered with a ragged, dark-coloured wrap, heaves at long intervals; the extremities begin to stretch; the face is devoid of expression; the eyes are wide open, staring, glassy; the lips parted; and on each side of the mouth-corners ominous wrinkles begin to form. The sufferer is a woman, and as we look closer we recognize her as Say Koitza, the wife of Zashue. He must hasten his steps if he wishes to find her upon earth, for she is dying!

It is very still in the room. The prayers which the medicine-man of the Tanos has been reciting are hushed, the little idols of lava with red-painted faces and eyes made of turquoises by means of which he hoped to conjure the sickness, lean against the wall useless. Those whose duty it is cower about the dying woman, and look on speechless. How faint the breathings grow, how the chest rises and falls at longer intervals, weaker every time! They listen as the rattling in her throat becomes harder and slower. They dare not weep, for all is not over.

Say Koitza is dying! Not the sudden death she once prayed for when Topanashka her father went over to Shipapu; but still she dies a painless death, — she dies from exhaustion.

What is going on in her mind while the fetters which tied her soul to the body are being dissolved? That body is henceforth powerless; it has no wants, no cravings. The soul becomes free. Can it already glance beyond? Not yet, for as long as earthly matter clings to him man cannot perceive the other world. Flashes of light gleam through the mist in which he is plunged, through both physical weakness and the efforts of the soul to become free. The body struggles for preservation, the spirit for freedom from its henceforth useless shell.

Are mind and body merely one? Does not death pui an end to everything that we ever were and can be? Does there remain after death anything beyond the memory of our former existence, preserved in the hearts of our fellow-beings? Nobody has ever returned from beyond the grave to tell us how he felt, what he thought, while dying. But a dying person always casts rays of light over his surroundings, and the surroundings of dying Say Koitza are not without their lesson for us.

What do we see? A man sits near the dying woman. He lifts up his hands and stares; it is the medicine-man, and he has done his utmost; he is powerless, his art useless. What he did was done in the conviction that spiritual influences, however grossly conceived and coarsely applied, could compel the soul to master the body's ailment, could prop up the sinking machinery and strengthen the motive power without regard to its decaying tools. To-day, provided the body is helped along with physical means, the soul would remain against its will, or against the will of what stands in closer relation to it originally than the form which it has animated here beneath. If mind and body were one, either method could be successful. Neither is, when death steps in to proclaim their separation.

By the side of the shaman a young man leans against the wall. He is well-built and lithe. His head is bent so low in grief that the dark hair streams over his face, concealing his features. The youth is mourning, mourning deeply. Over what? Over the body or its sufferings? No, he

mourns because of an impending separation. From what?
From the form of her whom he will miss? No, for that
form will not leave this earth in substance. He mourns
for something that goes beyond his grasp, and remains
beyond it so long as he himself moves upon this earth.

Mitsha also is here. She has properly no right to be
for she does not belong to the same clan as Say; but she
has remained, and nobody has objected to her presence.
She has not craved permission, it has come by tacit consent.
Mitsha has felt that Say was approaching the point when
the soul breaks loose and flits to another realm, and she
wishes to remain with her to the last. If that soul should
drop like a shrivelled fruit, to decay and perish forever,
nobody would bend to gaze fondly at it. But if it flutter
upward, we follow it with our eyes as long as we can, unconsciously thinking, " How happy you are, free now; and
how much I wish to be with you." The very grief caused
by the separation, the longing, the clinging to him or to her
whom we know to be leaving us, are signs that there is
something beyond, something which we are loath to lose
but sure to find again elsewhere. Mitsha has known Okoya's
mother but little, but the fearful distress of the past two
months has brought them together at last. Now the girl
weeps, but not loudly, at the thought of separation. If
death be annihilation, tears are of no avail. But if death
be a promise of life in another condition, then, child, well
may you shed tears, for your grief is a token of hope.

Shyuote stands at the foot of the beam, gaping. His
mother lies so still, she breathes so loudly. How well she
must be sleeping! Why did they call him down at all?
It would have been much nicer upstairs where there are
Koshare to be seen. He knows well enough that sanaya is
sick, but as long as she has such good rest she ought to feel
well. A child is not afraid of a dying mother, and when

she has breathed her last is convinced that she must be happy. To be well is compatible in the minds of children only with life. Death therefore appears to them as a step into a better and more beautiful existence. Children and fools tell the truth. The gleam of light which from dying Say is cast on her unruly son is but the rosy hue of a hopeful twilight.

The remaining occupants of the room stand with sad looks; they are all women but one, a middle-aged man. They do not feel the occasion except so far as there is a certain solemnity connected with it. Silent and grave, they watch a process going on whose real nature they cannot understand except as a momentous and appalling change. Change is only transformation, not annihilation.

Say Koitza has been lying thus for several days. The end is near at hand, and yet hours may elapse ere she dies. So still it is in the apartment that nobody dares even move. Rising and falling come the song and the noise of the dance from the outside, but they seem to halt at the little opening, as if an invisible medium would interpose itself, saying, " Stay out, for within there ripens a fruit for another and a better world."

Mitsha glides over to the young man with the dark, streaming hair and touches his arm lightly. He looks up and at her. It is Okoya, — Okoya, whom we believed to be dead, but who stands here by the side of his dying mother. He also looks emaciated and wan. After all the dangers and misery of a protracted flight this hour has come upon him. The eyes of the two meet ; their looks express neithei tenderness nor passion, but a perfect understanding that betokens a union which even death cannot destroy. It is that simple, natural attachment which forms the basis of Indian wedlock when the parties are congenial to each other.

That the two are one can be plainly seen. As yet no outward sanction has been given to their union ; but they are tacitly regarded as belonging to each other, and no opposition is offered to an intimacy which lacks but the bond of marriage. Passion has little to do with that intimacy ; the severe trials of the past have riveted them together on a higher plane.

Mitsha has made a sign to the young man. Both steal from the chamber noiselessly and climb to the roof. He goes first and she follows, as is customary among Indians. Once up there the dance attracts Okoya's attention for a moment. He has not seen anything of it as yet, for all day he has remained by his mother's side.

Shyuote improves the opportunity to slip out also. As he sees his brother and future sister-in-law go out, he follows. Why should he stay down any longer? His mother is well. She sleeps soundly and breathes so loud ! She certainly is improving, and up there he can see Koshare. But he is careful not to let Mitsha see him ; her positive ways are distasteful, so he creeps in among the spectators where her eyes cannot follow and soon has lost sight of everything in contemplation of the Koshare.

The appearance of Okoya and Mitsha on the roof attracts no attention. As long as the death-wail is not sounded, none but those of her clan have a right to be with the dying. Still one or other of the women casts an inquisitive glance at Mitsha ; a slight shake of her head is sufficient answer to them. The young pair go to one side ; he sits down on the parapet of the roof and she beside him. Their eyes follow the dance, but their thoughts are elsewhere. Okoya whispers at last, " Sanaya is dying."

Mitsha nods, and tears come to her eyes. Here she is not afraid to weep. Okoya continues, —

" I knew it would happen. Yonder " — he points at the

mountains — " I heard the owl, and I knew it meant what is now coming upon us."

The girl shudders. She weeps no longer; dread scenes of the past are looming up before her mind.

" In the kote," says she, " it was very bad. Do you remember over on the other side of the great river on the mesa, from which one can see so very far, almost over where we are now?"

" Not as far as that," replied Okoya, in a quiet tone, " but far enough. You are right, makatza; on the mesa we suffered much; there the Moshome did us a great deal of harm. If it had not been for you we should not be here."

" For me?" Mitsha asked in surprise.

" Yes, you. You saved me, saved the yaya, saved Shyuote from the fierce shuatyam! Yes, surely," he continued as the girl shook her head incredulously. " Do you remember, sa uishe, when one Moshome was holding my hands while another struck at me with his club? You took a big stone and hit him so that he fell and I could kill the other. Afterward you took the bow away from the dead Moshome, and you did as much with it as I did with mine. Yes, indeed, you are strong, but you are wise too, and good." He fastened his eyes on her with a deep, earnest look, and the girl turned away her face. She felt embarrassed.

" We shall be happy when you have built your house and you dwell in it as my koitza," Okoya whispered.

Mitsha cast her eyes to the ground, and a faint glow appeared on her bronzed cheeks. The young man was not misled by her manner, he knew well enough that she liked him to speak in this way.

" Sanaya goes to Shipapu," said he, moving closer to her, " and I must have a koitza. You said you would be mine and I should be your husband. It was the night of the council on the Tyuonyi. Do you remember?"

" I do, and so it will be," she said, raising her head. Her large eyes beamed upon him with an expression of softness and deep joy. " But whither shall we go? Here we are strangers; and the Puyatye, although they are very good to us, speak a tongue we do not understand. Shall we return to the Tyuonyi and live with my mother and the hanutsh ? "

" Are you sure that your mother is still alive? Are you sure that there is a single one of our people alive? " Okoya objected.

Again the eyes of Mitsha grew moist; she turned her head away and Okoya heard her sobs. Well did he understand her grief; it was stirred for the fate of her parents. Had he, had she, known all that had happened on the Rito !

A tremendous shout arose from the dancing crowd below. The distribution of gifts was beginning anew. Again the majority of the missiles were directed toward the Queres; a perfect shower of provisions, cooked and raw, pattered down upon the strangers. A large ear of corn tumbled into Mitsha's lap, and she handed it to Okoya, whispering, —

" The Shiuana are good."

" They are. They are good also to the yaya, for they take her away to Shipapu, where there is no hunger as on the shore of the great stream."

He sighed, and gazed to the west, where the San Francisco mountains stood. Beyond them, along the northern base of the Sierra de Sandia, in the sandy bottom of the Rio Grande, uninhabited at this time, they had suffered from hunger and heat. There misery had reached its climax. It is terrible even in our days to be compelled to flee from house and home in time of war into the cold, strange world. And yet nowadays one can flee to one's kind; and where there are human beings there are hearts. But in the days of old, and for Indians, it was not only distressing, it was ghastly to be obliged to fly. Nature alone stared them in

31

the face, and Nature has no heart, although it is said that we are one with her. The Navajos had driven away the fugitives, had tracked and tormented them fearfully, and yet once relieved from the enemy's clutches and thrust upon Nature alone, the wretched band regretted the days when the ruthless enemy swarmed about them. The Moshome at least fed those whom they captured, and those whom they killed were happy forever. Nature knows but law and force, and whoever depends upon her at a time when her laws will not tolerate the existence of man, falls a victim to the power of her forces.

Now all this was past. It rained gifts about them, and with a sad smile Mitsha gathered them into a little pile. Okoya looked on; he thought the girl was making provision for their future household.

The distribution stopped, for the dancers were resting. They began to sit down along the walls of the houses to rest and to enjoy the needed recess. Mitsha took some of the fruit on her arm, and said to Okoya, —

"Come, let us go down again."

"What do you want to do with that?" asked he, designating her little burden.

"I give it to the Chayan for what the Shiuana are doing for our mother."

Even in the state of most abject poverty, the Indian shows gratitude to Those Above.

The head of a man rises above the hatchway and signals the two young people gravely, sadly. They descend hastily; Okoya remains standing in the middle of the room, and Mitsha goes over to him as soon as she has deposited her burden. As nobody notices her she grasps his hand, and he presses it softly with his own. Say Koitza remains in the same position as before, but she lies more extended, and her chest heaves no longer. The by-standers are motionless like statues, expectant. A last rattle sounds from the throat of the woman; a deep heavy effort, and all is over. Light froth issues from her lips. Say Koitza has breathed her last.

It has become very quiet outside, as if men there had guessed at what was going on within. In the little apartment it is as still as the grave, — a stillness which speaks louder to the heart than the mightiest sound, and which is appropriately designated by the popular saying, "There is an angel flitting through the room."

This stillness might have lasted long; but now the noise and uproar arise again outside, and with full power the sounds of delight and mirth break into the dingy cell like mighty waves. With the departure of life from the body, it is as if a barrier that forbade entrance to noise from the outer world had been drawn away, permitting the sounds of joy to come in triumphantly, now that the soul is free. They find an echo inside, a dismal echo of lamentations and tears. Mitsha cannot weep boisterously like the rest, neither can Okoya. The two lean toward each other sobbing; the girl has grasped his arm with both hands, her head rests on his shoulder, and she weeps.

The lament below has been heard on the roof; it is a signal to rush down and join in it. Soon the room is crowded with people; the women grasp their hair and pull it over their faces. . Dismal wailing fills the cell. Among the others stands Shyuote, who has been told that his mother is dead. He plants himself squarely with the rest, and howls at the top of his voice. In front of the house the dance continues, and the monotonous chant and the dull drumming ascend to the sky; alongside of it the death-wail.

Tanos also crowd into the room; the throng is so great that the last comers must stand on the beam. Suddenly they are pushed aside; a tall young man rushes down and makes room, regardless of the weeping and howling crowd. Up to Okoya he forces his way; throws his left arm around him and Mitsha; his right hand seizes the hand of the youth and presses it against his breast. It is Hayoue, who has come from the north at last, — his heart guiding him to that friend whom he has so bravely, so unwearyingly sought.

Another Indian rushes down after Hayoue, his motions not less anxious, not less rapid and determined. He makes his way to the body and falls down upon his knees, staring with heaving chest but tearless eyes into the placid, emaciated face. It is Zashue Tihua. With a tension akin to despair he searches for lingering life in the features of that wife whom he formerly neglected and afterward suspected, whom he at last anxiously sought, and now finds asleep in death.

CONCLUSION.

AFTER twenty-one long and it may be tedious chapters, no apology is required for a short one in conclusion. I cannot take leave of the reader, however, without having made in his company a brief excursion through a portion of New Mexico in the direction of the Rito de los Frijoles, though not quite so far.

We start from Santa Fé, that "corner in the east" above which the Tano village stood many centuries ago. We proceed to the Rio Grande valley, to the little settlement called Peña Blanca, and to the Queres village, or Pueblo of Cochiti. There you will hear the language that was once spoken on the Rito; you will see the Indians with characteristic sidelocks, with collars of turquoises and shell beads, but in modern coats and trousers, in moccasins and in New England boots and shoes. Still they are at heart nearly the same Indians we found them in this story. I could introduce you to Hayoue, to Zashue, to Okoya, and the rest. If we strike the time well, you may witness the Koshare at their pranks, and in their full, very unprepossessing ceremonial toggery. At Cochiti we take a guide, possibly Hayoue, and proceed northward in the direction of the Rito.

For a number of hours we have to follow the base of the huge potreros, crossing narrow ravines, ascending steep but not long slopes, until at about noon we stand on the brink of a gorge so deep that it may be termed a chasm. We look down to a narrow bottom and groves of cotton-wood trees. To the north, the chasm is walled in by towering rocks; the Rio Grande flows through one corner; and on its opposite bank arise cliffs of trap lava and basalt, black and threatening, while the rocks on the west side are bright red, yellow, and white. The trail to the Rito goes down into this abyss and climbs up on the other side through clefts and along steep slopes. But we are not going to follow this trail. We turn to the left, and with the dizzy chasm of Cañon del Alamo to our right, proceed westward on one of the narrow tongues which, as the reader may remember, descend toward the Rio Grande from the high western mountains, and which are called in New Mexico potreros. The one on which we are travel-ling, or rather the plateau, or mesa, that constitutes its surface, is called Potrero de las Vacas.

For about two hours we wander through a thin forest. From time to time the trail approaches the brink of the rocky chasm of the Cañon del Alamo, near enough to have its echo return to us every word we may shout down into its depths. Suddenly the timber grows sparse and we be-hold an open space on a gentle rise before us. It is a bare, bleak spot, perhaps a quarter of a mile long, and occupying the entire width of the mesa, which here is not much broader. Beyond, the timber begins again, and in the centre of the opening we see the fairly preserved ruins of an abandoned Indian pueblo.

There are still in places three stories visible. The walls are of evenly broken parallelopipeds of very friable pumice-stone, and the village forms the usual quadrangles. In the centre is a large square; and no fewer than six, depressions indicate that the Pueblos had at one time as many as six circular subterranean estufas. In the ruins of the dwellings over four hundred cells are still well defined, so that the population of this communal village must formerly have reached as high as one thousand souls. Over and through the ruins are scattered the usual vestiges of primitive arts and industry, — pottery fragments and arrow-heads. Seldom do we meet with a stone hammer, whereas grinding-slabs and grinders are frequent, though for the most part scattered and broken.

The spot is well selected for an abode of sedentary Indians. An extensive view opens toward the east, north, and south. We see in the east the mountains above Santa Fé, in the south the ranges at whose foot lie the ruins of Hishi. In the north the high plateaus above the Rito shut out a glimpse of the Puye, but a whitish streak in that direction indicates the top line of the northern cliffs that overhang the Rito de los Frijoles. Right and left of the village, not more than a hundred yards from each side, begin the rugged declivities of the sides of the potrero. If we want to go farther we can proceed to the west only, and there we soon get into timber again.

A few steps within that timber, and we have before us a strange sight. A wall of rudely piled stone slabs planted upright, flags laid upon them crosswise, and smaller fragments piled against and between them, form a pentagonal enclosure which at first sight reminds us of a diminutive Stonehenge. There is an entrance to it from the southeast, — an open corridor flanked by similar parapets. The enclosing wall is not more than three feet high, and we easily peep into the interior.

Inside there are two statues carved out of the living rock Although much disfigured to-day they still show a plain resemblance to the figures of two crouching panthers or pumas. They are life size; and the animals seem to lie there with their heads to the east, their tails extended along the ground.

As we stand and gaze, our Indian goes up to the statues and furtively anoints their heads with red ochre, muttering a prayer between his teeth.

What may be the signification of this statuary? Do you remember the great dance at the Rito, and the painting on the wall of the estufa where the Koshare Naua sat and held communication with Those Above? Do you recollect that among these paintings there was one of a panther and another of a bear? The relation of the bear and panther of the estufa to the picture of the sun-father is here that of the two stone panthers to the sun himself. Their faces are turned to the east, whence rises the sun, in which dwells the father of all mankind, and the moon, which their mother inhabits. As in the estufa on the Rito, so in the outside world, the pictures of stone express a prayer to the higher powers, and here daily the people of the village were wont to make offer· ings and say their prayers.

We are therefore on sacred ground in this crumbling enclosure. But who knows that we are not on magic ground also? We might make an experiment; and though our Indian guide is not one of the great shamans, he might help us in an attempt at innocent jugglery.

Let us suffer ourselves to be blindfolded, and then turn around three times from left to right while our friend recites some cabalistic formula, incomprehensible of course to us.

One, two, three! The bandage is removed. What can we see?

Nothing strange at first. Surrounding nature is the same as before. The same extensive view, the same snow-clad ranges in the far east, the same silent, frowning rocks, the same dark pines around us. But in the north, over the yellowish band that denotes the cliffs of the Rito, we notice a slight bluish haze.

A change has taken place in our immediate vicinity. The stone panthers and the stone enclosure have vanished, and the ground is bare, like all the ground in the neighbourhood. Looking beyond we see that a transformation has also taken place on the spot where stood the ruin. The crumbling walls and heaps of rubbish are gone, and in their place newly built foundations are emerging from the ground; heaps of stone, partly broken, are scattered about; and where a moment ago we were the only living souls, now Indians — village Indians like our guide, only somewhat more primitive — move to and fro, busily engaged.

Some of them are breaking the stones into convenient sizes, for the friable pumice breaks in parallelopipeds without effort. The women are laying these in mortar made of the soil from the mesa, common adobe. We are witnessing the beginning of the construction of a small village. Farther down, on the edge of the timber, smoke arises; there the builders of this new pueblo dwell in huts while their house of stone is growing to completion. It is the month of May, and only the nights are cool.

These builders we easily recognize. They are the fugitives from the Rito, the little band whom the Tanos of Hishi have kindly received and charitably supported until a few months since, when they allowed them to go and build a new home. They came hither led on by Hayoue, who is now their maseua; for each tribe, however small, must have one. Okoya is with him, and Mitsha, now Okoya's wife, comes up from the bottom with the water-urn on her head, as on the day when we first saw her on the Rito de los Frijoles.

And now we have, though in a trance, seen the further fate of those whose sad career has filled the pages of this story. We may be blindfolded again, turned about right to left; and when the bandage is taken from our eyes the landscape is

as before, silent and grand.   The ruins are in position again ;
the panthers of stone with their mutilated heads lie within
the enclosure ; an eagle soars on high ; and our Indian points
to it, smiles, and whispers, —

"Look ! see ! the Shiuana are good !"

WESTERN NATIONAL PARKS ASSOCIATION is a nonprofit cooperating association of the National Park Service. Headquartered in Tucson, Arizona, the association was founded in 1938 as the Southwest Monuments Association to support the interpretive activities of the National Park Service.

Today we operate bookstores at sixty-six National Park Service sites throughout the western United States, plus an online store with more than 600 educational products. In addition to developing publications, **WESTERN NATIONAL PARKS ASSOCIATION** supports park research and helps fund programs that make park visits more meaningful.

One of our founding goals was to create and publish park-related information unavailable elsewhere. Currently we have more than 175 books in print with many new publications introduced yearly. **WESTERN NATIONAL PARKS ASSOCIATION** supports parks by producing more than a half million pieces of free literature annually, including trail guides, newspapers, schedules, and brochures. Since our 1938 founding, we've contributed more than $55 million to national parks, generated through store sales to park visitors and the support of our members.

Visit our online store and browse dozens of award-winning publications on national parks, military history, geology, American Indians, earth sciences, field guides to plants, animals and birds, cookbooks, children's books, prehistoric cultures, archeology, natural history, maps, and much, much more.

AFFIX STICKER
HERE

www.wnpa.org

CPSIA information can be obtained
at www.ICGtesting.com
Printed in the USA
JSRC021503190821
17893JS00015B/1